I0652623

TED

JOHN HOUSEMAN

TEG
By John Houseman
First published in Australia by Angela Houseman 2025

Copyright © Angela Houseman 2025
All Rights Reserved

A catalogue record for this
book is available from the
National Library of Australia

ISBN: 978-1-7641679-0-1 (pbk)
ISBN: 978-1-7641679-1-8 (ebk)

Cover artwork by Jake Minton © 2025

Typesetting and design by Publicious Book Publishing
Published in collaboration with Publicious Book Publishing
www.publicious.com.au

All characters and events in this publication are fictitious, any resemblance to real persons, living or dead, or any events past or present are purely coincidental.

No part of this book may be reproduced in any form, by photocopying or by any electronic or mechanical means, including information storage or retrieval systems, without permission in writing from both the copyright owner and the publisher of this book.

In loving memory of a wonderful husband to Pauline and father to Wendy, Gary, Mark and Angela, gone way too soon. Your words live on.

John Houseman 13 July 1942 - 30 August 1988 Age 46 years

"Be happy, try and make others happy and life will be good"
John Houseman 27th July 1987

Acknowledgements

Thank you to my husband of 40 years, Darren, for believing in me to achieve my dream of getting my late father's book published.

To Julia Andrews, I cannot thank you enough for all your amazing support, input, editing and knowledge that has made this book possible. Without you this would have remained a dream but because of your belief it is now a reality.

To Jake Minton, thank you so much for taking time out of your busy schedule to design the brilliant cover for TEG, forever grateful.

Thanks to my daughter Bailey for being my beta reader and becoming part of the journey with Grandpa's book. Hayes my son, thank you for your encouragement.

Finally, I hope this brings a smile to the faces of all my family and a whole lot of love to your hearts as it has to mine.

Angela Houseman
Cleveland, Australia
2025

Chapter 1

The room was busy with chatter and the clinking of glasses. Occasionally there would be a burst of laughter, quickly stifled. It wasn't that people were sad; they seemed quite happy, but a solemn countenance seemed more appropriate for Jason's Dying Day.

Only Teg was visibly unhappy. He sat on the floor in the corner of the room. He looked despondent and had, at some time, been crying. There was a sudden hush from one part of the crowded room; the silence quickly communicated to the rest of the gathering.

All turned to where the view wall was flickering into life. There were murmurings at the side of the crowded room and movement as people jockeyed aside to allow a tall, grey-haired man, still handsome despite his sixty-five years, to move to the front of the room and stand alone nearest the view wall.

He turned and held out his hand to a woman, some years younger than himself, who smiled shyly and shook her head. He, too, smiled and shrugged, not insisting that she join him.

The view wall had flickered with static and abstract images but suddenly cleared. On the screen, life-size and so clear that they seemed to be in the room, stood three men side by side. They wore long robes of white, and their hair was silver. Two men had hair that fell in gleaming waterfalls to their shoulders; the other man had a shiny pate. Behind the three men, about five meters away, stood twelve other people. Their ages ranged from mid-twenties to fifties, and each wore a cream-coloured robe. They stood in a semi-circle and watched respectfully as the three men in white bowed slowly towards the camera.

There were murmurs in the room near where Teg sat miserably. Above the camera, a monitor screen showed them the scene on the other side of the view wall where Teg's grandfather Jason now stood facing them. He could not resist bending to one side so that he could see the screen and stared in awe at what he saw. He heard close by one of the congregations murmur to his companion, "An honour indeed for Jason, they have assembled the full forum!"

"It is only right," replied the other man in hushed tones, "has he not been one of our cleverest and most caring physicians?"

They returned their attention to the screen where the middle one of the three men spoke. It was as though he was standing close to Jason and talking to him in person.

"Jason, we greet you; we honour you with our presence because you are worthy of that honour! To those of our people who we consider worthy, we give the distinction of having their histories inscribed and placed within The Sanctum of Honour. You have earned this right Jason and we commend you at your assembly for sharing with us now this sacred ceremony."

There were gasps in the room and murmurs of "such honour!" "His name will live on!"

Sarah, the woman who had earlier refused to come forward, could not now resist reaching out and clasping her husband's hand, her face aglow with pride. He looked down at her with such great affection that their love seemed to flow outward and bathe the watchers in warmth.

The man on the screen waited now as though expecting some response. Jason straightened to his full height and, still holding Sarah's hand, said, in a voice that trembled with pride, "President, I don't know what to say. It has been my honour to serve you and The Forum and, through you, the people of our world. That I have managed to do so with some success is a source of great pride and pleasure, and I consider it honour enough to have spent my life thus. On behalf of my dear wife and myself, may I humbly thank you for your great gift".

The President bowed briefly and then raised his hand palm upwards. There was a fanfare of trumpets, and from off to the side appeared a trolley pushed by two blue-robed young people. A trolley draped in brilliant, glittering silver material; on top of it reposed a pair of metal wings topped with a crown of laurel leaves, the whole creation being silver. Beneath this rested what looked to be a marble plaque covered with closely engraved writing.

The trolley stopped to the right of the three men, and again, the President raised his hand. Out of the semi-circle behind him, one of the cream-robed men stepped forward; he walked gracefully along and lifted the plaque off the trolley. Being made from lightweight material was shown in the ease with which he raised it, but even though they knew this, the watchers found it easy to imagine that it came from the finest marble, so good was the reproduction. The young man held the plaque out, resting it on his left upper arm, his forearm upright behind it with fingers curled over the top to steady it. He began to read from the plaque in clear, musical tones.

"Know you all that on this day, The Supreme Council of The Forum have, in their great wisdom, prepared a plaque of the history of Jason, of the family of Thorason, which shall be placed in The Sanctum of Honour so that all shall know he was a good citizen. For be it known that he has served the people well in his years. He has been a physician of note. He has obeyed the directions of The Forum to every degree and has never been less than a worthwhile obedient citizen. Thus we, in the name of the people and by the wisdom of The Supreme Council of The Forum, hereby consign the history of Jason, of the family of Thorason, to The Sanctum of Honour."

There was a further fanfare of trumpets while replacing the plaque, and the blue-gowned Attendants began to wheel the trolley towards the semi-circle of people who parted at its approach. A camera was obviously following the trolley because the people in the room saw its progress almost as though they were behind it. They saw it approach a set of large, heavily decorated silver doors which opened inwards as they neared.

The room they entered was circular with a high domed ceiling. Around the walls were many plaques similar to Jason's. The trolley stopped alongside a reserved space between two plaques. The Attendant who had read the tribute earlier appeared in the picture and lifted the plaque from the trolley; placing it in the vacant space, he stepped back and bowed, then walked away.

The camera remained trained on the plaque and slowly began to move backwards. As the camera started to move, the lighting in the domed room began to dim, and a bright beam of light shone down from the ceiling, neatly illuminating the newest addition to The Sanctum of Honour.

Finally, the camera was back outside the doors and paused there, showcasing the spot lit plaque as the doors slowly closed. As the doors finally came together, the scene changed abruptly, with the people of The Forum in view again. There was silence for a moment and then a spontaneous burst of applause from the people around Jason. He smiled proudly, looking around to acknowledge the applause, and then he looked down tenderly at Sarah, whose tears were of pride and happiness.

Attention quickly returned to the screen at the command of the President's voice.

"Jason, we of The Supreme Council and The Forum members salute you as you depart us. Go in peace. We wish you well!"

At his words, there was another fanfare of trumpets, and The Forum members bowed as the view wall abruptly went blank.

They returned once more to the status of a private gathering and immediately became a babble of voices. People pushed up to Jason, shook his hand and wished him well. They congratulated him on his honour, promising to salute him during his departure tomorrow. Many glasses raised to toasts, and as with all celebrations, some imbibed too freely and became loud whilst others nursed the obligatory drink and sought to engage in conversation with those of a like mind.

In time farewells were exchanged, followed by last handshakes and kisses until finally, there were just Jason and Sarah and their daughter Carolin with her husband, Peter. None of them seemed to notice Teg, the 15-year-old son of Carolin and Peter and grandson of Jason and Sarah, as he sat in the corner wondering.

Peter went to the tray and prepared four drinks which he handed around. They stood inwards and looked closely at each other; then Peter raised his glass.

"We salute you, Jason. We praise you for the honour you have received tonight. We wish you well!"

At the ritual salutation, they all lifted their glasses toward the group's centre until they touched. Then they drank in one quick motion. Peter collected the glasses and returned them to the table. He walked back to Jason and held out his hand. Their handshake was firm and sincere, and Jason bowed his head to Peter, who said, "I wish you well," before turning and leaving the room.

Carolin stepped up to her father and, rising on tiptoe, kissed him on each cheek. They held hands and looked at each other for a long moment, and then again, Jason bowed his head. Carolin said softly, "I wish you well," and she left the room.

Sarah now moved around and faced Jason. They joined hands. Sarah spoke proudly. "I was filled with pride tonight, my husband, but oh, how richly you deserved such honour. You have made me proud."

"For that, my wife, I am well pleased, for you have made me happy" They smiled contentedly at each other and then Sarah asked, "will you come to me tonight?"

He looked at her solemnly, then shook his head before replying, "I think not; I must prepare myself."

"I understand, husband."

Sarah rose onto her toes and kissed Jason lightly on the lips. They stood looking at each other, gentle smiles of love on their faces. Then Jason bowed his head. Sarah straightened herself and stood back a pace, still holding his hands.

"I wish you well," she said softly, then let go of his hands and walked, upright and proud, from the room.

Chapter 2

Believing himself to be alone, Jason poured himself another drink. He walked to the sizeable opaque window, not seeing Teg still sitting miserably in the corner.

When he reached the window, Jason touched a button on the wall. Immediately the window cleared brilliantly, and the lights of the town were revealed against the dark of the night. As his eyes adjusted, Jason made out the shapes of individual buildings and picked the different formations of stars that glittered in the clear night sky.

Jason allowed his gaze to move over the night-quiet town. His head lifted slightly as his eyes followed the contours of the hill upon which the central part of the town stood until he stared at the faint white shape of The Sanctum of Well-Being.

He recalled the friends who had so recently departed from his home and thought of his wife and daughter, whom he loved dearly, and he also thought of Teg, who had been a joy to him.

He could almost see them as they would be tomorrow, lined up on either side of the entryway to that dim white building, bowing in salute as he walked past. He felt no particular emotion as he thought of the morning. After all, he had known this day would come, and, like all good citizens, he was prepared.

Tomorrow would signal the completion of Jason's sixty-fifth year of life, and as was ordained, as the sun rose, he would walk into The Sanctum of Well-Being. The sun's rays topped the domed building and touched the outstretched wings of the giant monument in front of the building where Jason would die. His Dying Day would have come.

"Grandad"

Believing himself to be alone, Jason was startled by the voice of Teg, his grandson. He turned and stared at the boy who stood in the corner where he had previously sat.

"Teg!" exclaimed Jason "so there you are. I wondered why you hadn't come earlier to wish me well," he smiled teasingly "more important things on your mind, eh?"

Teg, obviously alarmed that Jason might seriously think this, ran forward, crying.

"No, grandad, that's not so. I was here all the time. He stopped and stared anxiously at Jason, who suddenly grinned and opened his arms wide invitingly. With relief, Teg ran into the open arms and was enfolded in a loving hug. Jason then held him at arm's length: and looked down searchingly at him before asking.

"Now then, young man, I don't understand. You say you have always been here, yet I've seen nothing of you. Is it possible you can make yourself invisible?"

"Don't be silly, grandad," laughed Teg, then pointed to the corner where he had sat for so long. "I was sitting on the floor over there," he explained.

Jason looked puzzled and asked. "Why would you want to do that? I am sad you did not want to wish me well."

"Oh, grandad, it's not like that!" the boy exclaimed. He stood there, eyes downcast, clearly struggling with a dilemma, but finally, he blurted out the heresy, "but grandad, I don't see why you should have to die at all!"

Expecting his grandfather's anger but anxious to retain his love Teg threw himself against him and wrapped his arms around him, crying, "Don't be angry, grandad, please don't be mad. I love you so much and can't bear the thought of not seeing you again."

The conflict in Jason clearly showed in his face. He stared out the window at the distant white building and stroked Teg's hair. After a while, he pulled Teg's arms from around him and indicated he should sit on the seat at the side of the window.

Jason sat opposite him and leaned forward, hands clasped as though in prayer, head bowed. Then slowly, he looked up until he met Teg's tearful gaze. He sighed deeply, then spoke sternly.

"Teg, you know that I should be very angry with you. Indeed, I must admit to being extremely disappointed that my daughter's child should speak such heresy. I will overlook your lapse because I love you dearly and because I am touched by your affection for me. I want to depart, however, while being sure that you are not straying from the path of rightness. You must promise me, Teg, that from this day onward, you will never again question The Way."

Jason looked expectantly at his grandson, but his expression became puzzled and irritated as Teg just sat there, bowed head. Finally, Jason rose to his feet and stepped forward to look down at the boy's bowed head.

"Teg, I have asked you for a promise," said Jason.

Teg remained looking down at the floor, but then he mumbled something. Jason smiled, relieved, and said, "come now, boy, a promise should not be made in a mumble; it should be made proudly! Now let us have it again, but properly!"

Teg's head came up slowly until he looked up at Jason. He swallowed nervously, blinked, and then said defiantly.

"I did not make a promise, grandad. I said that I could not."

Jason looked stunned and stepped backwards until his legs contacted the seat. He sat down and stared at Teg, shaking his head in puzzlement. When he spoke, his voice controlled, but Teg shivered as he heard the icy undertones.

"Explain to me, boy! What is this nonsense?"

Teg's fingers intertwined nervously, and he looked everywhere but at Jason as he spoke.

"I just don't see why you should have to die tomorrow, grandad, just because you're sixty-five."

"It is The Way!" Jason interrupted him in exasperation, then composed himself when he saw Teg cringe. "Go on, finish whatever nonsense you have to say!"

Teg began to sputter now; afraid he would not be permitted to finish.

"Grandad, just because your sixty-fifth year ends tomorrow, you must go to that place up there to be killed! Why, grandad, why? You're not ill, you are fit and strong, you are clever and wise, you are a physician who heals people. People love you. You make people laugh. You teach me things, you - you - you are my grandfather, and I love you, and I dream of all the things that I will do as I grow, and all the things you will teach me and - and - and I will make you proud and you will, and you will - oh grandad!"

Suddenly Teg was sobbing, his shoulders heaving, the tears streaming down his face.

Jason looked down, wanting to reach out and clasp the boy but knowing he had a last duty toward him. He began to speak, although this time, his voice had more sadness than anger.

"Teg, you must listen carefully to me. You were taught all this, you know, the reasons why things are as they are. Sometimes, I know, it is hard to believe what one is told without some hard evidence to support it. It's this that surprises me, Teg, because there is ample material available to tell you exactly what The Bad Times were like, to explain how The Wastelands came about and to show why it is necessary to stay with The Way. It mustn't happen again; this is important! You have been taught these things; is that not true, Teg?" The boy nodded, but his face clearly showed he still had doubts.

"Tell me what you know, Teg," said Jason. As the boy began speaking, Jason stared out of the window, and his eyes had a faraway look. Listening to his grandson's recitation was like going back in time, and he found it reassuring that the teaching had obviously not changed much.

"Before The Bad Times," began Teg, "there was no ordained way. The world was a place of wars and famine. There was no control over the population's growth or real control over the abuse of the environment. The cities became bigger and bigger, and the populations increased constantly. Crime became commonplace, and in most cities, criminals completely controlled whole areas. The air became poisonous with all the fossil fuels. The dumping of toxic wastes into the seas and rivers, and streams destroyed marine life that had provided a large part of the world's food. The land was needed more and more for food production to replace that lost from the polluted waters, but as the population grew, they also needed the land."

Teg paused and took a deep breath, looking sideways at Jason to try and gauge how his dissertation was being received. He, however, still gazed into the distance, and Teg wasn't even sure that he was being listened to as he continued in tones that showed he knew by rote the words he spoke.

"Populations became greater and greater, and food became scarcer. Crime was rampant, and the weakest suffered in all ways. There was no work for the great masses of the people. There was little money to give and scarce food to be purchased. Disease from pollution and malnutrition was rampant. Children died almost as soon as they were sick due to overburdened systems. Medical services could do little to handle the flow of ill and injured who sought their help.

Each year the problem worsened, and soon, the Governments of the people were incapable of controlling their own citizens. Riots became commonplace, and criminals became more contemptuous of the law. The law itself was unable to cope and became corrupt. Society broke down. Despair became a way of life.

A great plague swept the world, causing untold deaths. Aided by the polluted air and waters and inadequate medical services left to fight it, the plague destroyed the old world. When it was over, the wise men told us of The Way. No longer would there be an abuse of the environment, no longer would overcrowding be permitted; criminals would be destroyed, the incurably sick and the hopelessly lame would no longer be allowed to be a burden to society; and when each person had lived sixty-five years, they would surrender to The Sanctum of Well-Being where without pain or trauma be dispatched to the life after."

As he finished his discourse, Teg remembered again why he had begun it and looked with great sadness at Jason, who stared out into the dark. When finally, he did turn and face his grandson, Jason looked both confused and disappointed as he said, "You have learned the words well, Teg. How sad you have not learned the lesson in these words."

"I don't understand, grandad!"

"I'm sure you do, boy; your behavior tonight clearly shows that you have not absorbed the truth of the words you have learned. The unfeeling way you speak the words shows how little they mean to you. Do you believe that things were not as they say? Do you not believe that the world became poisoned through the incompetence of man. Do you not believe that The Wastelands exist. Let me tell you, boy - I have seen them!"

"I know you have, grandad, I have often wondered how it must have been, what you must have seen."

"Is it not enough that I have seen them, been there, and can confirm their existence! Do you dare to presume that a mere boy can question the wisdom of his elders, history, and even - why even The Forum itself?"

Teg looked up miserably at his grandfather, but there was a spark of defiance in his eyes as he started to speak, quietly and hesitantly at first but more intensely as he gained renewed confidence in what he said,

"I know I am only a child, grandad, but you have often told me, "You have a brain, Teg - use it!""

Jason couldn't resist smiling at the mimicry, it was so like himself and accurate, but his face sobered again as Teg went on.

"I can't stop myself from thinking about things, wondering why things are as they are. We are told about The Way and why it should be. We are not expected to question what we are told. I often wonder why we were encouraged to ask questions on all other topics so that we may learn, but we are not permitted to ask about The Way. Who decided that The Forum should control our lives? Who decided that The Supreme Council should have absolute power? Everyone knows, The Supreme Council dictates what the rest of The Forum will decide?"

Jason was staring in horror at his grandson, not having expected the heresy to be quite so definite.

"Teg, what are you talking about? They are our rulers; they have the knowledge and the wisdom to guide us. They protect us, inform us, and ensure that The Way is preserved. You cannot question the power of The Forum boy, have you gone mad?"

Teg was angry now. His beloved grandfather would not understand him and did not want to understand him.

Defiantly, he stood up and, looking out of the window, gazed up at The Sanctum of Well-Being as he spoke again.

"You see, grandad, even you, who has taught me so much and encouraged me to think and seek knowledge, even you will not answer my questions. No, grandad, please don't say anything; let me say what I have to say, and then I will trouble you no more. I remember the year before last when Thomas, the grandfather of my friend Jon, went to The Sanctum on his Dying Day. It didn't mean much to me, I had seen it so often, but I noticed Jon wasn't there. I can still see his family and friends smiling and wishing him well as he disappears inside. I looked for him, believing that he must have had an argument with his grandfather so that he did not want to salute him on his final walk. When I found Jon, he cried so bitterly, but it was a long time before I could find out why. He eventually told me how dearly he loved Thomas. He told me of their shared dreams as he grew up. His grandfather Jon knew of The Way, and accepted it, but he couldn't understand why his beloved grandfather should be taken from him."

Teg paused and turned to look at Jason, whose expression was patient.

"In many ways, Thomas and Jon were like you and me, grandad. Thomas was kind, clever and wise too. He had never been ill, and Jon's greatest pleasure was to be carried on his grandad's shoulders into the hills where they would study the birds, and the flowers and Thomas would teach him about them. Thomas had to be strong and fit to carry Jon like that." Teg paused for a moment and looked as though he was about to cry. He swallowed and went on in a voice that trembled slightly.

"And yet, one day, just because it was the end of his sixty-fifth year, he was killed, just as you are to be killed tomorrow!"

Now Teg did cry gently, his head turned away, Jason felt touched by the display of emotion, but his response was stern.

"You talk of it as though it were murder boy, or even as though it were punishment for murder perhaps!"

He paused as he remembered the last murder he could recall. It had been eleven years ago. It astonished him how a similar ceremony could be so different. The people who lined the approach to The Sanctum as the young murderer made his final walk had jeered and abused him, and even his own family had been there to heap curses upon him. They cheered and laughed when the sun's rays touched the monument's wings; it was not a typical solemn Dying Day walk.

"What is the difference, grandad?" Teg's voice broke into his thoughts, and momentarily Jason looked blankly at his grandson.

"The difference, the difference between what?"

"What is the difference between how criminals die and how anyone else dies?"

"There's a great difference; what a foolish question!"

Teg looked closely at Jason, sensing for the first time a faint shadow of doubt in his grandad's voice. Seeking to push his argument further, he probed, "Do you really believe there is that much difference, grandad? Walking into The Sanctum, you are fit, healthy, thinking, and feeling. Within minutes you no longer exist. Just like turning off a light, you no longer exist; whether you are a murderer or a physician!"

Jason's head jerked up at this, and Teg stepped back, fearful of his grandfather's wrath, as he roared, "how dare you bracket me with a murderer, how dare…!"

"But don't you see, grandad," Teg interrupted in frustration, "it is not I who does this, it is those who would take your life in the same way and for no other reason than your sixty-fifth birthday!"

Chapter 3

For all his youth, Teg sensed that his grandfather had never thought to question what he had been brought up to believe. He was convinced that Jason, until this last night of life, had never doubted the rightness of The Way. Teg wondered what his grandfather would think if he knew how deeply he thought of the rights and wrongs of how they were ruled. If Jason realised how deeply Teg considered the role and rightness of The Forum and The Supreme Council, he would turn him over to the police and the heretic tribunal, who would send him to The Sanctum of Well-Being. He shivered and wondered whether he might have gone too far. Despite his love for his grandfather and the undoubted reciprocal love, there was no guarantee that Jason would not consider this heresy so dangerous as not to betray him. He changed tack slightly, hoping to cast doubt in his mind without enraging him further.

"Has it never struck you as odd grandfather, that the place where we go to die should be known as The Sanctum of Well Being?"

He emphasised the last two words, and Jason shook his head in amused condescension as he replied.

"Clearly, they didn't teach you everything in school. Our history must surely tell you how great a responsibility we must ensure that The Bad Times do not recur. The Sanctum exists to preserve the well-being of our world!"

"By killing people?"

"Don't be impertinent, Teg! You keep talking as though The Sanctum is some charnel house. It is proven that the body begins to deteriorate, and the mind becomes enfeebled once the sixty-fifth year is passed. We cannot allow our world to become cluttered with frail, useless, senile people who serve no purpose other than to be a burden to society!"

We, grandad?"

"What?"

"You said 'we' cannot allow it. Who are we?"

"Are you deliberately being obtuse boy? You know full well that our laws and covenants are handed down to us by The Forum."

"Why should it be that we accept what The Forum says without question? We, after all, are the people it represents, and yet we have no say in the formulation of the laws it makes, in the way it rules our lives!"

It was clear from Jason's expression that he was beginning to realise how deeply his grandson had allowed his mind to wander along the forbidden paths of heresy. Teg read his expression and felt the clutch of fear in his heart. He sought to reduce the tension with a diversionary question.

"Grandad, how do we know that after sixty-five years, the body and the mind deteriorate so quickly?"

"How do we know? What a stupid question, we know; rest assured!"

"But grandad, how can we know it if nobody is allowed to live beyond sixty-five years?"

"What, what do you mean? There is enough documented evidence from The Bad Times, of course, that is why it was made part of The Way!"

"But you have often told me, with much pride, how the physician's skill and the technology at your disposal have helped improve the quality of human life by removing many diseases and controlling others. You have often pointed out people in their forties, fifties, and even sixties, who are fit and healthy but who The Forum considers deteriorating!"

"That is true, but what has this to do with your confounded obtuseness?"

"Is it not possible, grandad, that, with your improvements, people could live much longer than sixty-five years without being ill or senile. We know some people became ill much younger than sixty-five and cannot be cured. If they are sent to The Sanctum of Well-Being many years before their time because they are unfit to live, why should it not be that those who are fit to live at sixty-five should be allowed to continue to do so?"

"Because it is The Way, Teg! You anger me because you ignore the basic truths, forget our history, and ignore the terrible places; terrible, remember that I have seen them!"

"Grandad, do you remember the accident at the Institute of Technology before the summer?"

"Of course, I remember it; dreadful business!" said Jason, somewhat off balance by the apparently abrupt change of direction that Teg had taken.

"Do you remember Grandad how the breach in the chemical division store allowed the river at Castonville to become polluted?"

"I remember that very well, as you must do as well," suddenly, Jason looked inspired as he saw a way to show Teg the error of his thinking.

"There is a perfect lesson for you! You must remember how the fish and the waterfowl were poisoned. You cannot forget how horribly the water became discoloured and foul smelling. The grass and plants along the banks became cancerous and obscene to see or smell. That is pollution for you, boy. That must not happen to us again; that is how The Wastelands came about!"

Jason finished with a triumphant shout but felt disconcerted to see that, far from appearing impressed, Teg merely looked at him quizzically and asked, "is the river at Castonville clean again, grandad?"

"It is, and anyone who sees it now and remembers it as it was must surely understand how important it is to keep our environment clean. You would do well to remember that, Teg!"

"Grandad, how old were you when you went to The Wastelands?"

"What? Oh, let me see now." Jason's expression became far away again as he remembered the excitement, the trepidation of that expedition. A contingent of police, forty strong, went to the wasteland in the east. They got into trouble on the fringe of The Wastelands when their leading personnel carrier slid sideways into a gully, and many men were injured.

Jason remembered the pride he had felt to be chosen as Doctor Theo's assistant for the trip. They had found the policemen in a sorry state. The air was redolent with chemical smells and the reek of decay. They had long run out of rations and had eked a miserable existence from the scant vegetation they knew to be edible. Their medical supplies were exhausted, and there was much work for Doctor Theo and his young assistant.

They could see The Wastelands in the distance, vast caverns of skeletal structures that once had housed heaving masses of humanity.

Significant sweeping roadways and bridges soared on concrete columns twisting in and out of the monolithic forms. Decay had worked its poison on the once solid structures, and they were scabrous and falling apart in places. With imagination, one could see how once the ruins had been a great and thriving city. Observing the foul haze over The Wastelands, one could also imagine how life was choked out of the teeming masses.

Jason recalled how frustrated he had been as, with his inquiring mind, he had keenly tried to find out from the sick and injured policemen what it was like to go into The Wastelands. They refused to answer his questions, their eyes straying to the imposing figure of the commissioner sent by The Forum to accompany the rescue party. Jason realised that the men had been ordered not to speak and accepted this without question. Jason's fascination with The Wastelands remained long after he had returned home, but his unanswered curiosity gradually faded. His interest in The Wastelands now suddenly and unexpectedly revived in this incredible confrontation with his grandson.

"I was twenty years old when I went on that expedition!" he said proudly. "It was clear to see what terrible places The Wastelands were and why they no longer supported life. It must not happen again!"

Having heard the story of his grandfather's journey more than once. Teg could almost hear what he had been thinking. It was clear that Teg must often have thought about the story as he clearly had his questions well prepared.

"Grandad, why did the police go to The Wastelands?"

Jason's expression showed clearly that he had never had cause to consider the question before; he frowned as he replied.

"To do whatever duty they were required to do, what else?"

"But grandad, if there were no people in The Wastelands, why send the police there?"

"What? I don't understand, boy, why should the decisions of The Forum be questioned. Why should you concern yourself with such things' after all this time?"

Jason looked disbelieving at his grandson's next question, thinking that he had changed the direction of his enquiries.

"Grandad, when the policemen ran out of food, what did they eat?"

"What did they eat? How on earth should I remember after all this time?"

"But you must have some idea."

"They ate vegetation, edible vegetation, roots and leaves of various edible plants. What sort of a question is that anyway?"

"What did they drink, grandad?"

"Water, of course! What on earth are all these stupid questions about?"

Teg looked at Jason speculatively, wondering how much further he could go. Finally, he sat down and leaned forward, his hands on his knees, unconsciously imitating the way Jason often sat. He began to speak, slowly at first but gaining momentum as he endeavoured to complete what he had to say before being interrupted.

"I've often wondered, grandad, since you first told me about your expedition. There are many things I need help understanding. There are not supposed to be any people in The Wastelands, and a whole squad of police were sent there; why? Have there been other police expeditions to The Wastelands? I don't mind betting there have been."

"Why?"

"The air and the ground and the rivers, the whole thing was supposed to be too poisonous to support life, and yet the policemen ate the vegetation, drank the water and breathed the air, and they lived!"

Jason moved as if to interrupt, but Teg held his hand up in a gesture so imperious that, without thinking, he subsided.

"The river at Castonville was badly polluted so that, within days, the life in the river seemed all but destroyed. The vegetation along its banks withered and died. It was dirty, smelly, and foul, yet within half a year, it was clean again. Clean and fresh and full of life again!"

Once more, Jason tried to interrupt, but Teg leapt to his feet and paced up and down in front of the window as he went on.

"It's over forty years since you went on your journey, grandad, forty years! Surely, if there was vegetation and air and water suitable for supporting life all those years ago, isn't it possible that things would have significantly improved by now. Why don't they see if The Wastelands can be used again?"

Jason suddenly rounded on Teg, furious all at once.

"I assume by 'they' you refer to The Forum. How dare you presume to question their actions or to tell them what they should and should not do. It grieves me that my daughter's son should have so steeped himself in such heresies.

You question the wisdom of The Forum, ask about the existence of The Wastelands, and doubt the rightness of the Dying Day! I came here tonight to prepare myself for the ceremony. I was proud of the award bestowed on me; they have inscribed my history in The Sanctum of Honour. How would it be if they knew my daughter's son was a heretic?"

Jason pulled himself to his full height and stared down at his grandson, his voice stern and unyielding.

"You have caused me, in my last hours, to flinch from my duty. I should summon the police right now and tell them of your perfidy. I will not do so for your mother's and my dear Sarah's sake, but I beseech you boy, no, I command you to stop this nonsense, or you will bring nothing but hardship to those who would love you. Now begone."

Teg stood, trembling with fear at the outburst from his grandfather. His eyes were bright with unshed tears, his lower lip trembling as he gazed up at the man he so loved. Slowly he held out his hands in the traditional gesture. Jason gazed down at him but did not take the proffered hands in his own. After a minute, Teg looked at the floor and slowly lowered his hands. He looked up at Jason and said, in a tiny and quivering voice.

"I wish you well, Grandad."

When Jason continued to stand unmoving, Teg slowly turned and walked across the room towards the door. When he reached the door, he turned. The tears ran freely down his face now. He wiped at the tears with the back of his hand and then spoke once more, defiantly.

"I'm going now, grandad. I have said what I've said because I love you, and I don't understand why I can't continue to have you as my grandfather; I don't believe that it is wrong to question the things we don't understand. I wish you well, grandad, and I understand why you are as you are, but I must ask you one more question before I go. I will not wait for an answer because you will not give me one. One day perhaps, I will find the answer for myself!"

He stepped back so that he stood just outside the door. He just stood there, saying nothing until, as he had hoped, Jason could not resist turning towards him, curious about the question. Teg smiled shyly at his small triumph and asked.

"Grandad, if everyone must die after sixty-five years, how is it that The Supreme Council are much older than that?"

And then he was gone!

Chapter 4

Delmo felt bored. It was his turn to preside over the justice sessions, which he invariably found onerous. As the Second President of The Forum, he constituted one-third of The Supreme Council. The President was Aaron, and the Third President was David. Between them, they ruled over The Forum, which comprised twelve Attendants. These were the cream-robed people at the ceremony that Jason's gathering had watched.

There were also Acolytes, which fluctuated between thirty and forty members. Acolytes were chosen by The Supreme Council, and their function was to attend to the needs of their designated President; whilst being educated by the Attendants in the ways of The Forum. Acolytes wore blue robes and were hand-picked at an early age for training as Attendants. If they were fortunate, Acolytes could become Attendants one day, a position with many privileges. The ultimate achievement was to attain membership of The Supreme Council, but this was an honour reserved for very few and at very infrequent intervals.

One essential requirement for the Acolytes, should they wish to progress, was to do as they were told. The teachings ensured they learned not to question anything they may see or hear and to obey without question any command of one of The Supreme Council. Occasionally, these commands might be distasteful or have doubtful legitimacy to the recipient; however, this was no excuse for prevarication. To question or argue against such a command was to invite trouble. One who had dared to challenge such a command was Elene. She stood now, trembling, and afraid before the justice sessions. She was scared because she knew that invariably, an appearance as an accused citizen ended in a long walk into The Sanctum of Well-Being.

Elene had been thrilled when her parents informed her that the Second President of The Forum had selected her as an Acolyte. She did not understand why she had been chosen, but, at twelve years old, she had been happy to share her parents' pride in her selection. Her life at The Forum had been pleasant, although she missed her mother and father. Elene made friends easily among the other Acolytes. She had often, guiltily, imagined that it must be something like belonging to one of the families before The Bad Times when more than one child was permitted to a family. Fearful of the consequences, she had never voiced such heresies.

Mindful of the honour bestowed on her and her family, she quelled her misgivings and continued to imbibe her lessons and obey the instructions of her superiors. Even at such a tender age, her mind was active, and she saw and heard things that caused her disquiet. It seemed to Elene that she spent much of her time in the direct service of Delmo, the Second President. She guessed that, as he had selected her, he chose to keep an eye on her progress by ensuring that she remained within his orbit.

After her first year at The Forum, Elene had settled into a happy existence and had learned to close her mind to the things she saw and heard that felt wrong. She had little concept of justice but instinctively knew that the justice dispensed by The Supreme Council seemed arbitrary and often unfair. Although still young, she had learned enough to keep her opinions very much to herself.

In her second year at The Forum, Elene became aware of the budding beauty that she displayed. More than one male Acolyte and even a couple of the male Attendants had cast covetous glances at her young but quickly ripening body. She had been aware of it and had been flattered by it. She had also been puzzled and had to admit, somewhat disappointed, that any such admiration had remained unspoken, and its intensity only guessed at.

It was with a sense of shock and disbelief that she had begun to detect the same response from the Second President! As she became aware of his lingering gaze and it happening more and more, his hands seemed accidentally to touch her, and she began to fear his intentions. She found it difficult to believe that a man she so venerated and a man of such advanced years should have designs upon her. She spent many tortured hours alone trying to convince herself that it was all in her imagination.

Finally, her worst fears came to fruition when she was summoned late in the evening to the sleeping chamber of Delmo. She had been horrified to learn that he had expected her to remain there through the night. She was swiftly disappointed if she had expected him to understand her reluctance; instead, Delmo had raged at her.

"You dare refuse me? Why do you think I took you from where you were as a child? Do you believe it was for your brains, perhaps - do not make me laugh! Any fool could see the promise in you, girl. I decided when I selected you that you would be mine when you were of age. Now come here!"

His lust for her was such that he tried one more time to persuade her.

Trembling with fear and all illusions shattered, she cowered back and stubbornly shook her head. This enraged Delmo to the point where she thought he would strike her.

"Don't you see how lucky you are? To be part of The Forum is an honour that few can aspire to. To be selected by me and under my protection is a rare honour. Surely you can understand how foolish your childish refusal is!"

"It is not right!" cried Elene. "I am a child, and you are an old man; its…it's disgusting!" She crouched down on the floor, so furious was Delmo's reaction. Seeing that his evil plans were thwarted, he raged uncontrollably at her.

"Disgusting! Is that what you think, child? Then let me tell you what is disgusting!" He leaned over her cowering figure and seemed to delight in torturing her verbally.

"What's disgusting, my dear child, is to walk up to The Sanctum of Well-Being, knowing that your life will be snuffed out in a few minutes. Can you imagine what it must be like, girl can you? Can you guess how it must feel as each step takes you closer to those doors? And what do you think will happen to you when you are inside? Do you think you will die easily? Let me tell you this; when The Sanctum's Attendants know who you have offended, they will ensure your departure is not easy. Who knows what they might do with you? Perhaps you would have wished you had taken the easy way – with me! In any case, the result would be the same, except that their way, you will be used first and then exterminated like the worthless rubbish you are!" Delmo finished with a shout and then hung over Elene for a moment, hoping she might change her mind. When she just crouched there, shaking her head miserably from side to side, he snorted in anger and disgust and summoned the guards.

Now Delmo felt bored again. The procession of wrongdoers paraded before him was the usual collection of petty criminals displaying anti-social elements who had to be rounded up. What made the task so boring for Delmo was that there was little pleasure gained anymore from sending these people to their deaths. Once upon a time, he had enjoyed seeing the fear and horror in their eyes when they knew they were to die. Now it was too commonplace. He sometimes wished that one of the prisoners might make a break for it or even try to attack him. They wouldn't get far with the guards in attendance, but it would liven things up a bit, and he could enjoy watching the guards beat the miscreant.

Suddenly, as the guards escorted the next prisoner, Delmo sat forward expectantly. He grinned evilly as the slender figure of Elene was pushed into the accused's enclosure. She stood with head bowed as the charge was read.

"Accused citizen Elene, you have been brought before the justice sessions on a charge that you willfully and repeatedly refused to obey the lawful commands of a supreme council member. The charge will be considered by the Second President."

There was no invitation to enter a plea against the charge, no representation by counsel, and no offer of a chance to explain. Elene could hardly believe what had happened in such a brief time. All her childhood, she had learned of the wisdom, the honour, the infallibility of The Forum. Now she had seen a side of it that had left her numb. Her numbness faded and turned to anger as she heard Delmo speak.

"The validity of this charge is unquestioned as it was I who gave the commands that were disobeyed. The accused citizen knew full well the risks she faced for refusing to obey a lawful command."

"Lawful command?" shouted Elene, her voice high-pitched and trembling "how can you call that a lawful command. I will not allow myself to be raped by an old man, an old man who is supposed to be honourable, who is…."

Elene faltered and stopped as she shouted her protest. She had spun around to encompass all the members of The Forum who were present.

Her indignation was replaced by resignation when she saw the implacable, unyielding expressions. She knew that they were not interested in what she had to say. She stared at Delmo with loathing as he smiled down at her and said, in a sneering voice.

"Such a child, to believe that she can flaunt the wishes of The Forum." He waved a hand languidly towards the guards and said, with practiced indifference.

"Take her away. Tomorrow, she goes to The Sanctum of Well-Being!"

As the guards led Elene from the room, Delmo called out with an evil smile, "Guards, make sure The Sanctum Attendants know who the girl offended!"

Hearing his words, Elene turned and looked with defiant loathing at her tormentor, but as she was pulled from the room, her defiance was replaced by fear.

Delmo sat back with a satisfied look on his face. His disappointment in not fulfilling his designs on the girl was more than compensated for by his pleasure in sending her to her death.

Delmo became aware of the Attendants waiting patiently for proceedings to continue. Leaning forward, he called for the next accused citizen to come forth. He watched as the prisoner was led, but his attention diverted as a cream-robed Attendant hurried into the room and raised a hand to signify he wished to approach. Sensing the man's urgency, Delmo told the prisoner and guards to wait and summoned the Attendant.

"What is it?" he hissed imperiously "you can see we are in session."

"Forgive me, Second President," said the Attendant nervously, "I thought you would want to know, sir... it's Jason, sir, Jason of the family of Thorason."

"Ah yes, the one we honoured yesterday. What about him?"

"Well, that's it, sir. You see he didn't turn up today at The Sanctum for his Dying Day!"

Chapter 5

Jason changed position to try and ease the aching in his legs and back. He moved carefully, trying not to wake Teg, who slept peacefully curled up in a tight ball.

The space in which they hid was barely big enough to contain them both, but it served the vital functions of both hiding and sheltering them from the midday sun high overhead. The small outcrop of rocks in the face of the scrub-covered hillside had appeared much more extensive from below. By the time they had reached it and found how small it was, the heat and their aching limbs had dictated that they make the most of its limited shelter.

Jason felt a great weariness and wished only to close his eyes and sleep, but he knew he had to remain alert; the hunt for him must surely now be in full cry.

Jason recalled an event six years ago when a man who had been sent to The Sanctum of Well-Being after being diagnosed as incurable with arthritis had fled at night. When he hadn't appeared at The Sanctum, an intensive manhunt was launched. The man's condition made his journey slow and awkward, and his recapture was only a matter of time.

Jason well remembered the horror and disgust expressed by people at the time. People felt that the man should not have behaved so. As he recalled the scale of the search for that man, Jason wondered how big a search would be mounted for a notable citizen like himself.

That he should find himself as a fugitive was something that Jason still found hard to believe. He gazed down at his sleeping grandson with something approaching awe at the thought that a boy of Teg's age had persuaded him to discard all honour, leave his wife and daughter shamed, and turn on all his beliefs in just one night. He had to confess that he was not wholly convinced that all his life had been spent following a dubious path, but Teg had planted the seeds of doubt in his mind. The seeds germinated and took root as the long night progressed.

There was suspicion of dawn creeping up on the horizon when he finally decided and leapt into action. Going through the living quarters of his residence, he had gathered things he thought he might need. The selection had been random and ranged from a multi-bladed knife and a flashlight to a ball of twine and scissors. He had packed everything into a shoulder bag and went to the kitchen, where he grabbed various foods and drinks. By the time he had crept through the sleeping quarters, the bag was bulging and heavy on his shoulder. He had paused briefly outside his wife's and then his daughter's rooms. Listening to the gentle susurrations of their sleep. He had recalled the earlier joy and pride at the honour bestowed on him.

Jason wondered briefly if he had gone mad but quickly rallied determination to follow through on the course of action he set out upon. Sending a silent wish for forgiveness towards the untroubled forms of his wife and daughter, he went quietly to where Teg lay. Jason had stood looking down at his grandson.

Teg lay sprawled on his back, his pale face streaked with the marks of dried tears. Even in sleep, his face conveyed his sadness and confusion. Jason found it hard to believe that Teg had led him to this, but then he smiled resignedly, leaned down, and gently placed one hand over the boy's mouth whilst shaking him with the other. Teg's eyes had widened in sudden fear, his hand streaking up to pull away the fingers across his mouth, but then he recognised his grandfather, and his expression changed to puzzlement.

He had listened, wide-eyed, hardly daring to breathe, as Jason had explained his action.

"I have thought hard about what you have said, Teg. I've never thought about the things you have raised doubts about before. Once I started to ponder your words, other things intruded into my mind, and I realised there were too many unanswered questions. I may be mad, Teg, but I have listened to you, and I have decided that we will try and find some answers. To do this, I must flee and become a fugitive with a great likelihood of being caught. In that case, I will die with dishonour. Anyway, I am going to try."

Teg's face had transformed, and his eyes had a look of relieved joy as he listened. He sat up abruptly and grabbed Jason's arms, "grandad, please take me with you, please!"

Jason looked at Teg for a long quiet moment before answering,

"I knew you would ask me this, Teg, so I have thought hard and long about it. Taking you with me would immediately make you a fugitive and double the dishonour to our family. However", as Teg was about to protest, he held up a restraining hand and said, "I have thought long and hard about all you said tonight and how you have motivated my actions. You will never settle for The Way as you will always question. You will go too far one day, and I will not be here to help you. It is best, I think, that you come with me now. I can care for you, and you can inspire me when I have doubts."

Teg had been delighted and had quickly obeyed his grandfather's instructions. He had dressed and collected spare clothing together, which he had stuffed into a camping bag. Finally, they had crept quietly from the house and quickly headed to the east of town where the hills and fields were nearest.

Despite his age, Jason was fit and had no difficulty maintaining a good pace. By the time the sun rose above the horizon, they had reached the edge of town. They knew it would take about three hours for the sun's rays to come over the top of The Sanctum of Well-Being, and people would begin to wonder what had happened to Jason. Messengers would be sent to the house to see if he had been taken ill or had suffered an accident. By the time the truth dawned, Jason had hoped to be at least four hours journey from the town, but they had to keep up a brisk pace.

The Forum banned all internal combustion engine-powered vehicles. This rule led to the development of battery-operated cars and chemical-powered transport. Although some of these vehicles could hover and cross water and land. Such technology still needed to be applied successfully to flight, so Jason and Teg only had to watch for ground vehicles. Jason was thankful that they did not have to contend with the possibility of aerial surveillance.

By the time The Forum hunted them, Jason and Teg had made good progress into the hills. For a while, they kept going, keeping to the cover of trees and shrubbery as best they could. Fatigue and heat finally drove them up the hilltop to the rocky outcrop, where they now rested.

Teg murmured and rolled over. It looked like he would wake up for a moment, but then he settled down again, and his breathing resumed the steady sleep pattern.

When Jason saw that Teg continued sleeping, he decided to risk stretching his legs. Crawling out from under the overhang of rock, he remained on his knees while he scanned for police. Carefully getting to his feet, he winced as his knee joints protested. He arched his back to ease the kinks out and slowly stepped up and down on the spot to loosen his legs. Feeling better, he yawned widely, stretching his arms out, feeling the effects of his sleepless night.

He carefully surveyed the countryside again. The hill they were on sloped down a long way to a heavily wooded valley. He had thought at first of hiding there but had guessed that this was the sort of place the searchers would expect them to be. He had looked at the hill and, seeing numerous outcrops of rock, had decided that they would be better off hiding in one of them. The ground sloped up behind the trees to a low rolling hill. Beyond was a series of cultivated fields with occasional groups of trees.

Further on, the ground gradually became rougher, with shale and coarse scrub as the dominating features. This ground rose slowly at first but then suddenly erupted into a range of wild, low hills that stretched bleakly into the distance. Jason stared at them with distaste as he thought they must eventually cross these hills to hopefully get beyond the range of their pursuers. He wasn't sure where they would go or why, but instinctively felt they would find some answers at The Wastelands.

Suddenly something attracted Jason's attention. He crouched down as he looked to his right, where at some distance, but clearly visible, the moving speck of a vehicle glinted in the sun as it approached from the direction of town. Like a crab scuttling for cover, he crawled backwards quickly into the shelter of the rocks. He looked anxiously at Teg, sleeping peacefully.

Now Jason really felt like a fugitive, and the unreality of his situation hit him anew. When Teg had left with his parting question, Jason had stood there shaking with a mixture of anger and disbelief. When he had control of himself, he poured himself another drink. Very abstemious by nature, this alone had indicated the extent of his inner turmoil. As he crouched in the shade of the rock, he thought again of the thought processes that had brought him here. At first, as he had sat there, his thoughts had been mainly of Teg's treachery, and he was angry that his grandson had caused him to abandon his strict standards of duty and behaviour. He had cursed Teg for foolish questions but found himself considering the last question repeatedly. It was with shock that he realised Teg was right.

Jason had vivid memories of the last time The Supreme Council had changed two of the incumbents. Aaron, the Third President, had become President and Delmo and David had become Second and Third Presidents, respectively. There had been no explanation for the changes, and none had been expected. It was only now that Jason began to wonder about these events.

He recalled that it had been about twenty years before. He remembered that when Aaron became President, he was already losing his hair, the initial stages in the now familiar and distinctive bald head with the bushy, silver hair wings on either side. Jason's expression became thoughtful and then troubled as he recalled that when Aaron became President, he must undoubtedly have been in his late fifties or early sixties; the other two were clearly of similar age.

The doubts that Teg had planted in his mind began to grow as he remembered, vividly, that the two members of The Supreme Council who had been replaced had been much, much older than sixty-five. In fact, he recalled them from his youth, and they had seemed old then. The realisation that the stringent rules applied to the people were not applied to their rulers. This came like a cold-water shock to Jason, and he replayed Tegs words in his mind. He also found himself dissecting Tegs questions and considering the answers more deeply, and as the night slowly passed, he became more and more troubled. Jason felt so unsettled he was uncertain about what to do. He had doubts now, but it would not be easy to cast off the beliefs and teachings of a lifetime just hours away from his Dying Day. Something that, just a few hours before, he had been prepared to face without question.

Thoughts of his appointment with death made him again consider Tegs last question. As well as The Supreme Council and its immediate predecessors. Now Jason realised that, at various times over the years, there had been prominent Attendants, barred by lack of vacancy from The Supreme Council, who had served in The Forum until obviously beyond their sixty-fifth years. His doubts, evasions, and fears suddenly washed away in the realisation that Teg had a case. The thought struck him with the force of a hammer blow, and he could not recall ever having attended, or even having heard of, the Dying Day of any of those elderly members of The Forum. Suddenly Jason knew that he had to find the truth.

The road to The Sanctum of Well-Being was an incline paved with a smooth stone that threw back the sounds of the footsteps of those making their final walk. On each side of the road was a broad step, and beyond that, a series of narrower steps. On these steps, the family and friends, or just the curious, would gather to say farewell to those about to die. The atmosphere was generally relaxed with a little hint of sadness, and many of those making the final walk would be seen smiling proudly when they saw and heard how many had come to bid them goodbye.

Today there had been only a few celebrants, although the watchers along the steps were numerous. The reason for the presence of so many became clear as two police vehicles glided to a halt at the bottom of the walkway. The crowd fell silent, leaning forward to look down as the vehicles' doors were being opened.

The days of justice, when criminals took their final walk, were always well attended as people took the opportunity to demonstrate their own rectitude by reviling those whose character had been less robust. Whether the watchers knew how petty some of the crimes were that had led to this walk was doubtful, their looks of anticipation showed that they probably didn't even care.

As the prisoners assembled at the walkway's beginning, the crowd fell silent, readying themselves to hurl abuse as the unfortunate group took their walk to death. There were murmurs of surprise and anticipation as they saw that one was kept back as the prisoners began moving. They knew immediately that this one must be guilty of some heinous crime. It was common practice that such criminals were forced to walk alone so that the total condemnation of the watchers could be concentrated upon them.

As the group of dejected-looking men and women ascended the walkway, jeers and abuse were half-hearted; the main attraction was occupying the crowd's minds. The police at the bottom waited until the group had entered The Sanctum doors before pushing the lone prisoner forward. The crowd murmured angrily at the prisoner's approach, and their anger and fury seemed only to be fueled when they saw that the miscreant was a slim, quite lovely girl of adolescent years.

Elene had tried to prepare herself for this moment. She was determined she would not give the watchers the satisfaction of reducing her to a hysterical wreck, as she had often seen happen. Even as a disinterested observer on other justice days, Elene felt sympathy for the wretches who suffered the torments she now faced.

Bravely she held her head high and began to walk. She immediately realised how difficult it would be to keep her resolution. The sheer hatred and abuse that showered her from both sides were like physical blows, and she found herself hunching as if to ward off the verbal battering. She saw the doors of The Sanctum nearing. She remembered Delmo's words hurled at her to weaken her resolution. Her knees were weak, and her lower lip began to tremble as she struggled not to cry. She walked on, the vile language, the insults, the curses hurting and humiliating her.

Then, like a punch, she heard the screeching curses of her own family! She looked to her left and saw her mother and father joining in with the crowd screaming and shouting at her. Disbelieving, she turned, staring back at the distorted faces of her own parents. Unknowingly she wandered to the side of the walkway. Suddenly hands hit out at her, as verbal abuse was matched with physical. To her horror, she felt hands clawing at her body as some righteous watchers saw the chance for personal gratification.

Like a nightmare, she struck out at the screaming faces, catching somebody's head. Immediately she felt pushed, a mighty shove sent her reeling across the other side. Sensing a new entertainment, they immediately pushed her back the other way. Backwards and forwards, they shoved her from side to side across the walkway. She reeled and staggered, feeling her senses going. Bruised and bewildered, she spun across the walkway once again. She crashed into the watchers, and off-balance, two of them fell. Unable to stop, she tumbled over them.

Quickly she got to her feet, fearful of being trampled. She stared around, noticing she was outside the line of watchers. In front of her were the lawns that surrounded The Sanctum. Suddenly, without thinking, she was off and running across the grass. For a stunned moment, the crowd watched her, and then, with a howl of fury, they began to chase after her.

Already she had rounded the corner of the building and was out of their sight. It had now become a race against the mob racing around the side of the building. Gardens stretched in all directions. A shimmering white pergola stood at the junction of two crisscrossing paths. Trees had been planted along the sides of each track to provide peaceful shaded avenues to protect strollers from the sun's heat.

The mob came to a disorganised halt as the leaders looked here and there for their quarry. The grassy slopes were empty, the beds too low to provide a hiding place. Puzzled and frustrated, the mob milled about, angry at the loss of their prey. Some people ran right around the back of The Sanctum, but Elene was nowhere to be seen. One of the crowds wandered onto one of the pathways. He looked around and then suddenly peered intently along the long straight avenue.

"She's there!" he cried, pointing to where, in the distance, Elene fled parallel and kept close to the trees. Her ruse had given her a good lead on her pursuers, but she sobbed with frustration and exhaustion as she heard the clamour rising behind her. Heart pumping furiously, breath coming in great heaving gulps, the end of the avenue of trees was in sight.

As she burst out of the cover of the trees and ran full tilt across the road into the turning opposite, startling pedestrians who turned and stared open-mouthed. Pounding on, she ran down the side road. She crossed one intersection, came to another and turned. Tearing past an open-fronted garden, she suddenly came to an abrupt halt.

Running back, she looked where a child's bicycle lay on the lawn. Chest heaving, head throbbing, she stared down at the bicycle. She could hear the shouts of the mob coming closer. She dashed forward and picked up the bike. As she did so, a door at the house opened, and a cry of outrage told her she had been seen. Running with the bicycle, she tried awkwardly to mount it. The sound of the mob neared the corner, and the shouts of the woman from the house came closer.

She forced herself to stop and mounted the bicycle. Her tired legs and winded lungs made her weary, and her progress was painfully slow as she began to pedal. She glanced briefly over her shoulder and saw the woman racing up behind her, reaching to grab her. Behind the woman was the leading edge of the mob sweeping around the corner. Panting with frustration, she pedaled harder. She felt the woman's hand brush her shoulder, causing her to wobble. The wobble made the woman lose balance, and, with a scream, she stumbled and sprawled full length in the road.

The mob had seen that Elene was on a bicycle and howled even louder and increased the speed of the chase. Elene began to pick up the pace, the pedals flicking around quicker. She saw a side turning off to her left. Praying it wouldn't be a dead-end, around the sweeping corner, she nearly lost her balance. Groaning as she saw that the end of the road was fenced, then sighed with relief as she saw another turning off to her right.

Swerving into the side street, she nearly cannoned into a man helping his wife unload her shopping. There were shouts of anger as a bag crashed to the ground. Elene glanced over her shoulder and saw, to her relief, that the couple were not chasing her but were scrambling around after their groceries, sparing her only an occasional angry glance.

Suddenly, up ahead, Elene saw the white posts that marked the entrance to one of the bridges that spanned the river. Knowing that there were trees, hills, and winding roads on the other side of the river, she put even more urgency into her frantic pedaling. She quickly looked back as she soared up the incline that led onto the bridge, smiling triumphantly when she saw no sign of her pursuers.

Chapter 6

"This is an outrage-how did you let this happen? Delmo fought to restrain himself as Aaron ranted and raved. The Second President had known that his leader would be angry at the news of Jason's defection but had not expected the almost uncontrolled anger that had resulted. He felt a sense of injustice at the President's words but knew he must be careful how he responded. He was only one step away from the Presidency itself, but he knew full well that Aaron was still powerful enough to be done with him if the whim took him.

"President, the search for Jason was launched immediately after his absence was noted; I can assure you that no stone will be left unturned, no effort spared to bring the traitorous dog to heel" "Assure me! You can assure me? Nothing you say can assure me; you fool. How did this happen?"

"There is no indication that he contemplated treachery, sir. His own family insists that they are as surprised as we are!"

"His own family eh! No doubt they are as much a part of this as he. What else do you expect them to say? They must be made to tell us everything!"

"Rest assured, sir, they have been made to tell us everything. I doubt that anyone, least of all those trusting fools, could resist Garon's questioning" Aaron pondered this for a while. He well knew the persuasive nature of the Interrogator's methods. He sometimes wondered if Garon liked his work just a bit too much. Aaron suspected they had probably lost vital information more than once because of Garon's enthusiasm for his work. Privately, Aaron thought of him as the executioner rather than the Interrogator. He did have his uses, though, so his occasional excesses were tolerated.

"Did they have anything to say that might be useful?" he asked Delmo. Sensing a moderation of the President's anger, Delmo relaxed somewhat. However, he remained alert, feeling that Aaron was especially concerned about Jason's defection, "The only thing of interest that did transpire was that the grandson, Teg if I recall his name correctly, is missing. It's unlikely that Jason would have forced the boy to go with him; that would be so foreign to the man's nature."

"And I suppose this defection isn't foreign to his nature!" interrupted Aaron sarcastically.

"I have the feeling that the boy must have gone voluntarily - apparently, he was very fond of his grandfather."

"Do you really think that's the only reason he would have gone?" asked Aaron, in a tone that strongly suggested that he had his own opinion.

"He's only a child; it's not likely that he would have gone for any other reason, right?

Aaron's tone was deceptively mild as he started to answer, but Delmo could sense the anger beneath and tensed as he waited for him to explode.

He did.

"Only a child? Only a child, you say. Are you that stupid, you can't see that a child that age can be the most dangerous enemy we have!"

"I don't quite understand, President."

"You don't quite understand? That shows how stupid you are, then."

Aaron paced for a minute or so, gathering his thoughts. Initially Delmo was worried but could see Aaron's expression turn from anger to thoughtfulness, he sensed that now was the time to continue.

"The problem with children, my dear Delmo, is that they are curious. They are inclined to be nosy and to ask awkward questions. Fortunately, only some of our children have pursued their curiosity for too long. When we find out about it, we usually divert their curiosity satisfactorily. Where that doesn't work, it is an easy enough matter to contrive another solution. A visit to The Sanctum of Well-Being should sufficiently quell any curiosity. The danger comes from the one who might slip through our net. So far, we have been lucky. That is until today."

"But President, you make it sound like this boy, this Teg, is the big problem. From your reaction earlier, I thought it was this Jason who was your concern."

Aaron looked hard at Delmo, a long derisive look that made the Second President uncomfortable.

"Delmo, Delmo, dear, oh dear! How you became my Second President, I shall never know. Is it too much for you to understand that anyone with a keen, inquiring mind is likely to be a danger. A man only becomes one of this country's leading physicians if he has a good mind. Somehow, I doubt that he has ever really had any rebellious thoughts; it seems that the arrival of his Dying Day has led to his sudden conversion. I want you to find out all you can about this grandson of his - what was his name?"

"Teg"

Yes, this Teg. Find out everything: home background, school, his friends, everything. I have a sneaking suspicion that our friend Jason may not have led the boy astray; it could be the other way around!"

Delmo's expression showed that he found his leader's hypothesis hard to swallow. He was inwardly angry at the insulting way the President had spoken to him but knew that, for the moment, there was nothing he could do. Concealing his anger and doubts, he bowed to Aaron and began to walk out of the chamber. Reaching the door, he turned. He looked surprised for a moment when he saw that Aaron had turned to look out of the window, and his expression was worried indeed.

"Don't worry, President. We will find them. They will yet take their final walk to The Sanctum."

"No!" shouted Aaron. Surprised, Delmo stared at him, and then Aaron said, "No, they are not to be brought back here. The last place we want them is here. You will make sure they are found, without delay. When they are found, you will have them killed!"

Crouching low, Jason and Teg ran for the steep-sided gully that cut through the rough, stony hills about fifty meters away. They had broken from the cover about an hour before. The vehicle that Jason had seen in the distance had taken nearly an hour to reach the wooded valley below their hiding place. In case they needed to flee, Jason had woken Teg, and together they crouched in the shadowy space under the rocks watching the vehicles approach. By the time it was within a kilometer or so, they could see clearly that it was a police personnel carrier.

The tension had been almost unbearable as the vehicle approached the trees; a contingent of armed policemen was clearly visible in the back. They had been surprised and relieved when the carrier had continued through the valley and had emerged from the trees off to their left. They could see that the full complement of men remained in the back of the carrier and watched it until it dwindled into the distance.

They soon guessed why it was not stopping when Teg, seeing the tiny glint of another vehicle approaching from the direction of town, grabbed Jason's arm.

"Grandad, that must be why the other one didn't stop. I don't mind betting that the next one heads into the valley down there! They must spread them out to search an extensive area at once.

"You're probably right, Teg. They may start searching this hillside; it will only be a matter of time before they find us. It would be better if we ran for those hills now.

As they made their way through the trees at the bottom of the hill, they were surprised to find that the approaching vehicle could already be heard. Although they knew it must be a while before it reached the valley, the noise, borne on the still air so clearly, inspired them to push themselves harder. When they had crested the first low, shale-covered hill on the valley's far side and looked in the direction of the approaching carrier, they realised that it was just as well that they had hurried as it was now much closer than they had expected.; The loose shale and the occasional low scrub slowed their progress considerably, and it was with a sense of relief that they finally ran down the far side of that first hill. They had progressed along the dried-up stream bed that meandered between the mountains. So clear was the air they could plainly hear doors slamming and voices shouting as the search began. Every time Jason or Teg stepped on loose pieces of shale that clattered and rattled, they felt sure that the searchers would hear it. When they paused for a much-needed breather, they noticed that the shouts of the search party were now muted and guessed that they were searching the wooded valley. Knowing that they must put more distance between themselves and the searchers, they began moving at a tangent, which meant they must move up the stony hills and down the other side. Each time they crested a hill, they felt exposed, and half expected a distant shout or gunfire to greet them as they ran, doubled over, until they were once more below the skyline. The next hill they came to was higher than the others, and they were reluctant to expose themselves to the danger of discovery by going over the top. Walking along the side of the hill, they spotted the steep gully they were now headed for. They were relieved that the gorge led directly away from the searchers and appeared as though it went for a safe distance. They allowed themselves the luxury of gentler progress, giving their aching legs and lungs a chance to recover; they silently walked on for quite some time. The gully seemed to go on and on, sometimes petering out in a transverse valley but gradually deepening as they moved through the hills.

The sun was low in the sky when they finally stopped to rest. As though by common consent, although no words had been spoken, they headed towards a curving overhang in and around which grew shrubs and flowers. Gratefully, they sank onto the dusty, hard ground and, for a while, just allowed their breathing to settle and their feet to cool off. Jason rummaged in his bag and produced a container of fruit juice. They each took a grateful swallow, although again, without a word being said, they took no more than one swallow. Teg lay back against the sloping wall of the gully, his hands behind his head and closed his eyes.

"Tired, Teg?" asked Jason.

"Sort of, Grandad, but it doesn't matter how tired I am; I'm just glad we're here." He knelt up and looked searchingly at Jason, a faint edge of doubt in his expression, and asked.

"Are you sorry you came, grandad?"

"Sorry, Teg? My word no. I've had plenty of chances to think whilst we've been on the move, and I know I won't be happy now until I get some answers or die in the attempt!" He looked anxiously at Teg and reached out to pat his hand.

"I shouldn't have said that, Teg, don't take any notice of me."

"Don't worry, grandad, if it makes you feel any better, I can tell you that I know if we're caught, it means The Sanctum, but I'm not afraid to die, not if I know that I tried to do what I thought was right."

Jason was clearly moved as he looked at his grandson, and there was a catch in his voice when he spoke.

"Teg, oh Teg, what a revelation you are. All these years, I thought I knew you so well. The truth is I never even knew myself!" He smiled fondly as Teg moved so that they sat close together, side by side.

"Promise me one thing, Teg," said Jason, seriously.

"Yes, Grandad?"

"If there is a danger of my being recaptured and you have the chance to flee then you must do so. Now you must promise me that Teg, there would be nothing to be gained from both of us being captured. Now please promise me solemnly, Teg."

Teg stared at Jason for a long moment. He was weighing his grandfather's words carefully and showed that he realised their sense when he reluctantly nodded his head.

"I promise, grandad."

"Good, now how about something to eat?"

"To be honest, I'm not really all that hungry."

"No, nor am I. Considering how long it's been since we've eaten is surprising. I guess it's all the excitement."

Teg smiled, his face looking younger than it had since Jason had crept into his sleeping chamber. He almost chuckled as he asked,

"Do you really think it's exciting, grandad?"

"Well now, Teg, don't get me wrong, this isn't a game we're playing, as you know. I must be honest though and tell you that I feel as though I'm really alive for the first time in years."

"Really? You've always seemed happy enough., I've never thought of you other than one of the happiest people I've ever known!"

"The funny thing is that I was happy or thought I was. Understand me, there was a lot that I would never change. Your grandmother, for instance, whatever else may have happened in my life, or may yet, I will always be grateful that she is my wife. And any father would be proud to have Carolin as a daughter."

He leaned over and ruffled Teg's hair playfully, "and you, Teg, of course. I've always been so proud of you."

"Until last night, grandad!"

"Aha! Last night indeed. You know, you're right, Teg; I felt my whole world turned upside down. My grandson was speaking such heresies; I could not believe it. I must admit that I would never have dreamed I would let you turn me into a fugitive at that time."

"But it was you who came and got me!" Teg exclaimed with mock indignation.

"You may choose to believe that my boy, but I think my version is nearer the truth."

"You're not sorry, are you, grandad?"

"Sorry? Good lord, no. I'm sorry I didn't question a few things much sooner."

"I've thought about it for a long-time, grandad. It was rotten not being able to talk to anyone about what I thought. I knew that anyone I talked to could end up reporting me."

Chapter 7

"Tell me, Teg, tell me everything that you thought about. How did you start thinking about things? It's not the sort of thing that children normally occupy their minds with, not that you're much of a child anymore. I sometimes think you're more grown-up than many of us! Now, how about you tell me all about it?"

Teg seemed highly pleased by his grandfather's words and shifted about awkwardly as he sought to adopt the right attitude and find the right words. He investigated the distance and began tentatively recalling his early doubts and feelings. As he recounted them to Jason, his voice became more robust, his enthusiasm more marked, and his grandfather looked at him with what might have been awe.

"It was a silly thing that first made me think about things. I remember our teacher was telling us about The Bad Times. He was talking about one of the cities where things had turned awful, and I asked him questions about it. I wasn't being awkward. I didn't think much about the questions I was asking; they just came into my mind. Only when the teacher started to get angry did I begin to wonder why? My curiosity turned to doubt when I noticed he seemed frightened."

"Please, sir!"

"Yes, Teg, what is it?"

"Please, sir, when you talked about how the cities had become overcrowded, you said that some people had lived like that for years."

"That's right, Teg, what of it?"

"Well, sir, did The Forum make the people live like that?"

"The Forum didn't exist in those days, Teg. Now all you children listen because learning about this will do you all good. Before The Bad

Times, there was a form of government that was unwieldy, impractical, corrupt, self-serving, well, let's just say it was a bad form of government."

"Sir?"

"What now, Teg?"

"Sir, how did the government get power?"

"How did they get power? They had a system called democracy, meaning every citizen could choose the government they wanted."

"They chose their own government?" one of the students asked, astonished.

"Yes, and you know where it got them; The Bad Times!"

"But sir," asked Teg again, "If the government didn't make the people live in the cities, who did?"

"They chose to live there; they knew no better."

"But if they lived there for years like you said, they must have liked it there!?

"What is the point you are trying to make, boy?"

Teg flinched at the tone of exasperation that had coloured the teacher's voice but went gamely on.

"Well, it seems that if they liked it enough to live there for years without being made to, well, it couldn't have been all bad, could it, sir?

"You only have to look at where they ended up to see how bad it was, Teg!" the teacher said, exasperated.

"I know that sir, but if their government had done things properly, they could have stopped things from getting so bad, couldn't they sir?"

The rest of the class was getting impatient, not understanding the point Teg was trying to make. Teg was floundering somewhat, instinctively feeling close to something but not knowing how to reach out for it.

The teacher, sensing the unrest in the classroom, tried to turn it to his advantage.

"Well now, young man, it seems you have baffled the rest of the class, and you most certainly have baffled me; if you have some point to make, Teg, please make it quickly so that we may get on."

Teg shook his head in frustration, feeling that something was just below the surface of his mind but not quite sure how to articulate it. Finally, he burst out exasperated, "Oh, I don't know, sir, it just seems that if the government was good and did its job properly, there wouldn't be any need to have such strict rules for everybody!"

Teg was ready to expand on his theory and eagerly awaited the teacher's response. The rest of the class, still failing to follow Teg's thinking, merely looked on in boredom, but Teg saw that his teacher looked decidedly uncomfortable. He felt disappointed and perplexed when the teacher said, "Thank you for bringing up an interesting point, Teg. Now class, as you've just heard, there are rules we must follow to have a clean, safe and happy life. Who can tell me what the most important rules are?"

Now the class were back on familiar ground and miffed at Teg's domination of the lesson; they clamoured to win the teacher's attention.

"Yes, Daryl, you are first."

"Sir, one rule is to keep our environment clean, sir.!"

"Excellent, Daryl; who's next? Ah yes, Thanas, what about you?"

"One must always obey the commands of The Forum so that all may benefit, sir!"

As Teg listened to the platitudes and well-learned responses, he was aware of the teacher's relief, and his inner disquiet grew.

Jason smiled sympathetically as Teg paused in his narrative. He could imagine it was challenging for him to be so alone in his thoughts. Jason also felt a sense of embarrassment and shame that the same questions hadn't occurred to him. He listened with fascination as Teg went on.

"I tried asking the teacher things like that a few times, but he always seemed annoyed or nervous. He was not a bad person because one day, he stopped me as I was leaving the class. He asked some stupid questions about an essay I'd written. I couldn't understand why he had to ask me because everybody knew the answer. Suddenly, as the last boy left the classroom, he said, "Teg, please listen to me. The questions you ask will get you into trouble, please don't ask any more in my class. I won't always be able to pretend they never happened. Remember, Teg, you're too young to know!"

"I realised it was a warning, but now I realise what a chance he took. He should have reported me. If anybody had told The Forum the kind of questions I asked, I would have been in trouble, and he would probably have been as well for not reporting me."

Teg looked solemnly at Jason and said, almost sadly.

"It can't be right, can it, grandad, when people aren't allowed to say what they think?"

Jason smiled sadly and shrugged.

"No Teg, it can't; the sad thing is it's only now I'm beginning to realise just how wrong it is."

He looked around and then up to the sky.

"We've got about two hours of light left, Teg; what do you say we move on a bit before we find somewhere to settle down for the night. And while we walk you can tell me more about this inquisitive little mind of yours."

"After what Teacher Johansen had said to me, I made sure that I didn't say too much about what I thought; but there were things that didn't seem right all the time."

"One day I went with my mother and father to attend the final walk of one of the seniors at my father's work. Afterwards, we stayed for the justice day walk. Among the Accused, there was a boy; he couldn't have been more than my age. I don't know what his crime was. I only know it seemed wrong that he should have to die. I looked at the people who were jeering and shouting at the prisoners. I don't know why I was so surprised to see Teacher Johansen there, but he was, and he was behaving as badly as all the others. He seemed even worse when that boy walked past. I couldn't help noticing that as he shouted, he'd look around carefully every so often as if to be sure that people were observing how good a citizen he was. Afterwards, when we were walking home, I kept remembering the teacher and thought of what he'd said about me being too young to know about things. I couldn't help thinking that the boy I had seen must also have been too young to know about everything, yet he was being sent to die for some petty crime. It all seemed so wrong."

"I see the point you're making, Teg," said Jason sympathetically, "but you must keep a sense of perspective. There's always the chance that the boy had committed some grave crime."

"But grandad, isn't it true that if an accused citizen has committed a severe crime, he or she is made to walk the final walk alone?"

Jason looked at his grandson and nodded slowly, "A good point. It seems I have much to learn; go on, Teg."

"Do you remember you came into my sleeping chamber one night because you thought I had a bad dream?"

"Yes, I do remember. You were talking in your sleep. I was afraid you would wake the whole household. Why do you ask, was that dream associated with all this?"

"It wasn't a dream, grandad. It was so awkward not being able to talk to anyone about how I felt. It was like having to keep a big secret. You know, when you've promised not to tell anyone something, but you wish you could. I used to argue with myself when I was in bed."

Teg giggled abruptly at the thought of how foolish he'd felt when he'd first carried on a two-sided conversation alone. He looked embarrassed as he saw Jason grinning.

"I know it seems silly now, grandad, but it did work! It worked so well I actually ended up arguing with myself; that's the night you came in and thought I was dreaming."

Jason laughed out loud now. It was a pleasing sound, and he and Teg looked at each other happily, realising how much tension they had been under. Teg began to laugh, too and soon, they were rolling from side to side, their laughter echoing through the gully.

Suddenly they became aware of how much noise they were making and, looking guiltily at each other, they stopped laughing. They stared at each other for a moment, and then they were off again, spluttering and hissing as they tried to keep their laughter silent. The light was fading quickly now, and they felt exhausted, as much from their laughing spell as from their journey. When they located a suitable shelter, the darkness was quite profound. Exhausted as they were and disinclined to fumble around in the dark for food, they curled up under a thick spread of densely packed scrub and slept soundly within minutes.

Chapter 8

It was better not to look up. The bright light seemed to sear the eyes and burn into the brain. The straps cut cruelly into his flesh, and the hardness of the couch on which he lay numbed his body where it had lain for several hours. He wished very much that the soles of his feet and the tips of his fingers could be as numb; they, however, throbbed cruelly from the abuse applied. He thought it would be easy to go mad. To be wrenched from one's familiar surroundings and from the bosom of your own family was bad enough. To be subjected to unrelenting questioning in conditions that were almost guaranteed to terrorise one into saying whatever was required, regardless of its truth or otherwise, was an experience that, on its own, could practically guarantee madness; but to be subjected to sheer brutality, to be hurt cruelly, and worse, deliberately, is something any mind would find hard to comprehend.

Not knowing why this was happening was enough to make you think that perhaps you were insane already. He sought to collect his thoughts, believing that if he could control his mind's direction, he could retain some hope of eventually surviving this horror.

There had been no warning. There was a sudden rush into his chamber, a heart-stopping moment when he recognised an assassin among the men who burst in. Oddly, as they dragged him away, he felt relieved for he knew he would already be dead if that's what they had come for.

The journey had been like some incredible nightmare; pushed face downwards on the floor of the police vehicle, he had feared he would suffocate when his pleas for an explanation, and his protestations of innocence, had merely resulted in a jack-booted foot being pressed on the back of his head. He had been dragged from the vehicle and frog-marched backwards along brightly lit corridors so fast he could barely keep his feet tracking. The room into which he had been bundled had so clearly been an interrogation room of the worst kind. His insides had turned to water, and his legs weakened. He had fallen to his knees and begged for mercy without knowing why he was there.

The big man had come into the room then. Despite his abject terror and misery, he had been aware that the police officers manhandling him had suddenly backed away, leaving him kneeling, trembling and afraid, in the middle of the room.

He had a moment of hope, a feeling that perhaps this man would demand to know why he was mistreated. All hope fled when the big man stared at him contemptuously and said, in a voice fashioned in hell, "So this is the teacher of the little traitor; well, we'll soon find out just how much traitorous garbage this shaper of minds is responsible for. Strap him to the bench!"

Of all the pain, indignity and terror suffered in such a short time, the worst thing had been the complete and utter helplessness of being strapped so brutally and knowing they could do with him as they wished, and he couldn't raise a hand.

The big man leaned over him. There was something in his eyes that defied description. Cold, evil, anticipatory, he stared briefly down before snarling.

"You are the Teacher of the boy Teg?"

"Well, yes, but there must be some mistake, some nightmare, surely I…"

He had been cut off mid-sentence by a resounding slap across the face shaking his head agonisingly, bringing tears to his eyes and making his ears ring.

"Just answer my questions, do you understand?" the big man roared. He nodded fearfully.

"Tell me of what you and the boy Teg have talked about!"

"Why, only what I discuss with all the boys, the lessons that…."

"So, you try to make them all into traitors, do you?"

"Traitors? I don't understand; I talk to them only about the permitted things."

"You liar! If that were so, the boy would never have challenged the authority of The Forum; you have led him to it. Admit it!"

"Challenged The Forum, this is madness, we have talked of no such things, it is ludicrous - it's all a mistake, it must be!"

The beatings had begun, and the other nameless horrors had made him cry like a helpless baby. The agonising tortures had brought pain more severe than any rational mind could imagine. He had been reduced to a blubbering, whimpering, suffering wretch, and still, they had not believed him. The big man was enraged, yet it seemed almost as though the lack of the desired answers pleased him, although to describe his evil grin as a look of pleasure was to stretch credulity.

He'd known with a sudden clarity that he would die no matter what he told them. He felt an ineffable sadness with the thought that he would not see his beloved Andrea again and would no longer share the joy of long walks, hand in hand, across the pleasant hills above their home. He cried unashamedly at his loss and cared nothing for the sneers of his tormentors who thought he cried with fear.

He felt strangely calm as well, his rational mind letting him accept the thought of his inevitable death as preferable to this continued torture. He forced his mind to think again of his beloved wife, Andrea. He strove to keep her image in his mind as he pushed his tongue between his teeth and, raising his head as high as he could, slammed his chin down hard upon the bench. His tormentors were slow to see what he had done, but it was the big man who reacted first and, screaming at the policemen as though it was their doing, yelled, "you fool, get a surgeon, get a physician we must find out what he has to say!"

The policeman who ran to summon a physician did so with no great urgency. He could tell that the blood pumped from the severed tongue was the teacher's lifeblood.

Even though the music was loud, the hammering at the door could be clearly heard. There was something urgent enough about the clamour to still the conversation and create a strange suspension of activity as though the party had been captured in some time warp that slowed their actions and muted their voices.

The music seemed even louder above the sudden hush, and as the hostess ran to answer the urgent knocking, a guest leaned down and adjusted the volume so that the music was now just background noise. There were murmurs of shocked surprise as the door was opened, and Andrea almost fell inside, crying hysterically.

"They've taken him away; they've taken him away!"

They sensed immediately that something terrible had happened and there was tension in them as the host and hostess forced Andrea to sit down, and they listened to the exchange.

"What is it, Andrea, who's taken him?"

"The police, oh my god, they burst in and took him, dragging him away like some common criminal!"

There was an instinctive feeling among the more perceptive that Andrea had seen the last of her husband. There was also a barely noticeable but definite movement away from the distraught woman. It was as though the room's width could remove the orbiting danger. They were not uncaring people, but they knew what Andrea described involving the police was bad news.

Andrea was sobbing hysterically now; she also knew the probability of her husband's imminent return was low. Puzzled and alarmed, the host and hostess tried to discover more of what had happened.

"Did they say why they wanted him? Did they say what it was they wanted?"

"They asked him…they,…they said,…they asked him if he was the teacher of,…of the boy."

She broke down again, sobbing deep, wracking sobs.

"The Teacher of what boy?"

"They called him Teg. I think they meant the grandson of the traitor Jason."

"The one who didn't turn up for his Dying Day?"

"Yes, they dragged my husband away, saying something about the breeders of traitors not…not being fit to live."

She cried again, and so anguished were her cries they raised her from the chair and led her, near collapse, into a sleeping chamber. As the door to the sleeping chamber closed, the room began to buzz with alarmed speculation, and more than one shrill demand was made to be taken home.

In the excitement, nobody noticed the man who crept out of the back of the house and headed quickly across the street. Knowing he had little time to gather a few essentials and flee the town, Mr. Johansen also knew if he hadn't been replaced as Teg's teacher just two months prior, it might be him facing horror at the hands of the police.

There was a premise of heat in the warm wind that came with the early day. The morning sky was speckled with small drifting clouds. The trees whispered to each other, their leaves moving in time with the wind. Small creatures hopped tentatively toward the crystal stream that jumped and raced between the trees.

The animals advanced and then paused to look around carefully. Their ears and noses twitched before finally making a last dash for the water. Quickly they drank, raised their heads, and looked nervously around, then drank again.

Her early morning stiffness forgotten; Elene lay enraptured by the sight. She had travelled well after eluding her pursuers and had made good distance. She had often been forced to dismount and walk, pushing the bicycle beside her. She had instinctively cut inland, away from the city, and found few roads she could ride. She had cycled where the hills were smaller but still gave even coverage, with grass and flowers rather than rocks and scrub. It was not comfortable, but it was faster than walking. As night drew near and she found the stream, she followed its course, knowing she needed water.

She had thought often of the food she had eaten in the town, and her hunger intensified. Then she had thought of why she was running, and her desire didn't seem so bad. Her only food had been berries and occasional leaves that looked edible but had been sour.

Elene was thirsty now but so captivated by the scene before her she was reluctant to move. Suddenly she froze, and a small gasp of delight escaped her as a tiny deer appeared across the clearing, as if by magic. Hardly daring to breathe, she watched it trembling, sniffing the air. Reassured it moved a few feet closer to the stream. It stopped abruptly, ears pricked, looking hard in the direction from which it had come.

With startling speed, it turned and bounded across the clearing. There was a deafening roar, and the deer flew awkwardly through the air before crashing down, suddenly into an ungainly bundle, to lie still upon the grass.

All around Elene, small creatures scattered in alarm. She was hardly aware of them; her shocked senses concentrated on the still form of the little deer, its head a bloodied mess, its eyes unseeing.

Elene's blood froze when the cause of the tragedy was revealed. Into the clearing, laughing, and chattering strode two policemen. One of them carried the gun that had slaughtered the deer, and this, combined with the jackboots and the militaristic uniforms of the two men, gave them such a sinister aspect that Elene began to wonder whether she had done the right thing by running away. So cruel did the two men look, she suspected that if they should discover her, she might end up wishing she had accepted the end that had awaited her in The Sanctum of Well-Being.

"Well, that's two of us who won't be going hungry today," said the man with the gun, stooping to pick up the deer by its hind legs.

Elene could hardly believe what she was hearing. They were policemen, she thought; surely, they knew that eating wild animals was forbidden. It was part of The Way!

The two policemen walked to the stream. They knelt and with cupped hands, drank the crystal-clear water. The one with the deer laid it in front of him and pulling a wicked-looking knife from a sheath on his belt, began to skin and gut the carcass.

Elene felt ill. She wanted to turn her eyes away from the butchery but knew she must be aware of the two men's movements. To her eyes, the scene that had been so idyllic a few minutes before now resembled a vision from hell. The hide, loops, and coils of the deer's insides were slung carelessly aside, and the somehow obscenely denuded carcass was washed unceremoniously in the stream.

Elene's emotions were a mixture of sympathy for the deer and fear of discovery, and as the two men turned away from the stream, she retracted into the shadows beneath the bush that sheltered her. To her relief, the men appeared relaxed and unsuspicious as they retraced their steps across the clearing. One of them glanced casually around and stopped suddenly.

He clasped his partner's arm and pointed back across the clearing to beyond where Elene lay. As the men began to walk in her direction, she felt a sudden flush of fear as she realised she had left the bicycle lying out in the open!

As one of the policemen stooped and picked up the bicycle, Elene was sure he was looking directly under the bush where she lay. She held her breath, her heart thumping wildly as he straightened up, giving no sign of having seen her. She relaxed slightly as he turned to the other man and said, "Well, I don't know how this came to be here, but I reckon my boy will be well pleased with it!"

"It must belong to somebody; surely you can't just walk off with it?"

"Anyone who leaves a thing like this lying around in the middle of the countryside deserves to lose it; now take this deer for me; I can't manage both."

Elene teetered near to tears with relief as the two men began to leave the clearing. She laid her head on her arms and tried to still the shaking of her body.

"What the hell have you got there!"

Elene's head jerked up as the loud exclamation disturbed the quiet of the clearing.

Looking from her hiding place, she saw that the two policemen had been confronted by another, who was clearly an officer.

"It's a deer, sir, just a small one; I thought it might help the food situation!"

"Not that, you fool; the bicycle!"

"Well, sir, as you say, it's a bicycle."

The officer leaned forward and said, with sarcasm that made the two men blanch.

"I can see it's a bicycle cretin! Where did you get it?"

"I found it lying over there, sir. I'm sure it had been abandoned, sir."

"You are sure it had been abandoned, are you; tell me, who do you think abandoned it?"

"I wouldn't have a clue, sir."

"That is why you are a waste of space, you fool. A young lady has upset the Second President. If you noticed the bulletins circulated recently, you would know that she is the second fugitive we must look out for.

This young lady was sent to The Sanctum but decided she had a more pressing appointment elsewhere. However, one thing we do know, and what you would have learned had you been any kind of a policeman, is that she made good her getaway on a bicycle. The description of the reported bicycle matches remarkably well with the one you were about to steal!"

"Steal, sir? I wasn't stealing it. It seemed to be abandoned, sir."

"Well, now, let us see if you have any merit as a member of the law enforcement agency that provides you with your living. Tell me something; what is it that's wrong with the bicycle that led to it being abandoned?"

"There doesn't seem…."

The policemen, suspecting he might have nearly put his foot in it, stopped mid-sentence and looked carefully at the bicycle. After a while, he looked up at his superior, his expression puzzled.

"As I thought, sir, nothing seems to be wrong with it!"

The officer leaned close again, and his tone indicated that he would soon be losing his patience with his underling.

"Then why do you think it was abandoned?"

"I…I can't think of any reason, sir, to be honest."

How much do you know about being honest? Never mind that for now. Has it not occurred to you that, as the bicycle seems undamaged and there appears to be no good reason why it should have been abandoned, perhaps it hasn't been abandoned at all!"

The policeman stared at the officer, slowly beginning to understand his thoughts.

Seeing from the policeman's expression that the penny had finally dropped, the officer said icily, "I suggest you stop wasting your time and mine and begin searching immediately. You had better pray that wasting your time here hasn't given our fugitive time to escape. Now move it!"

The policeman leaned the bicycle against a tree, and he and his colleague dashed away to summon help for the search. The officer shook his head in disgust and walked out of the clearing.

Elene was frightened, so frightened she found it hard to think straight. She knew that if she tried to run for it, she would likely be quickly caught. She knew equally that if she remained, it would only be a matter of time before she was found. She reasoned that she must at least have some chance if she did make a run for it. Inching forward on her knees, she looked carefully around before pushing her head clear of the bush. Cocking her head to one side, she listened to the coarse voices of the policemen as they assembled a search party some distance away. She slowly rose to her feet, and then, as though the grassy floor of the clearing was some hollow surface that would betray her footsteps to the policemen, she ran on tiptoe to where the bicycle rested against the tree.

Breathing heavily, her heart trip-hammering, she looked around quickly and took hold of the handlebars.

At that moment, a big strong hand came around the tree and grabbed her wrist! She screamed and tried to back away, but the officer went around the tree, still holding her firmly.

"I thought you must be around here somewhere," he sneered, "and I knew you couldn't resist trying for the bicycle. That's why I'm an officer, and those other fools are not! He looked her up and down, and an anticipatory gleam entered his eyes.

"Well, now, we'll have to see what we can do with you, won't we!

Chapter 9

"It's always the way; there's no bloody justice," moaned the policeman who had earlier shot the deer.

"Not only does he get the girl, but he also takes the meat and won't even let me have the bicycle for my boy. Bloody officers!"

His companion looked around nervously, afraid his friend was overheard as then he too would be in trouble through association.

"It's only natural; that's one of the things about being an officer. You get all the goodies, don't you?

"I still say it's bloody unfair. Did you see that girl? My god, she's a nice piece, all right. That's how I like them, nice and young. She's too bloody good for him, I can tell you!"

"Do you reckon he'll give her one? After all, you know what they're saying, she gave old Delmo the elbow. It might be dangerous to dip your wick where the Second President couldn't. Might not go down too well, if you know what I mean."

"Don't be stupid. You don't think the council will find out, do you? When he's had what he wants from her!" He made a cutting motion across his throat, and they both looked through the trees to where the officer's tent stood in isolation.

"Seems a bloody waste to me," said the first man, to which the other one nodded gloomily, saying,

"Yeh, but what can we do about it?"

There was something repulsive about the man as he ate at the small table just outside the tent, his hands and face greasy from the meat that he greedily consumed. Elene's stomach was painful from hunger, and the smell of the meat and her fear made her nauseous. Her hands were tied tightly behind her back, and pain agonised through her arms and shoulders whenever she moved.

She was past crying now, her throat ached abominably from her sobbing, and her eyes were red and sore from the tears she had shed. She felt a great sadness, a sense of injustice that had befallen her when all had seemed so promising. In her misery, she had even wondered whether she might have done better to have surrendered to Delmo's demands; but then she dismissed such thoughts and took small comfort in her pride at having stood up for herself.

Elene saw her captor leering at her, and her small comfort vanished like a puff of smoke. She feared her fate when the officer returned her to his tent and tied her hands behind her. One of her feet had been loosely tied to the tent pole, and when he had finished tying her and had knelt, gloating, she had felt such a sense of helplessness and loathing she would gladly have died. He had reached out a rough, grimy hand and had run it down the length of her body. She shuddered and was nearly sick with revulsion. He sneered,

"I can just imagine how that will feel when I have those clothes off you, my beauty."

She had braced herself to face her fate with as much fortitude as she could muster but had been surprised when he stood up and, after looking down and murmuring,

"Yes, I shall look forward to that," then he left the tent.

The flap had fallen into place, leaving the tent semi-dark despite it still being before noon. Elene had heard the officer instructing a guard, and then it was quiet. After a few minutes, someone parted the tent flaps and looked curiously at her, she assumed it was the guard outside. There had been nothing for several hours since.

She had lain there in a semi-stupor, the heat in the tent and the exhaustion of her ordeal making her listless. She must have been dozing when the officer eventually returned because his sudden entrance through the flap startled her, leaving her heart beating wildly.

She had watched in agonised silence as he had stared down at her, grinning with lustful anticipation before sitting down and writing a report until an orderly arrived with his meal.

Now as she watched him finish the piece of meat, picking the bone clean with his teeth, Elene wished only that her ordeal could soon be over. She would welcome death that she knew instinctively must follow.

Having finished his meal, the officer leaned down and wiped his hands on the grass. He stood and belched loudly. For a moment, he stared out into the fading light, then turned to Elene, leering and said,

"Won't be long now, my lovely. Your patience will soon be rewarded."

She heard the faint shifting of his feet as he moved away from the tent, and then, she heard him urinating against a tree. This added to her disgust and revulsion so that she found it difficult to retain her composure when he returned and looked down at her in the half-light. She did not want to give him the satisfaction of making her cry for mercy, and so, as he unbuckled his belt and pushed his trousers down, she bit her lip and turned her head away.

When nothing happened after a few moments, she turned her head, curious. He stood there grinning and then laughed aloud as she jerked her head away.

At the sight of his full nakedness, Elene tensed and closed her eyes as he knelt. A sound like the clap of his hands preceded him, landing heavily upon her. She fought not to scream as she felt him move. Slowly she opened her eyes, sensing a pause. In the half-light she saw a person with a bloodied knife in his hand. Her heart beat rapidly as he bent over her, the knife held out before him. She looked in amazement at the officer's unconscious body being dragged away.

"Who are you? What are you doing?"

"My name is Teg. Now turn over quickly so I can cut you loose."

Chapter 10

Jason's relief at Teg's return was nothing compared to his astonishment at seeing his grandson's companion. They came running to where he stood, hidden, close to their cunningly contrived shelter of loose rocks pushed around a group of small scrubby bushes.

When they had awoken that morning, they had made a meagre meal from Jason's rations. Not knowing when they might be able to replenish their supplies, they had been careful to take only enough to quell their immediate hunger, but it wasn't long before the pangs returned.

When they prepared to move on, it quickly became apparent that the previous day's exertions, combined with his hunger and emotional stresses, had taken their toll on Jason. They had taken no more than a few steps before he had stopped, obviously in great distress. His joints seemed on fire from the prolonged, unaccustomed usage of the day before and he had been forced to sit down, wincing in agony. He had looked at Teg with some distress, and there was a tremor in his voice as he spoke.

"Oh Teg, oh Teg, what a foolish old man I am. How could I have imagined that I could hope to outrun the police? Now all I have done is lead you into danger."

"No, grandad, no. It's going to be okay. We made good time yesterday and covered a lot of ground. It's unlikely that the police will catch up with us today. You can rest all day, and then we can move much easier tomorrow. We'll be all right, grandad, don't worry!"

To Jason, it seemed as though the child he had known as Teg had disappeared almost overnight to be replaced by a young man brimming with confidence and excitement, despite being a fugitive from a court that would show no mercy whatsoever if they were recaptured.

Reassured by his grandson's confident air Jason smiled fondly and said, "It seems Teg that I need you to care for me and not the other way around, as I first thought. Well, my boy, I can't help but think I couldn't be in better hands."

Teg flushed happily at his grandfather's words. For a moment, he looked as though he would run into his arms, but thinking he was too grown up for that, he turned and stared into the distance, composing himself. When he turned back, he thought he detected a brief sadness on Jason's face, but it was gone quickly.

"You make yourself comfortable, grandad; make sure you stay hidden. I'll scout around to get an idea of which direction we should take when we move on. Don't worry if I don't return too quickly; I'll be alright."

"Take care, Teg, take good care," said Jason and then, as he was about to turn away, Teg hugged him. They both had tears in their eyes as Teg set out, turning at the top of the hill to wave and then he was gone.

Teg moved quickly down the other side of the hill and then, less quickly, to the top of the next hill, which was higher. Kneeling at the top, he looked carefully around for signs of activity or human presence. Seeing none, he stood and looked back at the way he had come, and then, turning slowly, he carefully fixed landmarks in his mind to help him locate Jason's hiding place when he returned. Still trying to figure out his or the town's direction, he shrugged and began walking.

Before fleeing, Teg had spent some time on weekends in the countryside when he and his grandfather went into the hills directly behind the town. There Teg learned about the birds and animals, the flowers and trees. Jason loved nature and communicated his love to Teg, who enjoyed freedom and space away from the town, albeit only a short distance.

Now, a reasonable distance from the town, he was astonished at the variety of trees, plants, and flowers that bedecked the land. He listened in astonishment to the differing birdsongs that filled the air. Like everyone in the town, Teg had been brought up to believe that The Bad Times had decimated nature so much that the only places where it thrived were within the confines of the few towns that had developed under the guidance of The Forum and the edicts of The Way.

Teg and nobody else he knew had ever travelled to other towns, and he had believed, as he was sure others believed, that the spaces between the towns, if not as bad as The Wastelands, were likely to be bleak and uninviting.

Now that he was savouring the beauty of the countryside, he realised with a deep bitterness just how restricted the townspeople were and how much pleasure and beauty was denied them by the restrictive rulings of The Forum. As he wandered along, all tension was gone; Teg happily sampled various leaves and berries that grew abundantly on the hills and valleys. He was staggered and delighted by the variety of tastes and textures of edible growth available. Occasionally he sampled something that made him grimace and spat it out, but having tasted everything without swallowing, he didn't suffer from the occasional mistake.

Occasionally, Teg would climb to the top of a hill to take his bearings, even shimmying up a tree to extend his range of vision if there was one convenient.

While he was up in the branches of a stately oak, he heard the crack of gunfire.

Crouching down among the leaves, he scanned the countryside. The silvery glint of a stream caught his eye first, and as he followed its course, in and out of the trees, he saw the tents of the police search party. He was about to climb down from the tree and go back the way he had come when he saw that one of the policemen had grabbed hold of somebody who, even at such distance, was clearly young and, if he was not mistaken, was a girl.

Clearly, the girl was being detained against her will, and instinctively, Teg knew he had to see if he could help her. Even as he dropped from the tree and ran down the hill, he was aware of the potential danger he was putting himself in, but an irrational surge of confidence and excitement surged through him as he crept through the trees.

As he had circled around the camp twice, Teg had come close to being discovered. Each time he had to lie perfectly still while, close by, policemen stood or sat and chatted and cursed. The police were unhappy being away from town, and their lack of enthusiasm for the task satisfied Teg.

Conversations between the policemen revealed the main reason for their presence was to find him and Jason, but The Forum also hunted the captured girl. Distracted and disgruntled by their senior officer, the police were content to spend the day as lazily as possible. Much of their talk centred on discontentment due to unfair advantages taken by the officer. Their primary complaint was the girl being disposed of rather than shared after the officer was finished with her. Sequestering the food and trapping the girl in his personal tent was causing unrest and the perfect distraction.

Teg listened with growing horror. He had found it hard enough to believe that the police officer would use the girl in the way the men suggested; that they could so calmly discuss the fact that the girl wouldn't be passed around; was unbelievable. More than anything, the suggestion that the girl would be disposed of made Teg seethe with a deep rage.

These were the people meant to protect The Way's followers and ensure the preservation of the law. These men were patently corrupt and evil. He felt a crusading spirit run through him and a sense of responsibility for the imprisoned girl lying in the officer's tent. He knew now, without a doubt, that he and his grandfather had been right to run away.

The onset of mealtime allowed him to slip from his hiding place and creep around to the clump of trees directly opposite the officer's tent. With hunger as his companion once more, he watched as the evil-looking man devoured the leg of the deer.

Teg was aware that the consumption of wild game was forbidden and saw the easy way the man ate the deer meat as another example of the deceit practiced on the people of the towns.

Teg froze and crouched down as small as he could as the officer, having finished his meal, approached the trees where he lay concealed. As he lay there, Teg looked around, hoping to find something that could be used as a weapon, but there was nothing. Despite his lack of a weapon, when Teg saw the officer returning to his tent and guessed his intentions, he knew he had to move.

Crouching, he ran to the side of the tent as the officer entered it. Sidling around the front, he cautiously looked inside. The officer was half undressed and kneeling. Desperate, Teg looked around. On the small table just outside the tent were the remains of the officer's dinner.

Glancing at the knife, Teg dismissed it as too blunt to be effective. He heard the officer's sneering voice tormenting the girl. And then he saw the answer. Hardly daring to breathe, he quickly crossed to the table and snatched up the leg bone that he had earlier watched the officer gnaw.

Looking inside, seeing he was unnoticed, he ducked into the tent and, with as much force as he could muster, swung the bone against the man's head just behind the ear. He felt sated when the man fell forward, out cold. Teg used the dinner knife to cut Elene's bonds, and soon, they slipped noiselessly into the trees.

They ran without stopping for a long time. When Elene lagged, Teg ran and grabbed her hand to help her along. He was surprised when she cried out in pain, and only then did he notice how her wrists had swollen now that the blood was fully circulating again.

He stood looking at her sore wrists, trying to imagine what pain she must have suffered, and then when he looked up, he saw that she was staring at him with a kind of wonder in her eyes.

"I haven't had a chance to say thank you," she said quietly, "I don't know how you came along when you did, but you were fearless!"

Suddenly Teg was all a dither. He had never seen a girl so pretty and particularly one who had looked at him this way. He could see that, despite her disheveled state and the dirty face streaked with dried tears, she was quite lovely. He had never thought of any girl in this way before, and his bashfulness was translated into brusqueness as he said, with what he hoped was sophisticated aplomb,

"There was nothing brave about it; it was just something that had to be done!"

"Well, I'll never forget what you did for me. My name is Elene, by the way."

Somehow, he had known she would have a beautiful name. Having heard it, he felt he wanted to say it out loud repeatedly. Seeing how she looked so intensely at him, he suspected that she must be able to read his mind. To cover his confusion, he became all business again and insisted,

"Come on, we must keep going, away from here!"

She nodded submissively and moved to his side. Just before they started moving again, he looked at her and said, quite shyly, "I'm pleased to meet you, Elene.

Chapter 11

It was almost dark when they descended the last hill to Jason's hiding place. Teg had more than once been glad that he had made such a point of memorising his way, and they had reached their goal quicker than he had hoped. When they reached the bottom of the hill, he crouched down, signaling to Elene to do the same. He looked hard at the spot where he knew Jason should be but could see no sign of him. Not sure if he was doing the right thing, he called softly, "Grandad?"

Somebody moved from behind a tree off to the right. Teg tensed, prepared to flee, and then ran towards Jason, Elene behind him.

David, the Third President of The Supreme Council, was quietly enjoying himself. He smiled ironically at what the people of the town would think if they were privy to what was going on in The Forum right now. He was cynically aware of the image of wise rectitude that he and his colleagues presented to the people when they appeared on the view walls, a common feature of all the homes.

The fact that The Forum building now rang with the rantings and ravings of an apparently demented old man seemed to please only David. The reason was that the old man who strode angrily up and down, berating the recipient of his wrath, was Aaron, President of the council.

The unfortunate who stood, tight-lipped and white-faced before him, was Delmo, the Second President. The Attendants assembled at Aaron's instructions were themselves tense and fearful, for they knew only too well how the anger of any of their seniors could abruptly turn against them.

That there would be rivalry between the second and Third Presidents of The Supreme Council was natural, but it was kept unstated and concealed as much as possible.

David was ambitious; that was how he had risen to his present position. He would not be content to stop there. Still, he knew he must tread carefully for any sign of further ambition on his part, if noticed by Aaron, would be seen as a challenge to him, and his power to remove a rival was, at this time at least, extraordinary.

Anyone who looked at David now would see only a rather bland, disapproving expression calculated to show his concurrence with the views being expressed by Aaron. That the Attendants should be there to observe any of them gave David further pleasure, for it was clearly done as a further insult to Delmo. Aaron knew his psychology.

"A boy! A mere boy! And an old man!" shouted Aaron. "How unfortunate for you, Delmo, that you had to come up against such powerful adversaries!"

As Delmo winced at the heavy sarcasm, he covertly observed David sitting watching. Inwardly Delmo seethed, knowing that had it been the other man presiding over justice sessions on the day of Jason's defection, then it would likely be he who would be facing this harangue over the failure of the police. His sense of injustice became even more pronounced as Aaron continued contemptuously. It was such an injustice.

"And then, of course, it was your misfortune to cross swords with one of the most dangerous revolutionaries our world has ever seen." He paused and glanced slyly at the Attendants, who tensed, ready to produce the proper response. Aaron nodded, satisfied, when the Attendants smiled at his cleverness as he said with bitter sarcasm, "Now then, what was this foul and dangerous criminal's name? Ah, Elene, wasn't it?"

Delmo struggled to keep his expression non-committal as he observed the grinning faces of the Attendants. He vowed to himself that one day they would be sorry. He felt some little satisfaction as the grins were wiped from their faces. Aaron enjoying himself immensely, suddenly whirled around, encompassing them all with a sweep of his hand and shouted angrily, "But you are all to blame! This forum has become a disgrace. There is no diligence, no discipline. There will be a tightening up, or I swear I will sweep the lot of you away.

What have we come to when children and old men can humiliate us?"

Aaron walked up to Delmo and, facing him, said forcefully, so everyone could hear, "I left you to organise the recapture of these miscreants. You assured me that it would be done before the day was out. That was twelve days ago! I'm giving you until the next full meeting of The Forum to do the job you were supposed to do. God help you if you fail this time. Now get out of here!"

They had established a routine now. Each morning they would rise with the sun. They would eat what meagre breakfast they could spare and then resume wandering. As they went, they would seek and gather all the berries and fruit they could find for their meals. Too weak to talk much and now so undernourished, their strength waned quickly.

As the sun climbed its zenith, they would shelter, where they would lie listlessly until the worst heat of the day had passed. They would continue walking until the sun was low and then seek shelter again, only this time for the night. They would be relaxed and happy when camping beside a stream or a water supply. When there was no water to be found, they were tense and downcast, knowing they must eke out what little water they had, with no clue when water would be available next.

Jason was fascinated by his new companion; Teg had enjoyed her girlish chatter and blatant hero worship. She had sustained him through the early days, giving him an added sense of purpose that enabled him to bolster Jason's flagging spirits. As time passed, with no improvement in their situation, no change in the grinding routine of their days, even Teg had begun to falter. Then, Elene showed great strength and depth of character that they had not expected. She strove to boost their spirits and reaffirm the correctness of their decision to flee.

As Jason observed her, he was moved by her courage. He saw clearly that her ordeal at The Forum, and since, gave her enormous strength. This strength enabled Elene to withstand their journey's tribulations. Their new living conditions were far from comparable to the comforts and conveniences they had grown accustomed to before their escape.

After Elene's rescue, she and Teg were mentally and physically exhausted when they found Jason. Once they felt adequately safe, they quickly succumbed to the demands of their tired bodies and slept soundly until the sun's warmth had woken them.

Although still stiff and sore, Jason improved significantly after his day and night rest and could keep pace with the youngsters. He even found that after a while, the stiffness in his limbs began to ease, and this, combined with the warmth of the sun, made him feel free and cheerful. At times Teg and Elene found they had to hurry to keep up with him. Alert to the dangers at their heels, the trio instinctively knew they must put greater distance between themselves and the searchers.

Continuing to press forward until the sun was high, the trio found a shady spot within a pile of tumbled rocks and gorse-like bushes where they sat and ate sparingly. They could finally listen to Elene's story for the first time since she had joined them.

Having heard the policemen's conversations and witnessing the officer's actions, Teg was more prepared for Elene's dreadful revelations than Jason. Even so, hearing it from her lips gave it a whole new dimension, and he listened with horror as she told them of her ordeal.

Faltering once or twice, Elene bravely carried on, only to break down completely when she recounted seeing and hearing her own parents revile as she walked towards The Sanctum of Well-Being.

Teg wanted to wrap her in his arms and comfort her, but instead, he blushed at the idea and sat awkwardly. Surprised, he felt slightly resentful when his grandfather leaned forward and stroked her hair, murmuring soothingly.

Elene had obviously been grateful for the kindness and had recovered sufficiently to finish her story. When she had finished, they sat silently for a while as she recovered from the telling. Jason and Teg absorbed the horror of what they had heard. It was Jason who finally broke the silence.

"Elene, you have suffered terribly and been remarkably brave. It is hard to grasp the awful facts about the people who have ruled us for so long. It's impossible not to wonder what other corruption exists within the system."

He paused for a moment as if thinking of something he had intended to ask her, and then, remembering, he said, "You said that when you were first taken to The Forum, "you woke up" and then later, when you told of being taken to The Sanctum of Well-Being you said you were woken up, before being pulled out of the police vehicle. It seems odd that at one of the most exciting times of your life, you should have slept through it. I thought you would remember everything about travelling to The Forum. And then, you slept through it all again at one of your life's most frightening times. That seems hard to believe!"

"Oh, it wasn't because I was tired or wanted to sleep. The police gave me something to drink that put me to sleep. Maybe the council suspected I might try to run away.

"Well, you certainly did in the end, sleeping draught or not, and now that you have done so, you can be sure that we will do everything we can to look after you. Isn't that right, Teg?"

Elene smiled gratefully at Jason and then turned to bestow the same smile on Teg. The effect was somewhat different, however. As he looked into her lovely eyes, Teg blushed furiously and suddenly found something exciting in a piece of ordinary-looking rock near his foot. Elene smiled secretly and nearly burst out laughing when she turned and saw the knowing smile on Jason's face.

As the days passed, a strong bond developed between the three travelers. Jason was aware of Elene's effect on Teg and secretly prayed that their feelings would grow to draw on each other's strength as they faced the dangers that inevitably lay ahead.

As more days passed and there was no relief from their situation, Jason began to fear that he was slowing them down and becoming a burden. He had thought of slipping away several times. This would leave them to move on faster and easier without him. Also, he rationalised that the food and water left would last much better between just the two people.

At one time, unable to sleep, Jason prepared to slip away in the middle of the night. He had even gone so far as to lay his bag, with what little goods they had, close to where Teg slept. With tears in his eyes, he wished the two children a silent goodbye. Only as he prepared to creep away did he realise he could not leave them a farewell message to say why he had gone. He knew they would probably spend a long time searching for him and thus increase their chances of being captured. Frustrated, he returned to his sleeping place and finally fell into a troubled sleep.

He had not been able to come up with a plausible explanation of how his bag came to be by the side of Teg when he awoke the following day, and more than once, he had caught his grandson looking at him with a speculative look that hinted he suspected his grandfather's intentions.

The night was still, clear, and bright from the moon's silvery disc, which seemed close enough to reach out and touch. Jason was once more unable to sleep. He was only too aware of how much he had slowed in the last few days. The amount of food they had been able to find was barely enough for two, let alone three, and he knew that they could not continue much longer like this without becoming sick, and the consequences of that were too horrendous to think.

He lay there, listening to the distant hum of traffic and wondering what to do. He recalled the enthusiasm and sense of adventure they had started out with. He wondered bitterly why it should be that such an obviously worthwhile venture should be stifled so easily and so pathetically.

Traffic?! He sat up, suddenly alert. He realised, with a start, that he had been hearing a vehicle or vehicles approaching. It indicated how he had become weakened and dulled by his ordeal that he had not immediately realised the significance of what he had heard. It had to be the police! Quickly he was up and running as quietly as he could to the top of the hill. Lying down, he investigated the distance, where a vehicle's lights shone brightly, even in the brightness of the moonlit night. It took only a glance for him to know that they were headed; directly for where he and the children hid. In an instant, he knew what he must do. He glanced down the hill to where the shadowy form of the hiding place concealed the sleeping children.

A lump came to his throat, and his eyes filled with tears as he sent a silent wish to where they lay, and then he was up and running as fast as his tired legs would carry him. He knew he needed to put as much distance as possible between himself and the children before revealing himself to the searchers. He hoped that he would be able to sufficiently divert and mislead the police to give Teg and Elene time to make good their escape.

When he neared, the vehicle came slowly forward, he was puffing badly, and his legs shook with exertion. He crouched by the side of the natural pathway through the gully that the vehicle was travelling and attempted to regain his breath and his strength. The car suddenly seemed to materialise behind the twin headlight beams, and Jason could see it was a police vehicle. He waited until he knew he must be seen in the headlight beams and then darted across the gully and started scrambling up the far side.

The screech of brakes hastily applied, and a sudden splash of white light on rocks to his right as a flood light was switched on confirmed that he had been seen. He deliberately paused as the beam of light swung around and impaled him before continuing to run up the side of the gully. As he came to the top, he paused again, vividly illuminated, and braced himself for the shot he was sure must come. Valiantly he prayed for the bullet that must end his life, knowing that the sound of the shot would wake Teg and Elene and alert them to the danger.

He stood, puzzled as no shot came, and then, above the sound of his harsh breathing, were sounds of pursuit. He began running down the slope away from the gully, praying that he could keep going long enough for his pursuers to lose patience and shoot him down.

He was staggering now, his legs tired and weak. When he suddenly felt a hand grab at his shoulder, he could do nothing to stop himself from falling forward, his pursuers immediately falling upon him and pinioning his arms. Determined to resist to the end, let his body go limp as they attempted to pull him along. When they began to force him to his feet, he started to berate them as loudly as his breathlessness would permit, hoping that in the still night air, his voice would carry to Teg and Elene, warning them to flee.

Not knowing what to make of his behaviour, his two captors merely shook their heads, believing him to be deranged. By the time they pulled him back down into the gully, he was so out of breath all he could do was lie wheezing when they threw him to the ground. He lay there for what seemed a long time. Slowly his breathing eased, and the trembling in his body subsided. He was aware of jack-booted feet moving about near him. Beyond them, the wheels of the police vehicle could be seen.

After a while, he was prodded in the back and ordered to sit up. Seeing no point in refusing and curious to look at his captors, he complied. There were four of them. One of them was clearly an officer, and he stood, legs apart and arms akimbo, and questioned Jason.

"You are the man known as Jason? Jason of the family of Thorason?"

Knowing his silence was futile, Jason nonetheless took some small pleasure in refusing to answer the peppering of questions. Finally, in frustration, the officer pulled a piece of paper from his pocket, consulting it briefly. After replacing it, he looked carefully at Jason "Perhaps it would interest you to know that your wife Sarah and your daughter Carolin are both dead!"

Jason couldn't help himself. His head jerked up, a look of rage and grief commingled on his face. He went to rise but was pushed brutally back down by one of the policemen.

Jason's voice trembled as he asked, "How, how did they die. Why?"

"They would not answer the questions they were asked. The persuasive methods used were more than they could take. Foolish of them to resist, really!"

"But they knew nothing, nothing at all. Why, why? They were good people, they were…"

Unable to continue, Jason bowed his head and wept. It had been distressing to him that he would have brought shame and dishonour upon his family. Never in his worst imaginings had he thought to be the cause of their deaths.

"Where is the boy?" demanded the officer suddenly.

Jason kept his head bowed; his grief almost impossible to bear. When the question was repeated, it slowly entered his consciousness that they obviously didn't know Elene was with them. Knowing that there would be little comfort or satisfaction for him now, he took what pleasure he could from the knowledge that he knew something that they did not.

Summoning up energy reserves, he put aside his grief and allowed his anger to grow, using the strength of that anger to resist and, if possible, mislead his enemies.

"Boy, what boy?" he asked, feigning surprise.

"Don't be foolish old man. We know the boy is with you."

Jason looked up at him and then deliberately and provocatively at the others before saying contemptuously,

"He must be some boy, this one you speak of. Are you so afraid of him that it takes four grown, armed men to hunt him down?"

"Don't waste my time! You know too well that the boy we seek is your grandson, Teg. Now, where is he?"

Deciding to try and mislead them, Jason forced himself to look regretful and to say, with contempt in his voice, "Damn the young, they are so weak, they have no character. He fled to the town too soft for this kind of adventure."

The officer looked searchingly at him, a seed of doubt in his mind.

"He has not been seen in the town. You are lying."

"Of course, he wouldn't be seen. He would hide, wouldn't he? With good reason, too, knowing that animals like you were after him."

"Watch your tongue, old man! You will find that..." The officer broke off as the headlights, and then the dark shape of a police personnel carrier came around the turn in the gully. As it stopped, Jason rose quickly to his feet.

Believing this to be his transport back to wherever they were taking him, he wanted to get them away from the vicinity as quickly as possible. As the carrier driver opened the door and climbed down, Jason followed him to the vehicle's rear. The officer followed him, still angry at Jason's taunts. He was about to say something to Jason when the driver of the carrier said,

"A little something here you might be interested in, sir."

Unlocking the rear doors, he pulled them open. A guard sat close by the door, a gun across his chest. A small light lit up the carrier's interior, and Jason's heart sank as he looked in at a downcast Teg and Elene.

"They were on us before we knew it" explained Teg,

The carrier bumped up and down as it was driven across the country. They could not see out and had no idea where they were heading. Teg and Elene had been relieved that Jason was safe, although they all knew it was precarious.

They sat in miserable silence for a time before Jason, seeing the extent of their despondency, determined to put aside his own depression and do what he could to cheer them up. "It may be a small consolation to you both, but I believe you should take some comfort from the fact that you have at least made a stand for what you believe is right. I have followed the rulings of The Forum without question and without caring. I have allowed myself to be used as a tool of a corrupt and self-serving hierarchy."

The guard, who still sat near the doors, looked decidedly uncomfortable at Jason's words but made no move to intervene as he went on,

"You Teg, at least you did question and look for the truth. How right events prove you. And you, sweet Elene, what trials you have suffered. My only regret is that we could not find the complete truth and bring it to the people. How corrupt a society it must be that does not protect the virtue of a girl so young, so worthy of our protection. We have been blessed by knowing you, child, and I hope you will take some comfort from the knowledge that you do not face your fate unloved."

Elene's eyes were full of tears as she leaned over and kissed Jason on the cheek before saying bravely,

"Thank you, you've been so kind to me. Even if I am to die, I will at least die happy having known you both."

She sat back, head bowed, tears beginning to spill from her eyes. Teg looked solemnly at her for a while and then, as he looked up, caught his grandfather's eye. Jason smiled gently and inclined his head towards Elene. Teg looked puzzled momentarily and then embarrassed, but finally, he moved closer to Elene and put his arm around her. She looked up at him and smiled uncertainly, then laid her head on his shoulder. Teg looked at his grandfather and grinned happily, his predicament temporarily forgotten. Jason thought they would die reasonably happy if they all died right now.

The heat in the carrier became almost stifling as the hours passed. Elene slept against Teg's shoulder, her head occasionally rocking backwards and forwards so that her hair brushed his cheek. His arm was numb and his shoulder sore, but nothing would have persuaded him to move for fear of disturbing her.

He thought deeply about how things might have been had they met under other circumstances. He imagined how it might have been to marry Elene and have his own family one day. He chided himself momentarily for his presumption, then told himself happily that he was sure she would not object if she knew the direction of his thoughts. He looked down at her sleeping face, lovely in repose and then across to his grandfather, who dozed fitfully. Teg felt deeply that it was his responsibility that they were in their present trouble and wished fervently that he could do something, even now, to atone. He realised his wish was futile and vowed instead to try and set an example by staying brave until the end.

They were jerked suddenly forward as the carrier was brought to a stop. The guard, who had also been dozing, looked up in alarm, his gun gripped tightly, relaxed when he saw no danger.

Elene, woken from her deep sleep, was bewildered for a moment. She looked up in surprise at Teg, and then slowly, she began to smile happily, and Teg felt a warmth in his heart when she snuggled against him and kept her head on his shoulder.

There was the sound of doors opening and then the rattle of a key in the lock of the back doors. They blinked and held up a hand to their eyes as daylight flooded into the carrier's interior as the doors were pulled open. They were summoned from the vehicle and climbed out stiffly, the cramp in their limbs making them move around awkwardly. They were pushed towards a sizeable grey slab of rock that dominated the clearing where they stood.

Around them, several policemen stood; their guns held aslant their chests. Instinctively the three prisoners drew close to each other. Teg found and held Elene's hand, and Jason, who stood to one side of them, laid an arm across their shoulders, his reach encompassing them both. He tried to think of something inspired, something appropriate to say but found himself too choked up.

Chapter 12

The officer stood and looked at Jason for a long time before he said, almost to himself,

"I just hope we're doing the right thing.

He turned and signaled to one of the policemen, who came forward and dropped two bulging satchels at their feet. The officer pointed to a direction behind them and to their right,

"Consider yourselves lucky! Go that way."

They stood dumbfounded as the officer and policeman walked to the vehicles and climbed in. The window of the officer's car was open, and just before the engine burst into life, they heard him turn to his companion and say,

"The Third President had better know what he's doing. If Delmo should find out about this, there'll be all hell to pay!"

They stood huddled together, suspecting some kind of trap as the police vehicles gradually dwindled into the distance. Finally, when all was quiet, Teg looked up at Jason and said, with wonder in his voice,

"They've let us go, grandad, they've let us go!"

Suddenly they were laughing, relief and surprise mingling with thankfulness.

"Why do you think they let us go?" asked Elene.

"Whatever the reason," said Jason, "I think we'd do well to get away from here in case they change their minds. The other two looked alarmed and glanced to where the police had last been seen as though fearful that they were on their way back already.

It was Jason who drew their attention to the two satchels.

Suddenly the bags assumed a sinister aspect, and they looked at them like they would explode or something equally disastrous. Teg said,

"I don't know why, but I'm sure those policemen wanted us to stay alive. I wouldn't mind betting it's something to do with what that officer said about the Third President."

"Um!" said Jason, "you could well be right. From what he said, I can only guess there's some kind of power play between David and Delmo."

"Well, if David's against Delmo, I hope he wins!!" said Elene vehemently, looking somewhat ashamed of her outburst. Jason smiled and gently touched her shoulder,

"You are perfectly entitled to feel bitter, my dear. Don't let it worry you."

"I'd rather just be able to forget it completely," she said. "I keep wishing that it had all been a bad dream."

Before he could stop himself, Teg said, half-jokingly,

"Then you'd never have met me; that's a nice thing to say!"

Taking him seriously, she looked distressed and cried out,

"Oh no, Teg, that's the greatest thing to ever happen to me. I love you so much!" She stopped abruptly, realising what she had said, there was an awkward silence as they stared at each other, and then Jason broke the tension; grinning, he said,

"Well now, seeing what we have in the bags might be a good idea."

As he moved forward, Elene ran to his side. Embarrassed by her outburst and fearful of Teg's reaction, she eagerly sought some distraction.

Anyone watching Teg approach the bags would have thought that he had walked. Only he could have told them that he was floating.

After so long on a diet of berries and fruit, and not much of that, the two satchels proved to be a veritable cornucopia. The variety of food was adequate for the three of them for a week at least. There was water and other things they had wished for more than once during their journey. The pack of chemical fire tablets was significant as they only required to be rasped with the implementation provided to ignite and provide a small but intense flame that would last long enough to set the greenest wood on fire.

They had noticed how the nights were becoming cooler and feared that the season would soon turn. The means of making fire would become more critical than ever.

They sat and enjoyed a meal that, while simple by the standards they had once enjoyed, now seemed like a meal fit for a king. Their relief from the unexpected end to their recent detainment and the chance to eat properly again made them light-hearted, and they began to walk again in a much better frame of mind.

It was clear that most of the day had gone by and that soon they must find a place to settle for the night. They had no idea where they were but instinctively knew to put distance between themselves and the spot where the police had dropped them. It was as if by common consent that they approached a large, almost square-sided rock, the size of a house, which stood among a stand of silver-grey upright trees that seemed almost to be standing guard. The base of the stone was eroded in places providing cave-like openings that would provide shelter and concealment. Before the light faded completely, they gathered leaves and dried grasses to make beds for themselves before crawling under cover of the rock to settle down for the night.

The excitement and relief they had experienced had exhausted them; it was not long before Teg and Elene slept soundly. For Jason, however, the sudden quiet and the cessation of activity gave him his first real chance to think about the dreadful news that nearly shattered him. He recalled the gentlewoman he loved so dearly and the daughter who, above all things, had given him Teg. He found it hard to believe that he would see them no more, but somehow, he knew that the policeman had been telling the truth.

He began to cry quietly, the tears falling hot upon his hands as he sat, head bowed, his mind in the past. After a while, his mind ranged further, and he thought of all that had happened since that fateful night when his grandson had disturbed his lonely vigil. He realised suddenly that had things not worked out as they had, he would still not have seen his wife and daughter again.

After all, he had been through, he now found it incredible to think that, not so long ago, he would have walked sedately and proudly to a compulsory death. He now knew how wrong it all was. He had learned quickly how corrupt and evil those were who ordered the lives of the men and women who blindly followed The Way.

The extent of the evil had been brought home to him by the knowledge that his wife and daughter had been cruelly destroyed because he had chosen to defy The Forum. He vowed silently to his departed loves, "I swear this evil will be exposed, and your deaths will be avenged. It's too late for you, and I don't have much time left. One day though, what has happened to us will have been worthwhile."

He conjured up a picture of his wife and daughter in his mind and whispered to them, "I wish you well!"

Immediately he shook his head irritably and murmured,

"No, that is the way we have been taught. No more of that; we know it is wrong." He thought momentarily and then whispered,

"Rest in peace, my loves."

He felt content somehow, as though that epitaph was far more fitting. He thought that it was original as well. As he prepared to settle down, he wondered how it would all end. He glanced across where Teg and Elene slept peacefully, about three feet apart. He settled down with a satisfied smile as he saw that their arms had bridged the gap between them, and their hands were intertwined.

Antony had often dreamed of moments such as this. Since ascending from Acolyte to Attendant, he had enjoyed a life beyond his wildest dreams. Son of an inept and insignificant man, he had been aware, even as a small child, that they enjoyed a less pretentious lifestyle than other families in their neighbourhood. That neither his mother nor his father amounted to much had been obvious to him for as long as he could remember. He was painfully aware that he mirrored his parents' condition. He, too, was insignificant and colourless. Physically he was weedy and the butt of many a bully's cruel humour. Weak-eyed, he had worn spectacles since being old enough to care for them.

It seemed only natural that he had been unable to cope with contact lenses and so, added to his other shortcomings, was the natural invitation to all those stronger and cockier than him, and that was most, to call him four-eyes. He had suffered in silence, mainly because he was too much of a runt and coward to do otherwise.

When he began attending school, he found a new host of tormentors and would have fled the premises if he hadn't fallen deeply and irrevocably in love with his mathematics teacher. He dared not reveal his love to her, fearing that perhaps, at age five, he would not be taken seriously. He worshipped her from afar and hung upon her every word as though it was holy writ. She had become a beacon on the dim pathway of his life.

The presence of this goddess in his world made life bearable and made school a place where for all the torments he was subjected to, he had a sanctuary where he could go to where his whole being was soothed by the object of his worship.

By the time he was old enough to realise that his math teacher was, in fact, a rather ordinary-looking woman, it was of little import as far as he was concerned. Even the most ordinary girls were beyond his grasp, his lack of physical allure and painful shyness ensuring instant rejection. It was easy to continue to worship the teacher, albeit not quite whole-heartedly, even though he now recognised her for her less than goddess-like countenance.

One thing he found he would never be able to do would be to forget or want to forget, the deep and abiding love and understanding of mathematics that had resulted from his long, unrequited love affair. He would never forget the triumph he had felt when he had been selected to go to The Forum as an Acolyte, his facility for figures and their uses having been recognised.

He had often watched and lusted after some of the more nubile. If he was honest, he even lusted for some of the ugly girls in the school. He was aware of his lack of desirability, so he avoided the trauma of rejection by keeping his desires hidden. Sometimes, he had to admit that this had been difficult and necessitated the employment of a convenient object carried in front of him or, failing this, a quick scurry to a quiet place bent over at an awkward angle.

Once his selection for The Forum had been announced, it had not been long before, seeking a conquest she could brag of; one of the more desirable girls in the school had overcome her distaste for his unprepossessing features had propositioned him in no uncertain terms. He had taken a perverse delight in looking her slowly up and down and saying grandly, "No thanks, I don't think so; I happen to have someone else on my list for tonight!"

He had gloated to himself at her crestfallen expression and her air of defeat as she had crept away. When, a couple of minutes later, he also walked away, bent into a deflated angle, he cursed himself for a fool.

His life as an Acolyte had been pleasant enough, and he had been content to be allowed to practice his skills as a mathematician and use them, as required, in The Forum's service. There were numerous desirable females among the Acolytes and the Attendants. He had spent many an hour daydreaming of the pleasures that might be enjoyed in the company of some or one of them…anyone!

It had not been difficult for him to avoid entanglements, chiefly because there was not one of them who wished to be entangled with him. His mistress continued to be his mathematics. His consequent mastery of the subject and his involuntarily blameless life soon led to his elevation to Attendant. He was a happy man indeed, well, almost.

He had gradually resigned himself to a life of abstinence from the pleasures of the flesh. However, occasionally a female would come into his orbit whose sexuality would guarantee his looking for something to carry or assuming an awkward stance to conceal from her the effect she had had upon him. One such female was Carla. Many of his night-time hours had been spent fantasising about her. So vivid had some of his daydreams been, he had almost expected that she would blush when next he saw her or throw herself at his feet in gratitude for how he had transported her to ecstasy.

It had come as an almost physical blow when, on the evening before, she had contrived to insinuate herself into Antony's company. She had made it quite clear that the greatest desire in her life was to spend the night at the beck and call of his sexual mastery. She obviously found his conversation brilliant or excruciatingly funny by turns. This fact puzzled him, as her nearness had made him feel as though he had two tongues and lips that would insist on operating in different directions.

They had obviously been more than adequate whatever his views on his conversational abilities, for she had indeed finished up in his bed, and many of his fantasies had been realised. He was too far gone in ecstasy to note the fact that it was she who provided the expertise. He was only too happy to be the material with which she could be an expert.

When she finally crept away from his chamber, leaving him a weak and grateful wreck, he fell into a deep and dreamless sleep without even questioning why he should suddenly have become such a desirable object.

When the summons had come, it had not caused him any alarm. He would often be required to meet with a Supreme Council member, even Aaron himself, to discuss some aspect of a report on some research or other that was going on in the town. The Presidents trusted nobody and kept their experts at The Forum to provide and check on the information passed through them for approval.

The importance of this had been made evident when, a few years before, a scientist at the Institute of Technology had submitted a new formula for a synthetic food compound that, if successful, would revolutionise the production of a whole range of foodstuffs that were synthetically produced from the same base.

The formula had been submitted to the various experts at The Forum for confirmation. Antony had discovered a subtle but nonetheless important error in the calculations. When The Forum's synthesist made up the formula, it turned out useless.

After the sun had risen over The Sanctum of Well-Being the next day, the institute began seeking a replacement scientist.

As Antony entered Delmo's chamber, he was in a more relaxed and tranquil frame of mind than ever since his arrival at The Forum. He still found it hard to believe that the previous night hadn't been a dream. There were specific physical reminders, however, tiny bite marks here and there, lipstick smudges on the pillow, the stale but somehow erotic lingering scent he always associated with Carla.

Any doubts he might still have had were wiped away soon after he had sat, as directed by Delmo, facing the view wall in his chamber. As the view wall flickered into life, he felt the slightly guilty nervousness one feels when watching a risqué movie in someone else's company and wondering how to react. He was shocked and somewhat disappointed when he saw that the female participant in the sexual athletics taking place on the screen was Carla. He also thought the man was familiar and was surprised that such a delectable woman should choose to disport herself, particularly on camera, with such an unprepossessing male partner.

It was a full minute before he felt himself break into a cold sweat as he understood why the man on the screen seemed so familiar. He recalled being glad he wasn't wearing his spectacles, as they would indeed have fallen off! He remembered that position well.

Antony had no idea why or how Delmo had obtained the film, but he knew for sure that it meant trouble. For some reason, on the screen of his mind, a parade of all the bullies he had ever encountered at school passed before his eyes. The funny thing was that as each one began to fade; he had assumed the face of Delmo. He closed his eyes, shutting out the scene before him.

"Well, now, what do you make of that?" Delmo's voice jerked Antony back to the present. He opened his eyes and saw with relief that the view wall was now blank. His relief was short-lived, however, when he saw the evil, calculating look on Delmo's face.

As well as being frightened, Antony was puzzled. Delmo's predilection for young girls was well known, and Carla could hardly be said to fall into that category, delicious as she was.

"I - I don't know what to say, Second President. I swear, sir, I had no idea that the young lady was, er well, one of yours sir!"

"One of mine? A bit too long in the tooth for me I'm afraid. Oh no, she's not one of mine not in that respect at least!"

Antony was trying to grapple with several thoughts at once. He desperately wished all complexities were mathematical equations; life would be much easier. He was astonished that a beautiful girl in her mid-twenties should be considered long in the tooth. If she was not Delmo's lover, the biggest and most concerning mystery would be why Delmo brought Antony here and showed the film.

"I don't understand Second President, if the young lady is not er, well sir, er, why…?"

"Well, she is one of mine in a way; she works for me, quietly, that is." Antony understood that quietly meant secretly, and he began to like what was happening even less.

Delmo fixed him with a half-amused, half-contemptuous smile as he said, in a pleasant tone that somehow still managed to drip with evil, "As a matter of fact, the young lady is a favourite of the Third President. To be more precise, she is the favourite!"

"The Third President, sir? Then how and why? I don't understand, sir."

"It's really quite simple. I doubt he would be too impressed if I told my colleague that a mere Attendant had been dallying with his favourite girl. Should I offer to show him the pictorial evidence of that encounter, I suspect he might choose to deny you the option of a sedate walk to The Sanctum.

He would prefer to see your final hours assisted by Garon's help. In any case, he would avail himself of Garon's excellent facilities in his workshop.

Antony had thought he was frightened earlier. He realised now that was just a prelude to the real fear gripping him. The sweat had returned, and he felt afraid to move for fear that he might disgrace himself all over the Second President's couch. He had seen Garon, a big, evil-looking man. He had heard of the man's love for his work and the excesses he was said to be capable of. Antony had almost forgotten about the Third President's part until Delmo's voice brought him sharply out of his reverie.

"Am I to assume that you would prefer me not to pass this information on to the Third President?"

"No sir, I mean yes sir, don't. I mean, sir, please don't tell him; I'll do anything, sir!"

Delmo smiled, satisfied.

"Ah, that is what I was hoping to hear. Very sensible of you indeed."

"I'm afraid I still don't understand Second President; why have you done all this?"

"It's straightforward, really. Call it politics if you like. I know that the Third President will be doing what he can to hasten my removal, knowing that my position with that old fool, er, the President is precarious. I don't intend to allow him to succeed. So, I shall muster what support I can, in any way I can."

"But where do I come in with all this, sir? How am I of use?"

"I'm not quite sure at the moment. I'll think of something, and when I do, I trust you will not be found wanting. After all," he nodded towards the view wall, "I have something you want!"

"And if I help you, Second President, will you give me the film, or have it destroyed?" Antony cringed as Delmo flew at him in a rage. Standing over Antony, he yelled, "Do you think you can bargain with me? Just remember who you are and what I am."

He moderated his anger somewhat and said, in a more reasonable tone, "However, we shall see how well you serve us when the time comes. Do well, and the film is yours. Now be gone, and remember, if any word of this should get out, I will personally deliver you to Garon."

Chapter 13

The thin branch bounced as the bird flapped its wings and twilled a love song. The musical notes soared up the scale and down again. The bird cocked its head to one side as if listening to the effect of its efforts and then, obviously pleased, repeated the exercise. The sound was so beautiful. Elene thought for a moment that she must be in paradise.

The early morning sun was warm on her face, and as she had woken, she had felt a great sense of contentment. The source of her delight impinged on her consciousness as she realised her hand was still held. Turning her head, she looked to where Teg's hand still held hers, and then she looked up, and her heart leapt as she saw that he was awake and looking at her.

They lay there looking solemnly at each other for a few seconds, and then Teg smiled. Elene's heart latched onto one of the descending notes of the bird's song and flew into the sky on the ascending scale. When her heart returned to her, it had clearly been exhilarated by its flight, for it beat excitedly. Teg's hand squeezed hers, and she felt so happy she wanted to fly to the treetops and join the bird in its love song.

She glanced to where Jason was still sleeping. She wanted to be alone with Teg, to explore this feeling that made her whole being sing. She looked up at the overhanging rock and then back to Teg.

"Shall we see if we can climb the rock?"

Teg looked relieved as if she had solved a problem for him; now, he didn't have to think of some excuse to get her on her own. They crept, occasionally glancing at Jason to be sure he was still sleeping. The morning was theirs, and they wished to explore it alone. Teg felt guilty as he prayed that Jason would at least sleep on for the moment.

They crept from under the sheltering rock and ran lightly, hand in hand, along its side. Jason watched them go through slitted eyes, smiled contentedly and, closing his eyes once more, pretended to sleep.

Once out of sight of the shelter, they slowed and walked around the huge rock, occasionally looking at each other and smiling shyly. They both looked as though they had a million words to say to each other, but neither spoke until they reached the far corner at the back of the tall rock. The rock was uneven and eroded, sloping gradually inwards towards the top. Teg stood looking up at the rock momentarily before turning to Elene.

"I think I could climb up here, but I don't know if you could."

"What? I can climb anything you can, and anyway, you're not leaving me here alone; I want to go with you."

She blushed shyly as she said this, and her heart leapt as Teg said, also shyly, "And I want you to be with me. You will be careful, though, won't you!"

She nodded, and then they stood looking at each other momentarily. Teg, suddenly bold, leaned forward and kissed her quickly and lightly on the lips, and then frightened by his own daring, he turned and began climbing up the rock. Elene touched her lips lightly with her fingers, and then she began climbing the rock. She wondered why she didn't just fly up as she sought footholds and handholds. She was sure she was capable of flight right at that moment.

The climb was relatively easy, and once they had reached halfway up, the inward-sloping face meant they only had to scramble up on all fours before they reached the level top. They pulled themselves onto the plateau and sat side by side, allowing their breathing to settle down. They looked over the trees to a long rolling range of hills dotted and blurred by early morning mist that rose with the warm sun. Teg's arm crept over and found Elene's, and they joined hands without looking at each other.

After a few moments of silence, they both turned simultaneously, about to say something and stopped half amused and half serious. Teg swallowed and then said nervously, "I hope you didn't mind what I did down there. I've wanted to kiss you for a long time. I was afraid you'd think it was silly or something."

Elene looked as though she wanted to say something. She also looked as though she might cry. Instead, she leaned over and gently pressed her lips to Tegs. The kiss lasted only a few seconds, but it was enough time for Teg to hear a thousand symphonies, see a hundred thousand rainbows and think of a million words to say. He said,

"Let's have a look around, shall we?"

Still holding hands, they climbed to their feet. Elene came close to him and rested her head on his shoulder. He placed his arm around her as they slowly turned around, the countryside below like a king and queen in a castle of love. They looked awkwardly at each other and then smiled, the light of discovery in their eyes.

And then they froze! Teg's arm dropped from Elene's shoulder, and he stepped forward, staring in disbelief. Elene came to his side, and they stood there, not touching, taking in the sight they saw before them.

Beneath them, the ground rose slightly at the back of the rock, then dropped away into a thickly wooded valley. The distant gleaming ribbon of a river wound its way through the countryside. On the other side of the valley, a series of hills rolled away, diminishing in size, finally levelling out in the hazy morning distance.

Teg stared beyond the river. He had never been here before, but he knew, without a doubt, that he was looking at almost exactly what his grandfather had described as The Wastelands!

The climb that had been so easy for the children was more challenging for Jason. He sat puffing for a while before climbing to his feet and turning to look where Teg and Elene excitedly pointed to their discovery. He stood silent and thoughtful for a long time. A thousand memories seemed to cross his face before he looked down at Teg and said, with something like wonder in his voice,

"Do you remember what you asked me that night, Teg?"

Teg instinctively knew his grandfather referred to the night before his Dying Day. He smiled as he recalled it and said, "I asked you a lot of things that night, grandad!"

"Indeed, you did, Teg, and how glad I am now that you did. What I meant, though, was your question about the river at Castonville and how quickly it cleared up."

"I remember Grandad, and I asked you if The Wastelands could have cleared up too."

As he said this, Teg looked out to the distant skyline of towers, slabs, and ribbon-like elevated highways. It was too far away to see the condition of the buildings, but something jarred in Teg's memory. He turned to Jason.

"But grandad, look the sky!...."

"The sky Teg, yes, the sky. The air above the town is clean. Even when I looked at The Wastelands forty years ago, there was a foul haze over everything. You were so right. One day everyone will owe you a debt of absolute gratitude for your insistence on seeking the truth.

Elene was staring in puzzlement at them. It was clear that Jason was being very complimentary about Teg, a fact that delighted her, but too much had happened too soon for her to keep up.

Seeing her puzzled expression, Jason laughed and, draping one arm over her shoulders and the other over Teg's, said, "It seems, my dear, that in many things, the people have been misinformed and misled. We have already experienced the corruptness and evil that bedevils the system that rules us. We can only guess what other rottenness lies at the heart of that system.

Were it not for Teg, I would no longer exist, and my life would have been wasted in the name of an evil lie. Teg had the vision to question the system. He dared to risk all by revealing his doubts to me. Most importantly, he has been right in everything he has contested. He suggested that The Wastelands may no longer be the noxious uninhabitable place we have been taught to believe. We are too far away, but when we reach The Wastelands, we may find that Teg was right!"

Elene had turned to look up at Jason, fearful anticipation on her face. "When we get to The Wastelands? You mean we're going right into them?"

"Of course, we're going in. Nothing could keep me away!" said Teg.

Elene stared, fascinated at the strange, distant skyline. She had been brought up to fear The Wastelands but knew she must go into them.

Alexander stared in disbelief. Delmo kept an excellent bar, and his variety of liqueurs was renowned. Among his duties as an Acolyte, he was required to attend to the personal requirements of Delmo. Those requirements included the preparation of his midday drink. He was fastidious about the condition in which the bar was preserved and was a stickler for having the drinks served just right.

Alexander had entered Delmo's chamber to prepare and serve drinks to Delmo and any guest he might bring. Just recently, there had been many guests, always single.

Alexander was required to leave before the conversations became serious. Today he had quickly moved around the living area, tidying the cushions, squaring off the ornaments that adorned the furniture and wiping any surface that showed the faintest suspicion of smearing or dust. He had turned his attention to the bar and stared in disbelief.

The Attendant, James, was a quiet unassuming man. He was known for his honesty and lack of affiliation to any one faction within The Forum. He had no ambition other than to serve The Forum to his maximum ability. Not only did James turn a blind eye to the questionable activities that he occasionally observed, but he was so dedicated to The Way it was generally believed that he imagined the right to stray from the paths followed by ordinary mortals was granted by divine dispensation to The Supreme Council members.

It had come as a surprise to him when Delmo had engaged him in conversation just a short time ago. He had never dreamed that the Second President was interested in the mundane activities of the supplies department which James oversaw. He had been flattered by Delmo's insistence that the department was in the best possible hands. When the Second President invited him to take a midday drink in his chambers, he accepted with alacrity.

As they entered the chambers, James was frantically trying to think of a few witty anecdotes he might regale his host with to foster his newfound patronage. Unfortunately, he was not the type, and he was still trying to think of a single witty thing to say when he almost bumped into Delmo, who had stopped abruptly with a scream of outrage.

"What do you think you're doing?"

James looked over Delmo's shoulder and saw a frightened, pale-faced Acolyte, a boy of thirteen or fourteen, who had been frantically trying to mop up a mess of various brilliantly coloured and very sticky liqueurs that had flowed and mingled on the top of the bar. Delmo's rage was a sight to behold, and James silently congratulated himself that he was, or appeared to be, a favoured friend of the Second President.

Alexander tried nervously to explain that it was not his doing, that he had come into the room and found the mess already there. James did notice that the extent of the spillage, and the already noticeable congealment at its edges, would indicate that the accident had occurred some while before.

Noting the extent of the Second President's rage, however, he prudently kept his thoughts to himself.

"You fool! You idiot! Look what you've done; how dare you. You embarrass me in front of my honoured guest!" He turned to James beseechingly, "Look at it. Can you imagine how I must feel, bringing you here to face this disaster?"

James didn't consider it quite the disaster that Delmo obviously did, but the flattery had not gone unnoticed, and he found it easy to sympathise with him.

"I can quite understand your feelings Second President, but I assure…"

"You are an understanding fellow; there's no doubt of that. I'm sure you'll understand when I say this bumpkin must go."

Observing the frightened boy, James secretly admitted that he thought Delmo was overreacting.

He asked nervously, "Go? Do you mean to The Sanctum?"

Delmo looked at the boy with a calculating expression and then, turning to James as though suddenly making up his mind, said, "I can see that thought disquiets you. Well, perhaps you're right, but he must leave The Forum. I'll have him return to town right away. I'm sure people will understand why it was necessary. After all, I have you as a witness."

Chapter 14

Amelia had often had to wait up late for her husband Peter, as she did now. She more than once had wondered if he had been detained by the police and whether she would soon receive notification that he would be making his final walk to The Sanctum, sent there as an undesirable citizen. No one who knew the gentle, soft-spoken woman would have guessed that in her heart, she prayed that she would receive that notification one day.

She was not in any way a vindictive woman, but she was a firm believer in The Way. In her mind, her husband drank far more than was good for him and, particularly at times such as when he was cruel to her, sometimes beating her until she begged for mercy. She feared for his immortal soul because his condition was more a cause for sorrow than anger. She believed sincerely that he would be better to make his final walk now, for his relatively less serious misdemeanors, before he did something terrible that would entail a far more severe loss of honour.

That she herself had not reported him to the authorities as she was entitled to do, stemmed merely from the fact that she believed that, as a concerned and caring citizen, she should do her utmost to convert him and bring him back to The Way. It had been an almighty struggle, and she had often wondered whether she would have the strength to continue for another four years until Peter was due for his final walk anyway, one year before she was.

She looked forward to her final year with pleasant anticipation, savouring the thought for a full twelve months without having to suffer the shame and abuse that her husband's presence meant to her. She sighed as she looked through the window and saw his familiar staggering figure coming over the brow of the hill. She reached out and adjusted the window controls so that the viewing panels became opaque enough for him to be unable to see her watching while she could still see what was happening outside. Her mouth was dry as she saw how drunk he was. In that condition, he was inevitably unreasonable and bellicose, seeking any reason, or even no reason, to lay into her.

Surprise replaced her fear as she saw a form suddenly materialise behind her husband. It was like watching a film with the sound turned off. She saw her husband turn, staggering as he became aware of the man behind him. As he turned, another figure joined them and then a third. A hand was pressed over her husband's mouth, and, at a run, he was rushed across the street into a side turning. She heard the whine of a vehicle starting and then the sound of it receding, unseen, down the side road.

She stood for a long time at the window before slowly turning and going to her chair. She picked up the book she had been reading and looked again towards the window. She smiled, was briefly guilty, and then smiled again. As soon as she recognised the uniforms of the policemen who had taken her husband, she knew that her nightmare was over. She had five years of peace and tranquility to look forward to instead of one.

The worst thing about being drunk, thought Peter, was waking up with no memory of any pleasures one might have enjoyed but with all the agonies of a hangover that would last far longer than the original pleasures. It didn't help that he was lying on the floor of a closed vehicle, his hands linked behind his back by what he assumed to be handcuffs. His head bounced on the vehicle's floor as it passed over unmade or badly maintained roads. The jarring of his body was agony on his manacled hands, and he struggled to roll over to ease them.

He wriggled into a sitting position and sat against the side of the vehicle as comfortably as possible. The throbbing of his head made thinking difficult, but he did his best to assess the situation. He was honest enough to admit that he had brought his plight upon himself. Many a morning, when he had been sober enough to think, he had gone cold at the thought of what might have happened had he been seen on his lurching, wavering journey home. He felt a twinge of fear at the idea that he had finally been caught, but he quickly dismissed his fear and resigned himself to his fate.

In truth, he had often wished himself dead. He was hopelessly addicted to the drink and was very aware of the pain and distress he had caused his wife. He had promised himself, time and time again, that he would mend his ways, but the lure of the bottle always proved greater. As he shifted position in the bouncing vehicle, he quietly prayed that Amelia would not be too unhappy at his going; after all, he did love her, even if she might find that hard to believe. He bolstered his courage by reminding himself that he had, in any case, only four years to go before this day would have come anyway, but as the vehicle slowed to a halt, his fear returned, and he felt a tightening in his gut. He hoped that there would not be a big crowd at The Sanctum to hear the charges against him and to jeer and abuse him, and he wondered whether Amelia might be here to heap her own ration of revilement upon him. As he heard the vehicle's rear doors being unlocked, he was struck by the lack of noise from the crowd that invariably assembled at the final walk.

The doors swung open, and he jerked his head away from the bright sunlight that flooded in. A policeman appeared, a gun held in front of him and motioned brusquely for him to get out. Unable to use his hands, he shuffled forward on his bottom until his legs dangled out of the vehicle. He stared around in astonishment. They were in a clearing in a forest. Trees, shrubs and grass were a lush and pleasant background for clumps of wildflowers and delicate ferns. The fresh and sweet air conjured up visions of a childhood spent running in the hills above town.

"Out!"

The command from the policeman startled him out of his reverie, and he jumped down to the grass, only to fall to his knees as his cramped legs gave out on him. He struggled to his feet and, at a signal from the policeman, walked around the side of the vehicle. He saw, to his surprise, that there was no one in the front of the car and guessed that the policeman with the gun had also been the driver. He was surprised to see a similar vehicle parked a few feet away.

Another policeman was opening the rear doors, and as he pulled them open, a young boy of about fourteen, who seemed to have been dozing against the doors, tumbled heavily to the grass.

Stunned and winded, the boy looked around in bewilderment. From the way he looked around, Peter guessed that he, too, had expected to be at The Sanctum. He, too, had his hands manacled behind his back and had to be helped to his feet.

The boy was pushed to where Peter stood. They looked at each other in puzzlement and their surprise increased as the manacles that held their hands were removed. The feel of the blood rushing back into their fingers made both shake their hands vigorously, and the policemen laughed mockingly. Then one of them stepped up to them and pushed them until they faced the far end of the clearing. Pointing ahead, he told them to start walking. They looked at him apprehensively, then with disbelief when he said,

"Go on then, on your way, we're letting you go!"

They looked at each other, clearly not believing what they had been told, and they both looked frightened when they were pushed in the back with the admonition.

"Go on, get going before we change our minds."

They began to walk, slowly, side by side across the clearing. From the way each carried himself tensely, it was clear that both expected at any moment to hear the stutter of the guns and to feel a brief but very final, tearing heat smashing into their backs.

Without turning his head, Peter said, trying to keep his voice steady.

"If we're going to die together, I'd sooner know my companion."

"My name's Alexander," the boy said, and it was clear he was near to tears.

"Pleased to meet you, Alexander; my name's Peter," he replied. The situation's absurdity hit him, and he chuckled, saying, "I hope our association will be a long one!"

The boy only smiled slightly, more from ingrained politeness than anything, and then he winced at a sound from behind them. They both braced themselves and then, relaxing, slowly turned and watched, incredulously, as the two police vehicles drove out of the clearing. They stood immobile as the sounds of the cars faded into the distance.

When all sounds, bar those of nature, had ceased, they looked at each other for a long time, hardly believing what had happened. Peter broke the silence, laughing in triumph and clapping the boy on the shoulders.

"Well, Alexander," he cried, "I don't know how it happened or why, but it looks as though our association could be a long one after all. What say we find out where we are, and then we can decide what to do."

They began leaving the clearing, looking around with delight at the clean, fresh greenery and the bright bursts of colour that dotted the grass. The boy stooped and plucked a flower from a clump, clearly pleased by its colour and form. He looked and saw Peter grinning and with an embarrassed shrug threw the flower away.

An almost pained expression crossed Peter's face and he went to a clump of flowers and picked two. Holding one out to Alexander he said, smiling, "Now we have one each. I hadn't thought to see such beauty again."

They walked down the long-sloping grassy way that led between trees that rose on either side in thick stands that marched up the hills. There was a movement, and they stopped abruptly, thinking some wild animal was about to cross their path.

They stared in shock as one, two, and then a whole squad of policemen emerged from the trees. An officer appeared last and pointed up the slope to where they stood. They didn't hear what he said but just had time to see the policemen level their guns before the bullets smashed into them, sending them staggering backwards in a grotesque dance of death, their blood and tissue spotting the grass for many feet on every side.

As the deafening roar of gunfire faded, the officer ambled up to the crumpled bodies, followed by the policemen whose guns still smoked.

As he neared the twisted, bloody heaps, the officer bent and picked up the object he had seen the boy drop. He stared at the flower briefly, shrugged as if wondering why anyone should carry such a thing, and then threw it to the ground. The flower was ground into the grass as the policemen walked over it at the officer's command to "bury them!"

Close up, the river was more expansive than they had thought. It flowed swiftly and powerfully, and it was clear that they could not hope to cross it at the point where they had approached it. Standing on the riverbank, they felt as though they could almost reach out and touch The Wastelands. They felt awe as they observed the mysterious towers and blocks that squatted on the horizon. The buildings seemed tantalisingly close yet were far enough away for them not to be sure how they were constructed.

Teg wanted to dive into the water and swim across the far bank, so anxious was he to explore the forbidden lands. He knew, however, that there was no way he could hope to cross the surging river, and he began to lead the way along the shore, seeking some point at which they might cross.

The sandy shore was very clean in some places, but in others, there were areas where the water no longer reached, where the rubbish and silt of generations had built up to form a barrier leaving behind an inland pool of debris from an earlier time.

Seeing the mass of junk and debris that had lain undisturbed for so many years, it was easy to imagine how once it must have floated in a nauseous sea of filth as the waste products of an overcrowded population poured into the river and carried with it the carelessly discarded disposables of an unaware society. Like great storage areas of a junk collectors' yard, the rubbish lay behind banks of silt and mud that, over the years, had imprisoned the assorted bottles and cups and containers that, thanks to the extraordinary advances made by that long-gone society, had been produced at infinitesimal cost and in unbelievable quantities so that they needed to be used but once. Year by year, they had flooded from the factories, their lightness, colour, long life and unbreaking ability making them the delight of the purveyors of everything from drink to oil, shampoo to weed killers, medicines to poisons, everything and anything that needed to be packed. Cups and bottles, cans and tubes and boxes, year after year. In their millions, they poured from the factories; in their millions, they flooded the shops, the supermarkets, the service stations, and the fast-food outlets.

And in their wake, they left the by-products, the waste chemicals, the polluted waters that had nowhere to go but back into the rivers from where they had come and the smoke that veiled the sky above the factories. Not just smoke but poisonous gases, unseen, unheeded by all, but the most caring, was dismissed. Those who cared were thought to be alarmist and reactionary, wishing to deny to society the benefits of science that brought them the fruits of multi-million investments that required a profit return. What they really needed were prophets.

Only a few heeded the prophets who forewarned of the dangers to the world. They laughed at thinking a few empty plastic bottles could be a menace. It was a nuisance, admittedly trying to get rid of the things. Some tried burning them but found the thick black smoke embarrassing as it blew across their neighbour's yards and stained their washing. They found the smell unpleasant, too, but didn't know what they smelled was poison.

They could have taken them to the city tip, but that required a conscious effort on their part. It was easier to bag and throw them from the car window when no one was looking. After all, there were plenty of open spaces. They bred a lot, and these people had many children. They needed more houses, and there was now less space. They required more bottles of this and cartons of that, and they needed more space to dump them in when they were empty.

There needed to be more jobs for the masses who swarmed through the huge conurbations. In idleness, they drank and gambled and fornicated. They had more children, children they could barely afford to feed. Their drinking diseased them, and their children were neglected. Sickness and malnutrition stalked the streets and avenues and found ample prey. So many people needed more and more bottles and cups and containers. The factories prospered; their chimneys polluted. They refined the ways of processing the chemicals that made the plastics that made the bottles. They needed fewer people to man the magic machines that poured out the millions and millions of white, red, yellow, blue, tall, short, round, square, and equally non-disposable containers that littered the streets the hedgerows and the few open spaces that remained. And they found a new place to throw their empty containers.

The river was a prominent place; a few containers thrown surreptitiously over the wall or off a bridge out of a boat were unimportant—first one, then ten, then a million. The ubiquitous plastic shapes bobbed and twirled and seemed to chat with the friends they found passing by. The river water seeped into the empty containers, and some were partially empty.

They found odd dregs of soft drinks and milk, sauces and soaps, bleaches and medicines, weedkillers and insecticides. The river water took these newfound friends and released them from their captivity.

It introduced them to the other friends who had come to populate the shifting, swirling streams and currents that flowed through the town. These streams fed the reservoirs and sustained the fish, crabs, shrimps, and all the multitude of marine life that provided so much of what was essential to the town.

The fish died, the crabs died, and the water became foul. Before it did, however, and before the creatures of the seas had succumbed, they were taken up as ever and consumed by the hungry masses. And the poisons that the people had thrown into the river were returned to them. "Cast thy bread upon the waters, and it shall be returned to you!"

"Pardon, grandad?"

"I was Just thinking out loud, Teg. It's a saying I heard once from the old Christian religion."

"The Christian religion, what was that?" asked Elene.

"Don't they teach you about that in school now? It's not surprising, I suppose. From what's become apparent, ancient religions would be anathema to our present rulers."

As they wandered along the shore. Jason told them what he knew of Christ and his teachings. The concept was complex for them to grasp, and it was clear that they regarded the story as just that, a story. Teg looked the most puzzled and was very thoughtful as he asked, "Grandad, you talk about this Christian religion as one of the ancient religions! Are you saying that there were more than one?"

"Oh yes. I am trying to remember the names of all of them. Christianity was one, there was another called, I think, Buddhism, one called Judaism, and several others, quite a few, in fact!"

"Who decided who belonged to which?" queried Elene, obviously having difficulty grasping so many ways.

"They decided for themselves," said Jason, then grinned as he realised how absurd it must sound.

"How is it that these religions just disappeared, grandad?" asked Teg.

"Well, you must remember that the world's population was decimated by the plagues that swept through them. Without the followers, the religions could hardly flourish, could they."

"But even so, there were survivors, grandad; how was it that they didn't continue with their old religions?"

"They weren't permitted," said Jason "When the new leaders emerged, they told the survivors that from then on there could be only one way. All other religions were forbidden. As they explained, and as the survivors must have been only too ready to believe, the old religions had served them badly. They had no place in the new world. The Way was everything."

"But grandad, how could they blame the religions for what happened. Didn't you say once that there were governments that the people chose and that these governments had been responsible for the laws and the welfare of the people who had chosen them? Are you saying that the governments and the religions were all part of the same thing?"

"Not at all, Teg. I hadn't given it much thought until now, but now that I think about it, it seems clear that the only reason to turn people from their old religions was to strengthen the new. It's never been talked of as a religion as such, but that's what The Way effectively is.

"The difference is that nobody has a choice anymore!" exclaimed Teg, and there was real anger in his voice.

Jason stared at his grandson with a look that had appeared increasingly on his face since the fateful night when Teg first shocked him with his heresies.

"Teg," he said shaking his head" If only I had been able to think like you. If I had questioned things like you do, perhaps I wouldn't have wasted so much of my life."

"You haven't wasted your life, grandad!" protested Teg. "You've done many good things, more than most other people, and you never hurt people, lied to them, or ill-treated them like our so-called rulers. They're more like prison guards if you ask me!"

Jason looked ruefully at Teg. He thought of how he had been horrified at even a suggestion of heresy on his grandson's part just a short time ago. Now he was listening to outright sedition, and he heard it with the conviction that it was right.

"Of one thing I feel sure, Teg," he said solemnly, "If anyone rights the wrongs that exist, it will likely be you."

Teg stared at him with a strange expression as though Jason had probed his mind and seen the dream that lay there. He was about to reply when a shout from Elene distracted him. They both turned and looked to where she pointed, and they became excited as they saw, low on the horizon, where the river swept around a bend, the small but nonetheless distinct outline of a bridge.

David was the most relaxed person as The Forum members assembled for their session. In truth, the function of this assembly was merely to rubber-stamp the decisions of The Supreme Council, and often this meant the wishes of the President alone. There was an air of expectancy today as they awaited the arrival of the last few members of The Forum. All were aware of the events that had so enraged the President. They all knew that anything that went against the wishes of any Supreme Council member was cause for anger, and rightly so, they believed. The more perceptive among them were aware that the defection of the physician Jason and his grandson Teg disproportionately affected the President. He had responded to the event with a fury such as they had never seen before and had insisted on being kept fully informed on a day-to-day basis of the progress of the search. Even the least perceptive of them was aware that the more significant part of the President's anger had been directed at the Second President.

Delmo, who had been made responsible for seeking the fugitives. The continuing failure of the pursuit had led to an ultimatum being issued to Delmo. Much of the air of expectancy stemmed from the knowledge that there had been no positive result so far. There was a stir and a murmur as Delmo walked into the chamber. He looked reasonably calm as he took his seat and looked slowly around at the gathering. He paused when his eyes met David's. They stared at each other for a moment, and then the Third President bowed his head slightly towards the Second President, who returned the salutation. Those who looked for fear in Delmo's face, or triumph in David's, saw only two well-controlled expressions that told them nothing other than what they already knew, that there were two consummate politicians.

All heads turned as the President entered. The Attendants stood until Aaron was seated. Delmo and David merely bowed their heads in greeting. For a long moment, Aaron looked at Delmo. His expression was hard to read, but more than one Attendant shivered at the thought of facing the President's anger and marveled at the equanimity with which the Second President returned his look.

As was standard practice, The Forum considered several submissions regarding new laws or changes to existing laws. Although discussion went on for some time on each individual item, it was only an opportunity for those Attendants who wished to do so to display their oratory abilities or to set out a position that might catch the favourable attention, and hopefully the patronage, of one of the Presidents.

One or two of those present, who found it more entertaining to watch The Supreme Council members than to pay too much attention to the speakers, observed a certain impatience on the part of the Third President as the speeches droned on. Once all had had their say, the President made his position known on the matter, and that was how it was decided.

As the mundane business of The Forum was completed, there was a stir among the Attendants as they readied themselves for what was to come. Even David was seen straightening himself expectantly and assembling his features into a suitably non-committal expression. It wouldn't be seen as too openly anticipating his rival's downfall. He showed a rare but definite glower of impatience as a Forum messenger came into the chamber and stood, hand raised, to signify his wish to be heard.

Unable to contain himself, David grumbled, "Can it not wait? Why should The Forum be interrupted so?"

Aaron looked slightly annoyed at being pre-empted and asked the messenger irritably, "Is this matter of any urgency? Can it not wait?"

The messenger, clearly nervous, had to clear his throat before saying, in a slightly high voice, "It is urgent, President; I beg your forgiveness for this interruption, but the sender of the message requested that it be carried to you at once."

Intrigued now, Aaron summoned the messenger forward. It was the first time he had been sent with a message into The Forum, and he gazed around curiously before snapping nervously to attention as Aaron demanded, "Well then, what is this message?"

"President, it is a message from the commander of the police search unit, sir. He wishes to inform The Forum that the traitor Jason and his grandson Teg have been tracked down and killed!"

Delmo wasn't worried as the old physician and his grandson never returned to town. He'd arranged for the police to intercept the old drunkard and the boy; yes, they had shot them down before they could flee, and they had buried them somewhere in the woods. How were they to know the difference between a physician, a drunkard, an ordinary boy, and a disgraced Acolyte without someone to tell them?

There was an excited stir in the chamber as the messenger was dismissed. Delmo beamed happily, David looked inscrutable. The President looked at Delmo and nodded once before saying, loud enough for all to hear, "It seems the Second President that your efforts have been rewarded. I had thought, I must admit, that you would fail me. What is important, though, is that the traitorous physician and his daughter's misbegotten offspring are no longer a problem." He turned so that he was directly addressing the assembled Attendants and said, very solemnly, "You must never forget that there always exists the danger that our society will throw up a sick mind which may go undetected despite our most stringent precautions.

We must all be alert for such creatures because they are like the worm in the apple. By the time the worm is found, it has often wreaked havoc upon the core. When the apple is picked, it collapses inwards, and its heart is eaten away. This must not be allowed to happen. Any sign of dissension with The Way must be notified so that it can be dealt with before it becomes a threat. I charge you all with the sacred duty of listening and learning.

Remember, The Way is the truth!"

There was an air of great solemnity as The Supreme Council filed from the chamber, and the talk began. Already, though, one or two looked suspiciously at neighbours, wondering whether there might be some hint of treachery or dissension in their apparently innocuous words.

Delmo returned to his chamber in time for his usual lunchtime drink. He had not invited anyone this time, his desire to be alone, possibly caused by the Acolyte who had become his new personal assistant. As she brought him his drink, he bestowed a kindly smile upon her. As he tasted the drink, he eyed her speculatively over the rim of the glass. He smiled again, drifting to indicate his approval, and the girl returned to the bar happily. She had much to learn to please her new master thoroughly, but she was only eleven and had plenty of time. And he seemed such a nice man.

Delmo enjoyed his drink more than usual for more reasons than one. He took great satisfaction knowing that the Third President would feel well cheated. Delmo knew that David would arrange for one or two of the policemen in that final search party to be brought in and questioned. It didn't worry Delmo because he knew the policemen only had to tell the truth. No doubt David would even enlist the services of Garon, who would take great pleasure in eliciting what information he could from his victims.

Chapter 15

The bridge's structure appeared to be sound. However, the roadway surface had myriad cracks and potholes. The rails and grids forming the balustrades had rusted and decayed, with significant snaggle-toothed gaps where whole sections had succumbed to the effects of wind, sun, and rain in ongoing cycles. The underlying concrete, however, had survived remarkably unscathed, showing corrosion only where the great pontoons stood in the water that slopped and slurped against them in a never-ending litany.

Molluscs and mosses had sought and found footholds on the rough surface of the concrete. They had marked and discoloured it where time had decayed them and made room for yet more, and then again yet more, as the unchanging cycles of life and death were played out on the manmade islands that towered up to the long arching span that once had carried uncountable numbers of vehicles and people from this side of the river to that, and, in equal numbers, from that side of the river to this.

There were tall, slender columns with decayed metal stems on top that once had held slim glass tubes that shone brilliantly into the night, lighting the way of the never-ending traffic streams. Here and there, the surface of the bridge was dotted with the remnants of the long glass tubes that, losing their precarious hold on the tall, stately columns, had plummeted to the ground with a resounding crash that went unheard because the people and the cars that carried them hither and thither had long since gone.

They stood at the beginning of the bridge and looked along its length. The sheer size of the bridge and an awareness of how long it would take to cross it had surprised them. So wide was the river that the straight lines of the bridge merged in infinity as perspective drew its width and height into a point. There seemed something daunting about the way the far end of the structure was hidden from their sight, distance behind, the only intervening factor. Jason broke the silence, striving to keep his voice matter of fact, knowing that the other two were overawed by this moment when they were about to set foot upon the creation of a long-gone generation, on a journey into an alien and unimaginable strangeness.

"I wonder if they ever dreamed it would end like this?"

"Who, grandad?" asked Teg, glad to hear voices bringing normality again.

"The men who built this bridge conceived and designed it. It served a need and met a demand. Just imagine what that demand must have been. What kind of commerce and to-ing and fro-ing could require a structure such as this? Imagine what it must have been like when this bridge was thronged with vehicles that hurried back and forth, here and there, always on the move. Imagine this bridge full of cars, trucks, buses, and bikes filling it from end to end."

"Filling it?" exclaimed Elene, "You mean that the whole bridge was full?"

"From end to end, believe it or not. I have seen old and almost unbelievable films of the cities in the times that led to The Bad Times. It was like pushing a stick into the heart of an anthill and seeing a heaving mass of metal-clad ants scurrying one way and another, belching fumes, smoke, and all manner of evil gases into the air."

"Films!" exclaimed Teg, "Did you say you had seen films of The Wastelands?"

"Yes, hadn't I told you? Mind you, they weren't The Wastelands then. They were still thriving cities, with many people and industries and commerce that made them wealthy and gave them the means to produce more of the things that, in the end, led to their demise and, inevitably, to The Wastelands!"

"Why do you say inevitably?" asked Elene.

Surprised at her perspicacity, he raised an eyebrow in an oddly comical gesture that made her giggle. However, her face became serious again as he considered the import of her question.

"A good question," he began, "and one that seems complicated to credit when considering how controlled society is now. From what I know, I've only been permitted to know a limited amount about how society functioned in those days. Society back then seemed destined to lead to self-destruction. Society became divided between the haves and the have-nots. There was a belief that the most crucial thing in life was acquiring wealth and material things.

Little consideration was given to the effects of one group's lifestyle on another group. Those who had seemed inconsiderate of those who didn't have. They believed that the have-nots were what they were because of a lack of effort or determination. That the haves put so many obstacles in the way of the have-nots, thereby preventing them from displaying the virtues they were criticised for not having, seemed unnoticed."

"So why do you say the end was inevitable? Surely there must have been some people who could see what was happening?"

"Indeed, there were, but people's selfishness meant that while they had what they wanted, they saw no reason to concern themselves with the responsibilities of others. The poor believed their situation stemmed from the wealthy, but by the time they understood this, it was too late, as they had no means to improve their situation."

As Jason talked, something had been troubling Teg, but he waited politely until his grandfather had finished before speaking.

"Grandad, I can't help wondering about the films you saw; why haven't we seen them? Haven't they got them anymore?"

"I assume they still have them, but I wouldn't know for sure; I was at school when I saw the films. You can imagine how long ago that was. Strangely enough, it was very soon after that the films were banned. As far as I know, they've never been shown since."

"Why should they have been banned, grandad?"

"I don't know, Teg. I hadn't even thought about the films again until now."

"It seems strange that they would stop showing the films," said Elene. "After all, if they showed how crowded it was, it would make people realise how lucky they are now."

Teg had been very thoughtful, and what Elene said made him look up and nod as though concluding.

"Maybe they don't show them because they show what it was like before The Bad Times, and they're afraid people will see something that will make them wonder if everything they say is true."

Once again, Jason found himself regarding his grandson with a sense of wonder at his ability to see beyond the obvious.

"Well, are we going across or not?" asked Elene.

It was what they had wanted ever since they had reached the river, so they put aside their apprehensions and set foot on the concrete causeway that would take them to The Wastelands.

It was a strange journey they made. Their slow progress was made so by the cracked and crumbling upper surface, which threatened to trip them or turn an ankle. They progressed in silence, intent on watching where they trod. The only sound was the soft crunching of their feet and the occasional squawk of a gull that would soar overhead. They walked well away from the sides, fearful that a sudden stagger or fall might send them crashing against and through the decaying railings.

The wind was cool out here, and they shivered and pulled their clothes tighter around them. They stopped to rest and were astonished to see that the place from which they had started was now just a mere point at the converging lines of the bridge. Ahead, the point they aimed for was more significant, and as they moved on, it assumed proportion quickly so that they could make out the stark, skeletal remains of what had been some structures spread out across the bridge. When they drew close, they saw that the glass was now uncountable pieces on the ground, once the structures had been windowed. There were remnants of timber, plastics, and whole plastic seats that looked like a good scrubbing would restore them to their original condition. Unable to resist it, Teg sat in one of the seats.

He found it hard to believe that he sat in one of the seats where someone had sat all those years ago. He tried to imagine the sort of person who had used the seat and for what purpose. Then he thought of the fate that had befallen the unknown person, and he felt sad and quickly went outside again.

The bridge swooped down in a gradual decline until it met the land and became a road. It was impossible to imagine how the road had once looked because it ended in chaos, blocked in places, partially blocked in others, by tangled creepers and vines that had spread across the highway, finding tenuous holds in small, dirt-filled cracks that had split and widened to accommodate the growing roots. Vines had attached themselves to what had once been lighting columns and to decorative faces of buildings that now resembled great piles of empty boxes stacked one upon the other to incredible heights. The vines had found their way up, floor by floor, crawling in and out of windows and reaching great heights. Standing on the other side of the structures, they stared in awe at the view of The Wastelands that now confronted them.

As the three tired travelers came down the slope to the choked and overgrown road, they stared up in amazement at the vast buildings, long abandoned, dirty and corroded in places where acid-laden air had wreaked havoc and where the rains had, long ago, brought filth from the atmosphere to stain and streak the once glittering facades of a dead empire.

The buildings marched into the distance, with here and there, a heap of rubble, enormous and grotesque, where an older or less well-made building had felt the weight of its years and knelt tiredly before crumpling gradually, its parts spilling outwards, making huge barriers across the road and piling up against its sturdier neighbour, much of its rubble pouring into the long unattended lobbies and gaping windows.

"Did people live in these buildings?" asked Elene, staring up in amazement at a tall slim, delicate edifice that seemed to have a hundred levels.

"Some of them lived in, but many were workplaces. They'd come here in their thousands every morning and depart each evening again. Many of them lived miles away in the surrounding countryside."

"No wonder they needed such a big bridge," said Elene, "Just imagine what it must have been like!"

"Grandad - what's that?"

They turned, startled at Teg's exclamation. A creature had emerged from a mass of tangled, twisted vegetation. Teg instinctively drew close to Jason as they stared fearfully at the odd-looking animal.

"What is it? What is it?" said Elene with alarm. Both she and Teg turned in surprise as Jason burst out laughing. Seeing their disconcerted looks, he tried to look contrite but failed. His face wreathed with smiles as he said,

"It's only the second I've seen in my life, and it's obviously a different breed, but if I'm not mistaken, it's what used to be called a dog."

"A dog! What on earth is that?" asked Teg, "It sounds-well, funny. A dog, a dog," he repeated the sound a couple of times, much to Jason's amusement.

"Once there were many dogs," Jason explained, "people regarded them as what they called: pets." Seeing their puzzled expressions, he elaborated. "Pets were favourite animals that people kept in their homes and treated as one of the …"

"Kept in their homes!?"

Teg and Elene exclaimed simultaneously, staggered at the notion of animals being not only allowed into the home but also encouraged.

"Yes, I suppose it does seem hard to accept," said Jason, "but from what I understand, it was a common practice, and as I was about to say, they were often treated as one of the family. They even gave them names."

"It's still there," said Elene.

"What? Oh - the dog. Odd-looking thing isn't it. UH, OH! It's coming over."

Teg and Elene moved quickly to get behind Jason. Although he had prior knowledge of some animals, he still felt apprehension but tried to hide it as he watched the dog approaching. It came forward slowly and then stopped a few paces away. Its head was held on one side, its tongue lolled pinkly from its mouth, and its tail waved slowly from side to side. It looked almost comical as it surveyed them, and Teg and Elene found the courage to gradually emerge from behind Jason and stand at his side.

"Perhaps he's hungry," said Jason and fumbled in his bag for a small piece of a synthetic compound that looked and tasted like beef, something the people of the Town had to take on trust, never having tasted the real thing.

The dog had backed off a few paces as Jason had withdrawn the morsel from his bag. Crouched, ears laid flat, tail poised to flee, but when Jason held the offering out, it came forward slowly, sniffed the piece of the compound and then quickly and delicately picked it from Jason's fingers with its teeth and swallowed it in a trice. Immediately its tail wagged furiously, its nose twitched, and it came right up to Jason, nudging at the bag, a look of joyful expectation on its face.

"Now then, now then," said Jason, "I can't keep giving you our food; we need it for ourselves."

Undaunted, the dog continued to fuss around them until Jason gave it one more piece of the compound. When he made it plain that there would be no more offerings, the dog seemed content to frisk around them, inviting them to join him at play. They found its antics amusing and were delighted when Teg ventured to stroke it, to see it roll on its back, its tail brushing the ground ecstatically. Elene reached out and tentatively stroked its side but jerked her hand back when an enthusiastic tongue licked her affectionately. They soon realised that the dog meant no harm and enjoyed the light relief its presence had brought them. They were disappointed when the dog suddenly stood stock still, its ears pricked, and then bounded off, disappearing into the greenery that spread between the buildings that lined the road.

They stood watching where the dog had disappeared, expecting it to return. When it hadn't come back after a while, Jason broke the silence.

"By the colour of the sky, we don't have much daylight left. I suggest we find somewhere to bed down for the night."

They stared around at their strange surroundings. The shadows under the sprawling greenery had deepened, and the glassless windows looked black and sinister as the shadows lengthened, the sun sinking behind the enormous buildings. Without speaking, each knew that the others found the prospect of spending a night here without first having explored fully a daunting prospect, and they were all relieved when Elene suggested,

"Would it be a good idea to return to those buildings on the bridge? At least we've looked them over and know they're safe."

"An excellent idea, young lady" beamed Jason, "and if we hurry, we'll have time for a meal before it gets too dark."

"No, no, no - please, no more, it's the truth, I swear it!"

David watched, dispassionately at first but with growing distaste as he observed the apparent pleasure that the Interrogator got from the infliction of pain and his victim's cries. The man's cries were piteous to hear and were the latest of many that had issued since Garon had begun to seek the truth from him. The Third President had wondered more than once at what stage the big brutal man would decide that the recipient of his techniques was finally telling the truth. David suspected that it probably mattered little, and even if it were clear that a person being interrogated had told the truth right from the start, Garon would continue with his harsh questioning just for the pleasure of it.

David was aware that he could order him to stop anytime he wished and that the big man would no doubt obey him, but he was equally aware that this would only antagonise him, and the Third President needed all the friends he could get at the moment. He knew that he now had an enemy in Delmo and that the Second President would seek ways to remove him from The Supreme Council, hoping to pave the way for someone of his choosing to take David's place. He knew that Delmo was a capable foe and that he was capable of trickery of any kind to get his way. Because he suspected trickery had occurred in the case of Jason and Teg, David had arranged for two of the search party to be brought, secretly, to Garon's frightening workshop.

The first policeman had been a disappointment, revealing nothing of any value and dying far too quickly for Garon's liking. Still, the second man had lasted much longer and was no doubt cursing his more robust constitution as his pain-wracked body twitched and strained against the restraints.

The Third President was concerned that both the policemen had told the same story and that they had insisted that they were telling the truth with monotonous regularity. David was sure that something was wrong, but nothing that Garon could extract from the two men had revealed it to him. The Third President was becoming desperate now, sure that somehow Delmo had survived by trickery. He was also desperate because he could see that the man who had howled, sobbed, screamed, and cried under Garon's ministrations was not likely to last much longer. If he had told the truth, it was a truth that David hadn't wanted to hear. The Third President climbed down from the stool where he had sat throughout the interrogation. He smiled at Garon and said, almost subserviently,

"Why don't you rest for a moment, my friend? You have worked very hard. I could ask the wretch a few questions."

The policeman's anguished face looked up at David with beseeching eyes. The man looked almost grateful for David's kindness when David questioned him in gentle, pleasant tones.

"You say you found the man and the boy in the woods?"

"Yes, Sir"

"How did they come to be there?"

"I don't understand, sir."

"Well, had you chased them there from somewhere else, were they camped there? Did they fall out of a tree?"

"They came over the hill, sir; they were just walking. They came straight towards us."

"Were they surprised to see you there?"

"Not at first, sir. We were hiding, but they were sure surprised when we stepped out before them!"

"You were hiding. Why?"

"Our officer had told us to, sir."

"You mean he knew something was going to happen, somebody was going to come along?"

"He didn't say so, sir, but now you say it, he must have done. He had us hiding in the perfect place and at the right time!"

"I see; that's very interesting. Now, think very carefully. Is there anything else that you can remember about that incident?"

The man shook his head, wincing as the movement reminded him of his agonies. The Third President was about to turn away when he noticed a puzzled expression on the policeman's face.

"You've thought of something else?" he asked.

It may be nothing, sir, but now I think back, I can remember just before we saw the man and the boy, I heard a vehicle, maybe two vehicles, starting up, away over the hill, and then they drove off. It was very still, sir; sound carried a long way."

The Third President was triumphant; now he knew surely there had been trickery. He turned and walked quickly from the chamber. As he entered the doors, he heard Rian's cries renewed as the questioning resumed. David couldn't understand the need for more investigation, but he shrugged at the realisation that he mustn't antagonise Garon.

Chapter 16

Teg sat up in alarm. He had been touched. He had been dreaming that they had been captured by the police and being questioned. One of the police officers had slapped him around the face. The hand strangely had been wet, but it had been accurate enough to penetrate Teg's sleeping mind.

He stared, startled, then slowly began to laugh as the dog once more bounded forward, tail wagging furiously, to lick him under the ear. Disturbed by his laughter, the others stirred and began to sit up. Immediately, the dog bounded to Elene, jumping upon her and licking her face joyfully. She screamed and curled into a ball, her arms over her head. The dog, enjoying the new game, ran around her, darting in every so often to try and find her hiding under her arms. Hearing Teg's helpless laughter and realising that the dog wasn't trying to hurt her, Elene gradually emerged from hiding, much to the dog's delight. She still ducked her head as the dog enthusiastically wanted to demonstrate its affection, but finally, in amused exasperation, Elene shouted, "Oh, do sit down!"

There was a brief, startled silence, and then they all burst into laughter as, on her command, the dog immediately sat perfectly still, its tongue lolling, its tail wagging.

"Well, well, well, it clearly recognises the voice of authority," chuckled Jason.

"That's incredible," said Teg, realising, to his surprise, that he was slightly envious.

Looking thoughtful, he suddenly said to the dog, "Come here!" and was delighted when it jumped to its feet and ran to him.

"Sit down!" he commanded, and the dog sat, waiting expectantly.

Elene looked peeved for a moment, and Teg felt guilty, but it was Jason who enabled the moment to pass when he said,

"I thought we'd seen the last of that thing last night, but he's decided to adopt us."

"You mean he's going to stay with us?" asked Elene, pleased.

"Well, I'm not sure for how long, but certainly, he's made up his mind to come to us for the moment. The only problem is if he does stay with us, can we afford to feed him?"

"Oh, grandad, surely we can spare enough for one little dog!" Teg protested, as keen as Elene to retain the animal's company.

"You may well find that it eats a deal more than you might think," said Jason, but I don't see how we can send it away anyway. I think it will decide when it wants to go."

"You mean we can keep it?" said Elene delightedly.

"I think it's more a question of him deciding whether to keep you," laughed Jason.

They rose and stretched their limbs, cramped from the shelter's hard floor and the night's cool. They cleaned off the plastic seats at each side of the booth, and Elene and Jason sat on them while Teg sat on the floor, the dog at his side. They fed the dog titbits, enjoying how it sat expectantly, eyes flicking from one to the other as it awaited the next offering.

Still having to eke out their rations, the breakfast was, of necessity, small, and they were soon finished. As they stood and prepared to move out, the dog, sensing the coming journey, bounded out of the booth and ran excitedly round and round, returning each time to the booth so that it was there when they emerged and began walking alongside them.

As they began walking, they stared ahead at The Wastelands they were about to enter. An early morning mist shrouded the upper floors of the taller buildings, and the soft grey light that filtered through gave the scene a new, mysterious quality.

The three felt nervous as they once more walked down the long-sloping approach to the tangled vegetation at the intersection. Sensing the mood, Jason tried to lighten it by pointing to the dog, running from side to side, sniffing here and there like a bloodhound on the trail of clues.

"Perhaps we should give our friend a name," said Jason, "After all, he seems to have offered himself to us as a pet".

Distracted by the idea, Teg and Elene took delight in throwing up potential names for their new fellow traveler.

"How about Jon," said Elene cheekily.

"Jon!" said Teg.

"I think he looks like Peter," said Jason.

"Peter?" They both exclaimed in disgust, and Jason held his hands in surrender.

Oblivious to its future title being decided, the dog ran happily ahead of them. Suddenly it stopped, squatted, and unceremoniously emptied its bladder. The three watchers seemed slightly embarrassed for a moment, and then Jason broke the spell by laughing aloud and saying, "I doubt that our friend, were it capable of stating an opinion, would have been too impressed with any of the names we've just chosen as; it's a girl!"

Teg and Elene stared at the dog, which had resumed its peregrinations unconcernedly. They seemed fascinated by the fact that it was a female, and Teg seemed puzzled. He looked as though he would question Jason about how he had reached his conclusion, but before he could do so, Elene claimed their attention.

"Well, if it's a girl dog, then it's only right that I should name it!"

"Very well then, you do so," said Jason.

Elene looked surprised at the speed with which her suggestion had been adopted and frowned momentarily before her expression brightened, and she said "In a story I heard once at school, a girl saved her father's life when the evil Mictorans attacked the town. She was called Tara; that's what we'll call the dog."

"Tara, that's silly," said Teg derisively; Elene looked hurt momentarily and then defiant. Turning, she called to the dog, "Tara!" and was surprised and delighted in equal parts when it came bounding up to her and stood waiting expectantly for the following command.

"Good girl!" said Elene, patting its head. As it bounded off again, she looked at Teg with such a triumphant look that he couldn't help but laugh. The sun was beginning to break through the mist in places, changing the quality of the light and warming them. They strolled, knowing they had plenty of time. Now fully involved with the dog, Elene ran with it and took great delight in calling it to her and getting it to obey her commands.

Jason and Teg walked side by side in companionable silence. Teg decided to break the silence with a question.

"Were the Mictorans real people, grandad?"

"The Mictorans? Oh, the ones that Elene mentioned. Yes, they were, very much so. It was while I was still at school that Mictor was captured."

"Mictor?"

"Yes, that's how they got their name; he was their leader."

"Did you get to see him, grandad?"

"Me? Oh no, once he was caught, he was very quickly disposed of, as were his followers. As The Supreme Council said at the time, cancer such as that had to be cut out quickly before it could spoil the clean, whole body of the people."

"Cancer, grandad?"

"It was a metaphor. The disease is unpleasant and unspeakable, and they likened the Mictorans to it to emphasise evil intent."

"Were they that evil grandad?"

"Well, we were told they were, and, quite naturally, we believed it, as we believed everything we were told." Jason looked at Teg with an embarrassed grin and shrugged apologetically.

"Unfortunately, Teg, we didn't have someone like you to show us the error of our ways."

"What exactly did this Mictor do that was so bad, grandad?"

"To tell you the truth, I don't know. All I remember, as I was still a schoolboy then, was a great deal of trouble. Everyone was ordered to assemble in their homes, and the President addressed them on the view wall. I don't remember everything he said; my attention span was quite limited for adult matters in those days.

I remember he said that there was a great evil at work, that it was trying to destroy The Way and that everyone must be on the alert for the Mictorans and report any suspicions about anyone they thought had anything to do with them. It was terrible for a while because it seemed there were people you wouldn't have dreamed were evil who were arrested and dragged away, sometimes in the middle of the night. They were never seen again. I'd go into school some days, and one of the boys' fathers or mothers had been taken.

One day it was terrible because one of the boys in my class cried all day, and we finally found out what was wrong. He told us that, for a joke, he'd told his father that his friend was a Mictoran. He'd found out that morning that his friend had been taken away at night. He never saw him again."

"That's terrible, grandad. Couldn't he have told the police it was just a joke?"

"He wanted to, but his father wouldn't let him; he said that if he went to try and help a Mictoran he would disappear too."

"But you said he wasn't a Mictoran!"

"He wasn't. That's what the boy said to his father. The trouble was it had got to the stage where everybody was frightened."

They walked on silently while Teg tried to absorb the import of what he'd just heard. He shook his head occasionally, a grimace of distaste crossing his face as his imagination conjured up the turmoil and fear that must have infected the whole population. He finally turned to Jason and shook his head as though unable to conclude.

"What exactly were the terrible things these Mictorans did, grandad?"

Teg's mind had prepared itself for a catalogue of evil deeds that would make the blood run cold. He was unprepared for Jason's answer.

"Well, I don't know the full facts, of course, as I told you they kept many secrets, and I was only a boy, but the main thing was that they tried to tell people that The Way was no good, that The Forum and in particular The Supreme Council were themselves evil, and that people should do as they pleased."

"But did these Mictorans kill people or torture them? Did they attack the town or what?"

"I don't think so. Now that you have asked the question, I must admit there was never any sign of anything like that. I never actually heard anybody talk about killings or torture or anything. It seems they were just people who wanted to change things."

Teg's face was filled with disbelief as he faced Jason. They had stopped in the middle of the road, a hundred feet from the intersection, and Teg was intrigued by and angry at the story he was hearing.

"Are you trying to say, grandad, that because these people didn't believe in The Way and felt that some of the things The Supreme Council did were wrong, they were hunted down and killed? People who had nothing to do with them were taken away and killed just because other people said they were Mictorans. But imagine, grandad!

If there was somebody you didn't like or had a grudge against, you only had to tell the police they were Mictorans, and they'd be taken away; that's terrible!"

"As I've said, Teg, it was a horrible time. It's to my shame and the shame of many people that we did not question or doubt The Forum's rule. As you can see, those who did were ruthlessly dealt with."

"What did they do, these people? How did they operate?"

"Oh, they tried to tell people things about the past that were different to the teachings of The Way. They got into the communications station once and put an old film onto everybody's view walls. I remember walking into our chamber while it was on. I remember how excited and fascinated people were watching it, hoping it would disappear because they knew they shouldn't be watching it. I remember being amazed that they should be so frightened because it was the same film I'd seen at school."

"What, the one you told us about with all the people and the thousands of vehicles."

"That's the one. The strange thing is, now that I think of it, it was right after that that films were banned."

"What was Mictor like grandad?"

"Mictor? I couldn't tell you. We never actually got to see him. All I know is that we were told he was a very evil man who threatened us all. For a long time, I remember mothers used to threaten naughty children, that Mictor would get them, used to frighten them silly."

"Grandad, doesn't it seem strange that we're out here, all alone, just because I felt the same way the Mictorans did all those years ago?"

"After what we've learned these last few weeks, Teg, I suspect your question is sound."

Chapter 17

"Tara, Tara!" Elene's shouts attracted their attention. Turning, they saw her at the bottom of the slope, bent overlooking the tangled thicket of vines and creepers that adorned the intersection. Tara had run into the shelter of the greenery, and it seemed no amount of calling would bring her out.

Jason and Teg drew level with Elene and joined her in calling the dog. After a while, Jason said reassuringly.

"Don't worry, my dear. She's come back before, and I'm sure she'll return again."

He peered at the thick growth that confronted them, then looked over it into the vast canyon formed by the giant dead buildings. He looked back at the miniature jungle and then squared his shoulders.

"Well, we've come all this way. It's about time we had a good look at these wastelands. Shall we go?"

They had to duck low to enter the greenery, but they could stand upright at places. The light that filtered through the leaves overhead had a strange, almost underwater quality. In places, their feet crunched on glass that had lain undisturbed since plunging to the street untold years ago. Once they had to crawl, heads held low, backs rapping against intertwined branches and vines. They could stand and look around them as they emerged into an open space. There was more of the wild vegetation ahead of them, although it was less plentiful and, from what they could gather, appeared to peter out altogether a bit further along. They saw that the bridge was now hidden as they looked back toward where they had come. They looked nervously at each other and then all around them. They looked up to where the buildings on either side of the street soared high, seeming to taper elegantly as perspective narrowed them. Small white clouds floated in a clear blue sky, and as they stared upwards, it was as though the clouds stood still and the buildings moved, seeming to sway towards them, threatening to topple. They looked down, shook their heads, and then grinned foolishly at each other, knowing they had all experienced the same feeling.

They began to move on, their footsteps thrown back at them by the open doorways and windows of the empty buildings. They walked in the middle of the road, their feet crunching over powdery asphalt, broken glass and other debris of the decaying metropolis. Teg walked to the side of the road and peered cautiously into the gaping maw of an entrance. Huge metal frames had collapsed into the street, the glass still intact in places, smashed in others. Teg carefully stepped over the obstacles cluttering the entrance and ambled into the building.

He stared in awe, trying to imagine how it must once have been in the vast hall. Ahead, there was a large staircase. Four flights of stairs rose to a mezzanine level supported by great round columns that once had been decorated with small shiny tiles. Most of the tiles had long fallen to the floor, but here and there, patches clung to the concrete, making the columns look like strange totems designed by an imaginative artist.

To the right of the hall stood a long counter, thick with the dust of many years but otherwise seemingly unscathed. Its glossy black surface sprang immediately into brilliance as Teg wiped his hand across the top. Teg turned as he heard Jason and Elene enter the entrance hall. They stared around, equally fascinated as he was, and when Jason spoke, his voice boomed in the cavernous space.

"Just imagine, we are the first to set foot here in over a hundred years. I wonder what the last occupants of this place were like."

"I imagine they looked a bit different to that at the time," said Elene. Attracted by her apparent attempt to be flippant and the underlying tone of nervousness, they turned and looked to where she pointed. Across the hall, the scattered remnants of a human skeleton lay in a dark corner. They moved towards it slowly, almost reverently, and stared down at the remains of someone who, like themselves, had walked into this hall but in an age long gone by. The bones had become brown with the passing of the years and had begun to crumble in places. The skull lay against the wall, seeming to grin at them with some secret mirth from down the years.

It was clear that only some of the skeleton was there. When Jason suggested that dogs had probably been responsible for removing the missing bones, Elene looked offended, as though the suggestion was slightly against Tara.

Teg looked away and began to explore the enormous hall with his eyes. He noted the wires that still protruded from the high ceiling and looked down to see the shattered remnants of the colossal chandeliers that had once hung above the crowds flocking through the hall.

Teg smiled as he imagined the sounds the huge glass fitments must have made as the slow corrosion of their fixings finally took its toll, and they hurtled to the floor. His smile faded as he remembered that there would have been no one to hear it. He wandered towards the counter and around it. On the far side of the counter was a series of shelves and pigeonholes. There were still a variety of panels and grilles with buttons and coloured lights that were in outstanding repair.

In one of the spaces, there were sheets of paper that had once been written on but now faded into an indistinct blur. He reached out and took hold of the article, but it crumbled to dust at the touch of his fingers. Another minor and less imposing counter was in the hall's far corner. It had a timber frame that was now crumbling and powdery in places, still relatively well preserved in others. It had been covered with a faded and broken fabric at some time, leaving shreds of an indeterminate colour clinging precariously to the rotting timber. Behind this counter, shelves had gradually collapsed as nails and screws that held them had corroded away. The remains of the glasses and bottles on the shelves lay scattered on the floor.

The corroded remnants of metal tops still clung to the necks of some of the bottles, but the contents had long evaporated. Behind this counter, there was a door. The rusting, pitted metal facing the door had pulled away in places, showing the dried splitting wood beneath. Teg held the handle of the door and tried to turn it. At first, it didn't move, but as he was about to give up, it slowly turned with a dry grating sound.

Hearing the noise, Jason and Elene came over to see what he was doing. Teg pushed the door, but, as he had expected, nothing happened. Jason came to his side and added his weight to Teg's. For a moment, the door resisted, then, with a jerk, it opened an inch or so. Gathering their strength, they pushed on the door, and, with a horrible screeching, it slowly, reluctantly, opened. They let go of the door and stepped back abruptly.

On the floor of the room lay two complete skeletons. Between the two skeletons, dusty bottles and glasses lay scattered, indicating how the two people from long ago had decided to spend their last days. Remnants of hair still clung to their skulls, and the tattered remains of what had once been clothes still, here and there, adorned the yellow-brown bones.

Without a word, Jason and Teg pulled the door shut and quickly left the building with Elene. The sudden sunlight on their faces and the fresh air, after the dustiness of the building, seemed like a refreshing shower, and they stood there in the middle of the ghostly street for a few moments before slowly resuming their exploration.

It was one of those days! Everything that could go wrong seemed to be going wrong. At the beginning of the day two of the supply clerks had been reported as sick, the third time in a week that the staff had been depleted by illness.

Later, he discovered an error in a stock sheet that meant only three of the test retorts were in stock instead of the seven he thought he had. He could imagine the fury of the Head of Technology when he only received three units instead of the four he had requested.

Being conscientious could be tiresome at times, and there were occasions when James wondered whether being head of the supplies department was worth all the hassles. And now, to top it all, he had been summoned to the chamber of the Third President. Walking through the quiet passageways, he felt their high-ceilinged coolness calming him. He finally gave up frantically trying to think of what errors might have occurred in his department, severe enough to warrant a reprimand from one of The Supreme Council. He would know soon enough, he told himself, and allowed himself to enjoy, as he always did, the elegant ambience of The Forum building.

When he entered the Third President's chambers, he was surprised to find him not sitting behind his desk waiting to hand down punishment but relaxing on his couch, a drink in his hand. James stood there momentarily, remembering the last time he had been summoned to the chamber of one of the Presidents, and it was almost like déjà vu.

"Help yourself to a drink, James. I don't have a server here, as I wanted to talk to you in complete privacy."

James' hand shook slightly as he mixed himself a weak drink. Somehow, he didn't like having private conversations with a Supreme Council member. It didn't fit well with his image of himself.

James stood nervously by the bar sipping his drink when the Third President indicated he should sit; he hurried to comply.

"How are things in the supply department?" James was surprised that the Third President should be interested in the activities of his department, particularly following the unexpected interest shown by the Second President recently. He wondered whether some great scandal was festering unseen in his department and was about to break over his head. He found it hard to believe, knowing how conscientiously he applied himself to the day-to-day running of his empire, and he was greatly reassured when David's voice was friendly.

"I understand you're doing good work for us there; I take it you enjoy the job?"

"Yes, Third President, very much," responded James, wondering why such an innocuous question should, to him at least, seem to have such disquieting undertones.

"Good, that's good," said David heartily, "You wouldn't want to lose the job, of course!"

"Lose it, sir? No sir, I'm thrilled to serve there" The disquiet had returned, and he nervously sought to ingratiate himself with the Third President.

"Of course, sir, I'd be only too happy to serve you in any capacity you wish. My only desire is to serve The Forum, The Supreme Council, and the Third President."

"Of course, of course. Still, there's not necessarily any reason why you shouldn't continue to serve in your present position, is there?"

"No sir, not that I know of sir."

"There's nothing you've done, or perhaps not done, that could jeopardise your position in any way?"

Innocently as the question appeared to have been put, James felt the clutch of an icy hand around his heart. He had no idea what the Third President was driving at, but he instinctively knew that his earlier misgivings about the summons to these chambers had been justified.

"There's nothing I can think of sir. Indeed, it would grieve me to think that I'd been remiss in my duties."

"There's nothing you should have reported and didn't?"

The icy hand tightened its grip. Frantically he searched his mind for whatever he had failed to report. He drew a complete blank.

"I'm sorry Third President, I can't think of a thing."

I should refresh your memory. I understand you recently received an invitation from my colleague to have a drink with him in his chambers."

"Your colleague, sir?"

"The Second President, man, who else!"

"I'm sorry sir, yes, yes I did."

All James' misgivings were coming home to roost. From the very start, he had known that he was different from the type to be a sought-after drinking partner for members of The Supreme Council. For some reason, he was reminded of the test retorts that had caused him problems that morning.

They were used to apply opposing forces to various materials to determine their breaking strain. All at once, James felt that he knew how those materials must regard the first applied pressure. He was puzzled because he still didn't know where the pressure would come from.

"I believe something untoward happened while you were there."

"Something untoward, sir, I don't understand."

Chapter 18

"Something involving a young Acolyte who was serving the Second President!"

"Oh, that, well actually, sir, it didn't happen while I was there, sir, it happened before we got there!"

"What are you talking about, man? What happened before you got there?"

"The drinks, sir, the er, the drinks got spilled. The young Acolyte knocked several bottles over."

"It's not that I'm talking about, idiot! It happened after you got to the Second President's chamber."

"Afterwards, Third President? All that happened, sir, was that the Acolyte was dismissed."

"Dismissed?

"Well sent packing, sir; the Second President was outraged, sir."

"The Acolyte was sent to The Sanctum, you mean?"

"Well, no Third President he was-er, he was sent back to town, sir."

James' voice faltered as he felt the trap closing in on him. He knew, without knowing why, that this was where the cause of his trouble lay.

"Did it surprise you that he was sent back to town, not to The Sanctum?"

"Well, sir, it seemed," he had been about to say…" I considered The Sanctum an unduly harsh punishment," but stopped himself in time, deeming it unwise. He changed tack and went on.

"It was a surprise, sir, but the Second President obviously felt that he should show clemency, sir."

"Tell me, James, did you not say that the Second President was, and I quote-very irate?"

"Yes sir, he was indeed Third President."

"Under the circumstances, did you not think it odd that he should set aside this intense anger and show mercy to a mere Acolyte?"

"I must confess, Third President, that I did not give it much thought; I did not consider it my place to question the decision of a Supreme Council member, sir."

"No, and quite right too. Tell me though, James, you are aware that such a transgression on the part of an Acolyte requires that he or she be sent immediately to The Sanctum?"

Despite his loyalty to The Forum, James had often felt that the stringent rules regarding the behaviour of the Acolytes were sometimes rather cruel, but he knew better than to say so; instead, he merely replied

"I am aware of that Third President."

"And yet you witnessed a breach of the rules?"

"Well, yes, sir, but it was the second...."

"Did you report this matter?" demanded David imperiously, and James felt the trap slam shut.

"It was the Second President, sir," he said nervously. "I didn't think it was necessary, sir."

"You didn't think it necessary. Tell me, when were you given leave to decide when to obey The Forum's rules and when not to?"

James merely gulped.

"You realise what the penalty for such a blatant disregard for the rules should be, don't you?

He did indeed, and his heart sank at the thought. He felt a faint glimmer of hope as his mind snatched at the words the Third President had used.

His voice trembling. "Should I, sir?"

"Yes, you should. The penalty should be a walk to The Sanctum, James. The very place where Alexander should have gone!"

"Alexander, Third President?"

"The Acolyte, you fool, the one you so graciously permitted to go free!"

The injustice of it all swamped James, and he forgot himself for a moment, protesting vigorously.

"I, I permitted, but that's unfair, I..."

His voice died as he remembered where he was, and he waited with trepidation for the Third President's following words.

"Tell me, James, did Alexander ever get back to town?"

The question took James by surprise, and he stared open-mouthed at the Third President, wondering the reason for such a question.

"I don't know, sir. I assume he must have done; after all, it was the decision of the Second President!"

"Well, I'll let you into a little secret, James. I don't think Alexander did make it back to town. However, I need to be certain of this. How would you like to find out for me, James?"

"Me Third President, but - but sir, surely the police, they could….."

"The police must know nothing of this!" snapped David. "Nor, for that matter, must anybody else. Let's say it's between you and me, shall we? I shall arrange a leave of absence for you. You will return to town in some suitably nondescript guise, and you will find out about this Alexander".

"But Third President, it's a job for,...well sir it, I don't know sir, I don't know!"

"I know, James. I know that you will do as I ask, and when you have done so, you will resume your duties as head of the supplies department. Should you fail me, James, it is very likely that your lapse from duty will be met with the penalty it so richly deserves. The choice is yours, James: a walk to The Sanctum or a trip to town?"

James left for town that night.

It looked like a giant had tired of his game of cards and thrown away his hand. Great slabs of concrete, rough and pebbled on one face, smooth and polished on the other, lay in disarray all over the road where they had fallen from the face of the towering building. In places, they had lodged precariously one against another in varying angles and formations as though the same giants' children had tumbled their house of cards before departing.

They made their way carefully through the crazily leaning slabs, fearful that one false move could bring them tumbling upon their heads. Emerging unscathed, they quickly put distance between themselves and the tumbled panels. They reached a crossroads, like many other crossroads they had reached in the past few days. They had decided on a system where each of them, in turn, would decide which direction to take; this time was Elene's turn. She looked left and right and then ahead. The choice was academic, really. Each change of direction had brought them to yet another canyon of buildings, another great mausoleum of blank-eyed monsters that stared unseeing across the great divides, unaware of the midgets who crawled at their feet.

"We'll go that way", Elene decided, pointing left.

Without a word, the other two followed her, the routine of their days already established. They would wander along, occasionally entering a building to explore its long, quiet lobbies and rooms. They found incredible amounts of undamaged equipment that only needed a battery or an electrical supply to get them humming and moving. They had no way of knowing whether the delicate circuity inside had survived the changing seasons or the dust that clogged everything, and in any case, it didn't matter.

They found objects they recognised only from pictures they had seen in books, and they found others whose function they couldn't fathom. On a few occasions, their wandering had brought them to a sudden open space filled with trees, creepers, vines, and grasses that grew wild and had encroached in great carpets of green across the roads and up to the very perimeters of the buildings. They found edible fruits and nuts, and berries. They learned to fix the location of these places in their minds so they could find their way back to them when they needed to replenish their meagre food stocks.

They knew their diet was inadequate, but somehow, they remained cheerful and determined. If occasionally one of them became depressed, the others would do their utmost to lift their spirits. Still, as the days passed and the vastness and the sameness of the substantial dead city impinged on their consciousness, they began to wonder quite what they were achieving.

The sun was high above as they followed the road Elene had chosen. Their exploration was desultory now, and when they reached the next intersection, as if by common consent, they wandered over to a shady gap between two buildings and sat wearily against a wall. They had learnt to be unembarrassed by the requirements of nature and, when Elene rose to her feet and wandered off around the corner, they merely gave her a casual glance before shutting their eyes and resting gratefully in the shade.

The shriek that rent the air was unmistakably from Elene, and they scrambled to their feet in alarm. Hearts thumping, they began to move in the direction she had taken. They broke into an urgent, fearful run when they heard small whimpering sounds mingled with gruff noises.

Rounding the corner, they saw Elene grappling on the ground, her cries sharp and urgent; they rushed up to her, and they skidded to a halt, recognising sounds as excited laughter. They stared in amazement as Elene's assailant detached itself and ran to them before standing, tail wagging, tongue lolling in greeting.

The return of Tara lifted their spirits immensely, and they resumed their exploration with renewed enthusiasm. Elene, perhaps, spent more time frolicking with Tara and was clearly happy that the dog had found its way back to them. She was less happy when the dog came running to her, limping very noticeably on her right hind leg. Concerned, she called the dog to sit and anxiously examine the injured limb. There was a small cut on the pad of the paw, and Tara looked very much as if she was lapping up the attention she was getting.

"Hey, what are you doing with my dog?"

Elene rose to her feet and returned to where Jason and Teg stood. They all spun in amazement at the shout and watched astonished as Tara, all signs of a limp gone, bound to the corner where a boy of about Teg's age stood staring at them. The boy stood motionless, watching them suspiciously. Jason broke the silence, his voice sounding strained and excited.

"Who are you? What are you doing here?"

The boy didn't reply but continued to stare at them. Tara sat quietly at his side, obviously used to being with him.

"We didn't know it was your dog", called Teg "We didn't know anyone was here. I'm Teg; what's your name?"

As Teg spoke, the boy began to back slowly away. Then suddenly, he turned and sprinted around the corner, Tara bounding playfully after him.

Chapter 19

They stood as if frozen; together, they broke into a run for the corner. They ran into the intersection and looked anxiously around. They were waiting to see Tara chasing around another corner, clearly in pursuit of her owner. Instinctively, they knew it would be futile to run after the boy, but they did scurry in the direction he had taken.

They rounded the corner where they had last seen the dog and found themselves on yet another road of dead, derelict buildings. The difference this time was that the road turned left a few hundred feet along, and there were no intervening turnings. They knew he must have taken the left-hand turn unless the boy had entered one of the derelict buildings.

The road continued for only a short way before the buildings ended abruptly. They continued in that direction. When they turned the corner, they stopped in surprise. Between the buildings, they saw a great space beyond which was a sharp rise before the giant towers of the metropolis continued their march. The space was some great plaza that must once have echoed the passage of thousands of pairs of feet as the inhabitants of the great monolithic office blocks sought brief relief from height and enclosure by escaping to the open area that the three travellers now entered.

The original paving remained, although cracked and risen in places. Grass and weeds encroached across what had once been well-trampled pathways. Trees were dotted about the great space, and rusty iron fitments and rotted fragments of wood showed how seats had once been provided beneath the shade of the overhanging branches.

A river bisected the plaza. Although only narrow, it moved swiftly, and its banks had been ornamented with walkways and seating areas that now were overgrown with the wild descendants of many plants and flowers that had once been tended daily. There were bridges at several places along the plaza. All but one bridge had succumbed to neglect and the ravages of the seasons and had fallen into the waters beneath, leaving landlocked remains that jutted from the banks like broken teeth. One bridge was almost intact. It was newer than the others and had been made of concrete, which had better survived the years. A metal plaque had been set into the concrete at the beginning of the bridge.

They wondered what great event led to the bridge's construction and the installation of the commemorative plaque now corroded, illegible, and broken. It seemed natural to cross the bridge, although the other side offered only a fare similar to the one they were leaving.

They stood atop the bridge and looked down at the water. They were surprised and delighted to see many fish swimming in the waters below, waters that were clear and clean.

"If anything demonstrates the validity of your theory about The Wastelands Teg then the presence of those fish must surely do so," said Jason.

"They're beautiful," cried Elene, "and look how fast they move!"

"They may be beautiful," said Teg pensively," but what I see down there is a change of diet! What do you think, grandad, fish for supper?"

Surprised that the thought hadn't occurred to him and delighted at the thought of some other fare than berries and fruit, he was about to agree with Teg when, like the others, he whirled round at the shout that echoed again and again across the plaza.

"Alright, hold it right there!"

They came onto the bridge, ambling, and three men passed in front of Jason, cutting them off from both ends of the bridge. Elene sidled to Teg's side, her hand seeking his. Jason moved to be with them, positioning himself between them and the men approaching the bridge. They came from behind trees, and two of them carried guns. There were seven men, and beyond them, Jason could see the boy they had followed kneeling beside Tara.

Nothing was said for a while, and the two groups looked at each other curiously. The clothes that Jason and the children wore were dirty and torn by now, but the quality of the cloth and the fine workmanship were evident when compared to the rough garments of the others.

The silence was broken by Jason, who said, in as confident a voice as he could muster.

"We are pleased to meet you; we had hoped others might be here."

When the men just continued to look at them without speaking, Jason went on.

"We mean no harm. As you can see, we are unarmed. We seek only to be friends."

One of the men stepped forward and felt the sleeve of Jason's tunic. Nodding his head in satisfaction, he stepped back and said roughly,

"That's quality, that is. That didn't come from around here, I know. These are Waypeople!"

There were murmurings among the other men, which were quickly muted when one of the men with a gun raised his hand. It was clear from the way they looked at him that he was their leader, and they quickly encircled the three travellers when the man with the gun ordered,

"Bring them along; we'll let the master have a look at them!"

Staying close together, Jason, Teg and Elene were herded off the bridge and marched across the plaza to the slope leading up to the waiting ranks of buildings. They could see the boy running, Tara leaping and bounding beside him. Nothing was said as they walked. Occasionally, Jason would try to engage their captors in conversation. Still, they did not respond, and it was noticeable that they were alert and wary as though expecting to be attacked at any moment.

They walked for nearly two hours, gradually leaving the vast, cavernous streets of multistoried buildings behind and entering an area that had once been more residential than commercial. There were whole blocks of crumbled ruins, overgrown with weeds and brambles. At odd intervals, houses that had been new and modern at the time of the demise of the metropolis still stood, some seeming almost intact, at least from the outside. They looked quaint now, like ancient dwellings in history books or sets erected for historical films. More prominently among the ruins stood the tall box-like structures home to many families whose quality of life depended on the elevators continuing to operate or the lighting not being destroyed by vandals and not being at risk of attack when they ventured from their box-like abodes. As The Bad Times worsened, as the streets became more and more avenues of lawlessness and crime, their worlds became more and more bounded by the encroaching walls of their regulation-size dwellings, and perhaps the end came as more of a blessing than anything else. As to their mental well-being, that was a story that they could best have told had they known the right words.

Jason shook his head sadly as he pondered the irony of the worst homes having the greater permanence. Still, as he looked around and thought of the huddled masses who had lived in all these dwellings, he knew that even the finest of the homes must have become a prison, a fortress, a place to die, as the end came. The silent party turned into a corner formed by the solid concrete walls of what had been some kind of factory. The blank walls continued either side of the road for a reasonable distance. At the far end of the road, a heap of rubble appeared to be sprawled the width of the road.

Jason and Teg glanced at each other, both sharing the feeling that they were under some observation. As they drew closer, they saw it was a carefully constructed barricade, higher than a man and seemingly solid across its width. The barrier appeared deserted, but as they reached within about twenty feet of it, the party stopped and stood there silently.

Suddenly a head and then the shoulders of a man appeared on the barricade.

"I see you, Roger", he called down. "Who are the strangers?"

"They are Waypeople. We captured them at the trying grounds!"

"Why have you brought them here?"

"They seem harmless enough; we thought the master might wish to question them before they die!"

Elene gasped as she heard this and looked at Jason and Teg, mutely seeking reassurance. Both knew there was no point in saying anything for the moment. They tried to smile reassuringly at Elene but were only too aware of how artificial their expressions must seem.

"The Master isn't here at the moment" the voice on the barricade called, jolting them from their thoughts.

"They'll have to be kept below until he comes; bring them through."

The barricade was constructed from a seemingly haphazard collection of assorted junk, most of it great slabs of broken concrete. Metal also formed a large part of the heap. It became clear that the barricade wasn't just a random pile of rubbish when a large, almost vertical sheet of metal began to move to one side, seeming to disappear magically into the barricade.

As they passed through, Jason could see that a great deal of thought and work had gone into the design and construction of the barricade, and he guessed that it would be a formidable obstacle to overcome. The concrete walls continued on both sides of the road for another hundred feet, and then suddenly, there was a great space. Why it was there, he could not imagine.

Different from the plaza they had seen, this had never been a place of beauty. Stained so dirty even the passage of years had had little effect, crumpled walls and broken columns lay all around. Great intertwining skeins of rusting metal stretched as far as the eye could see in both directions, continuing in reducing numbers as wrecked and desolate buildings formed wide passageways at either end. Metal frames and gantries in various stages of disrepair and decay stood surprisingly upright or lay drunkenly upon the heaps of rubble across the area.

Teg and Elene stared in mystified wonder at the strange place and seemed only slightly enlightened when Jason explained,

"It's what used to be a railway marshalling area, I should imagine. Judging by the number of rails, I think it must have been quite busy!"

"Quiet there, no talking", snapped the man they now knew to be named Roger. Jason looked angry and seemed about to make some retort but, glancing at Teg and Elene, remained silent. They turned and walked along the side of the yards along the high concrete wall on their left; the wall suddenly became a series of high curving arches with gloomy, cavernous spaces within. The interiors were littered with a multitude of junk and, in places, what were the lingering remnants of large vehicles. There was something almost menacing about the dark, echoing spaces. The three prisoners shivered with cold and apprehension as their escorts suddenly turned into one of the archways and led them to the rear.

They halted when they had nearly reached the back of the space, and it was almost too dark to see in front of them. There was a scurry of movement, and then suddenly, a small but bright flame hissed into life. Almost immediately, the small flame illuminated a bright flaming torch, and they stood in a pool of yellow light, grotesque shadows moving around with the dancing of the flame. The party began to move again and almost immediately came to a dark, dirty door that could hardly be seen against the equally discoloured walls. The door opened onto a stone staircase that led downwards.

They walked down the stairs slowly, the flickering flame of the torch confusing their eyes, making their steps unsure. There was another door at the bottom of the stairs, and as this was pushed open, a sudden babble of sound hit them. As they crowded through, the door pushed shut, the three captives were pressed against the wall with one of the armed men standing facing them. The man, called Roger, and the others who had accompanied him walked away into a scene in which Jason, Teg, and Elene stared in disbelief.

At least thirty people worked in the vast cellar; some were women. They were in an underground cellar that stretched for a considerable distance. The cellar roof was supported regularly by square columns upon which electric light bulbs in protective wire cages hung. Throughout the cellar, there were a variety of workbenches. At most of them, it was clear that the work being carried out was either the manufacture or repair of various weapons ranging from simple spears to efficient-looking, though old-fashioned, guns.

Gradually as the new arrivals circulated among the workers, or they became aware of the presence of the three captives, the work was put aside, and they began to wander over to where Jason, Teg and Elene stood. There seemed to be nothing overtly hostile about the people, but their eyes had the wary look of those used to the necessity for alertness. When they had all assembled in front of the captives, Roger stepped forward and, looking grave, addressed them.

"We captured these three out on the trying grounds. They claim they mean no harm, and that may well be true. We're sure that they're Waypeople."

There was a murmuring among some of the assembly, and one rough-looking man called out,

"What the hell did you bring them back here for? You should have put them away where you found them and be done!"

"You should know that is not our way Marcus" responded Roger." They posed no immediate threat to us; it seemed safe enough to bring them back. It may well be that the master will wish to speak to them."

"The Master will be gone for days yet. In the meantime, we must watch the dogs, who knows what mischief they'll get up to."

"We are no more dogs than you are, sir!" Jason shouted angrily, finally losing his patience. "We are travellers who have suffered greatly and come here without evil intentions. By what right do you presume to decide our fate so lightly?"

The cultured authority in Jason's voice brought looks of respect to many of the faces, but Marcus stormed forward and angrily thrust his face close to Jason, spitting out his words furiously.

"You listen to me, old man. You keep your mouth shut; do you hear me? We've had all the spies we need in this place, so if you don't want me to shoot you down now, you just shut up!"

As he said this he reached out and snatched the rifle that their guard had been holding and pointed it threateningly at Jason. It looked like he was about to pull the trigger, but he reeled back in stunned surprise as Teg darted forward and slapped the gun aside, shouting.

"Don't you dare point that gun at my grandfather! What kind of cowardly bully are you? My grandfather is a fine physician, far better than you. Do you think you're brave with all your friends around you and a gun in your hand?"

Teg stood there, chest heaving, eyes flashing, his fists clenched tightly at his sides. As his fury ebbed, he looked almost as surprised as the others, and his face paled as Marcus, recovering, snarled at him,

"You little bastard, I'll break your damned neck for you."

Chapter 20

"Wait!"

The command from Roger was so compelling that Marcus fell instantly silent. The others stepped back a pace as Roger marched up to Marcus and snatched the gun from him. Surprised, he allowed Roger to push him back to join the others, and although his eyes were still fiery, he listened in silence as Roger turned to Jason.

"Is what the boy says true? Are you a physician?"

"It's true I was...I am a physician."

"We have people who need your services. Would you treat them?"

"Of course, I will look at them. I only hope I can help. You must forgive me if I appear hesitant, but I don't know what facilities you have or what medications."

"We don't have much, I'm afraid," said Roger, "but anything is better than nothing. Just having a physician will be an improvement."

"You mean you don't have any physicians at all?"

"We did have, but both of them have been killed in recent raids."

"Raids?"

"The police raids. They are brutal affairs. Being a healer is no guarantee of safety when they descend on us."

"I don't understand. What are these police raids you talk of?"

"Hark at him!" jeered Marcus. "He tries to pretend he knows nothing; if you ask me, his only purpose in coming here is to gather further information for future raids!"

"You're mistaken, sir!" protested Jason angrily, "it seems your obsession with spies blinds you to the basic humanities. What kind of society do you have here that feeds upon mistrust and hate? You might just as well not live!"

"And I'm sure we wouldn't if it were your choice" sneered Marcus.

Jason shook his head in disgust and turned to Roger.

"I am ready to look at your sick if you wish me to."

"Very good, but I hope you will understand that it will be necessary to blindfold you as we have to be very security conscious, I'm afraid."

"I understand. I'm beginning to understand many things."

They were led back up the stairs and through the archways to the derelict railway yard. They walked in the same direction they had previously and entered another archway further along. Their nostrils were immediately assailed with rich, pungent odours, and they stared in amazement at two fine-looking brown horses tethered to wooden compartments that looked to be very old but still strong.

Roger, noting their amazed expressions, smiled and, stroking one of the horses on the forehead, said, "We have to have some form of transport for those who find the distances we have to travel too great or for the sick and wounded. Normally, the journey we are about to undertake would be made on foot, but it won't be any picnic for you, being blindfolded, so we'll travel in style."

They watched as two men who had come up from the cellar with them pulled a simple, two-wheeled cart from the back of the stables. One of the horses was quickly and efficiently harnessed to the cart, and Roger indicated they should climb aboard. They were blindfolded once they had settled themselves as comfortably as possible on the tray-like coach.

It was strange to be jogged along at slightly more than a walking pace. Not being able to see initially gave the trio a feeling of insecurity, but once each adjusted to the rhythmic bobbing of the cart, the movement was almost pleasant and soothing. The group travelled in silence for a while until Teg tried to engage Roger in conversation.

"The police raids you talked about were they police from the town?"

For a long time, there was no answer, and Teg had resigned himself to the fact when suddenly Roger said,

"I don't know what town you mean, but I do know they are the police of the Waypeople."

"When you say Waypeople, I assume you mean people who follow The Way?"

"Naturally, what else could I mean?"

"But surely you don't blame the people for what the police do!" exclaimed Teg.

"Who else are we to blame? They're your police, after all!"

"They're not my police," protested Teg, "and in any case, it's not the people who control the police; it's The Forum."

"And it's The Forum representing the people, so it's the same thing," insisted Roger.

"That's ridiculous," Teg growled, "the people don't get any say in The Forum running, so how can you blame them?"

"Are you going to put up with the brat's cheek?" snarled another voice, and with a sinking feeling, Teg recognised it as belonging to Marcus. He hadn't realised that he was on the cart with them, and for a moment, he felt afraid at the realisation of their disadvantage.

In a tone of voice aiming for conciliation, Jason asked, of no one in particular, "What exactly is the purpose of these raids?"

It was Marcus who answered in his usual angry voice.

"What do you think? They want to destroy us; that's what they want."

"Why would they want to destroy you?"

"To listen to him, you'd think he didn't know what was going on," sneered Marcus.

Jason flinched as he felt the other man's breath warm on his face. He leaned close and said, very deliberately, "As you well know, mister physician, they want to destroy us because we are a threat to their way of life because we don't conform because we want to be free!"

"But what on earth's wrong with that?" piped Teg, who was astounded when Marcus burst out laughing, finally managing to say, "My word, you're a cool customer, sonny; you very nearly had me going there. Try and get me talking, eh? Get all you can out of me, and then sweet talk these other soft bastards into letting you go. Then, straight back to The Forum to report, like a good little spy."

"I've never heard such nonsense!" Teg began to protest but was choked off in mid-sentence when he felt the front of his tunic grabbed, and the spittle of the angry man sprayed his face as he rasped.

"Nonsense, nonsense? I'll tell you what's nonsense, my fine friend. Nonsense is you walking in here thinking you can spy on us and then walk out again. Well let me tell you this: I intend to see that you get what's coming to you and I'm going to demand the right to put the spear right through your guts, all three of you!"

The stars were plentiful and more brilliant than ever graced the skies. Music more beautiful than ever composed by mere mortals filled the heavens, and angels sang an accompaniment.

That it was all in Antony's mind didn't bother him at all; it was the only suitable backing to the raptures he was going through. He had no illusions this time as to why his humble body should be the subject of such ardour on the part of Carla—the why was not significant. The mere fact she was here was sufficient. The idea that she might be his again some other time was reason enough for joy. Carla looked up at him, smiled briefly, and then moved against him again. The celestial orchestra struck up the second movement.

Gradually putting the trauma of his encounter with the Second President behind him, Antony immersed himself in his work. At first, he had frequently anticipated some demand for his services as the price for Delmo's silence, but it had not come. He had almost wished it would relieve the tension that kept him highly strung. Each time he saw the Third President, he felt sure that David was approaching him with a challenge regarding his alliance with the lovely Carla. Each time, after David had passed, Antony would be cold and sweating at the same time.

Needing additional modules for his computer to assist him in checking a complicated formula related to the ongoing search for a clean system of flight propulsion, he had gone to the Supplies Department to requisition what he needed. The absence of James from the department had prompted a merely casual query about his whereabouts. The equally calm reply that he had gone to town on some errand or other for the Third President had been followed by a simple plea that he does not say anything as even his informant was not supposed to know.

Antony didn't dream that the information would be important to the Second President. Still, he ingratiated himself with him as a first step to securing the handing over or the destruction of the incriminating film. When he saw the interest with which his information was received, he suspected that he might have advanced further in his ambitions than he had hoped and asked,

"Does this mean, Second President, that I can have the film, at least see it destroyed?"

Delmo had laughed at the mathematicians' naivete and replied, "Oh dear, I'm afraid not dear fellow, your information is of interest for sure, but I will need much more before your wishes are granted" He paused, and smiled, "However your diligence should not go unrewarded how would you like the original instead of the film, for tonight at least?"

Carla had been summoned, and Antony could hardly believe her prompt arrival into Delmo's office, where his wishes were made known. As Antony had followed Carla from the room, he had imagined himself as a great lover 'porting his mistress to the boudoir. He would probably have been deflated if he had known that all Delmo saw was a donkey following a carrot.

If James had had moments when he would gladly have given up his position in the supplies department and all the Attendant problems that went with it, now he swore that such thoughts would never enter his mind again.

The familiar surroundings of the department would have been like paradise to James right now, and the thought only served to increase the misery he felt as he wrapped his tunic tighter around himself to ward off the night-time chill.

He had anticipated no difficulty in locating the home of the Acolyte Alexander. It had required several days of waiting and watching before he could engage Alexander's father in conversation at a bar near his workplace. It had come as something of a shock to James to discover that the man still firmly believed, and proudly so, that his son was still an Acolyte at The Forum. He talked expectantly of the day when Alexander would become an Attendant and it was clear that that moment would be the only moment of glory the man would ever expect in his life. James was cautious not to let on what he knew.

Not understanding why Alexander hadn't returned to town but having established that the Third President's suspicions were apparently correct, James would have been delighted to return to his department and remain there forever. However, his last instructions from David were to spend a few days seeing if he could find out anything about an old man who might have disappeared under unusual circumstances. It had been pure coincidence that in a bar less than a mile from where he had met Alexander's father, James had overheard a unique conversation between two women who clearly regarded a daily visit to The Sanctum of Well-Being as necessary entertainment. They considered it their moral duty to farewell those upright citizens who, having reached their age limit, did their duty to the community by making their final walk.

The two women also regarded it their duty to add their portion of abuse to those heading to The Sanctum by force.

James listened casually at first as they chatted but then more intently as he caught the gist of their conversation.

"If anyone deserved to go to The Sanctum, it was him, such a wicked man!"

"Strange we missed him, though, as we were there all that week."

"I sometimes wonder whether he upped and left, and she's too ashamed to say. This story about seeing him being grabbed by the police could just be a cover."

"If I was her, I'd be delighted if he'd left me. In all the years I've lived next door to them, I've never known a week go by without him coming home and giving her a beating, always drunk, of course!"

"Well, if he's pushed off and left her, I bet she hopes he's not coming back."

The two women had been so wrapped up in their conversation as they left the bar that they hadn't noticed James following them. It had been his good fortune that they had walked together as far as the home of the woman who lived next door to the one, they had been discussing.

From their comments and the direction of their looks, he could establish which house the woman lived in. To avoid arousing suspicion, he had walked past the two women and up the street, doubling into a side street where he had waited until the coast was clear. Now he waited, concealed in a dark recess across the way from the woman's house.

Chapter 21

James wondered how to proceed from here. He had seen the woman several times through her window and noted that she was an ordinary-looking, homely sort who didn't seem to be distressed at her husband's loss.

James forced himself into action with the cold really getting into his bones now and the knowledge that he was achieving nothing. He could only guess, but he thought it would be a good guess that an ordinary citizen confronted by a Forum member would be on the defensive. Gambling on this, he straightened his tunic and smoothed his hair, then walked across to the woman's house.

It was effortless.

Flustered at the presence of a Forum member, Amelia had nervously answered his questions. He had not even bothered to give her his name, deeming it wiser not to do so.

"I am a Forum representative; I must ask you some questions regarding your husband."

"My husband? I'm afraid he's not here, sir."

"I realise that, it's his absence I wish to discuss."

She looked frightened as if he suspected her of having done away with her husband. She looked only slightly less fearful when James asked, "Why didn't you report your husband's disappearance to the authorities?"

"Well, sir, I thought that as it was the police who had taken him, it wouldn't be necessary."

"Did the police tell you why they had taken him?"

"They never told me anything, sir, not that they had to; it had to happen one day!"

"What do you mean they never told you anything?"

"I never talked to the police, sir. I only knew they'd taken my husband because I saw it from the window."

James felt sorry for the woman. After ascertaining her husband's name and obtaining a photograph of him, for record purposes, he assured her that his inquiries were only routine and that she would hear nothing more of the matter.

Highly satisfied with himself, James left her home, sure that he had information the Third President would be delighted to receive. He wasn't sure why the information should be so important, and he knew it was probably better that he didn't know.

Curiosity has a way of getting hold of people, and James was no exception. He decided it would be interesting to see what he could find out. He allowed himself to believe that his successful excursion into the world of intrigue had shown that he had a natural aptitude for the task.

After Marcus's angry outburst, an uncomfortable silence had settled over the travelers. Blindfolded, they needed help knowing how far or in which direction they had travelled. For a long time, the sound of the horse's hooves, the grinding of the wheels and the creaking of the cart were the only sounds. Gradually, however, they began to hear the occasional call of people and a brief but friendly reply from one of their escorts. Then there would be the occasional shouts of children or a dog's bark.

They were aware of passing through a busy place with many voices, shouts, and laughter. There were rhythmic cries at intervals and the sounds of bartering and haggling. They guessed they were passing through some kind of marketplace, although it sounded more like the imagined marketplaces of history books.

Then suddenly, the cart stopped. The trio sat for a long time while voices were all around them. The voices chattered and giggled, and many were obviously children. Then, to their relief, the blindfolds were removed. It took much squinting and blinking before they could see comfortably, but they looked around in astonishment when they could.

They were indeed on the edge of a large marketplace. Crude stalls were scattered about in seemingly random patterns. They offered a variety of foods, drinks, implements and clothing. There were none of the modern appliances that were so taken for granted in the town.

They were staggered to see the number of people in the market, and they looked apprehensively at the large number who had gathered curiously around the cart. The people's clothes had the same homespun quality as their original captors. The great majority of faces seemed either friendly or just neutral. There were some who were openly hostile and reacting to Marcus, who was grumbling about Waypeople being brought into the heart of their community.

It became clear that although Marcus disliked Roger, he respected him, or at least the position he represented. He, therefore, didn't openly face Roger and challenge his decision to bring captives here, but he made sure his grumblings were heard and passed through the crowd.

Attention focused on Roger, who loudly announced the Waypeople were to remain among them, under guard, and that they would be caring for the sick under the supervision of Jason, the physician.

The three prisoners were led into a narrow passageway between two buildings. As they went, the noises of the marketplace faded, but they could still hear the protests of Marcus as he made his views known to the locals.

The surprises continued as they emerged from the passageway and saw they were in a village. There were formally laid out rows of tiny houses of a staggering variety. Despite this eclectic nature of styles, the homes had their own charms and, more importantly, had an air of permanency. They were obviously made from any and every kind of material that their builders had been able to scavenge from all over the city.

There was so much to see they didn't know what to look at first. Teg and Elene bumped into each other and nearly fell when they looked back at two men and a woman standing outside one of the houses.

Wide-eyed, they observed that the youngest of the three had to be at least seventy and the oldest eighty, but they looked quite robust and were most certainly happy. There were many children in the village, and gradually, a few of them, becoming aware of the presence of strangers, abandoned the games they were playing and ran to look at the newcorners.

As the children skipped alongside the cart, Teg and Elene stared, fascinated at one group of three. Although of varying ages, ranging from about four to ten, they were so alike as to clearly come from the same family. Teg called out to the oldest of the three,

"You look so much alike!"

"That's because we're brothers, silly," the boy responded with a surprised grin.

"What are brothers?" asked Teg, and the puzzled expressions on the children's faces were no less intense than the look of surprised sympathy on Roger's face.

"You don't know what brothers are?" he asked.

"I suppose they're children who look like each other," Teg replied, slightly embarrassed.

"But they're children of the same family; boys are brothers, girls are sisters, didn't you know that?" Roger asked incredulously.

"You mean they all share their mothers and fathers?"

"I mean, they're all from the same parents?"

"Really?"

"Yes, they are," said Roger, "but I almost forgot, you're Waypeople; what a terrible thing that must be."

One of the children overheard what Roger said and relayed it to the other children. Immediately their mood changed. Elene came close to Teg, held his hand, and in turn walked close to Jason as suddenly the children became abusive and began jeering at them, dancing from side to side in weird, ugly movements, chanting "Waypeople, Waypeople, die, die, die!"

They were relieved when Roger led them into a long low building, leaving behind the jeering taunts of the children. They passed through a large, deserted hallway and then into a long narrow room with low beds down either side. Every bed contained a patient, and most of them looked very sick.

Jason stared around in dismay at the primitive conditions. A cursory glance was enough to show the crudity with which wounds had been dressed, and the number of patients who wandered between the beds or sat on the floor against the walls spoke of drastic overcrowding.

Roger walked between the long lines of beds and spoke to a woman at the end of the ward who looked back to where Jason stood and began sauntering towards him. She was a tired-looking woman who had once probably been quite beautiful. Now aged somewhere in her fifties, she had retained an air of almost regal dignity. She was coolly polite as Roger introduced them.

"This is Margarita; she has been looking after the hospital as well as possible. As you can see, it's not the easiest of tasks."

"Indeed, I can see that," said Jason. "I hadn't imagined that conditions would be so poor, or these poor people would be in such circumstances."

The woman glared angrily at Jason and drew herself haughtily erect before saying bitterly,

"It is easy to criticise. However, there has been little we can do thanks to the barbaric efforts of your damn police. Feel free to go if you feel that the hospital is beneath your dignity; we will manage somehow, as we have done before."

"But no! You misunderstand me. Please forgive me if I gave the wrong impression. I intended no criticism, believe me. My comments were merely meant to express my admiration for what you are doing. It is clear to see what heroic efforts you are making. It grieves me to think that you should think so poorly of me!"

Jason's hurt was so evident and his old-world charm so irresistible that Margarita's expression relaxed somewhat. She still looked slightly hostile, however, until Elene suddenly stepped forward and said, shyly but determinedly,

"He really is a very good man, and he is very kind. Please don't be angry with him."

Jason looked pleased but embarrassed at Elene's interjection, but the effect on Margarita was remarkable. Her face suddenly broke into a broad smile, and there was a hint of tears in her eyes as she looked down at Elene and said,

"Well, now, that's a thing. I'm sure if a young girl like you speaks up for him, he can't be all bad. Now tell me, what's your name?"

"I'm Elene, and this is Teg; he saved my life."

"Hello Elene, hello Teg. I suspect that when he saved your life, he also stole your heart, isn't that so?"

As Elene blushed furiously, Margarita put back her head and laughed, and she was transformed.

Jason stared at her in fascination, and when she observed his scrutiny, she shrugged and, leading him away from the group she, said,

"You must forgive my strange behaviour, Doctor. I must confess that when I heard you were Waypeople, I was prepared not to like or accept you, but Elene, well, she is so much like a daughter I once had. I'm afraid my intention to dislike you went by the board."

"I can assure you, Margarita, that we are here only because we do not wish to be Waypeople, as you call them. Because we consider The Way wrong, we have fled and now find ourselves here."

"Well, I fear you may find it difficult to convince our more die-hard citizens of that. The activities of your police...."

"Please, please, don't call them my police!"

"Very well, the activities of the police have not endeared them to our community, nor have they any love for even the ordinary Waypeople."

"We know nothing of these raids! Can you tell me something about them?"

She looked at Jason with a doubting expression. He looked back with such an honest face that she softened and said, We should let you see exactly what you've let yourself in for first.

Chapter 22

Jason's sense of inadequacy increased as he toured the crowded hospital. Many of the bedridden had received gunshot wounds, and some had severe burns from the latest type of chemical laser weapons used by the police. He was impressed by the fortitude with which they had borne their suffering and touched by their apparent faith in him when they learned that he was a physician. He wondered what they would think if they knew he was a Wayperson.

When they had completed their inspection, they returned to where Roger waited. He had been talking to Teg and Elene, and they were on good terms. Margarita led Jason and Roger to a small room that she used as an office. There was not much in it and Jason imagined that she most likely used it to escape as a refuge when things became too much for her.

They sat there silently for a while, and then Margarita grinned ruefully.

"I can see you are beginning to regret agreeing to help us, Doctor."

"Oh no, not at all," said Jason, anxious not to give the wrong impression. "No, I was thinking about how poorly equipped you are, mainly concerning medicines. Tell me, how do you get your medications?"

"Well, when our other physicians were alive, they were able to manufacture some drugs themselves when they were able to find the necessary ingredients. Otherwise, we got what we could from any police patrols we might be able to overcome, not very often, though, I'm afraid."

"Well, dear lady, we must get ourselves organised. It's a long time since I studied pharmacology, but I recall many basic drugs. I will draw up a list of ingredients, and we must hope that your people will be able to obtain some of them, although where from, I wouldn't have a clue."

He paused, dragged a piece of paper and a pen towards him, and began to write a list of odd-looking names.

"As to the immediate future, we must work straight away. We will be able to do much with natural drugs, and that is one thing I have retained an interest in."

"What do you mean by natural drugs?"

"I mean natural in the truest sense of the word. There are many drugs that nature has provided for us in the roots and leaves and bark of plants and trees. We must gather as much as possible and do what we can for those poor people."

"But these plants and things you require, who is to gather them? Even if you are the only one who knows what is required, it's unlikely that they will allow you to roam the countryside. Regardless of what you say, you are still a Wayperson, and they see you as the enemy."

She looked at Roger for confirmation, and his gloomy nod indicated clearly that he shared her opinion. He looked thoughtful, however, when Jason announced,

"It's no great problem! My grandson, Teg, has spent many hours in the hills above town with me. I have taught him to recognise many of nature's wonders. He will know many of the things I require, and it will be simple enough for me to sketch and describe some things he might not know."

"How are we to be sure he won't just run away?" asked Roger.

"You can rest assured that as long as Elene is here, Teg will return," said Jason grinning. "In any case, he will need help, so whoever you send can supervise."

Now, we must also organise the beds."

"Just a minute, just a minute," said Roger in exasperation," you act as though it's all settled; what if it's decided that Teg can't go out on this nature ramble of yours?"

"In that case, my friend, your comrades out there will continue to suffer and die, and there will be nothing I can do."

Roger stared at Jason for a long moment and then looked briefly at Margarita. There was something in the way she looked back at him that clearly indicated who she would side with. Roger rose to his feet and shrugged.

"I'll organise some of our people to go with Teg. I suggest they start out first thing in the morning."

When Roger had left, Jason and Margarita sat looking at each other for a moment, and then she gave a small, satisfied smile and said,

"Well then, Doctor, what were you saying about organising the beds?"

"First of all, many people in that ward would be just as well off at home or even back at work. There are quite a few that have nothing more than sniffles. This hinders patients who need space, rest, and plenty of attention.

Perhaps our first step should be to do some weeding, Margarita?"

She rose to her full regal height and looked down at him almost affectionately. Then she smiled a warm smile that did something peculiar to his insides.

"You may be a Wayperson, Doctor, but I will enjoy working with you."

The sun had barely cleared the horizon as the cart jolted away from the barricade. Teg still felt half-asleep, and he shivered in the early morning air. He had enjoyed the ride to the border. The horse had been allowed to stretch its legs this time, and the journey had been accomplished in half the time.

Teg turned suddenly as a warm, wet tongue licked his ear and grinned happily as he looked at Tara. He had been surprised when, on reaching the barricade, the boy they had seen in the city the day before had been waiting with the dog at his side.

Teg had been accompanied from the hospital by Jan, a big, strong-looking blonde boy who said very little but was always alert. Teg guessed that he was to be more of a guard than anything. Also with them on the cart was Daniel, a boy about Teg's age and whom Teg had taken an instant dislike. He had tried to avoid showing this, not that he felt it would make much difference. Daniel's constant sneering and unfriendly manner soon made it clear to Teg that he was not somebody with whom he would become close.

Teg's spirits had lifted somewhat when he had seen Tara, and he had felt even better when the boy had grinned cheekily as he climbed on the cart and said to Teg,

"You were the one who had my dog yesterday. I didn't think I'd see you again."

"We really didn't know it was anyone's dog," said Teg, "but I suppose we should have guessed when it was so obviously used to doing what it was told."

"Oh, it's a good dog alright, when she doesn't wander off. Mind you, she always comes back in the end."

"What do you call her?"

"Call her; what do you mean to call her?"

"What's her name?"

"She hasn't got a name. Why give a dog a name?"

"My grandad said that long ago, before The Bad Times, lots of people had dogs, and they used to give them names."

"How would your grandad know that?"

"He knows lots of things. When he was a boy, they taught children many things. He's very clever, my grandad. He got a special honour from The Supreme Council."

The moment he had said it, Teg regretted it. The man driving the horse and cart turned and scowled. Daniel sneered even more, and Jan stared hard and suspiciously at him.

"Not that he wanted it," said Teg, trying to retrieve the situation. "It was a complete surprise. They probably were furious when they found out he'd run away the next day."

The atmosphere on the cart had cooled considerably, but suddenly, the boy with the dog grinned.

"Here," he said. "I bet you don't even know my name yet; I'm Zack!"

To Teg's delight, Zack held out his hand to be shaken. His grasp was warm and firm, and for the first time in a long time, Teg felt he had a friend other than his grandfather and Elene.

"I'm Teg," he said, grinning.

"I know that" said Zack, "you told me yesterday, remember!"

There was something pleasant for Teg in recalling earlier events with Zack, as though their friendship was long-standing, and he nodded happily as he recalled their rather odd first meeting.

Suddenly they seemed stumped for something to say, and Teg, remembering their conversation before he had blundered, said,

"Before we knew she was anybody's dog, we called her Tara."

At the mention of the name, the dog's ears pricked up, and she happily licked Teg's hand.

A disgusted snort of "Tara? How ridiculous" from Daniel threatened to spoil the moment, but Teg felt a warm glow of friendship for Zack when he looked defiantly at Daniel and said to Teg,

"Tara, that's a great name; that's what I'll call her from now on."

When they had reached the ruins of what had once been an imposing but obviously ancient building, the horse had been pulled to a halt, and the driver had dismounted. As he unhooked a bag of feed for the horse, he said to the three boys,

"Beyond these ruins, you'll find the beginning of some pretty wild country. From what I can gather, it's the country where the physician fellow thinks you should find most of what you want. Now I'll be back here before dusk. Make sure you're here in plenty of time for us to return to the barricade before dark. And watch your step."

He stood feeding the horse whilst his eyes constantly scanned the surrounding streets and buildings. Teg was beginning to understand the kind of tensions they lived under, and he felt as relieved as the others when they ran up the weed-choked heath to the ruined house and began to make their way through it.

As they emerged from the rear of the old house, they came onto a scene of such wild splendour. Even as a ruin, the house retained much of its grandeur, and it was easy to imagine how the big vine and creeper-clad columns and walls that still stood in places had once been part of soaring rooms and palatial corridors. Teg would have been happy to have stayed there for the rest of the day.

The ground immediately behind the house was level for a hundred feet, and then it began to rise in a series of symmetrical slopes. Even though the grasses grew untended, the roses and the flowering shrubs had long reverted to wildness, and the once formal hedges were unkempt and overgrown, it was easy to see that once these gardens had been formally laid out and scrupulously cared for over a long period.

Teg imagined it would be possible to spend a couple of years of hard work on the gardens to restore them to their original splendour. He had been wandering through the wild growth and trailing creepers and only gradually became aware of the other three standing impatiently on top of the first slopes that led up to the trees in the distance.

He felt strangely embarrassed and tried to cover his discomfort by calling to them,

"This place has such a variety of plants I thought we might find some of the things we need right here."

They looked at him in disbelief, but then, to his delight, he spotted the familiar leaves of lemon balm growing wild at the base of what had once been a red brick wall.

Excitedly he called them.

"I was right. Look here, there's lemon balm and even apple mint."

They looked oddly at him as he scrambled happily through the tangled undergrowth, finding various herbs that once had graced the formal garden. Daniel looked on with his perpetual sneer, and Jan was busily looking around as though expecting to be attacked at any moment. Only Zack seemed to share his enthusiasm.

When Teg had identified half a dozen of the herbs they required, he turned to the others and said, very pleased with himself,

"What we'll do is leave these until we return. If we leave ourselves enough time to gather some of these before the cart comes for us, it'll save us a lot of time out in the country, and we can concentrate on the others we need. Come on, let's go,"

As he started to trot off up the hill, Zack ran after him, Tara emerging from the ruins to happily follow.

Teg suddenly became aware that Jan and Daniel had remained where they were. He trotted back down the hill to where they stood and looked at them curiously.

"What's wrong?" he asked.

"Who do you think you are, giving orders?" demanded Daniel angrily,

"I wasn't giving orders," said Teg, surprised, "It just seemed the best way to do it."

"Well, just you remember who you are, Wayperson; it's you who'll do what you're told!"

"I wasn't trying to annoy you or anything, Daniel, I realise what the situation is, and all I want is to get the things my grandfather needs."

"Oh yeh, your grandfather, the great physician! Well, he won't look so great with a spear stuck through him!"

Teg stared, horrified at the other boys gloating expression.

"How can you say a thing like that? After all, it's your people he's trying to make better. Why should you want to see him dead?"

"Just don't forget that it was you, Waypeople who put our people in that hospital in the first place," Daniel spat out, "the only good Wayperson is a dead one!"

Chapter 23

Teg couldn't believe the bitterness that emanated from the other boy and shivered at the thought of how deeply he had absorbed the lessons of hate that someone had no doubt preached to him.

Realising that nothing was to be gained by further dispute Teg quietly asked,

"What do you want to do next?"

Seeing that he had apparently regained his authority, Daniel grandly announced,

"We'll see what we can find out in the country, then pick up what we need from here on the way back."

It all seemed so foolish to Teg that, as he turned and started back up the slope to where he had stood listening to the exchange, he couldn't stop a slight grin from starting on his face. When he saw Zack watching him, he tried to control his expression, but as he drew alongside Zack, who turned to walk alongside him, Teg saw that he, too, was grinning, and suddenly, he felt better.

It felt good to be in the countryside again, and Teg was pleased to think that a real friendship was developing between him and Zack. The other boy seemed impressed by Teg's knowledge of the various trees and flowers they saw and joined enthusiastically in helping to collect any of the leaves, barks and roots needed. They chatted amiably about themselves, and Zack listened in awe as Teg described their flight from town, the circumstances under which he had met Elene and their subsequent adventures up to being captured in the plaza.

Zack began to describe his life in the so-called wastelands, but he was interrupted by Daniel, who said, still sneering,

"You watch what you say to him; you know he's a Wayperson, and they're all spies."

Zack rounded on him angrily,

"Be quiet, Daniel, I don't have to do as you say, and there's no need to talk about Teg like that; he's alright!"

Daniel started towards Zack, looking as though he was spoiling for a fight, but suddenly Tara was between them, teeth bared, growling at Daniel. He stopped abruptly and then took a pace backwards. Trying to appear unconcerned about the dog, he said, "Alright, Zack, I can see you're a friend of the Waypeople; maybe you've even been spying for them. I know a few people who'll be interested to hear about you."

Teg looked distressed, seeing his new-found friend in trouble on his behalf, but Zack grinned at him and said heartily,

"Oh, don't worry about him, Teg, he's full of wind. He's never happy unless he's being nasty to someone."

Despite Zack's outward appearance of unconcern, Teg was sure he could detect a glimmer of anxiety in his eyes. He suddenly felt very anxious about the future.

David always felt a shiver of distaste when he entered Garon's quarters. He knew the horrors committed there in the name of The Supreme Council. There was always the underlying knowledge that, should a power struggle within The Forum result in his own downfall, he was just as likely to end up in the merciless hands of the Interrogator.

The only good points in Garon's favour, as far as David was concerned, were that he was good at his job, albeit to excess sometimes, and he appeared never to side with any particular faction within The Forum. By this means, he had survived many years of change and intrigue and made few real enemies, even if he had made even fewer friends.

Garon had escorted David to the cells on either side of a wide corridor one level down from the interrogation chamber. Although clean and dry, the underground passages were cold, and David shivered, equally from the cold as from being close to the Interrogator.

"Will you need me?" asked Garon, his voice booming around the bare stone walls.

"No, no, I'll be able to handle this myself; just be on hand in case of any trouble'.'

"Oh, I don't think you'll have any trouble with him, Third President," said Garon, with a grin so evil, David shuddered.

The man on the bed cringed back as David entered, fear in his eyes. He seemed puzzled as he heard the Third President's voice instead of Garon's, and there was a flicker of hope in his eyes as David sat on the edge of the bed. It was all David could do to keep his voice regular as he looked at the haggard features of the policeman. He had been surprised to learn that the man had survived Garon's questioning and could only assume that it was because the Interrogator had found a more exciting subject.

David shuddered as the policeman grasped his wrist. The man's emaciated frame shook with the effort of speaking.

"Third President, thank heavens you've come. You must know I'm innocent, sir. You have come to arrange my release, haven't you?"

"We'll see what we can do," said David, not knowing what else to say, "but first, there's something I'd like you to help me with."

He produced the photograph James had obtained for him and held it before the man's face.

"Do you recognise this man?" he asked, waiting expectantly as the policeman peered intently at the photo.

"There's something about him, but - I'm not sure Third President."

He sounded despondent, clearly wanting to help and secure his deliverance.

"Perhaps I could jog your memory. Do you remember the man and boy who were ambushed and shot?"

"Of course!" he said triumphantly, "that's the physician."

Smiling, David disengaged the man's hand from his wrist and stood up. The man attempted to sit up, feebly reaching out for him.

"You will have me released, Third President," he gasped weakly, "you will get me out of here?"

"I'll see what can be done," said David, opening the door. He looked back at the man but quickly looked away again, unable to stand the look of hope in his eyes. He left the chambers without speaking to Garon.

James was beginning to wonder whether he was in trouble. He had reported in triumph to the Third President and described his adventures in the town in detail. He had been pleased to note how the Third President's interest had quickened, and it was with a flourish that he finally produced the photograph. He had been astonished when David had almost snatched the picture from him and rushed out of the chamber with the admonition,

"Wait here until I get back!"

At first, James had waited in a relaxed frame of mind, but as time passed and the Third President hadn't returned, he had become fidgety and, finally, anxious. He had sat still for as long as he could bear it, but then his nerves had moved him to get up and wander around.

Passing David's desk, he could not resist looking at the various papers there and had just had time to quickly move away from the desk and head back to his seat before David re-entered the chamber.

Now James sat there wondering if he had been seen at the desk and, consequently, was in trouble. He was relieved when David smiled and said warmly,

"You have done well, James. The information you have provided has been valuable. I am pleased with you. Even though I still recall your original transgression. I will give more thought to thinking of some little reward for your efforts in this matter. I'll see what I can come up with. In the meantime, remember, you must reveal nothing of this to anyone, understood?"

"Oh yes, of course, Third President; rest assured you have my full discretion!"

"For your own sake, I hope you're right."

As James left the Third President's chambers, he wasn't sure whether to be elated at the prospect of his coming reward or worried about the continuing threat of his 'transgression' being used against him. Of one thing he was sure though, He would love to know what the Third President had meant when he had doodled on the desk pad, Jason and Teg, where are they now?'.

If James was curious, it might have helped him to know that his fellow Attendant Antony was no less interested. Despite his delight at once more sampling the delectable Carla's charms, Antony would, in all honesty, have preferred that he had nothing more to do with whatever it was that the Second President was plotting. His summons to Delmo's chamber had depressed him, and his depression hadn't been lifted when the Second President had cheerfully announced that he had a little job for him.

You were very bright to spot that our head of the supplies department was absent from his duties recently. Well, you may or may not know it, but he is back. I want you to find out exactly what it is he was doing during his absence and what, if anything, he found out.

"But, Second President, he's not likely to tell me that, sir, particularly if he was acting under the orders of the Third President!

"Then it will be up to you to make him tell you, won't it."

"But, sir, how am I supposed to do that?"

"I don't care how you do it; just ensure you do. Otherwise, you may have more reason to fear the Third President than James."

Margarita found it hard to believe that so much of a change could have been wrought quickly. Despite much grumbling, some of them were reasonably good-natured and some very hostile, they managed to reduce the hospital's population by at least forty per cent. She was embarrassed when she saw how right Jason was about the condition of many of the ward occupants and confessed to him her shame that she had failed to spot the malingerers.

She had been warmed by the way he had hastened to assure her that it was not her fault and that she had far too much to do without the burden of weeding out. In addition to the reduction in the number of patients, the whole ward had undergone thorough cleaning. An army of women had been recruited as 'volunteers', and Margarita had watched with admiration as Jason had chivvied and charmed them to great efforts. Several of the women had later volunteered to help with the nursing of the sick, and Margarita was sure that it had a lot to do with the gentle, cultured man who had already caused a transformation in the hospital.

The patients, too, had responded to Jason's presence, seeming to take heart merely from the fact that he was causing changes to be made. He had done what he could for the worst off among them with the available supplies but was impatiently waiting on whatever Teg was bringing him. Even so, the psychological health of many of the patients had been improved by a program of bed baths and the washing of the assortment of materials that masqueraded as bed linen.

The ribald comments of the men, and some of the women, during the bed baths had created an atmosphere of good humour that was clearly doing a lot of good for many of the patients. By the time the evening was approaching, there was a feeling in the hospital that things could only get better now, and as Jason walked wearily between the long lines of beds, he was moved by the friendly smiles and nods he received, particularly when he heard one of the patient's remarks,

"He may be a Wayperson, but he's a damn good doctor!"

His whole-body aching, he collected a steaming drink from the cooking area at the back of the hospital and then followed Margarita into her small but blissfully quiet room. They smiled as they saw Elene curled up in a corner sleeping soundly. An affectionate rapport had developed between the girl and the woman. Elene had hardly left Margarita's side all day, working at everything she could manage until exhaustion finally drove her to a quiet spot.

They sat down carefully, not wanting to disturb the sleeping girl, and for a while, they just sat and sipped their drinks. Jason looked up and found Margarita looking at him with affection and puzzlement. When she saw that he was aware of her gaze, she looked slightly embarrassed and said, "I hope you don't mind me saying it, but you're remarkably resilient for someone your age. I can hardly believe the amount of work you've got through today."

He waved a hand deprecatingly, "I couldn't have achieved one-tenth of what I did without some damn fine help, and most of that was due to you."

She looked almost girlishly pleased with his compliment, and then her expression changed and became thoughtful and sympathetic as he went on.

"I've enjoyed myself today. I've learned what real doctoring is about. It's one thing to have all the equipment and medicines available and to have special doctors for special things, but when it comes down to it, the real test must be under conditions like these."

He investigated space, a faraway expression on his face for some time. When he suddenly began speaking again, Margarita was about to ask him if he was alright.

"You know what I find hardest to grasp? If it hadn't been for my grandson Teg, I would quite happily have walked to my death a few weeks ago. My knowledge, my thoughts, my ideas, my expertise; all those things would have died with me. It seems so incredible now that I, and so many other supposedly intelligent, thinking people, should have allowed ourselves to be so ruled, so brainwashed, that we would placidly walk to our deaths simply because a ruling body had decreed that our lives must end when we had completed sixty-five years. Here I am now, proving that I still have so much to offer, and I feel sure I will have a long time to come.

I am astounded to think that when Teg first questioned these things, when he first suggested to me that perhaps The Way was wrong, I was angry with him. It was as though he had committed some grave sin. I actually toyed with the idea of turning him over to the authorities."

Jason had become quite agitated as he recalled the traumatic night when Teg had come to him. His hands moved nervously on the tabletop, and Margarita reached out and laid a hand gently on top of his. He stared down at her hand for a moment, slowly turning his hand over and clasping hers. He looked up, almost shyly, as if fearful she would be angry, but all he saw was her warm smile. He went on.

"I have learned things about our so-called leaders, The Forum and The Supreme Council that are so horrendous and obscene. I want to raise an army and drive into town and destroy them. They are evil, of that there is no doubt, no doubt at all!"

Jason's voice trembled as he finished saying this, and tears collected in his eyes. Still holding his hand, Margarita leaned forward and said,

"There's something else, isn't there."

Jason sniffed, blinked back his tears, and said quietly,

"When they found out I had not turned up for my Dying Day, they took away my wife and my daughter, Teg's mother; he doesn't know that they killed them both."

They quietly sat, staring at each other as Jason finished, and Margarita also had tears in her eyes now. Then they jerked around as Teg's voice said quietly, but stunning them like a shout,

"Don't worry about it, grandad. I've thought often that's what would happen."

"Teg, oh Teg!" said Jason, rising to his feet, "I'm so sorry, I didn't know you were there."

Teg looked sadly at Jason and appeared near to tears as he said quietly,

"I don't want you to think I don't care what happened to Mother and Grandmother; of course, I do. It's just that I'm not surprised. I somehow knew we would never see them again. All I care about now is that the evil people who could cause such things to happen should be destroyed."

Jason could think of nothing to say as he looked at his grandson. He had a feeling that Teg wasn't just speaking idle words.

They were distracted when Elene, awoken by Teg's voice and scrambled to her feet, running to him, quickly and lightly kissing him. Teg looked embarrassed but pleased and said proudly to Jason, "Come and see what we've got grandad."

They went outside to where the horse and cart still stood. Zack sat on the edge of the cart, Tara on the ground.

When Elene emerged, she was obviously thrilled when the dog jumped up and ran to greet her. The cart was piled high with an assortment of leaves, roots, and barks and even flowers that gave the cart the appearance of a carnival float.

Quite a few people had gathered around the cart and were chatting happily. Many of them had already heard of Jason's good work in the hospital and nodded in a friendly way if they caught his eye.

Jason was delighted with the bounty and began sorting through it happily, giving quick instructions to Margarita as to how different things should be stored ready for preparation.

He was chatting happily when he became aware that his voice sounded unusually loud. He realised that it was because all the other voices had stopped. Surprised he looked up and saw the people who had been around the cart had backed away and that he, Teg, Elene, and Margarita were surrounded by a ring of hostile looking men. His heart sank as he recognised their adversary from the day before, Marcus.

"Well now," Marcus sneered. "We decided to wait until the brat got back so we could save time and take you all together."

"Take us where?" demanded Jason.

"To the Trying Place old man" Marcus snarled, "you're going to be tried and then you'll be put away, for good!"

"No, you can't, it's wrong" Margarita protested. Before she could continue Marcus had stepped forward and pointed a finger accusingly at her. "You keep your mouth shut, woman, I'll be quite happy to shove the spear through you as well as these three if you're going to side with them. It's bad enough having spies in our midst without having our own people helping them."

"You fool..." began Margarita, but before she could say anymore Marcus had slapped her around the face. Immediately Jason sprang forward. Marcus swung around and smashed a fist into his face. As his grandfather crumpled to the ground Teg also made as if to spring at Marcus but, on a snarled command of, "Take them!" He found his arms pinned behind him and could only struggle helplessly as he, Jason, and Elene were bundled unceremoniously onto the cart.

Chapter 24

They were joined by three armed men, and Marcus and the horse were set into motion. As they began the journey back to the barricade, excited people began to follow the cart while carrying flaming torches, which cast weird, dancing shadows in the gathering gloom as the strange procession made its way up the road.

The only consolation for Teg and Elene on the frightening journey was that they could sit together. Teg placed his arm protectively around her shoulder, and she laid her head against his chest. He thought sadly of how it would be if he could sit with her thus, under other circumstances, and he looked down fondly at her as he thought of how much she had come to mean to him. Looking up and seeing the expression on his face, she smiled shyly. They both looked around anxiously as Jason groaned and opened his eyes. He looked around, and an expression of hopelessness crossed his face as he saw the escort and the guns they carried. With a little despair, he lay back and closed his eyes.

When they reached the barricade, they were surprised to see how many people were streaming through it. There was an air of excitement about them which increased in the vicinity of the horse and cart as it inched its way, with very little space to spare through the opening in the barricade. There were a few hostile cries as the cart: went past, but mostly the people looked with curiosity more than anything.

They became aware of a murmuring sound like a hive of disturbed bees. The sound increased as they approached the last turn to the plaza, and as they made the turn, the sound hit them with almost physical force. Even Jason was moved to sit up and take notice of his surroundings, and he, like Teg and Elene, stared in astonishment at the transformation in the plaza.

Darkness had closed in now, and the scene below them was lit by hundreds of flaming torches, either held aloft by the crowd or fixed to posts that had been driven into the ground. A stage had been set up in the middle of an ample open space, and flaming torches were set around three sides of it. The wavering flames, the smoke swirling into the air, and the movement and murmuring of the crowd gave the whole scene an eerie quality.

The crowd fell silent as they became aware of the horse and cart moving down the slope towards the stage. A path opened through the public and the carriage was brought to a stop close to the location. Marcus jumped down and walked over to talk to a group of men who stood by one corner of the stage.

In the meantime, the three prisoners were ordered to step onto the stage. They stood in the middle of the bare platform and tried to see around them. The primitive lighting and the surrounding darkness made it difficult to get a clear impression, but it was easy to tell that there were a great many people assembled there. From parts of the crowd came angry shouts of, "Kill the traitors!" "We want no Waypeople here!"

Other hostile cries occurred with an almost rhythmic cadence as though being orchestrated. There were also shouts of "Let's be fair!" "They're entitled to a fair trial!" and similar calls for justice. However, all chatter and calling ceased when Marcus suddenly climbed onto the stage and held his arms out wide above his head. When silence had settled, he began to speak in a voice that clearly and obviously had tons of confidence and leadership. It was also possible to detect hatred in his voice as he pointed at the three captives and called the crowd.

"My friends, you see here before you three of the Waypeople. They are our enemies and must be done away with!" There were some supportive shouts and some murmuring, but many people looked almost embarrassed and seemed not to want to look at the three on the stage as Marcus went on.

"We have enough problems, enough dangers in our society without inviting murderers into our midst!"

The shouts began again, a few more this time, as people started to respond to the hysteria in Marcus' voice. They became quieter, though, as Roger suddenly appeared and scrambled up onto the stage and held up his hands for silence.

"Listen, my friends, this is not our way! These people are entitled to be treated fairly, and you know that the master should be here for any trying. The Trying Grounds should not be dishonoured with this mockery of a trial. By what right does Marcus presume to bring them here? On what does he base his charges of spying and murder? Let us wait for the master's return and not fall to the level of animals."

Roger's speech appeared to be well received by most of the crowd but there were rising shouts of anger at places, again seemingly orchestrated, and Teg's eyes narrowed as he noticed that the group of men Marcus had earlier been talking to had dispersed. He could guess who was directing the hostility.

Marcus, who had listened to Roger with barely concealed contempt, now sprang forward angrily and cried out, "He dares to ask how I know they are spies. I wonder why he should be so anxious to protect them?"

It was clear that Roger had many supporters in the crowd, and when Marcus heard their angry murmuring in his attempt to discredit him, he quickly changed tack.

"I'll tell you why I know these Waypeople are spies. I know because they have condemned themselves out of their own mouths."

The crowd had become silent again and stared curiously at the three accused. Roger looked puzzled at Marcus' words and looked towards Jason to see if he knew what he meant. Jason looked equally puzzled, and so did Teg.

Marcus strode up to Jason and stared straight at him. Looking around quickly to see that he had the full attention of the crowd, he said loudly so that they could all hear,

"Are you going to deny, physician, that the very night you supposedly fled from the town, you were given one of the highest honours possible from the…" Marcus paused in mid-sentence as a cry went up in the crowd. He stood and looked to where all heads had turned. His expression seemed part anger, part apprehension, as he observed a vehicle's headlights moving slowly along the top of the slope that rose from the piazza. Teg was surprised to see the outlines of a police personnel carrier, but he soon saw, as it moved down the slope towards the stage, that it was painted a neutral colour and that its condition indicated that it had been used far, far longer than any police vehicle would typically be.

Roger, glancing around and seeing their puzzled expressions, smiled and gestured towards the vehicle, "We captured it from a police patrol about four years ago, one of our very few successful engagements, unfortunately. It's seen better days, of course, but it still enables the master to move about the country when he needs to."

"The master," said Teg, "You mean he's here now?"

As if in answer to his question, the vehicle stopped, and the door opened. Two men ran forward and assisted the passenger out of the front. Having done so, they stood back almost reverently. The crowd had fallen silent, and the feeling of respect emanating from them was almost palpable as the new arrival began to walk past the stage to where a seat had hurriedly been produced in front of it. Having reached the seat, the man stood looking up to where the three accused waited.

Teg felt a strange feeling as he looked down at the man. He was very old, although upright. His hair and his beard were long. He wore a simple brown tunic that reached the ground and had the most hypnotic eyes Teg had ever seen.

The master's gaze travelled from Jason's face to Elene's and then to Teg's. Teg felt compelled to stare back at the old man, and their eyes locked. Teg had never felt such strength of personality before, and as he gazed into the master's eyes, he felt almost as though he was going to fall forward; so powerful was the attraction. Then a brief smile flickered across the old man's face, and he looked away. Teg felt as though he had been left dangling over a great height. His heart pounded, his legs felt weak, and he knew he must know more about this man. Instinctively he took a step forward and then stopped abruptly as Marcus jumped ahead to the front of the stage and shouted,

"You see, the Wayperson would attack the master; he must be punished!"

"That's ridiculous!" shouted Teg, "I wished only to speak with him; I would know more of him!"

"So, you'd have more to tell your evil leaders in the town", Marcus sneered.

Teg shook his head in despair at the determination of the other man to distort anything he might say. The crowd had begun to murmur again but abruptly fell silent as the master lifted his hand. There was a reverent hush as the old man began to speak, and Teg listened with awe, not so much to what he said but more to the quiet authority and wisdom that seemed to be part of his words, even the most mundane of them.

"I am surprised to return and find this Trying going on. Is there a good reason why it could not have waited for my return?"

"There is our master," called Marcus. "These spies have come among us and, by their own words, have revealed themselves to be our enemies!"

"A serious charge Marcus, and one which you should be able to substantiate. Otherwise, your actions have been inappropriate indeed."

There was a suggestion of uncertainty on Marcus' face for a moment, but then he recovered and said confidently,"If you allow me, master, I will prove what I have said."

The master looked thoughtfully at the three prisoners, his eyes seeming to linger on Teg a moment longer than the others, and then he sat down. Resuming where he had been when interrupted, Marcus once more confronted Jason and asked loudly.

"Is it untrue, physician, that on the very night, you supposedly fled from the authorities in the town, you were awarded one of the highest honours possible?"

"That is true," said Jason simply, and there was a murmur in the crowd.

"Did you refuse that honour? Did you turn it down?"

"No, I did not."

"So, you freely accepted from the evil men who rule you, a great honour that could only have been given to someone who was a good and loyal servant, and then, you would have us believe, you flee in revulsion and terror from the very same rulers. You must think we are mad."

"At the time I received the honour, I had no intention of running away", Jason began to say but was interrupted by loud derisive laughter from Marcus, which was taken up by some in the crowd. Jason stood in dignified silence until the laughter petered out, and then he went on.

"There were things I had not realised, things I had not thought about, that were made clear to me."

"And who was it who enlightened you so?" interrupted Marcus.

"My grandson Teg," said Jason, turning and smiling reassuringly at Teg, who was feeling dreadful because he knew that he was the source of Marcus's information. He had seen Zack near the stage and wondered whether he had revealed their conversation to Marcus, but he had guessed the truth soon after when he had seen Daniel staring up at him, his perpetual sneer and a look of triumph on his face.

Teg turned angrily as he heard Marcus say, scathingly, to Jason.

"So, you are trying to tell us that in just a few short hours, this boy, this mere boy, was able to persuade you to cast aside the beliefs and teachings of a lifetime. Come now, physician, he must be a very persuasive child!"

Jason turned again and looked at Teg, a look that seemed to convey a great deal, in a split moment and said simply, "He truly is."

Teg felt proud at Jason's words but also sad that he had led his beloved grandfather to this undignified end. He looked down, disconsolate for a moment, but then he became aware of the master's eyes on him, and at once, he straightened up and felt renewed energy surge through him.

He turned on Marcus and shouted, hoping his voice would carry.

"Only men whose minds are closed to new thoughts find it impossible to understand the facility in others. You are filled with hatred, with loathing, which has robbed you of compassion and understanding, but worse, it has robbed you of the concept of justice."

There was a surprised, and what sounded like an approving murmur, at Teg's words, and Marcus wet his lips nervously as though appreciating, for the first time, that his adversary was Teg and not Jason.

He recovered quickly, however, and launched into the next phase of his attack. This time he walked up to Teg and addressed his question to him.

"Tell me, how did you get here?"

"We walked," said Teg, surprised.

"All the way?" asked Marcus.

"Of course, we…" Teg stopped, realising where the question was leading and the impression the answer would create. He glanced down at the sneering Daniel and knew that his eavesdropping was the cause of their present problem.

"No, we didn't walk all the way; I've just remembered we were arrested and driven in a police carrier for most of a day."

Marcus was laughing sarcastically, obviously enjoying Teg's discomfort.

"Let me get this right," he asked, "you say you were arrested and driven all day in a police vehicle. Then what happened?"

The look on the questioner's face showed anticipation. He was looking forward to the answer; the look on Teg's face showed how much he wished he could answer with something else.

"They let us go," he said.

Marcus seemed to be laughing genuinely this time, and there was a lot of disbelieving laughter from the crowd. Tegs' only comfort came from knowing that the master wasn't laughing but looked thoughtful.

'They let you go?" Marcus asked dramatically and began laughing again before suddenly changing, his laugh disappearing abruptly to be replaced by an angry snarl as he rounded on Teg.

"You try to make fools of us, boy. You expect us to believe your lies. You expect us to believe what the old man tells us. Do you really want us to believe that foul and evil police would arrest you and then release you unscathed? What sort of fools do you think we are?"

Marcus stood, breathing heavily, his hands on his hips. There was a look of satisfaction on his face as he heard the crowd's increasing support. He smirked as, when he straightened up, the public immediately became silent. Enjoying his moment of triumph, he strode up and down the front of the stage a couple of times before stopping suddenly and, holding up his hand, exclaiming,

"You are spies, liars, cheats. You take us for fools. You must be made to pay the penalty. You come here for one reason and one reason only, and that is to destroy us?"

The crowd had begun to rumble angrily and to close in on the stage. Teg stared around at them, and then, suddenly inspired, he stepped to the edge of the stage and held up his arms. Not knowing what had made him decide to do what he was doing but somehow knowing it was their last chance, he addressed the crowd, making sure his words could be heard by the master. Nobody was more surprised than him when the public fell silent.

"You all appear to believe that the town's rulers, the enforcers of The Way, are evil. There is much hatred among you towards the Waypeople and their rulers. Such hatred is understandable when set against the corruption and evil that infests The Forum and its servants. Why is it that, knowing how evil and oppressive that rule is, you should find it difficult to believe that there are some among the Waypeople, as you call them, who would want no part of that evil? Is it so hard to believe that some would rather flee than have more to do with such a corrupt system?"

The silence was intense now as Teg's young but somehow impressive voice rang out over the heads of the crowd. Marcus looked around, and his face grew angrier as he saw the attention Teg was getting. Suddenly he stepped forward and cried.

"Enough of this. It is time."

"Let him be heard!" a voice shouted, and there was a mumble of agreement. Marcus looked around furiously but then retreated to the edge of the stage sullenly when the master signaled him to do so. Seeing this, Teg was heartened and went on with renewed strength.

"For all the Waypeople, The Way has been a part of their lives since birth. People have not questioned it because it is all they have ever known. For several generations, the town's rulers have perpetuated their evil dynasty. There may have been those who challenged The Way but have been ruthlessly disposed of.

Rest assured, my friends, I would have had you as my friend if I could have known you existed. The people of the town that spoke out were silenced. Fortunately, we got away and reached what we had been taught to identify as The Wastelands.

We now see how false the description of The Wastelands is. Ask yourselves what else the Waypeople believe simply because they know no difference? You should not hate the Waypeople because they are victims. Hate their rulers, just as we do, because they are evil; they are evil not just towards you people who do not subscribe to their system, but to their own people who do as they are told."

Teg stared around at the silent crowd. He knew that things could still go badly for them, mainly if Marcus pursued the question of the police 'assistance' they had received. He thought hard about what else he could say and was about to give in when suddenly inspired, he said,

"We were asked to explain why we came here. I have told you why. I can say it in many or fewer words though, my friends, we are Mictorans, and proud of it!"

Teg hadn't known what he would say until almost the moment he said it; therefore, he could not have anticipated what reaction he might get. He would probably not have expected what happened if he had thought about it. There was a collective gasp at his final words, and all eyes turned towards the master, who had risen to his feet. His face was stern, and Teg's heart sank as he imagined he had made a dreadful mistake.

Chapter 25

Teg stared down at the master as he slowly walked to the stage and looked up at him.

"Come down here, boy."

Teg immediately jumped down from the stage and stood before the old man. Looking into the clear shrewd eyes, he felt more awe than fear.

"There have been no Mictorans for over forty years, boy; how do you presume to call yourself such?"

Teg felt an aura about the old man and wanted to impress him. He suspected, however, that the simple truth would be most impressive.

"We know of the Mictorans, sir; my grandfather has told us of them. I know they failed in their aims, but they were good, and there is no reason their name should not live on and their aims be renewed."

The master looked at him for a long while, and there was sadness in his voice when he finally said,

"If you know the story of the Mictorans, then you will know that their abortive attempt to fight The Way led to the most dreadful orgy of death where friend was set against friend, neighbour against neighbour, and family against family. That is not a comfortable responsibility to bear."

Teg was angry. He wanted to like the old man, not to be at odds with him, but his fury spilled over.

"How dare you lay the responsibility for what happened at the feet of the Mictorans. If you knew the story, you would know that the awful events that followed the Mictoran's defeat were the sole responsibility of The Forum. Can't you see what they did? They created fear and mistrust. Encouraging citizens to accuse each other created confusion. By acting on accusations that could not possibly be proved, they created fear.

The Forum even involved children in their dreadful plot. They struck at the very roots of society, and why? To create fear against the Mictorans, to make people believe that all the evils that had befallen them were the fault of the Mictorans. By doing all this, they successfully created fear and confusion, and in so doing, they divided society. This division meant they ruled the people more easily. They were and are evil and corrupt men; it is a bad system. This was the work of The Forum and The Supreme Council.

To blame the Mictorans for the terrible things that happened, you effectively exonerate The Forum. It is shameful, a disgrace! I don't care what the consequences are; I say, "Long live the Mictorans!" The brave people who tried to fight evil should be honoured and upheld as an example to all freedom-loving people, lovers of justice and admirers of courage.

Teg stopped, breathless, hot, excited, and not a little scared at the fury with which he had ranted at the master. As he ceased speaking, there was complete silence for a moment, and then he was astonished as the crowd suddenly began wildly cheering. He stared around in disbelief, saw smiling faces and waving arms, and heard their shouts of support. Hardly able to believe what was happening, he turned back to the master and looked at him in puzzlement.

To his surprise, Teg saw that the old man had tears in his eyes and, as he spoke, indicating the crowd with a wave of his hand, his voice trembled slightly.

"A fine speech, young man, and one which, as you can hear, has the wholehearted support of the good people here. I have tried to make them forget about these things. I have believed for so long that what happened all those years ago was so bad it must never be allowed to happen again. I can see now that they have never truly believed me, that in their hearts, there has burned a secret flame that has waited with longing for a chance to be rekindled. You have told them what they want to hear.

You have a gift with words, young man, and there is a fire in you that will spread and spark new fires among these people if I but give them leave. Perhaps even if I do not give them leave."

"With respect, sir, I do not understand. I realise they have great love and respect for you, but why should they require your permission to fight for what is right?"

"I am gratified that what you say about their love and respect is true. I know this, and they know I return it in full measure. It is that very love and respect that would make them hesitate to resurrect something that is such a painful memory to me."

"A painful memory?"

"Yes, Teg, I believe I have known all my life that this moment must come and that one day someone such as you would come along and start it all again. I see how happy it makes my people, and I see something given to very few in you. You will be a great leader Teg, and now that you have arrived, I will do what I know is right for my people and give you, my sanction."

"Your sanction Sir, for what?"

"To take up the fight again, Teg. You see, I am Mictor!"

Antony knew that James was always the last to leave the supplies department at the end of the day. As he hung about at the intersection of the corridors, from where he could see the entrance to the department, he prayed that he wasn't about to make a fool of himself.

He had thought, more than once, of abandoning his plans and returning to the tranquility of his chambers, but the recollection of Delmo's anger earlier in the day had made him persevere. The Second President had waylaid him in the entrance to The Forum building and demanded to know his progress in finding out what James had discovered in the town. He had been furious at the negative report and had requested an answer by the next day. He had softened then and hinted that as well as diverting his anger, a positive response might bring a reward.

As he stood now waiting for James to be alone, even the thought of Carla's charms did nothing to quell his disquiet. He tried to look inconspicuous as two people came out of the supplies department and walked away down the corridor. Knowing James would be alone, he hurried to the door and quickly entered. He carefully shut the door and turned to find James watching him.

"I was about to close up. Was it anything urgent?" asked James, quite pleasantly. Suddenly the scenario that Antony had prepared seemed to him woefully inadequate, but he plunged on in the absence of anything else.

"I - I wish to discuss the department's business with you."

"The business of the department, in what way?"

James was puzzled, and Antony knew he would have to sound convincing.

"Er, is there somewhere we could sit and talk? It's quite important."

"It seems rather odd, to say the least, but if you say it's important, I suppose we could go into my office."

"Hadn't you better lock the door? It might be better if we're not disturbed."

"I'm sure that won't be necessary; we're not likely to get anyone in here at this time of night, at least not usually!"

They walked to James' office, and he sat at his desk, clearly impatient.

"I'd appreciate it if we could make this as quick as possible", he said. "I am rather hungry and anxious to get to my meal."

Antony felt very uncertain about how to begin but finally decided to proceed with his planned strategy.

"You'll no doubt be aware that my duties, among other things, include attending to the care of the central computer. You should also be aware that the records of the supplies department are kept on the computer.

When James nodded noncommittally, Antony swallowed hard and went on,

"You must know that any misdealing's in the movement of goods in and out of this department would eventually show up on the computer."

James now sat forward slightly, his eyes narrowing. He seemed more curious than alarmed, and Antony wondered if his ploy would fail immediately. He ploughed on, "It would be a simple enough matter to process the various dealings of the department over a given time to show any misappropriation of supplies".

James was frowning now and asked disbelievingly,

"You're not trying to tell me you have found such things?"

Antony tried to look inscrutable, but a slight case of nerves made him grimace suddenly so that it looked as though he briefly grinned.

"Is it some kind of joke?" asked James, utterly baffled.

"No, no, it's no joke", said Antony, recovering. "I just want you to consider that the computer can reveal such things."

"Most impressive, I'm sure, but what do you tell me all this for? I know there have been no misdealing's in my department."

"You realise you would be in great trouble if such things did show up?"

"Of course, I do, and rightly so. But why all this charade? What is your point?"

"My point is that you would be in a lot of trouble if the computer highlights malpractices of any kind or if the computer detects malpractice."

"What on earth do you mean? It's the same thing, surely?"

"Not if the computer was manipulated to point out malpractices, even if they hadn't taken place."

"What do you mean, if the computer made a mistake? I thought they never…."

He broke off as another thought hit him, and he looked carefully at Antony before saying, with some anger in his voice, "Or do you mean if the computer was made to make a mistake?"

Antony tried to smile confidently, but again it came out as a nervous grin. He suddenly felt as though he wanted to giggle, and to prevent himself from doing so, he spoke, "It would be straightforward, and nobody would know the difference."

"Why are you telling me all this?"

"Knowing this, you might be open to a little deal."

James rose to his feet, outraged, "How dare you! You dare to suggest that I would enter into some dreadful scheme to misdirect goods from my department, and have you cover it up on your damned computer? I would never even think of it; now get out!"

"No, no, no, you misunderstand. I don't wish for anything from your department. I want something from you. I suggested that if I didn't get what I wanted, I might falsify the computer to make it look like you misdirected goods for yourself."

James sat down again, stunned. His face reflected anger one moment, bafflement the next, and then slowly, with the realisation of what the other man could do, came the first stirrings of fear.

"But why, why me? Why would you do this thing? And what do you mean that you don't want anything from my department but want something from me? What have I got that you could want?"

"Information."

"Information, what information?"

"I want to know what you did and what you found out during your recent trip to town."

"You want to know…you? Let me tell you that I was on an errand for a Supreme Council member, and your audacity could land you in serious trouble."

"Oh, we know you were doing the Third President's bidding."

"You do? How…Who's we?"

"Never mind, just believe me when I say you should tell me."

"This is ridiculous! I can't divulge the business of the Third President to a mere Attendant; he would have me killed."

"You may find, my friend, that someone will make that choice anyway."

Suddenly James looked scared and insecure, and Antony found that he felt sorry for him and was embarrassed by what he was doing.

"Look, James, if you just tell me what you found out in the town, no one else need know, and then you can forget all about it."

"But someone else will know, won't they."

"Who?"

"Whoever sent you here."

"Yes, but you don't need to worry about that."

"How can you say that? Anyone who can stoop low enough to send you here to blackmail me would think nothing of exposing me as a source of information if it would suit him."

"Blackmail?" said Antony. "I hadn't thought of it like that."

Indeed, he hadn't, and all at once, he felt sickened by what he was doing. He looked miserable at James and said, pathetically, "I hadn't thought of it as blackmail. It was a suitable ploy to get the information from you. I dare not go back empty-handed."

James could see the other's misery, and his fear and anger were replaced by an unexpected sympathy for the other man's dilemma.

"This isn't really your kind of work, is it?" he asked kindly. When Antony just shook his head, James asked, "Who was it sent you here?"

Antony looked at him for a long time, conflict on his face, then finally lowered his head and mumbled, "The Second President."

James sat and stared at him for a moment and then said softly, almost to himself, "So, we are pawns in a fight for power between Delmo and David. What a sordid prospect that is."

"Why should there be a fight for power?"

"Surely you're not that naive; there's always a power struggle. Once in a while, the struggle becomes more intense. This time, the other Presidents think Aaron's days are numbered. It's a fight to see who will remain to take Aaron's place."

"But how have we become involved?" asked Antony, scared now at the picture his fellow Attendant had painted.

"Well, I know how I got involved. The Third President picked me up on a minor transgression, and he's used it as a lever ever since."

"I'm afraid what happened to me was rather more sordid than that," said Antony, blushing.

"But the result was the same. I just wish I knew our part in this.".

"I suspect it has something to do with Jason and his grandson Teg."

"What, the physician who ran away on his Dying Day?"

"That's right, there was a note on the Third President's desk the other day about where they might be."

"Where, who might be?"

"Jason and the boy."

"But they were shot; you were in The Forum when it was announced."

James sat very still, his face white. He was clearly thinking furiously, and an expression of horror was dawning on his face. Finally, he whispered.

"Oh my god, that's what it's all about."

"What, what is it all about?"

"I went to town at the Third President's bidding to check up on an Acolyte and an old man who had gone missing. There was no trace of either of them. It's clear now what happened. Delmo must have arranged to have the old man and the boy kidnapped and killed to make it appear that Jason and Teg had been killed."

"You mean that he would cold-bloodedly have innocent people murdered just to save his own position, but that's dreadful!"

"You really are naive, aren't you. Things like this go on all the time. The Supreme Council thinks nothing of having people killed or even tortured if it suits their plan. Why, how many times have you watched as the justice sessions send people to The Sanctum for the most trifling of offences?"

Antony was aghast.

"I never thought of those things this way. They were part of the system."

"Yes", interrupted James", a system that we have supported and, by our support, have encouraged. Now, for our sins, we have become ensnarled in the dirty acts of our good Supreme Council."

Antony looked around nervously as he heard the disgust in James' voice. He was clearly stunned by events and nervously asked.

"What do we do now? I can't see any way out of it. We're in it, like it or not."

"Well, we'll have to agree on some story you can give to the Second President for now, but we're going to have to think of some way of getting out of this rotten system.

"Getting out, how?"

"I don't know, but I'm sure, if we can't get out, we'll have to see what we can do about changing what we're in."

"Changing, what you mean, revolution?"

Chapter 26

James looked alarmed as if suddenly realising what he had been suggesting, then he pulled himself together and said solemnly,

"Whatever we do, Antony, I know that I suddenly don't want to be a part of a system that can kill and torture innocent people. I don't know where it will all end up, but from now on, I shall be looking for a chance to change things. I realise you can get me into a lot of trouble for what I've just said, but I think I'd sooner be dead than go on this way. I'd like to think I'd got you on my side."

Suddenly Antony was thinking of his schooldays and youth when there were no friends, only bullies. He thought of later years when there were still no friends, only fellow Acolytes and fellow Attendants. Now he looked at James tentatively held out his hand, and as he reached forward and clasped it, Antony felt like crying.

Teg stood at the top of a slight rise in the clearing. Around him, the trees moved lazily to and fro as the wind moved gently around in their leaves as if seeking something. The sun was warm, and the early morning mist had just about burned away. From where Teg stood, he could see through to where the small river bubbled quietly. The tents on its banks lay deserted, as if sleeping.

Teg looked down the slope and saw Marcus standing there with a long, wickedly pointed spear. Teg tensed as he saw the other man's feet move, and then, all at once, Marcus was charging up the slope at him, the spear held out in front of him. As the gap closed, Teg went into a slight crouch and then, as the spear looked as though it was about to impale him, he dropped to one knee, his hands flashed up and grabbed the spear shaft, and he fell backwards.

Still gripping the spear, Marcus was jerked forward and sideways, his momentum carrying him on so that he was thrown into the air and crashed to the ground behind Teg. Teg jumped to his feet, the spear now in his possession, and looked down at his opponent, slowly rising to his feet, breathing heavily. He brushed leaves and grass from his tunic, then smiled at Teg.

"You learn quickly, young fellow."

"I have a good teacher. You have a natural talent for aggression."

Marcus smiled uncomfortably as he recalled the antagonism he had shown to Teg when he had first arrived three months before.

"Only joking", called Teg, seeing the other man's discomfort.

They began to walk side by side down the slope towards the camp. They made an odd pair, Marcus big, stocky, and aggressive looking. Teg was slim and youthful looking but with muscles already hardening under the intensive regime that Marcus had introduced.

As they sat by the river and rested, having been practising combat for nearly an hour, there was an easy friendliness between them, although it was clear when Teg spoke that Marcus listened to him very respectfully. Despite his youth, Teg had an air of authority, and he had gained in height and confidence in the months since Mictor had revealed who he was.

Teg's expression became thoughtful as he remembered that night. He remembered every moment and how he had stared at Mictor in disbelief. He could never have imagined that things would work out as they had.

"Mictor? But you're dead!"

"Do I look dead, my boy?"

"I'm sorry, sir; I meant I was told you had died."

"Oh, I know that well enough. The Forum didn't want people to believe that I still lived. They wanted them to believe the revolt had been completely crushed to enhance their image. Fortunately, I managed to escape, although there have been many times since I have wondered if I might have been better off not to have escaped. The aftermath of our efforts has lain heavily upon me for many years. Still, all that has changed now with your arrival. I see hope where there was despair and fire where there were ashes. We must leave this place and return to the relative safety of our homes. We have much talking to do."

The old man seemed invigorated and signalled to some of his followers to lift him onto the stage. He walked first to where Jason and Elene stood. He looked closely at Jason and, holding out his hand, said,

"So, you are the boy's grandfather. I can see in your face where his intelligence comes from."

He turned to Elene and lightly touched her cheek as he looked into her eyes and said,

"And I can see where his inspiration comes from in your lovely face."

He laughed as Elene blushed. She glanced down to where Teg stood. He looked up at her in such a way that she blushed even more and was glad when Mictor indicated that they should leave the stage and return to the community. As Jason and Elene climbed to the ground, Mictor walked to the front of the stage and stood quietly until the whole plaza was quiet. He began to speak, seemingly without effort, yet his voice carried clearly over the entire crowd.

"My friends, you have given me your loyalty for many years. Over the years, you have asked me to lead you. When I have said do this thing, you have done it; when I have said do that thing, you have done it. When I said go, you have gone; when I asked you to wait, you waited. I understand those who feel the wait has been far too long. I realise now how much feeling there was, and is, in the hearts of many of you for the dreams and ideals that once were so much a part of my philosophy. There was a time when the concept of freedom and universal justice was so strong nothing else mattered."

"When I was younger, young enough to feel the fire in my heart and the steel in my bones, I battled the evil demons. Not demons, perhaps, but men in the guise of monsters, who would take away not only the freedom of thought and action that is rightfully everybody's but also dignity and the right to life that belongs to everyone. I went, and many followed me."

"We learned that ideals and lofty thoughts are no match for the sophisticated weapons essential to any tyranny. In the wake of our abortive crusade, a great purge arose that caused untold suffering to many innocent and misguided people. Many died, many suffered, and I confess I lost heart."

"We had gone, with so many hopes, to liberate. The burden was too much for me to carry, and though I escaped with my life, my spirit was left prisoner. I have been blessed by your love and devotion towards me in many ways. It has been years since those black days, but I always knew the dream you carried in your hearts would not be realised through me.

Today my friends, someone has come among us who carries the same dreams and ideals that once burned in me. I see in him the hopes that faded for me all those years ago. My spirit has been set free, and I have felt it in my heart since his arrival; he is the one who can do what I could not do and free the people."

Mictor had become emotional as he spoke, as had many who listened. There was complete silence as he turned to Teg and said,

"I know you came seeking freedom for yourself, your grandfather and your girl. However, in your heart, there is the wish that all people should be released from the evil bondage that binds their hearts and souls. If this is so, Teg, will you take up the awesome task that I believe you have been ordained by fate to do?"

Teg felt he was suffocating and intensely emotional at Mictors words. It was as though his whole life had been directed towards this moment, and while he felt proud at Mictors words, he was only too aware of his lack of years and of the tremendous responsibility the old man wished to place upon his shoulders. He looked at Jason and Elene.

In Jason's eyes, he saw a look of expectation, and he shivered as his grandfather said, "Throughout these weeks, Teg, I have thought often of your words and the depths of thought and understanding behind them. I have seen that you are something special. Mictor is right; this is your destiny."

Teg stared at Jason for a moment and then turned and looked at Elene; she stared at him with eyes that shone. Her face reflected her love and pride, and she said simply,

"Wherever you go, Teg, I will go as long as you wish me to."

He smiled and said quietly, "That will be forever."

He turned around to face Mictor again, noting as he did the tense, expectant faces of the crowd. He tried to think of the right thing to say, and he knew he had done right as he heard the enthusiastic cheers of the crowd when he said,

"If this is to be my destiny, then so be it, but if I am to set out on this path, it will be with you as my guide Mictor."

They returned to the settlement in the vehicle that had brought Mictor to the Trying Place. The drama and emotion of the night's events drained them, and Jason and Elene dozed as the car sped through the night. Teg, however, remained wide awake, his mind full of the night's events. He wondered whether he could live up to the expectations that Mictor had for him and, equally important, Elene's faith in him.

Chapter 27

When they returned to the hospital, where Jason had asked to go, they were surrounded by a welcoming crowd who had seen the master's vehicle. They were surprised when they saw Jason, Teg, and Elene emerge from the car and enter the hospital but listened raptly as the driver explained what had happened.

Margarita had just finished binding the wounds of one of the wounded men when she saw the party entering the ward. She looked as though she could hardly believe it but then was up and hurrying to them. Whether she was more delighted to see Jason or Elene wasn't clear. Still, when Jason detached himself and began wandering between the beds asking the patients how they were, she hugged Elene happily and listened delightedly as she was told of the night's events. She looked up when Mictor entered the ward, and it was clear that she had respect for the old man as she hurried to greet him.

He had last been in the hospital a week before and was impressed with the changes. He listened, with a twinkle in his eyes, as Margarita extolled the virtues of Jason and laughed outright when she blushed as he said, "It would seem, my dear, that this physician is a healer of hearts and bodies."

Margarita was anxious to show Jason how, in his absence, she had arranged for the various herbs and other materials that Teg had collected to be stored. Sensing her desire to be gone, Mictor excused her.

Elene looked as if she wished to follow but seemed embarrassed at wanting to leave Teg's side. Her problem was solved when smiling at her, the old man said, "I am sure there are many ways you can be helpful here, my child. If you allow me to steal your love away, there is much I wish to talk to him about. Perhaps Teg will come back here for you when he is finished."

They watched as she ran down the ward after Margarita. As Teg watched her go, he felt he had known her all his life and couldn't imagine how life would be if he no longer had her.

However, as he turned and followed Mictor, all thoughts of Elene and everything else was driven from his mind as he prepared to face his destiny. Mictor's home was surprisingly humble, the only concession to his position being discreetly constructed watchtowers at a reasonable distance from each corner of the house.

Mictor explained to Teg that when he was at home, these watchtowers were manned constantly and, in the event of an attack, the alarm would be sounded by the blowing of horns.

"Have you had any attacks, Mictor?"

"Oh, yes, indeed. I'm afraid that The Forum is determined to see us wiped out, Teg, and they periodically send police squads here to try and eliminate us. Fortunately, we have a good system of lookout posts and usually get early warning of their approach.

Constant practice has enabled us to perfect evacuation, and one blessing about our settlement here is that there are innumerable hiding places. There are vast underground areas to many of the more prominent buildings and the underground railways, or what used to be an underground railway."

"An underground railway?"

"Yes, in the days when this was a thriving city, before The Bad Times, as you would put it, there was a system of tunnels beneath the city in which trains ran. There were stations at various places in the city where the underground trains could be reached and left. It was a bustling system."

"Do these tunnels still exist?"

"Some are no longer usable; they've become unstable and dangerous, but many are in perfect condition."

"Um, I'd like to see these tunnels if possible."

"Whenever you're ready, you just say so Teg; you only have to ask."

Teg felt uncomfortable at the way Mictor was clearly already treating him as a leader and felt compelled to say,

"Mictor, doesn't it bother you that I'm just a boy? You seem to have such great hopes, and I'm afraid I might let you down."

"You're not a boy, Teg, but an extraordinary young man. Mankind can think, reason, and question. This sets us apart from the animals, birds, and sea creatures. These gifts are, very sadly, all too often misused or not used at all. Most people are content to go through their lives caring for nothing but their creature comforts, their immediate families or whatever pleasure they find the most beguiling. They are pleased to have their thinking processes carried out for them by someone else and will subscribe to the views of the one who shouts the loudest, rewards, or promises them the most.

It is one of history's greatest mysteries that, throughout the ages, at all levels of culture and civilisation, people have allowed themselves to be led by men whose main aim leads to the destruction of the very lifestyle their followers aspire to. This is why there will always be leaders. There will always be men who seek power and wish to be leaders, but for many, their personal desires make them unsuitable for the role. Hence the gravity of having the right leaders guiding those who are too weak, lazy, or stupid to do their own thinking.

People have often allowed their so-called leaders to restrict them, curtail their freedoms, retard their progress, and, through ignorance or sloth of the mind, have even believed that what their leaders did to them was for their own good. Thus, dictatorships are perpetuated. There have been good leaders, of course, great leaders, but invariably they do not put themselves forward as leaders; they are called upon to lead. They lead not by imposing their own will or philosophies but by providing maps and examples. Such leadership qualities are rare, found in very few, and when they are found, they are to be cherished and encouraged, not put down because of some preconceived and erroneous notions.

You question your ability to lead just because of your age Teg. If I were to take you from here and put you against each man in this settlement, I doubt there is one who could match you in logic, reasoning powers, determination or caring, all the qualities of a true leader. How many great thoughts have been lost? How many perceptive questions have gone unasked, and therefore unanswered, because the originator of these thoughts was enjoined to stay out of grown-up affairs? How often have these thoughts been denied to the world by people whose thought processes were infinitely inferior to those they would suppress. No, Teg, your age is no barrier to leadership. I see in you qualities that, if given the means and the opportunity for fulfilment, you will be a true leader of men.

I am a man, Teg, who has seen much and who has, in his own way, been a leader, but I know enough to say that I will happily follow you, Teg, because I see in you the ultimate fulfilment of the dreams I once held for my people."

When Mictor finished speaking, Teg sat in silence for a while. He still felt embarrassed by the old man's fulsome praise, but he was also uplifted by his simple sincerity. He smiled at Mictor,

"I am honoured by your words and confidence in me; I will try not to fail you. Now, tell me more about these police raids, this underground railway, and anything else you think I should know.'

As they settled down for what they knew would be a long session, they were both aware that a subtle change had occurred in their relationship. Teg felt awed at the knowledge that the old man opposite him, a man he so admired and respected, was now his follower and that he Teg was now the leader. He listened as Mictor began to answer his questions.

"The police raids occur at irregular intervals. They try to take us by surprise, but fortunately, we have a system of lookouts that usually provide forewarning. We have worked hard perfecting the evacuation of civilians into the underground shelters, but sometimes the speed at which the police break through our outer defences is such that we lose some of our people."

"By lose, you mean they get killed?"

"The men, yes; the women and children, not necessarily. If they can, the police prefer to capture them alive."

"For what purpose?"

"You really don't know? You will perhaps better understand why some of the people here have such hatred for Waypeople. It's because they believe that you all know about, and subscribe to, the system of slavery to which our people are put when they are captured."

"Slavery? For what?"

"They serve the members of The Forum, their families, and their friends. They are worked brutally, and their lives are pure misery."

"But The Forum has Attendants and Acolytes for this purpose; why do they need slaves? How is it that we knew nothing of this? I'm sure my grandfather doesn't know either. It seems so incredible."

"The Attendants and Acolytes have a special place in The Forum, they are selected for whatever qualities they may have, and they may progress, given the right circumstances, to positions of luxury and power. They all, however, the Attendants, the Acolytes and The Supreme Council have their own servants, or slaves more like, who are treated no better than animals, and who are replaced, if necessary, by the simple expedient of raiding our settlement and taking a few more prisoners. As to why you know nothing of this, I believe you and I must take a journey, Teg. Many of your answers may be found at the end of it. If it is your wish, I will organise it as soon as possible."

"Whatever it means, it is an important journey. Yes, please organise it as soon as you can. Now, tell me, you mentioned civilians. I presume you mean women, children, and those too sick or weak to fight?"

"Not exactly. The choice of fighting the invaders or hiding is left to the individual."

"You mean that there can be able-bodied men hiding instead of fighting?"

"I realise it sounds bad, Teg, but you must remember that those who fight are required to do so with primitive weapons and limited skills against the sophisticated weapons and training of the police. It is not a pleasant prospect, and we have always believed that it is wrong for an individual to be forced to do something they don't want to."

"How are the ones who fight organised?"

"How do you mean organised?"

"Well, how do they train? Who is responsible for organising them into groups? Who directs their efforts?"

"I'm afraid there's nothing as organised as that, Teg. When the alarm is raised, those who would fight go to the danger and do what they can to protect us."

"Then that is the first thing we must change, and I think I know just the man I need."

Chapter 28

Marcus was brought in at Teg's request; he approached with a look of resignation tinged with fear. He seemed surprised when invited to sit down and even more surprised at the friendly tone in which the invitation was given. Teg smiled reassuringly.

"Well, Marcus, we meet under somewhat different circumstances."

"We certainly do. I can hardly blame you for thinking ill of me. However, what I did was done with the best intentions. We are not vigilant enough and are open to too many dangers because of our lack of preparedness. It may seem an inhuman approach, but I consider it a necessary evil that perhaps one or two innocent people may die rather than jeopardise the wellbeing of the settlement."

Marcus sat back when he had finished with the air of one who was resigned to his fate and pleased to have been able to say what he wanted. He was puzzled when Teg asked,

"There is a better way, surely?"

"I don't understand."

"Wouldn't the answer be to increase the vigilance of the settlement so that in the event of strangers, such as myself, coming along, you would feel sufficiently secure to hold them until their true nature had been determined?"

"There's very little chance of that, I'm afraid. How can we be secure if we have to fight with primitive arms and untrained men against the might of the police and all the technology available to them?"

"Well, first of all, nothing says your men can't be trained."

"Trained? Trained, you say, when half of them hide in the ground and shiver when we are attacked, and most of those who do fight, brave as they may be, hardly know one end of a spear from the other."

"That surely is a good enough reason for them to be trained, right?"

"I can hardly argue with that, but who will train them?"

"How about you?"

Teg almost had to laugh at the expression on Marcus' face. He wasn't quite sure whether Teg was serious or not and showed it when he answered,

"Oh yes, I can imagine you putting me in charge of the fighting after how I treated you!"

"Do you think you could train the men?"

Marcus realised that Teg was serious and sat forward, his face alive with excitement.

"Do you really mean that?"

"Of course, I do. You seem like a natural fighter to me, you have a strong personality, and, most importantly, you are aware of the problems the settlement faces, and the need to do something about it."

There was clearly much that Marcus wanted to say, but he seemed embarrassed to speak until

Teg, looking at him shrewdly, said, "Would I be wrong if I assumed it was something you had often thought about?"

Marcus looked startled and then laughed admiringly, "The Master was correct; there is something special about you. How on earth did you know that I have often wished I had the power to make the men train correctly.

Oh, I don't mean that I want power in the way you might think I do; it's just that it's so frustrating to see men dying and being defeated simply because they are disorganised and untrained."

"Well, Marcus, I agree with you all the way, and if you want it, the job is yours."

Marcus was overcome with excitement and had a host of ideas running through his mind, but then he became serious and said, "I am honoured and will do my best, but any efforts may be doomed to failure by the number of men who don't wish to fight. Even those who are prepared to fight may not take kindly to working under my instructions."

"That is my problem!"

Marcus looked at the young man before him with a calculating look. When he saw the strength and determination that seemed to radiate from him, he stood up, almost at attention, and said,

"Yes, Sir!"

"If you sign these here, I'll get the packs for you."

James was the only one left in the department; the last of his staff had left early because there was a party being held on the grounds to celebrate the President's eightieth birthday. James would have to attend for some of the time for appearance's sake, but in the weeks since he and Antony had talked, their revulsion and disquiet with their rulers had grown to the stage where the thought of attending any celebrations in their honour was distasteful.

He returned with the packs of ammunition requisitioned by the policeman and, having checked that the papers had been signed, pushed them over the counter. He turned away to place the documents in the appropriate tray for processing. When he turned back, he was surprised to see that the policeman hadn't taken the packs and was looking nervous, as though he had something on his mind.

"Can I help you with something else?" asked James.

"Oh, I was just wondering, well, could you tell me how my friends got on?"

"Your friend? Who's that?"

"Er, well, it's Policeman Tanner; he was assigned here some weeks ago."

"Policeman Tanner? I'm sorry, the name doesn't ring a bell."

"Well, even if the name doesn't ring a bell, perhaps you'll remember his face; he would surely have come in here, if anywhere."

The policeman took a photograph from his wallet and passed it across the counter. It showed a pleasant-looking man whose smile was more of a simper than anything. James looked carefully at the policeman and said, "No, I can't say I've seen him. I'd probably remember him if I had."

"That's strange. I was sure he'd be here, hoping I might see him."

"Why are you so anxious to see him?"

The policeman coloured slightly and looked embarrassed as he answered, "We were good friends; we spent a lot of time together. It's not always easy to find good friends in the police force" He looked suddenly alarmed, as though he might have said the wrong thing.

James knew that it was not unusual for relationships between policemen in the all-male environment. Although such relationships were supposedly frowned upon, a blind eye was turned if they were discreet. Feeling surprisingly sympathetic towards the man, even though he was a policeman, James smiled and said reassuringly,

"Don't worry, I know what you mean. I'm sorry I can't help you. Tell me, what made you so sure he was here?"

"Oh, after they came and took him away, I asked my officer how long he'd be away for. He told me he wouldn't be coming back because he'd been assigned special duty at The Forum. I was worried about him; he'd been distraught when we shot the old man and the boy. He didn't like killing and felt that it was just too cold-blooded this time."

James was suddenly very alert, the icy fingers of premonition tickling his spine.

"This killing you talk about, why should it have mattered so much to him?"

The policeman looked worried now, his eyes darting about as if suspecting a trap. Seeing this and understanding how the man felt, James patted his arm reassuringly and moving from behind the counter, he went to the door and locked it before saying,

"Don't worry, you won't be overheard, and I promise you, whatever you say will be safe with me."

The policeman looked at him for a long while, his face uncertain. He must have seen something in James' face that reassured him because he seemed suddenly to collapse inwards, almost as though he was going to cry. Feeling sorry for him, James led him to his office and, when they were seated, said gently, "Now, tell me all about it.

The man seemed glad of the opportunity to unburden himself and began talking in a low, unhappy voice so that James had to strain to hear at times.

"It's hard to understand how he ever became a policeman. He's such a nice guy; he's not suited to it. He was too weak to say no when they recruited him. It couldn't have been easy for him; there are some right bastards in the force. The only thing that made it bearable in the end was our friendship.

I know that having him around made it bearable for me. I know some think we're weirdos, but we're not really. We're just two people who care about each other."

There was something defiant in his voice, almost accusing, then he smiled apologetically and continued.

"We'd heard about this man Jason who'd run away just before his Dying Day; we knew that they were hard on anyone who broke the rules of The Forum, particularly those who tried to avoid the Dying Day. It's always amazed me that there aren't many more who run. Anyway, in this case, all hell broke loose. From what I could gather from The Supreme Council, the President, in particular, worried that this intellectual guy Jason, might be a menace to them because he had the potential to influence people to question due to his intellect.

Strangely, the President seemed even more worried about the boy than Jason. Anyway, the orders went out that they were to be found and killed. Just like that, no return to town, no trial, just killed. I felt a bit uneasy about it, but Tanner, well, all I can say is he took it badly; I think the truth is he really sympathised with what they had done although he too didn't say as much, not even to me. Anyway, as I say, the boy showed up, and I can tell you, it was pretty sickening, just shooting them down like that."

"So, how did he come to be selected for this apparent duty here at The Forum?"

"Some special police turned up one day, the police that answers to The Supreme Council. They spoke to several men and took one other beside my friend. I sometimes wonder if I might have been selected if they'd spoken to me first."

"Why is that?"

"Well, the first man they took, and then my friend, were both selected when the special police found out they'd been with the patrol that had killed Jason and the boy. I assumed the selection for special service was some kind of reward for the squad's success".

"I see, and was anything else said about this selection?"

"Not really, oh only that I guess it was being looked after by the Third President."

James was suddenly very alert, his pulse racing.

"How do you know that?"

"Well, I hadn't had a chance to say goodbye to my friend, so I went to where the special police had parked their vehicle. It's a shame my friend is not here. I wanted to say hello to him. I was too late to say goodbye, they were already inside, but I did hear one of the policemen say that he was sure these two would satisfy David. I could only assume they meant the Third President.

James kept his expression inscrutable as he considered what he'd just heard. He felt sure he now knew where the Third President had gone with the photograph of the old man. He had an awful feeling that the man before him was unlikely to see his friend again. He also instinctively felt that he had a potential ally in the policemen, so he set out to win him over.

"Listen to me," he said carefully," it may well be that your friend is at The Forum."

He held up a hand to forestall the policeman's question and went on.

"I can't explain at the moment, but I promise you I'll do what I can to see what I can find out. Leave me your name and details, and I'll contact you if I hear anything. I suggest in the meantime that you say nothing to anyone about your friend coming here, just wait until you hear from me."

The policeman looked reassured as he left the supplies department. James looked very thoughtful.

The party was in full swing when James arrived. As unpleasant as he now found any dealings with The Supreme Council, he knew he must do what was required of him. He went to where Aaron sat, flanked by Delmo and David. Bowing to the President, James offered his congratulations. The President smiled, secure in the knowledge that here was one of The Forum's most loyal and faithful servants. The looks James received were somewhat different from the second and Third Presidents. From Delmo there was a speculative look. The Second President had been told by Antony what James had discovered in the town. However, Antony had made it clear that James had absolutely no idea as to the true meaning of the information he had obtained.

As the weeks passed, it became clear that the Third President could not produce any hard evidence of the fraud, Delmo had relaxed. He had, however, persuaded Antony to keep an eye on James in case he should be sent on any other errands by David that might spell danger for the Second President. Delmo was aware that David had probably worked out the deception that had been enacted with the old man and the boy, and he knew that if the occasion arose, David would try and use that information.

Having done what was necessary, James hastened away to find Antony, anxious to tell him about the policeman's visit. He found his friend sitting disconsolately beneath a tree, a new drink at his side. Sitting beside him, James looked around to be sure they could not be overheard and said quietly, "Why so glum, my friend?"

"Hello, James. Oh, I was sitting here thinking about how things are and how we'd like to change them. It entirely depresses me when I see what we're up against."

"I know what you mean Antony, but there's no reason to get depressed. We will wait to change things, and we should expect it to. What we must do is wait and watch. We must gather what we can and hope to be able to use it when the time is right. I have something to tell you that may or may not be useful, but let's see what you make of it."

Antony listened, without interruption, as James told him the story of the policeman's visit. When his friend had finished, Antony sat quietly as he digested what he had been told. Finally, he asked, "What do you think happened to these two policemen. I've certainly not seen any new faces around?"

"I believe that they were delivered into the hands of the Interrogator."

Antony shuddered at the mention of the dreaded name, and they both looked automatically to where Garon stood in the company of three fawning Attendants who looked very much as if they would rather be somewhere else.

As he looked at the big brutal man, James became thoughtful and said, almost to himself, "It would be instructive if we could investigate the domain of our friend, the Interrogator."

"Please don't describe him as our friend," protested Antony.

"Ah, but that is exactly what he will be, at least for now."

"What on earth do you mean?"

"I doubt that Garon has many, if any, friends. Perhaps he will be gratified enough to show a couple of real admirers the place where he carries on his trade."

Antony looked horrified. James chuckled at the expression on his friend's face,

"I don't know what horrifies you most, Antony; the thought of being friends with Garon or setting foot in his chambers. Come, we must go and greet our dear friend."

"But James, he'll be suspicious; he'll guess somethings up."

"Oh, Antony, anyone can see that Garon is already half-drunk, as he always is at these functions. By nightfall, he will be too drunk to stand, and by morning he will remember nothing."

Chapter 29

Being in the Interrogators company was uncomfortable, but when he wished to talk with you, it was wise to pretend to be honoured. It was astonishing to the three Attendants who surrounded Garon that James and Antony should voluntarily seek out the big man's company. They were delighted when the two monopolised Garon's attention, so they could slip away, with sighs of relief, to enjoy the party as far away from their erstwhile companion as they could get. It had been easy enough for James to commandeer Garon's attention because he had hit on the one subject that was of significant interest to him.

James tried not to notice Antony wincing as he heard the flattery that dripped from his lips.

"I trust that, in celebrating his continuing good fortune, our President is aware of how much he owes you, Garon."

Garon, half drunk, considered what James had said. He smiled slowly and nodded his head,

"I hope my efforts do not go unnoticed."

"Rightly so, rightly so. For myself, and I know my friend Antony here shares my sentiments, it is reassuring to know that we have someone as staunchly loyal and devoted to our defence as you are."

Garon obviously liked the sound of this and, having taken another long drink from his glass said simply, "Go on."

"I have often told my friend here how much I would like to introduce myself to you and tell you how much I admired you, but I always felt too humble. I always feared that you were too fine a man to concern yourself with those such as me."

Antony took a drink from his glass. It seemed it must have gone down wrong because he coughed and spluttered. Giving him a concerned look, James ascertained that he would recover and then continued with his paean of praise.

"I have often wondered how it must be knowing that you are such a vital cog in the machinery of our society. When one thinks of the tremendous responsibility that rests upon your shoulders, one imagines that you must, at times, consider yourself the resting place of the trust and confidence of all our caring citizenry."

Garon's bleary eyes focused and refocused on his newfound admirer. He was clearly having trouble with the flowery language but not with its intent. His brutal face creased into a grin, and he laid a big arm companionably across James's shoulder. James tried not to cringe as Garon said, "There aren't many who understand the way that you do. It can be a lonely job, but it is essential. We must forever be on our guard against spies and troublemakers. Some imagine I have an easy life, but I can tell you it can get very lonely in the kind of life I lead in my chambers."

Garon became maudlin as the drink took further control of him. James looked delighted when Antony, deciding he should contribute, seized on the opening that the Interrogator had given him.

"We have often wondered what it must be like for you, living alone like you do. We have often talked about how interesting it would be to visit your chambers and see where so much important work is done. Sadly, we are merely ordinary Attendants, and you are too important, and rightly so, to consider the likes of us worthy of a visit to your chambers?"

Garon was gratified to have friends who had volunteered their time in his presence. He had difficulty seeing them and had already forgotten their names. Still, he was aware enough to know that here was an opportunity to make a gesture befitting such an important man as himself. He tried to focus on his newfound friends, but finding this too difficult, he merely waved an arm in the air and said grandly, if in a somewhat slurred voice.

"You are fine fellows; you deserve a treat. If you would like to see my little workshop, then you shall. Come, I will take you there."

Had Garon wanted to be literally as good as his word, the visit would likely never have occurred. He was incapable of taking anybody anywhere. Fortunately, James and Antony knew only too well where the Interrogator's chambers were, and they took him. As they left the party, almost unnoticed in the increasing noise and drunkenness, Antony took the opportunity to snatch up a full flask of wine which he carried carefully in one hand whilst using the other to help support the weaving and awesomely heavy Garon.

The corridors of The Forum building echoed hollowly to Garon's loud, drunken voice as they weaved their way towards his chambers. They prayed that no one would see them if they should wonder at the strange spectacle of two of the soberest and most respected Attendants in the company of one such as Garon. However, they saw no one and were able to relax when they finally entered the Interrogator's rooms.

Antony immediately found a glass he filled from the wine flask and handed it to Garon. The wine ran down his chin and to his tunic as he tilted the glass to his lips. Having taken a satisfying swallow, he gestured to his companions.

"I'll show you my little workshop. That's where the work really gets done."

He staggered and nearly fell once but managed to reach the level below, where they stared, trying to conceal their horror at all the torture apparatus that adorned the room's walls. The centre of the room contained a couch with many restraints, and it didn't take much imagination to guess what horrors had occurred here.

Antony had prudently brought the flask of wine with him and re-charged Garon's glass as he slumped into a chair, grinning drunkenly. He waved his free hand, nearly knocking his drink out of the other hand, and said, in a voice that was now barely coherent, "There we are that's my workshop. I do everything here. It's important; I'm important."

Antony hastened to reassure him that he was indeed essential and, at a signal from James, positioned himself between Garon and the door so that James could slip out unobserved.

Recalling some of the flattery James had used, Antony began to apply it to the wavering figure before him, occasionally topping his glass and praying he would pass out. James went down the stairs as quickly as he could, his heart beating wildly. It was cool down here, and he shivered as he surveyed the line of doors down each side of the wide corridor. He mentally tossed a coin and ran to the right-hand side.

The first door opened easily onto an empty cell. The second was the same, so it was all along the right-hand side. Perspiring freely, James ran back to the stairs despite the cold and listened carefully. All he could hear was Antony frantically extolling the virtues of Garon and his work. He smiled grimly and ran to the first of the doors on the left-hand side. Again, the cell was empty, as was the second. Nervously he opened the third door and automatically began to close it again when he realised the cell was occupied.

He was surprised that the cell should be unlocked when occupied, but as he moved to the bed and saw what had been done to the man's feet, he knew that locking the door was unnecessary. He knelt by the side, the terrible anger welling inside him as he saw what had been done to the man. He suddenly realised that the man's eyes were open and that he was staring at him with terror. He placed his hand on the man's shoulder and said gently, "It's alright. I'm not going to hurt you." There was a brief flicker of something like hope in the man's eyes, but it soon faded to be replaced by puzzlement when James asked, "Are you the policeman: Tanner?"

The man's face screwed up in concentration as if he was trying to recall something from a time long ago. Suddenly his eyes filled with tears, and he nodded his head.

"We will try to help you," said James. "It may take time, so don't despair. Whatever happens, you must tell no one I was here, do you understand?"

There was hope again in the man's eyes, and he nodded. James patted him on the shoulder and went to the door. As he shut the door, he looked in again, and his heart lurched as he saw the eyes staring at him, full of hope and trust.

He was shaking as he ran back to the stairs. He wasn't sure whether his trembling was more the result of fear or of rage. He felt hopeless as he thought of the risks he was taking, but then he looked determined and sprinted up the stairs. Antony stood before Garon, rattling almost hysterically about the valuable part the Interrogator played in protecting them. He jumped as he felt James's hand on his shoulder, and he looked round at Garon foolishly when James said, "It's alright, Antony, he's out cold."

It was with great relief that they crept out of the chambers and hurried back to the party. They spoke again once they were back, standing beneath the tree where they had met earlier. Using the noise of the party as cover James explained what he had found.

"It's ghastly!" exclaimed Antony, "but I'm afraid there's nothing we can do about it."

"That's where you're wrong," James said vehemently and, seeing his friend's surprised look, went on.

"Don't you see that's why our system is so rotten? Dreadful things like this happen, and we turn away. Well, this time, we're not going to turn away."

"What on earth do you intend to do?"

"We're going to get that poor bastard out of there. I don't know what kind of life he can lead now, but I'm sure I'm not leaving him to rot in that foul bastard's cells!"

Antony looked surprised and frightened.

"You mean you're going to try and rescue him from there. You must be mad, James; what chance have the two of us got?"

James smiled, gratified by his friend's use of 'the two of us'. He clasped Antony's arm and said grimly, "We won't be alone, my friend, and as far as I'm concerned, it's do-or-die; what do you say?"

Antony sighed exaggeratedly and then smiled, almost shyly, "It used to be such a quiet life here. I hope you won't mind me saying, James, but you're the first person here I've been able to think of as a friend. I can't live with myself if I don't help you now. What do we do?"

Not being sure of just how willingly most people would accept him as a leader, particularly in view of his youth, Teg had wisely decided that his initial approaches to them should be with the assistance of Mictor. The old man nodded approvingly as Teg outlined his strategy and was even more approving when Teg announced his intention of taking one of the settlement's people as his right-hand man.

"Have you anyone in mind at the moment?"

"Yes, I certainly have; I've asked Marcus to send him here. He should be arriving any minute."

The old man regarded Teg with renewed admiration when Roger presented himself a few minutes later. He clearly believed that he couldn't have chosen better. If there was any doubt in Teg's mind as to whether he had made the right choice, it was soon dispelled when Roger, having listened to his proposal, said simply, "Teg, don't let your age bother you. Already the people are talking of you as the leader. They don't care about how old you are; they care only about what you can do for them. They see your appointment of Marcus as commander of the defence forces as a brilliant and positive step. They really feel that you can make things happen. As for myself, well, I heard you at the Trying Place, and I don't mind telling you it made me shiver. I saw right from the start that you were special. I certainly hadn't expected you to honour me when you called me here, but I can only say that I am yours to command."

Touched by the other man's trust and loyalty, Teg had asked him to set plans for a complete and detailed tour of the settlement in motion. He had also requested that a general assembly of the people be organised for that evening and that the able-bodied men should be encouraged to attend. It was agreed that, as the less mobile members of the settlement may wish to attend, the Trying Ground and the railway yards where Jason, Teg and Elene had first been brought, should be the venue.

Wishing to see how Jason and Elene were fairing, Teg went to the hospital, leaving Mictor to rest before the evening demanded his energy.

The hospital had been transformed by the volunteers who, inspired by Jason's example, worked hard to improve the conditions. The air was redolent with the scents of herbs that had been crushed or boiled or just simply applied to the wounds of injured men.

There was a stir as Teg entered the ward, and he saw how the men and women there looked at him with a new look. He felt slightly uncomfortable at the respect they showed him as he walked between the beds, but he felt better when he saw Elene, entering the ward at the far end, break into a run on seeing him. She ran to him excitedly, and he was aware of the grins and sly nudges of the others in the ward as she threw herself into his arms.

"Teg, oh Teg, isn't it exciting. Aren't you just over the moon? It's so wonderful here, and people are so friendly now. Margarita is such a lovely person, she treats me as though I were her own daughter, and it's so good working in the hospital because they are so happy when you do things for them."

Teg was laughing as Elene finally came to a halt, partly from lack of breath, partly from embarrassment at how she had prattled on. He was delighted to see her so happy, and as he looked at her, he felt a surge of emotion, and his face became solemn.

"What is it, Teg?"

He leaned down and whispered conspiratorially, "I was just thinking how much I'd like to kiss you," he said, grinning. Elene stepped back, blushing but looking absurdly happy. Then she stepped forward and quickly kissed him before running away down the ward, followed by the approving cheers of practically everyone in the hospital.

Seeking out Jason, Teg went to Margarita's room and found him there writing out instructions for the preparation of an ointment to be made from some of the herbs that had been gathered. He looked up as Teg entered, and his face broke into an affectionate grin.

"Teg, my boy, how are you?"

"I'm fine, grandad, but what about yourself? You look exhausted?"

"Exhausted is the word Teg, but let me tell you, I've never been happier in my life. It's as though I've found a whole new reason for living. Now, tell me about yourself. I hear you're already setting the world alight."

"Hardly that, grandad, but things do seem to be moving. There's obviously so much to do."

"Well, Teg, if anybody can get things done, I'm sure you will."

"I hope you're right, grandad. It all seems too much to believe at times."

"Yes, I know what you mean, Teg. When I think about everything that's happened, I sometimes think I'm dreaming. I tell you what, though, if it is a dream, I don't want to wake up."

"I know how you feel, grandad."

Teg paused, obviously feeling embarrassed about having to talk to Jason as a leader, but then he shrugged and said, "Can you prepare a report about the facilities here? This place would be totally inadequate if a major crisis arose. The other thing that worries me is how vulnerable this place is. From what I hear about these police attacks, this site doesn't seem too secure."

Jason looked at his grandson with open admiration.

"You don't miss much, do you, Teg? Margarita has been telling me a few things, and one thing is for sure, you're right on both counts. Apparently, about three years ago, the children had an outbreak of measles. The hospital was already overcrowded and not really coping when a police raid left many wounded. Obviously, the hospital couldn't cope, and quite a few died.

Then about eleven months ago, there was a police raid, and some of them got as far as the hospital. There was no way of stopping them from gaining access, and, in the end, the staff, including Margarita, had to flee, leaving the non-ambulant patients to the mercy of the police."

"What happened?"

"When they came back, they found one barely alive patient. The rest had been murdered. The one man still alive said that when the police realised that all those in the ward were either men or unsuitable to be slaves, they shot them where they lay."

Teg shook his head at the tale of infamy and could understand even more the hatred some people felt for the Waypeople. There was one point that intrigued him, "You mentioned that the patients were either men or unsuitable to be slaves. What exactly did you mean by that?"

"Some of the patients were children; one was a woman. They were all victims of a house collapse and had broken limbs. They were murdered as well."

There seemed nothing adequate to say, and Teg rose. Having been promised a report within a couple of days. He left the hospital and returned to Mictors house to prepare for his night's visit to the railway yards.

Chapter 30

The Railway yards were reminiscent of the night before at the Trying Ground. The difference was that this time as Teg arrived, there was scattered applause and even a few cheers. The torches that had been lit created odd shadows as they moved in the breeze and gave an air of unreality.

Teg was astonished at the size of the turnout, and as he looked at the crowds strung out across the debris-strewn yards, he wondered if they would all be able to hear him. He turned to Roger and murmured, "It would have been better if they were all nearer to me; it would be easier to make myself heard."

He watched, surprised, as Roger went to a group of men and spoke to them, gesturing towards him. He felt slightly embarrassed as they turned, bowed slightly towards him, and then trotted off into the crowd. Soon their efforts showed as small groups of people began to move from their earlier vantage points to join the crowd already assembled in front of the platform from which he would speak.

When the large crowd had settled before him, he signalled Roger, who went to the arches and emerged with Mictor and Marcus shortly. They came through the crowd and were assisted onto the platform. Teg smiled a greeting and went and stood by Marcus while Mictor went to the front of the platform to make the speech they had agreed on earlier. The crowd fell silent as the old man stayed there, and it was clear from their expressions that the people still revered him.

"My friends", he began, his voice carrying well, "I spoke to many of you last night and told you of the one who had come among us. I told you how he had freed my spirit from the prison where I had placed it for so long. I knew this young man would be a leader among men, and

I was sure he would rise to the daunting task imposed upon him. I have been fortunate to see him go about this task, and, in just one night and one day, I have seen him apply himself to the things that matter with a deftness of touch and a confident air that clearly indicates how right I was about his leadership qualities.

I have already seen an air of optimism about many of you, a feeling that great things are about to happen. It is true to say that as well as freeing my spirit, he has lifted the spirits of the whole community. He will apply himself to the arduous days ahead with dedication and devotion, but he is the first to admit that he will need your help and support. I know you all well enough to say that I am sure he will receive your support. Over the years, you have shown great loyalty and affection to me, for which I will be eternally grateful. The finest thing that you could do for me, if you wish to put the seal on that loyalty and affection, is to join with me in giving that same tribute to your new leader, people I give you, Teg!"

As he said this, Mictor stepped back and held out his hand. Teg bowed in his direction and stepped to the front of the platform. He stood looking out over the large crowd. There was a smattering of applause in front of him, then from the side and the back. The applause spread and became continuous. Someone cheered, then someone else. They all began cheering. The cheering swelled and rang in the night air. Teg stood there in disbelief as the crowd cheered and cheered. He felt a lump in his throat as, discordant at first, but then picking up rhythm, came the cry "Teg, Teg, Teg…"

He stood there until the cheering subsided. When it had done so, the silence was almost palpable. He felt agitated as he opened his mouth to speak. Just as he did so, there was a short sharp babble of noise from a baby that someone held. Quick as a flash, someone at the back of the crowd called out, "Bloody Hell! I knew our new leader was young, but I didn't know he was that young!"

The crowd roared with laughter, Teg helplessly joining in. As the laughter died down, the tension was gone, and suddenly, he was ready.

"My friends," he began, then paused and, looking out over the assembly, began again.

"My people!"

An outburst of cheering threatened to equal the earlier one until Teg held up his hand. Silence fell immediately. He felt a surge of power in himself and went on with confidence. "When I started my journey, I knew nothing of what I might find. I knew only that it was a journey I had to undertake. You see, my friends, I had to know the truth."

The air seemed to vibrate with his words, and he felt his strength growing as the crowd listened with rapt attention to his every word.

He went on, "And what is the truth I found? The truth is that for generation after generation, evil and corrupt people have, for their own purposes, persuaded, cajoled, bullied, and coerced the people of the towns to subscribe to and follow a path that they have designated The Way. They have been able to do this because, in successive generations, they have, by evil means, been able to beat out of the people the capacity to question or resist the repressive rules imposed upon them. They have imposed their will upon the people by the evilest means imaginable and have taken away their spirit. They have turned people into unquestioning, obedient, unthinking drones who allow themselves to be used and abused and who then, without even thinking to resist, allow themselves to believe that by walking passively to their deaths at the end of a specified time they are serving the good of the community. No matter that they may be healthy, no matter if they are of sound of mind, no matter if they have much to offer their families and community, no matter if they are loved. The people do not matter. All that matters is The Way.

How did all this happen? You have all heard of The Bad Times. It is hard to imagine what The Bad Times must have been like. However, it does not take much imagination to know that they must have been catastrophic. Indeed, we know they were catastrophic because we see the evidence of that catastrophe all around us. If there is one truth in what The Way preaches, The Bad Times must never be allowed to happen again.

The rulers of the towns, the people who call themselves The Forum, have used the facts of The Bad Times to create a fiction that has enabled them to maintain their evil hold on those you call the Waypeople. The Waypeople, my friends, know this place and all the other places that were once great thriving cities as The Wastelands. They are told of how these great cities became uninhabitable, of how the waters became: cesspools, the air became noxious, and the dwellings became prisons and death cells for the people who could no longer drink the water, breathe the air or eat the food which had become so contaminated it was no longer edible. They were fearful of leaving their homes, and lawlessness was rife. There was no authority, no control. It is a grim and dreadful picture that should chill the heart of every right-thinking man, woman and child.

It is this dreadful picture that The Forum has used as one of the means of subjugating the Waypeople. You see, my friends, the Waypeople are told, and they believe, that these so-called Wastelands are still just that. They think the air is unbreathable, the water undrinkable, and that vegetation cannot grow because the land is poisoned."

There were some laughs in the crowd at the absurdity of the notion, but they were quickly stilled when Teg raised his hand, "It is easy to laugh, my friends, to think how ridiculous such ideas are, but the only reason these notions are absurd to us is because we know the truth. How can the Waypeople be expected to know the truth when all they are taught is lies?

I want you to consider this, my friends. I know that many of you have a deep hatred for the Waypeople and for what their police have done to you."

There were murmurs in the crowd that threatened to swell until Teg called out sharply, "But wait! How can the Waypeople know what their police do to you when they don't even know you exist?"

There were puzzled looks in the crowd, but gradually more and more heads nodded as the truth was absorbed.

"The truth is", Teg went on ", that the Waypeople are also victims of their police as you are, though they do not realise it. At the bidding of The Forum, and in particular The Supreme Council, the police commit atrocities and suppress freedom when they are the very force that all right-thinking citizens would expect to protect them.

There is no worse betrayal than a betrayal of trust. There are those among you who would do something about this. There are many more who would ask what we can do. There are no easy answers, but there are answers. First, we must let the Waypeople know the truth and make them as desirous as we are to return freedom and justice to the world. Secondly, we must help the Waypeople know we are not their enemies and that we seek to achieve a world where we may all live in harmony."

There were some angry murmurs among the crowd at this. Teg allowed them to continue for a moment before raising his hand. When silence had fallen again, he turned and, pointing towards Mictor, said, "Some of you find this notion of how Waypeople are your friends hard to take. For many years, you have revered this man Mictor, the man you call the master, and rightly so. You have revered him because when he was a young man, he showed great courage, wisdom, and compassion and tried to change the order of things. He will tell you that he failed. Let me tell you now, my friends, he did not fail.

He planted a seed that has lain dormant for many years, but a seed that will germinate and sprout will grow and flourish and when, as is inevitable, the forces of good and right triumph, it will be said that he started it all. For this, you have revered him; why then do you murmur angrily when I tell you that in bringing the Waypeople to our side, as our friends and allies, we are only completing the work that the master set in motion all those years ago?

I have discussed two things that must be achieved to achieve our goal. There is a third. Let there be no doubt in your minds; there is only one way in which, ultimately, we will triumph; we must destroy evil!"

There was a burst of cheering and clapping and a few shouts of "Down with The Forum.'

Teg waited patiently until the noise had subsided and went on.

"Of one thing, I am sure; there is no way at all that we will be able to win the fight that faces us unless we change how the fight has been fought until now."

Teg paused for a moment. He looked briefly towards Mictor and shrugged resignedly, knowing that what he was about to say might turn many people against him. He turned to face the crowd again and, squaring his shoulders, went on. "I came here and found a society that, in its own way, has maintained the traditions of man's history. There is no restriction on the number of years a man or woman may live. The sick and the lame are cared for, not cast into some institution to have their lives terminated. Men and women may say what they think and believe what they want to believe. There are no restrictions on the number of children in one family. Until I came among you, I did not know what brothers and sisters were. This is the evil that has been visited upon the Waypeople. The sanctity of life, the value of the family, and the nobility of the mind have been destroyed, and why? To enable the power-hungry, self-serving despots who control the lives of the Waypeople, cling to and strengthen the hold they have.

You have the right of choice and to live your natural term, and you are permitted to know the joys of family in the truest sense of the word. These are truly precious things. The only threat to them is those evil rulers and the demons they send against you to kill, maim, and enslave! And how do you meet this threat to your very existence? How do you protect the rights and freedoms that are so precious? How do you ensure the continuity of your society for yours and your children's children? There are those of you who fight and care enough for and believe enough in the priceless freedoms that are man's rightful heritage. How much more difficult your task is made by the fact that there are so many who run and hide; cower in the ground, leave the protection of their lives to others!"

Teg's voice had risen as he spoke the last sentence, and he deliberately brought it to a ringing climax so that the ensuing silence seemed even more pronounced. There was an uncomfortable stir among the crowd, and many men looked down at their feet. Others stared defiantly at Teg, and there were murmurs of, "We're not soldiers", "How are we supposed to fight."

Teg began to speak again in a more conciliatory tone.

"There is no shame in being afraid; it is a natural condition that sets man above animals in recognising and overcoming his fear. It is not an easy thing to be a fighter, and it is not an easy thing to kill, but when these things are essential for the very survival of your way of life, then it is something that you must do.

I have today asked Marcus, whom many of you will already know, to take over the task of setting up the defence force that will be the cornerstone of our fight against evil. I do not ask that you walk naked and unarmed against your enemies. There is in all of you the ability to be trained as fighters. With a concerted effort, improving the availability and quality of the needed weapons, will be possible. The only way that these things can be brought about is by the setting up of an organised system of defence whereby every able-bodied man, and woman if they choose, can be trained in the basic skills of fighting and the use of weapons, so that they may take their place alongside their fellow citizens in defence of their lands.

We must do many other things, but they're only worth something if our first objective is achieved. I call on you now to come forward and to make it known that you will take your place in the ranks of those who will fight for freedom."

Immediately some men came forward; they were men who would always fight. Some came forward hesitantly but eventually stood alongside the others. Some waited, looking afraid, wary, or indifferent.

There was silence apart from the sounds of moving feet. Gradually the eyes of all those in the vastness of the yard turned on those who were able, who were strong, but who still did not come forward. The silence continued. One man walked along, his head down. As he walked towards the front, Teg spoke, "What you do now is not the thing to be ashamed of. You have already left that behind."

The man's head came up, and he smiled gratefully at Teg and walked head high to stand with the others. And then they came, in ones, two's threes until there were none left who had reason to be ashamed. They stood below the platform in a great crowd. Marcus came to the front of the platform and stood beside Teg. He seemed stunned at the response to Teg's call, and as he turned to Teg, his eyes looked hopeful.

"Perhaps now it really can be done."

"Now it has begun", said Teg. "Here is your army, Marcus; use them well."

He held out his hand, and Marcus shook it vigorously, beginning to grin.

He turned to the crowd of men assembled in front of the platform, "Men", he shouted," tomorrow we will begin.

We will assemble here at first light. I see the beginnings of a significant era, the start of a great crusade. We will learn together, we will train together, we will fight together, and we will win. We will destroy the enemy!" The cheers this time were for Marcus, and as he watched and listened to him, Teg smiled to himself. He had chosen well.

Chapter 31

Policeman Valdor arrived as instructed. He perused the forms on the desk in puzzlement and looked up at James. "I don't understand. These aren't the forms I filled in last time I was here."

"I know," James interrupted." I had to talk to you; the forms were just a ploy."

The policeman looked nervous as James leaned forward, but his expression shifted from concern to anger as James said, "When you were here before, you asked me about policeman Tanner. I have located him, but I'm afraid I have some bad news for you. Your friend was taken to the Interrogator for questioning. Garon is not known for being gentle, and I'm afraid your friend has suffered greatly at his hands."

"But why, what has he done? He's a good man."

"He has been caught up in a power play between the second and Third Presidents. The result is that he has been brutally tortured. I must tell you that physically, he will never be a well man again; I'm sorry."

Valdor stared at James, disbelieving. However, something in the other man's expression conveyed the truth of what he said, and suddenly, a tear slid down his cheek. He made no effort to wipe it away nor the others that followed. His voice trembled when he spoke.

"Please forgive my emotion. I can't imagine why someone so good and gentle would suffer so. Is there any chance I can see him?"

"Do not apologise for your emotions, my friend. It is the mark of a man who still has his humanity, which is more than I can say for our so-called rulers. As to whether you can see your friend…he paused and looked carefully at the policeman, then, making up his mind, he went on, "I fear there is only one way that will be possible; we must get your friend out of there."

Policeman Valdor looked at him as though he was mad. "Get him out of there, you mean out of the Interrogators?" Words failed him, and he sat back, looking stunned. James leaned forward, "One thing is sure, if your friend is left there, he will die. He will die either from neglect or because finally Garon will tire of him and kill him."

The policeman shuddered and then asked, "But how I mean, it's impossible, surely?"

James grinned, surprised at himself and his feeling of devil-may-care confidence.

"We won't know until we try, will we?

"We, you mean us?"

"Oh yes, we will help you, my friend. We will help you because we are sickened by the things done in our name. We have no wish to be a part of a society that can allow the things that have been done to your friend, and many more like him, no doubt, yet to be done."

"But you'll be in great danger."

"At least we will be true to ourselves. Now, are you prepared to join us in rescuing your friend? You are aware of the dangers; you must know that if we fail, it could well mean our deaths."

"If we don't try, it will certainly mean the death of my friend. I'm not sure I would want to live anyway then; can you understand that?"

"Yes, I think I can. Right then, we must see what we can do. Either I or Attendant Antony will contact you soon. In the meantime, have courage and remember, not a word to anyone."

"Of course. I don't know how to thank you; it all seems incredible.

If something should go wrong, if my friend should die before we can get him out, I would very much like to serve you in some way if you really mean to challenge The Forum. I would feel I was doing something for him."

"Well said, and I know that Antony would join me in welcoming you to our side. Let's see what we can do. We'll be in touch."

James didn't see Antony that day, nor the next, but when he did, his friend was aghast at trying to spirit the prisoner away from Garon's cell. This didn't, however, prevent him from agreeing to help in any way he could, and it was decided that if either of them thought of any means of achieving their objective, he would immediately contact the other.

As it transpired, Antony had the idea and committed himself to helping James with the rescue plot, so he whole-heartedly began planning with James.

"Gregory, the Attendant at The Supreme Council offices, is having a party for some friends tomorrow night. It's to celebrate his forthcoming marriage."

I've never really got to know Gregory very well. I'm unsure if I could get us an invitation if that's what you want."

"That's the last thing we want!" He laughed when he saw his friend's puzzled expression. Suddenly, he was enjoying the intrigue.

"No, my friend, what we must try and do, is arrange an invitation for our dear friend Garon."

James looked at him briefly before smiling as the idea took root, but then his expression became serious again, "I see. You mean we get him away from his chambers, and while he's gone, we get our policeman friend out. It's a good idea, but how do we make it work?"

"I've thought about that as well", said Antony, looking pleased with himself." It's risky, but it's the only thing I can think of. I'm working on the preposition that Garon, not being very bright, will fall for the simplest of tricks. What you must do, James, is arranged to have policeman Valdor here tomorrow to help get his friend out if my little ploy works."

Antony prayed that no one would come along and see him. Fortunately, it all seemed quiet. It was the afternoon of the following day, and he nervously approached the door to Garon's chambers. As he neared the door, he hoped fervently that Garon would be below, in his 'workshop'.

Looking around and seeing nobody, Antony carefully opened the door. He investigated the room with a fixed smile on his face in case the Interrogator should be there. There was nobody there. He listened carefully and soon heard sounds below that indicated Garon was tinkering with some of his apparatus.

Looking around, Antony saw a small stool, which he pulled across and popped against the door, holding it open. His heart was racing, and he felt breathless as he crept to the top of the stairs. Mentally, he rehearsed the voice he would use and then called out.

"Oh, Garon!" in a voice much higher than average. The moment the sounds below stopped, and he knew that Garon had heard him, he called out again in the same high voice.

"Don't forget Gregory's party tonight, we're all hoping you'll be there, must run, see you later!"

Quickly, he hacked across the room. He held the door, pushed the stool away with his foot, and was out of the door and closing it in no more than two seconds. He walked quickly away down the corridor, wanting to break into a run. To his relief, there was no one around. When he reached the intersection, he risked a quick glance back. There was no one in sight. He rounded the corner, and although he moved quickly, he began to relax. He felt like laughing when he knew he was safe, but his legs shook.

They were beginning to wonder if Antony's scheme had failed. The light was already fading, the night drawing in, and there had been no sign of Garon leaving his chambers.

The three of them were concealed in the darkness at the far end of the corridor that led to Garon's door. Whilst they were in darkness, the passage at the far end was brightly lit.

Antony was despondent. As he had explained to James and policeman Valdor how he had attempted to trick Garon, it had sounded ridiculous to his own ears, and he could tell from the other two's guarded expressions that they didn't think it had much chance of success.

"Something tells me that…" began James.

"Just a minute," interrupted Antony.

They held their breath and crouched down in the shadows as Garon's door opened, and he emerged looking happy and obviously dressed for a party. To judge by his walk, he had already begun drinking, and he carried a flask of wine in his hand.

Suddenly, the three watchers were tense and nervous and looked at each other speculatively. It was policeman Valdor who moved first. He began to walk forward, then stopped, and turning to the other two, he whispered, "If you want to, you can leave this to me now, you've taken a great risk, and I'm truly grateful. It might be better for you if you left now."

"You'd never manage on your own", said Antony, "and in any case, now that we've started this, I won't feel happy unless we see it through to the end."

"I'm with you there," said James. "let's go," and they moved off down the corridor.

To their relief, the door to Garon's chamber wasn't locked. They had previously discussed how they would approach the rescue and decided that they would continue without hesitation once they had started. So it was that they crossed the stairs the moment they were through the door, James leading the way. Swiftly, they went down the stairs to the bottom level and straight across to the third cell on the left. As they opened the door, James was relieved that policeman Tanner was still alive. His eyes showed fear as the three men crowded into his cell, then incredulity as he recognised his friend.

Policeman Valdor stood still, stunned, and shocked, as he saw his friend's condition. Tears were in his eyes, and his shoulders began to shake as he started to sob. Knowing that time was of the essence, James slapped him on the shoulder and, almost brutally, said, "No time for that now; if you really care about him, let's get him out of here."

The sharp words had the desired effect and stooping, the policeman lifted his friend off the bed. Antony quickly arranged the covers as best he could to try and give the impression that someone was still in the bed. It would stand up to no more than a cursory glance, but that was hoping that Garon might just take a quick look in now and then rather than making detailed inspections.

By the time Antony had finished, the others were already ascending the stairs, and he hurried to join them, closing the cell door behind him. They made an incongruous sight as they hurried along the corridor to the dark end, where a door led to the grounds at the back of the building. By the time they stepped cautiously through the door into the cool night air, they were all sweating from the tension. Policeman Valdor had parked his vehicle beneath a group of trees, and anyone looking casually in that direction would probably not have noticed it in the shadows. They hurried across the open ground, glancing nervously around but seeing no one.

When policeman Tanner had been laid inside the vehicle, Valdor turned to James and Antony, his face emotional, and said, "I don't know how I'm ever going to be able to repay you, my friends, but I pray that somehow there will be a way. Please call on me if you ever need me."

"How will we find you? Surely, you'll be fleeing from here now?"

"Oh no, not at all. I will find somewhere safe to keep my friend and care for him, and then I will return to my duties."

"Is that wise?"

"Nobody knows of my part in this, other than us, and by carrying on as normal, it's improbable that I will be suspected. In any case, my friends, if I am to help you in your fight against the bastards who rule us, I will be better placed if I remain with the police."

He drove away, keeping the vehicle's lights off until he cleared The Forum grounds.

As Antony and James returned quickly to their quarters, they felt frightened but exhilarated by what they had done. They thought they had struck their first blow in what they knew would be a very long and dangerous campaign.

The invaders swarmed over the hill; their weapons held high. The defenders reached them, and, as they clashed, the air was filled with shouts, cries, oaths and flying bodies. The battle raged furiously for ten minutes or so, and then gradually, the invaders gained ground, pushing the defenders further and further back until they could break through and around the last line of defence. They charged on down the hill to where women and children of the settlement were working in the fields harvesting the new season's crop of potatoes.

The workers stopped what they were doing and watched as the invaders came to the field's perimeter and waited. The scattered defenders were regrouping and coming slowly down the hill. When they reached the waiting group at the edge of the area, they sat down, exhausted.

They turned expectantly as Marcus came striding down the hill and stood looking at them.

"Better," he called, "much better. You are beginning to look like fighters now. What do you think, Teg?"

From among the weary defenders, Teg arose and came to stand alongside Marcus. He was breathing heavily, and his cheeks were flushed from his exertions, but he was grinning. He spoke so that the scattered men could hear him.

"As you say, Marcus, much better. I would feel much happier about dealing with the enemy should he arrive now. Let's hope he doesn't trouble us for a bit longer. The way things are going, another couple of weeks and these men will be good enough to fight anybody".

The men cheered and laughed as Teg waved to them and walked away. He stood at the top of the hill and watched as Marcus dismissed the men and walked up to join him.

"There's no doubt about it, my friend," Teg said admiringly. "You have worked miracles. They really are looking like fighting men now. They're fit, skilled, and most importantly, you've inspired them so that they're keen to do well. Things are looking much better."

"I'm glad you're happy, Teg, although I'm sure they get inspiration from how you have worked alongside them. You've asked for no special treatment and worked just as hard as any of them. I'm thinking of making you, my second-in-command".

They both grinned at the joke, but as they began to walk away, Teg became serious.

"We've been fortunate, Marcus, that we haven't had a raid in the three months or so I've been here. It's enabled us to prepare to defend ourselves and has meant that we have yet to commit any men to battle until they're ready. I've got a feeling our luck will not hold much longer, and I'd like you to spend a few hours with me, reviewing a few ideas I've got and letting me know what you think".

It was hard for either of the men to remember how badly their first meeting had gone. Since recognising Marcus' natural aggression and leadership skills and putting him in charge of the defence forces, Teg had developed a great respect for the other man, which he knew was reciprocated.

Their mutual respect grew into a firm friendship that made it easy for them to work together.

They walked quickly, fit now, and enjoying the ease with which they could use their bodies. When they came to Mictor's house, they found him sitting outside, enjoying the sun. As always, he was surrounded by an admiring group of young and old alike, who enjoyed his tales of the old days and listened carefully to any words of wisdom he felt disposed to utter. Seeing Teg approaching, they rose and respectfully withdrew, leaving him and Marcus alone with the old man.

"Well then, how go the warriors?" the old man called cheerfully.

"Good, good", said Teg as he sat down at Mictor's side. "I'm looking for Roger. I want him to come with Marcus and me to look at a few things I have in mind".

"Oh, he's been gone a while now. It seems one of the horses has taken a walk. He's not very happy, I'm afraid."

"I don't suppose he would be. They're invaluable to us, those animals. How did it get away?"

"That I don't know, but if there's any negligence involved, I pity the culprit from how Roger went off."

They laughed good-naturedly at the thought of the ordinarily placid Roger in a temper. However, Teg was aware that it was one of his virtues that he took his responsibilities seriously.

"In a way", Teg said, "the horses feature in what I want to discuss with Marcus and Roger. I've often thought that we are hampered by a lack of mobility. The value of the one vehicle we have is inestimable, but the one on its own is insufficient. We must look at ways to secure another or even more."

I'll run down to the market in the morning and get one," said Marcus airily, at which they all laughed, but even as he laughed, Marcus was looking at Teg shrewdly and asked, "What have you got in mind?"

"Well, you'll agree that we must have more vehicles and modern weapons. The one vehicle we've got and the very few reasonably modern weapons we've got were obtained only because you happened to come off best in a skirmish during one of the police raids. We've got to go on the offensive. Instead of waiting for the police to raid us and, hopefully, make an error we can capitalise on, we must set out to lure them into a fight where we have stacked the odds in our favour. I've got a few ideas of how we can go about it, and I've no doubt, my good friend Marcus, that you'll be able to come up with a few."

Marcus was staring at Teg almost in disbelief, then he began to grin and shout happily.

"At last, at last, how good that is to hear. Oh, Teg, if only you knew how often I've dreamed about something like this. It's the only way we're going anywhere, that's for sure!"

"Good", said Teg, grinning, "and as I see our good, if not very happy, friend Roger approaching, I suggest we get going straight away."

They walked to meet Roger, who had yet to have a successful day.

"Now then, Roger, why do you look so glum? Has one of your horses turned into a bird and flown away? Roger smiled ruefully and replied, "It's a mystery, I'm afraid. There appears to have been no carelessness on anyone's part nor any sign of the horse having broken its tether, but it's gone right enough."

"Never mind, my friend, if Teg here has his way, we won't need your horses anyway."

"Oh, how's that?"

"We'll always need the horses, Roger, if only so that we'll remember what horses look like," said Teg, "but what Marcus means is that I think it's time we considered ways of obtaining more of the kind of vehicles we need if we're to ever hope to mount any sort of an offensive against The Forum."

A few weeks previously, Mictor had shown Teg around part of the underground railway system. Much of it was in a poor state of repair and dangerous, but a surprisingly large proportion was in sound condition. One stretch of tunnel ran straight for almost a mile before ending abruptly, where the roof and the ground above it had collapsed, creating a solid wall across the tunnel. Teg now led Marcus and Roger to an area about half a mile outside the barricade at the railway yards and east of the plaza or Trying Place. The site had been mainly commercial, judging by the ruined buildings that dotted the landscape, and many isolated concrete walls were still standing. Leading his companions to a spot close to where three concrete walls stood, not connected to each other but forming a rough U shape, he gestured down at the ground.

"I have spent some time in the past few weeks studying some of the old underground railway system." He gestured to a mountainous heap of rubble that had once been a brick building of several stores.

"When that building came down, it caused a massive collapse in the tunnel system, effectively cutting off a long straight run of the tunnel that, beneath this spot, is still usable. The tunnel must carry on somewhere on the other side of that heap of rubble. I can only guess at what condition it's in, but from what I can make out, there are no other large buildings down, on a line running for at least a mile, so if the tunnel was originally straight, then we should be able to locate where it continues. I propose that we open an entrance to the tunnel somewhere around here, and if we can locate the tunnel on the other side of the collapse, we open an entrance there. We find out how far it continues, and if it's safe to use, we open another entrance further along the way somewhere."

"That's going to mean an awful lot of work, Teg. What's the reasoning behind it?" asked Roger.

"First of all, the tunnel we open here will give us quick access to and from the heart of the settlement. With some luck, the tunnel we can open on the other side of the ruins will provide us with access to a spot a fair distance away. First, we should lure a police patrol into this area. It's far away from the settlement that if anything goes wrong, there'll be time enough for the people to go into hiding as they normally would. Hopefully, though, everything should go smoothly. Using the tunnels, we can outflank the enemy, get behind them, take them by surprise, and quickly get back to base. The tunnels will also serve another purpose. I believe it should be possible to lure the police into the underground passages where, by using the element of surprise, we should be able to disarm or kill them if needed."

"If what you propose is to be any good, there'll be no doubt that we'll have to kill them," said Marcus, "if we don't, if we let them go, or if any of them were to escape, our strategy would be ruined for any future use."

"I'm a bit concerned that a tunnel that can get us into the settlement quickly could also serve the same purpose for the enemy", said Roger. "Otherwise, it sounds like a brilliant idea."

"Naturally, there would have to be safeguards, but we're now forced to do something ambitious soon, or we're just wasting our time. What do you think, Marcus?"

"What are we waiting for?"

It was agreed that the tunnel project be kept as secret as possible. There was concern that if the existence of the tunnels and the new entrances were made known, some of the more reckless children might find them too much of a challenge. So it was that the men who were to start work on the tunnel entrances left the settlement ostensibly to go to the training camp and then approached the work site by a devious route. Teg was there to meet them and explain what the scheme was about. Pleased at the chance of taking matters into their own hands, the men set to work with a will. Groups created natural-looking rubble mounds around the proposed entrance sites on either side of the collapsed tunnel section. By the end of the day, unless one knew, there appeared to be nothing but piles of debris and tumbled houses as far as the eye could see. The men camped the night in the fortress-like areas within the rubble walls so they could start excavating at first light. Roger oversaw the work gangs, but so enthusiastic were they that he merely had to direct the digging following the instructions left by Teg.

Chapter 32

In the meantime, Teg had taken Marcus with him to the settlement entrance to the tunnel, which they entered carrying torches, measuring implements, and writing materials. They spent all day exploring and making notes. By the time they emerged into the evening light, they had drawn up plans for hiding places to be constructed in the tunnels, for elaborate booby traps to be rigged and for emergency escape tunnels to be camouflaged so that entrances to them would only be known to those who had been told.

They were tired and dusty when they returned to the settlement, but as they washed before sitting down to eat together, Marcus turned to Teg and said, "Teg, I've lived here all my life. As a child, I ran and hid. I've listened to the screams of my friends and neighbours being cut down and captured. As I've grown, I've learned to hate the people who inflicted misery on our people. When I was old enough, I began to join in the fight against the attackers, but it was always just a holding operation. It had become a way of life. We would be attacked. We would try to fight off the attackers until as many of our people as possible had concealed themselves. Then we, too, would run and hide.

We hoped that not too many would be killed or captured; we hoped that the police would not find their way into the heart of our settlement, forcing us to move elsewhere. All my life, I've lived through this pattern. You, Teg, have been here just over three months. In that time, you have given our people hope, you have created an army, you have revolutionised our hospital and nursing facilities, at least that marvelous grandfather of yours has. Now, we are making plans to take the fight to the enemy. I shudder to think, Teg, what it might have been like if I had prevailed at the Trying Place that night.

You know I would gladly have had you killed. How incredible that all seems now. I'm saying, Teg, that I am beginning to believe that we can eventually achieve absolute freedom and justice thanks to you. Whatever happens here, we owe you a great deal, Teg. You've given us back our pride and dignity."

Teg was touched by his friend's moving speech and reached out and clasped his arm for a moment but didn't say anything. They moved into the house for their meal. The house was one that Teg, Jason and Elene shared, although it was scarce for them to be there simultaneously. Jason was so involved with the hospital that he found minimal opportunity to be away from it, or so he said.

Teg suspected that even when things were quiet, Jason was reluctant to leave because he enjoyed being with Margarita. That the feeling was mutual was obvious. A very warm and affectionate friendship had grown between the couple. Teg was delighted for his grandfather but sad for himself because the demands of his leadership meant that he saw very little of Elene. When he saw her, he realised that his fondness for her had deepened, and he felt sure that she also cared greatly for him.

"A penny for them, Teg," said Marcus.

"What? Oh, sorry, Marcus, I was miles away."

"No need to apologise. You're not really in the mood for company. Look, if you don't mind, I'll leave now, have an early night. I'll get out first thing tomorrow and see how the diggings go. Goodnight, Teg."

"Goodnight, Marcus."

Teg felt a bit guilty about his withdrawn manner of sending Marcus away, but now that he was alone, he was glad of the chance to sit quietly and just think.

He arose from the table and cleared away the dinner things. Having done this, he went to the couch and, taking off his boots, lay back and closed his eyes. Half awake, half asleep, thoughts and impressions ran through his mind.

He relived the whole adventure in his mind, as he often did. He still found it hard to believe things had turned out how they had. He was thrilled and honoured to have been accepted as leader by the people of the settlement. He had a burning ambition to lead them from the restrictions of their previous life to an entire and free life alongside a liberated Waypeople. Sleepy, he thought of Elene again and wondered what their future held. He really did miss seeing her and knew he must do something about it. He smiled at the realisation that he was thinking about her so hard, he could almost imagine her and hear her calling him.

"Teg, Teg."

Startled, he sat up. Elene was bent over him, her face anxious, "are you all right, Teg?"

"Elene! Am I alright? Of course, I am. I was dozing. Why shouldn't I be okay?"

"Oh, it's just that Marcus came to the hospital and said it might be a good idea if I called in and saw you. I thought maybe you were sick or something."

Teg looked at her blankly for a moment, then slowly smiled. He held his hand to her, and his heart leapt as she sat beside him.

"You know something", he said softly. "I think maybe Marcus isn't such a hard man as he makes out to be."

"Mister, are you a member of The Forum?"

"I am. Why do you ask?"

"I've got some information you'd like. It's about Teg."

"Teg?"

"Yes, he's the boy who ran away with his grandfather. They're in the settlement now, and he's planning to cause you a lot of trouble."

"The settlement?"

"It's what you call The Wastelands. Teg's getting an army together to fight you."

"I see. You'd better come with me; someone else will be interested in your story. What's your name, boy?"

"Daniel, sir."

"So, you're Daniel. My colleague tells us you have some important information regarding this young man, Teg."

"Yes sir, he's been taken on as the leader of the settlement, and he aims to fight you."

"Why should we believe you, Daniel?"

"I can tell you what I know about him. You can check that, can't you? How else could I know about him if I hadn't seen him?"

"Why should you want to do this if he's trying to help your own people."

"I just don't like him. Why should he be a leader? He's no older than I am. It's ridiculous. I'd expect you to reward me well for information like this. Then I won't need them."

"Where exactly is this settlement, you talk of?"

"It's almost due North of here, about six days ride."

"Ride?"

"Yes, I came by horse."

"By horse? Where on earth did you get a horse from?"

"They've got a couple at the settlement; I stole one."

"This settlement you talk about, how would we recognise it?"

"There are three tall buildings that you can see from miles away. Although you wouldn't know it from a distance, they're in bad condition. Anyway, the two outer buildings are shorter than the middle one, and the middle one has lookouts on the top floor that can be seen for miles around. You'll have to travel the last few miles at night or on foot to take the settlement by surprise."

They questioned him for another hour before escorting him to a small room where he was given food and drink. They both looked very thoughtful when they returned to where they had questioned him.

"Arrogant little bastard, isn't he," said James.

"Yes, that sneer of his seems to be a perpetual feature. What do you think of what he says, though?"

"Well, if what he says is true, it's a coincidence that he approached you, Antony. You did well to get him here without being seen."

"What we do with him now is what worries me."

"Yes, we certainly can't keep him around here. If he was discovered, he'd blow the whole thing sky-high. The only really safe answer is to kill him."

"I was afraid you'd say that, it's not an option I'd really want to consider if I could help it. Killing a child, however obnoxious he might, would bring us down to the level of the very people we want to remove."

"I know what you mean, my friend, but we must remember this is a kind of war we're fighting, and that boy has now become our enemy. Even so, I must agree that I'd rather not just kill him in cold blood".

"Why don't we just send him back to the settlement?"

"Send him back, how do you mean?"

"Well, if he's back there, he won't tell anyone what he's done, right? He'll be out of our hair and away from any chance of accidental exposure here."

"How would you get him to go back?"

"We simply tell him that his continued absence from the settlement could arouse suspicions that could jeopardise any attempts by The Forum to capture this, Teg. We also clarify that any reward he may receive will depend on his doing as we say."

"I think you're right. It is the only way. That's what we'll tell him then."

"I tell you one thing, though; I wish we could make contact with this Teg. Imagine how effective our efforts would be if they were coordinated."

"Well, at least we know he's there now. All we need is to find some way of contacting him and convincing him that we're on his side!"

"You want me to go back?"

"Yes, Daniel, it's the only way. Everything must run smoothly with our chances of capturing this, Teg. If you don't go back, there's every chance they'll suspect what's happened. In any case, now all you've done is give us information. Imagine how much greater your reward will be when that information leads to the actual defeat of this rebel."

"Yes, I see what you mean. I don't want to return, but I have no choice. There's one thing though that I do want as part of my reward."

"Oh, and what's that?"

"There's a girl, her name's Elene. She's to be left for me when Teg is taken."

"Ah, a pretty girl, is she?"

"She's beautiful, and I want her. I want to take her from Teg."

"I can see better now why you hold such a grudge against this Teg. He stole this Elene from you, didn't he?"

"No, he brought her with him. She ran away from The Sanctum, something or other. She'd been sent there to be killed for upsetting some President, somebody called Delmo. I made up my mind when I first saw her that I wanted her, and nothing gives me greater pleasure than to take her away from that bastard."

"We'll keep what you say in mind. Now, we must get you out of here. You mustn't be seen by anyone else. We always need to find out whether this Teg might have spies here. You won't want to jeopardise your chances of getting this, Elene, will you? How did you get into the grounds anyway?"

"I climbed the fence out by the big lake."

"You climbed the fence? You took a gamble, young man. It's patrolled by the police, and they have instructions to shoot on sight."

"I came over in the dark. The fence by the lake is the only stretch I could find that could be more brightly lit. Anyway, I wasn't seen."

"It will be safer if we create a diversion when you go out. You may not be as lucky again."

"How far would you say we'd walked?" asked Teg.

"Difficult to say when you're underground, having no points of reference, but I'd say at least a mile," said Marcus.

"It seems longer than that to me, but as you say, it's difficult to judge. This tunnel is undoubtedly in good condition, though, apart from a few minor bad spots, and there's no sign of it ending just yet, although it's difficult to see too far with these torches."

"You realise that when we decide to open up this end of the tunnel, we will have to do it from inside."

"Why's that Marcus?"

"There's no way that I can see that we're ever going to be able to pinpoint the tunnel from above. It's not absolutely straight for a start."

"I don't like the idea of opening it up from underneath. For a start, it will be dangerous work; secondly, there's no way of knowing where we'll come up. We're either likely to come up right in the open, or we'll come up right under a building and bring it crashing down on top of us."

"And there's no way of knowing just how deep underground this end of the tunnel is. We were fortunate at the far end that it was only about ten feet down, much deeper, and we'd have had problems building ramps down into the tunnels."

"There might be a way."

They both spun around, almost forgetting the other man was behind them.

"How's that, Roger?" asked Teg.

"It may be too farfetched, but it might be worth a try. Where the tunnel roof has caved in, in places, it has caused settlement and dislodgement of the ground and any structures above.

"The whole damn place is like that anyway" protested Marcus.

"Yes, I know that, but if my theory is correct, then the ground above the cave-ins must be looser than the rest and has probably got rubble mixed in with it. What I was thinking is, if we found some way of sealing off the tunnel, say just the other side of the cave-in, and a bit further on from there, and then fill the sealed-off section with smoke, we might find that the smoke would find its way up through the looser, rubble-filled ground into the air above. If it does we can then plot the tunnel's position from above quite well."

"You must be joking!" protested Marcus, "you don't really think that would work, do you?"

"Wait a minute, Marcus", cautioned Teg, "there might be something in Roger's idea. Unless you've got any other ideas, I think it's worth a try."

They returned to the newly completed entrance. A hard-packed earth and rock ramp sloped up to ground level and emerged into an open space surrounded by rubble walls. In one place, the walls had been skillfully erected with a slalom entrance so that unless someone knew it, they would only find it by accident. To a casual observer, the walls of rubble looked continuous.

Marcus gave instructions to the work crews who were resting in the redoubt, and, with some good-natured grumbling, they set about finding quantities of thick hardwood that would, hopefully, burn slowly but with much smoke.

Meanwhile, Roger walked around the massive pile of debris that rested above the collapsed portion of the tunnel and made his way through another cunningly concealed entrance into a second cleared space with an earthen ramp leading down into the tunnel's darkness. Gathering whatever men were there, he sent them to collect wood to be taken to the other stretch of the tunnel.

Seeing that the work was well in hand and knowing it would not be complete before dark, Teg began to make his way above ground to the settlement. He had given instructions for a large quantity of torches to be prepared, and these would be kept at each end of the tunnels so that they would always be available when needed. In the meantime, however, he was content to take the long way back, having spent most of the morning underground.

Leaving the concealed entrance behind, he began picking his way over an old house's ruins. As he clambered over what had once been the roof, he suddenly paused and, straightening, stared out over the tumbled landscape.

He smiled and began to climb over the ruins back in the direction he had come. Seeing Roger emerging from the rubble walls entrance, Teg cupped his hands and shouted.

"Roger, you'd better send a couple of men out here. Make sure they can run; they might need to. I've just seen your missing horse."

Chapter 33

On his return to the settlement, Teg called into the hospital. He saw very little of Jason these days and liked to talk to him when he could. He was delighted at how his grandfather had settled down and particularly happy at the companionship he had found with Margarita.

Elene, too, was firm friends with the kindly woman and had all but adopted her as her mother, an arrangement Margarita found eminently acceptable.

Teg and Elene, when the chance arose, spent hours together just walking and talking. They were clearly in love, and each knew how the other one felt, but they had tacitly agreed to wait awhile before making any real commitment. They knew that much could, and probably would, happen soon and were afraid that any obligation might burden the other one when it came to the action that would ensue. As Teg entered the hospital and saw Elene tenderly ministering to a sick child, he felt the familiar tug in his heart and a yearning for his loved one. She looked up, saw him, and looked like she wanted to leave the patient and run to him. However, she continued with what she was doing, and when she looked up again, her face showed the disappointment that he was no longer in view. She patted the child on the head and stood up, then jumped, startled, as a pair of arms encircled her from behind, and Teg's voice said,

"Guess who?"

"Mictor?" she asked and then giggled helplessly until Teg turned her around and kissed her lightly. All at once, her face became serious, and she said softly, "Good to see you again, Teg."

"Good to see you too."

"I thought you could get away for a couple of hours. I'd like to spend some time with you."

"I'd love to, Teg. I'm sure Jason won't mind. It'll leave him alone time to make eyes at Margarita."

They both laughed and then quickly had to control their laughter as Jason and Margarita walked down the ward towards them, smiling happily and obviously delighted to see Teg.

"Hello Teg," said Jason heartily. "I wondered when we might see something of you, although I know you've been mighty busy. I was hoping I might get a chance to chat with you."

"Sure, Grandad. Hello Margarita, is he behaving himself?"

"Unfortunately, yes," she said, then blushed as she realised what she had suggested. Jason gave her an odd but affectionate look, and Teg and Elene, exchanging glances, had to fight hard not to break into a fit of giggles again. Fortunately, one of the patients called out to Margarita, and as she went to him, Elene followed, giving both herself and Teg a chance to recover.

"What was it you wanted, Grandad, anything important?"

"Well, it's important to me, Teg, but I wanted to discuss it with you before I did anything about it. Look, can we go outside somewhere and have a chat?"

They wandered away from the hospital and strolled between two rows of the oddly formed dwellings that comprised most of the settlement. Teg never tired of admiring the ingenuity of how the houses had been constructed from various recovered materials, but sensing the seriousness of Jason's mood, he gave his whole attention to him.

Just past the rows of houses, the ground sloped quite sharply away, giving a view over a wide area of deserted and derelict buildings. The three buildings the settlement dwellers called 'The Lookout' were sharply etched by the afternoon sun as it descended towards the horizon. The bright ribbon of a river glinted beyond the lookout, and beyond that, the dark, dense greenery of a forest of trees showed where the boundaries of the old city had ended.

Teg and Jason sat on a low stone wall that had stood the test of time. Sensing that his grandfather was gathering his thoughts, Teg waited in patient silence for him to begin.

"Teg, when we first came here, you found out, accidentally as it turned out; your mother and grandmother had been killed by the authorities back in the town. We've never really talked about it since

Teg, and if you'd rather not talk about it now, I'll understand, but I would like to know how you feel about it."

"I have thought about it a lot, grandad, and I must be honest and say that I've often felt guilty that I can't feel sadder than I do. It's not that I didn't love my mother or grandmother. It's just that, well, the way life was there somehow reduced the value of life. I don't know if you understand what I mean. Still, when life is reduced to a set number of years, when it can be taken away at the whim of people like The Forum simply because you are ill or crippled or have committed some so-called crime, then the actual value of a life doesn't mean so much. Life was no longer precious to people; it was given up without a struggle. Someone else said it was time to die. I find it incredible to believe, grandad, that even today, there is, back in that town, a system where people are happily, and I really mean happily, walking to their deaths. What is so obscene is that they're doing it because they've been virtually brainwashed into doing it by a bunch of men who, from what I saw on the view wall that night, are clinging to life for as long as they can."

Teg had become animated as he spoke, his frustration and anger boiling. Now he smiled ruefully at Jason and, calming down, went on quietly,

"You may have wondered, Grandad, why I seemed not to show much grief when I learned that mother and grandmother were dead. As I've said before, you may not understand, it's difficult to say. I don't want to say anything that would offend you; Mum and Gran were your wife and daughter, but I know you'd like me to say what I believe."

Teg paused and stared into the distance, seeking the right words. He shrugged and went on.

"The system that I talked about not only brainwashed the people to sacrifice themselves at the bidding of The Forum, but it also brainwashed them into expecting, even demanding, it of each other. I believe that had mother and grandmother been allowed to live, and had we been caught and taken back and made to take the final walk, they would have been outside The Sanctum, joining others in abusing. They would have jeered and been ashamed of us. They had made a virtue of dying. It's obscene, Grandad.

Where is the love? Where is the living together, the affection, the sense of family? How can it be that all these beautiful and wonderful things that make life worth living were discarded immediately because you have defied the evil law, an unnatural law? Because you wish to live, you are wrong, a lawbreaker, someone to be ashamed of."

Teg was on his feet now, his emotions high; he paced backwards and forwards, trying to find the words to encapsulate his feelings. Suddenly, he stopped and, facing Jason, said in a bewildered and sad voice accompanied by tears that had built in his eyes and now spilled down his face.

"Grandad, how on earth do you think Elene must have felt? Dear sweet Elene, a child with so much love to give, promise, and beauty. Sentenced to die for refusing to let some foul, evil old hypocrite rape her? If that wasn't lousy misfortune enough, how must she have felt when she heard and saw her parents reviling her? Those same parents probably still hate her because she shamed them by refusing to die and wanting the right to live that should be everybody's. You know, Grandad, when Elene first told me her story, I was horrified. I was horrified at what she had been through, but I was also stunned because I knew that had we been taken back and had mother and grandmother been alive, they would have done to us what Elene's parents did to her. That's why I haven't cried for them. Oh, I'm so sorry, Grandad!"

For the moment, he was a boy again, and he fell to his knees at Jason's feet and threw himself into his arms. They remained there for a while, the old man rocking the boy backwards and forwards and stroking his hair until his sobs subsided. Finally, Teg recovered and rose to his feet before sitting again beside Jason. He saw that the old man had also been crying and shrugged disarmingly, trying to lighten the atmosphere.

"What would my people think of their great leader now?" he asked in self-mockery.

"Dear Teg, if they had any perception, they would see that your compassion and sensibilities make you the leader you already are and the great leader you will inevitably become!"

They sat quietly before Teg looked at Jason, suspecting he still had something to say.

"I hope my words didn't upset you too much, grandad".

"No, Teg, no. It always amazes me how someone as young as yourself can articulate the very thoughts and feelings I have so much trouble expressing, and I've always thought of myself as an intelligent man. No, Teg, you did not upset me because you spoke the truth. I will not deny that I feel a certain sadness when I think of my dear Sarah, but it is more the sadness of nostalgia. What you say is true, Teg, and if we are to mourn, we should mourn what might have been. You know, of course, that I loved and respected your grandmother very much, Teg, even if, because of the reasons you have so succinctly expressed, I seem not to grieve for her?"

"Yes, grandfather, I know that."

"It's just that I wouldn't want to do anything that might, shall we say, make you think I was being disloyal to her memory."

"It is the present that counts grandad. We've just been through why we must not dwell on the past."

"Yes, Teg, I know, I know. I just wanted to be sure, that's all."

"Sure, about what?"

"Well, that you wouldn't be upset."

"Upset? Upset about what?"

"Well, if I did something that seemed, as I say, disloyal to your grandmother."

"What are you on about, grandad?" asked Teg exasperatedly, although beginning to suspect the truth. His suspicions were confirmed when Jason looked bashful and looked away from Teg as if suddenly seeing something of absorbing interest on the horizon. Still looking away, he almost mumbled.

"I want to ask Margarita to marry me!"

There was silence. When no sound came from Teg, Jason slowly turned, fearing his grandson's disapproval. He stared at Teg, who sat smirking and began to grin. Jason heaved a big sigh of relief as Teg said happily, "Grandad, that's marvelous news. Do you think she'll say yes?"

"That, my boy, is the question. I'm unsure I can pluck up the nerve to ask her."

"What if I made it a command from the leader?" Teg said cheekily, then ducked away as Jason pretended to cuff him around the ear. Then Jason became very serious and, looking intently at Teg, asked, "Do you think that would work?"

They paced up and down, their eyes flicking from side to side, scanning the landscape. The broken buildings and heaped rubble made their task difficult, and occasionally, one of them would clamber to the top of one of the more immense heaps and stare around intently. They had been at it since the fires had been lit in the early morning, and so far, all they had seen had been broken buildings and rubble.

"It's not going to work, is it?" said Roger miserably, "and after all the time and effort the men have put in. I don't know if I'll be able to face them again."

"Well, one thing, Roger, it'll have cleared any rats out of that tunnel section."

"Talking of rats", Roger said jokingly, "here comes one now, no doubt, to have a good laugh at my expense."

Marcus approached, a grin on his face. Secretly, he had hoped that Roger's idea would work, but now that it seemed to have failed, he knew that it would be expected that he would get some mileage out of it. He wasn't intending to let him down.

"Hello there, Teg, hello Roger, looking for something?"

"Yes, Marcus," said Roger in mock seriousness, "we were having a look for a brain for you. As your last one was a ruin, we thought this would be the obvious place to look for another."

Marcus grinned, and then, adopting an eager childlike pose, he lisped, "When I get a brain, Uncle Roger, will I be able to look for smoke growing in the ruins as well?"

Teg burst into laughter, and Roger smiled ruefully. He began to look a bit discomfited when Teg continued to laugh, his laughter becoming almost hysterical as he pointed at Marcus. Finally, Roger thought that Teg had gone too far.

"I'm prepared to be amused, Teg, but I don't think it was that funny. After all, I did my best."

"Oh no, Roger, it's not that, it's Marcus. He hot footed it over here to laugh at you so fast he must have caught his boots on fire."

The other two looked down to where Teg pointed, and the smoke was seeping up through the ground around Marcus' feet.

Chapter 34

She was sobbing hysterically, huddled in the corner as James strode down the corridor. She did not see him until he was almost upon her, and then, when she did, she whimpered in fear and seemed to be trying to back herself right through the wall. She was no more than twelve years old and near collapse from anxiety and distress. Kneeling, James reached out his hand. She recoiled, her eyes wide, her teeth chattering.

"What is it, child? What on earth is wrong?"

There was a faint glimmer of surprise in her eyes at his gentle tone, but then her fear returned two-fold as the sounds of angry voices and heavy footsteps were heard from around the corner. Instinctively, James grabbed the girl's hand. She resisted fiercely, pulling away.

"Don't be a bloody fool!" he hissed. "They'll catch you if you stay here. Now come with me."

As he tugged again at her hand, the sounds around the corner became louder, and suddenly, she moved, coming towards James and running frantically after him as he raced off down the corridor. By the time he reached his chambers, the sounds had faded, and quickly unlocking the door, he ushered the girl inside and relocked the door. When he turned, the girl had backed away from him and stood against the wall, wide-eyed with fear. He conspiratorially put a finger to his lips and placed his ear against the door. He could hear muffled sounds in the corridor and then, abruptly, the clatter of feet rushing past. He had jerked back instinctively but placed his ear against the door again. He remained there until all sound had faded and then slowly straightened and turned to face the girl. She looked less frightened now but still tensely poised as if ready for flight.

James smiled reassuringly at her and walked to the dining area, calling for her to follow. He busied himself for a while, hoping she would be relaxed by his normality. When he next turned, she had sidled inside the door and stood, her back against the wall, eyeing him nervously. His chest tightened with sympathy as he looked at her big, frightened eyes in the waif-like face. She was poised there like a deer in the forest who had heard a footstep and wasn't sure how to flee. He spoke softly to her, "Come now, child, I'm not going to hurt you. I don't know what kind of trouble you're in, but I find it hard to believe that you could have done anything bad enough to warrant a full-scale manhunt. What seems to be the problem?"

He thought he detected a relaxation in her, although she didn't move or speak. He sat down and, smiling reassuringly, waved his hand around to encompass the whole room.

"Why don't you sit down, child? There's no point in tiring yourself, and, in any case, you must surely know that if I did mean to harm you, there would be very little you could do about it, now would there?"

She looked at him curiously, trying to determine whether his words were a threat.

Suddenly, she caved in. Now, she cried the tears of a child needing comfort rather than those of fear. Not knowing quite what to do, afraid to touch her, James went to her and, holding out his hand, said very gently, "Please believe me, child, I will not harm you. I am your friend. Now, why don't you come and sit down and tell me all about it?"

For a while, she just stared at his outstretched hand and then slowly reached out her own hand and placed it in his. He led her to a seat and waited whilst she sat down, then sitting opposite her, he leaned forward.

"My name is James; what's yours?"

"Melinda"

"A pretty name, and what do you do in The Forum, Melinda?"

Her eyes widened again, and her lower lip trembled, but she controlled herself and whispered, "I am, I was, the personal servant to the Second President." As she said the name, she looked like she would cry again. She bit her lower lip and avoided looking at James.

"Is it the Second President you're running away from?" he asked, already suspecting what the girl's trouble was. She merely nodded. James pondered how best to approach the subject, then asked, "Did he hurt you?"

She looked hesitant as if wondering how to answer, and he asked instead, "Did he try to hurt you?"

This time, she nodded. Believing his suspicions correct, James asked, "How did he try to hurt you?"

She lowered her head and didn't answer.

"Did he try and make you do something you didn't want to do?"

She nodded again, slowly looking up until her solemn eyes met his. She looked at him for a long while as he gazed sympathetically back at her.

Finally, she sighed as though she had made a big decision, and then she began to speak in hurt, puzzled tones.

"He has always been a nice man. I worked for him since his last girl did something bad and had to be sent to The Sanctum. I was thrilled with him, and he seemed to think I did my job well, and then and then, the other day, he tried to make me...he tried...."

"I think I know what you are trying to say, Melinda."

She looked at him surprised, seeming shocked at the thought that anyone else should know about something so dreadful. She burst out, "But you can't know, he-he tried to make me go to his bed!" She sat back and looked at him defiantly, expecting him to recoil in horror perhaps.

Instead, he said gently. "I guessed that's what it was, Melinda, and I can understand why you ran away."

"Oh, I didn't run away then because he left me alone when I cried. He said I would have to do what he said the next time; otherwise, I would be badly punished. Today, he - he tried to make me go with him again. He hit me and told me I must do as he said, or he would send me to The Sanctum of Well-Being.

I couldn't believe it. I couldn't, I couldn't,"

She began crying again, bewildered. James reached out and placed a hand on her shoulder. She looked at it but didn't try and pull away.

"He wouldn't really send me to The Sanctum, would he?"

James thought deeply for a while. He knew that the girl must be made aware of the fate in store for her, but he didn't want to frighten her any more than she already was. He felt a deep revulsion for Delmo, who could be so corrupt. Already, he had ruined the girl Elene's life. James suddenly sat up straight, wondering why he recalled the first girl's name; then he remembered the boy, Daniel, and he knew what he must do all at once. He looked closely at Melinda, ensuring she could see his seriousness.

"Melinda, you've already mentioned the girl who served the Second President before you; her name, if you didn't know it, is Elene."

Intrigued that he should have known her predecessor and interested to hear what he was about to say, she sat up, more alert now.

"You say that the Second President told you she was sent to The Sanctum for doing something bad. Well, I can tell you that she did nothing bad at all. She was sent there because she did exactly what you have done. She refused to do what the evil old man wanted. She…."

"You mean I will be sent to The Sanctum!" she said, alarmed, tears again in her eyes. James patted her shoulder reassuringly and said soothingly,

"No, no, no, just wait, listen to what I have to say."

When she had calmed down, he went on, "Although you were told she was sent to The Sanctum, as indeed she was, I suspect you weren't told that she escaped."

"Escaped? From The Sanctum?"

"Not from within The Sanctum, no, she was actually making the final walk when she made a run for it; she got away."

"But that's against the law'!" Melinda exclaimed.

James stared at her, then couldn't help laughing, ironically.

"My dear child, do you believe she should have allowed the Second President to abuse her like he tried to abuse you?"

"No, of course not, but…"

"Never mind about but. Do you think the Second President was entitled to demand that she does what he wanted, or you, for that matter?"

"No, no, it's wrong, it must be!"

"Of course, it's wrong. Surely then you can see that it cannot be right for someone to be punished for refusing to do something they know is wrong."

"I suppose so. It just seems hard to think of someone running away like that."

"But aren't you running away?"

"I suppose so, but I don't know where I was supposed to be running to. I just got so frightened."

"Well, one thing is certain, Melinda, you can't go back, and I know you don't want to go to The Sanctum. There's only one answer."

"What's that?"

"We're going to have to get you away from here."

"Away from here? Where to?"

"Hopefully, to the same place that the other girl, Elene, went to."

"Where was that?"

"Well, if I tell you, it was The Wastelands, you'll probably not think much of the idea, but I can assure you it's not quite as you think."

He sat with her for a while and told her what he knew of Teg, Elene and Jason. He told her about the settlement, what little he knew, and how Teg was planning to try to end the kind of evil that had led her to where she was now. Then he told her about himself.

"There are things that have happened, Melinda, that make me, and some others, think the way this young man Teg does. I need some way to contact him to let him know that we are here and support him. If we can arrange to get you there, you will be able to give him our message, and you will be safe."

"But how will you get me there?"

"We must consider that, but I think I know just the man. In the meantime, we must ensure you are kept well hidden."

Chapter 35

"Jason, you do realise that any of a dozen women out there would gladly tear my eyes out and take my place, don't you?"

"My dear Margarita, I'm sure you exaggerate my charms beyond all reason, but I love it, so don't stop."

"They really do think the world of you, Jason, you know that don't you?"

"It has always been the way with doctors, my dear. Women, for some reason, find them irresistible. In my case, it's quite understandable. There's my good looks, my incredible intellect, my…."

"Why, you old braggart…."

"Margarita, I seek only to boost my confidence because I fear that at any moment, you will see me for what I am and cast me aside like a used bandage."

"Oh, you fool, Jason. I see you for what you are, and I love you because of it. I never dreamed I could be so happy again. I feel blessed that you came into my life."

They stared into each other's eyes, as much in love as any couple had ever been. Misty eyed; Margarita rose on her toes and kissed him just as Teg came through the door.

"Have you no shame? I leave you alone for a few minutes, and you lose yourselves in an orgy of passion. …"

"Jason!" Margarita interrupted, "Do you hear this grandson of yours? You should put him over your knee and spank him!"

"I'm not sure it would do his image as leader much good, my dear, and honestly, I'm not sure I could manage it anymore. With how he's growing up and developing under Marcus' training, I might be smacked."

Teg looked fondly at the pair of them. The change in him was decidedly marked. He had grown taller and more mature and trained with the rest of the men as Marcus had hardened them and molded them into a tight-knit fighting force. It had been five months since Teg had become leader, and the settlement's fortunes blossomed under his leadership.

He had the knack of seeing where significant improvements could be made and had a careful selection of people to spearhead the improvements he sought. Marcus and Teg had set substantial changes in motion with food production, building weapons, the way information was circulated and the general attitude of the people of the settlement. There was a sense of unity and purpose that was creating a feeling of hope for the future.

Teg felt sure that the wedding of Jason and Margarita would help to cement and improve the sense of unity and purpose that had grown up, and he was delighted that nearly all the people had gathered for the wedding and the celebrations that were to follow.

He had learned that there was no formalised wedding ceremony in the settlement and had yet to be within the memory of even the oldest members. Although generally lasting, relationships were formed out of either love or expediency. They became accepted purely on an announcement from the couple or simply because it became evident that a confident man and woman were living together. Teg had suggested to Mictor that some ritualised wedding services might be good in fostering the growing sense of community and permanence, and Mictor had readily agreed. The only wedding ceremony Teg had witnessed had been in the town and had been based on The Way, which was sufficient reason for it to be discarded as a model right from the start.

He and Mictor had spent many hours discussing the form the ceremony should take and had even discussed it with Jason and Margarita. They had agreed the service should be simple and that the words that would be spoken were what mattered most. Now that the time for the wedding had arrived, Teg found himself reviewing the terms that he and Mictor had finally settled on: to act as a message for the whole community and give them the ideals they would learn to accept as a sound basis for living.

"Well then, are you ready?" asked Teg.

Jason and Margarita looked at each other and smiled, then began to move, hand in hand, out of the door. A platform had been erected outside Mictor's house, and a great crowd had assembled to witness the wedding. Mictor stood with Elene on the platform. He would conduct the service with Elene assisting him.

As Jason and Margarita ascended the steps to the platform, the crowd began to clap and cheer. Then, as Teg came onto the platform behind them, the cheers became continuous and were sustained for a couple of minutes until he stepped forward and raised his hands for silence. As he did, more and more, he felt a great sense of kinship with the people welling up in him, and his voice was emotional.

"My friends, we are all here today for a very happy occasion. Since my grandfather and I were accepted into this community, we have learned to love and respect you. We like to feel that we are a part of you. There is no doubt that you have made us welcome and that together, we have brought this community to a stage where it shall soon be possible for us to decide our destiny and secure all the freedom that is our birthright.

I have seen with much pleasure the growing love between my grandfather and Margarita, and it gave me much joy to learn of their intention to marry. I believe, my friends, that this marriage is a symbol for us all. May this union symbolise unity, love, and confidence in the future that has become the spirit of this settlement. I know you will join me in wishing them long life and love!"

As he finished speaking. Teg turned and bowed to the bridal couple, and the crowd began to cheer. Their cheers faded as Jason and Margarita stepped forward with Mictor on one side and Elene on the other.

Mictor turned and faced the crowd. He was clearly ready to enjoy his role, indeed he had remarked to Teg that he hoped the formal ceremony would catch on and that he might have the opportunity to conduct many of the services. It was then Teg had realised how much the old man needed some reason to exist. As the months passed since Teg assumed the leadership, Mictor's function gradually ceased. He was still regarded with much respect and affection by the people. Still, they soon realised the changes taking place, the air of optimism in the community resulted from Teg's efforts, and their primary loyalty was now towards him.

"My dear friends," Mictor began, "as Teg has already said, today marks an auspicious occasion in the life of this settlement. When Teg and his grandfather, our excellent friend Jason, joined us, it did not take long to see that these were extraordinary people. The service they provide to our community has been and will continue to be, of inestimable value.

That Jason has now chosen to bind himself, by taking a vow of marriage, to one of our friends who has also served this community so well is a cause for celebration. You will all know that since the arrival of Teg and Jason, the thoughts and efforts of our community have been directed towards the day when we may walk freely in all parts of this land, free from fear and attack. The most critical word today is 'free'. We have long dreamed of freedom. We have long believed it would be allowed to us once Teg arrived. Since then, we have come to believe that freedom is attainable. Our minds have been directed towards that expectation. In that spirit, Jason and Margarita will pledge their love for each other today and declare their dedication to the ideals that will pave our way into the future."

There was some scattered applause as Mictor finished, but most attention was focused on Elene, who had come forward carrying a crude cage where two small birds hopped about. She stood between Jason and Margarita as Mictor addressed them.

"Do you believe in the sanctity of life?"

"I do," they both proclaimed loundly.

"Do you believe in the sanctity of the mind?"

"I do."

"Do you believe that the freedom of one's thoughts should be at the mercy and control of another?"

"I do not."

"Is it your wish that in committing yourselves to this union, the sanctity of thought and speech that you have defended shall remain forever the right of each of you even though they may not coincide?"

"It is"

"Will you care for one another truly and honestly as long as you are both together?"

"I will."

"Do you freely enter into this marriage without coercion and of your own choice?

"I do."

Mictor signaled to Elene, who opened the cage and lifted it high. One bird flew out almost immediately and fluttered into the air. It circled overhead until the second bird flashed out of the cell and flew up to join it. They both flew high into the sky. The crowd watched the birds as they diminished, and then they looked back towards the platform as Mictor spoke again.

"The birds are a symbol of our freedom. The vows we have heard today tell us that the celebrants, Jason, and Margarita, do not view their marriage as a cage; they do not view life as a cage. Together, they will fly the paths they choose, but they will each be as free as those birds in their hearts and minds. Thus, what they do together is done by choice. What they do for each other, they do from selection. The thoughts and affections they may share will be of their own choosing. Neither will wish or choose to engage the other.

They will sanctify freedom by choosing to stay together to care for each other. Love is freedom, and without freedom, there is no real love."

He turned towards Jason and Margarita,

"May you find true happiness together; may you find true freedom together;"

The simple ceremony ended, and as Jason took his bride in his arms and kissed her, the crowd cheered. Jason released Margarita and turned to speak to the masses. As he did so, he was aware that the cheers were dying away and, to his surprise, he saw that most of the group were looking away from the platform towards the east. He stared to where they were looking but could see nothing untoward, and then he heard, faintly at first but louder as the signal was picked up and relayed on from stations nearer to home, mournful wailing of the horns, signaling a police raid.

He stood there stunned as the crowd scattered. In a remarkably short time, the only people left who were not on the platform were those who were too old or too infirm to move fast, but they, too, were making their way towards their hiding places.

Teg was already off the platform, running to where Mictor's ex-police vehicle was kept. By prior arrangement, the guards on Mictor's house, one of whom was the driver, were already making their way to the car. As soon as Teg arrived and climbed in, they were in motion, gathering speed as they departed from where the platform had been erected. Teg had time for a brief wave to a concerned-looking Elene before they went through a gap between two buildings and heading towards the east.

This was the first raid that had taken place since Teg had become leader, and he felt a fluttering of nerves at the thought of what might lie ahead. He also felt a sense of exuberance that Marcus would finally get the chance to put his troops and his theories on defence to the test. The outcome of this battle and the lessons learned could determine the future fight strategy against The Forum.

As they neared a barricade, not the one that Teg and Jason had initially been brought through but equally as well constructed, they began to pass between groups of men, running towards the same barricade. They waved cheerfully as the vehicle passed, and Teg was impressed by the easy way they moved and the air of purpose about them. He remembered how they had been before the training had started and was delighted at the changes that had been wrought. As they slowed down at the approach to the barricade, the guards began to move a large section of steel to permit the vehicle to pass through, but jumping from it, Teg indicated that they shouldn't open the barricade any further.

"We'll leave the vehicle here," he said. "There's no point in risking having it captured." He turned to the driver, "You stay here at the barricade. If there's any sign that the vehicle is threatened, take it back into the settlement."

Teg finished speaking. The crackle of small arms fire could be heard faintly in the distance. The groups of men who had come up behind Teg were mustered around the barricade and, on hearing the guns, looked impatient to be moving. Teg suddenly realised that they were waiting for his permission and, jumping up onto the barricade, shouted at them.

"This is your chance to prove that you have learned your lessons, that the past few months have been worthwhile. Take no unnecessary risks. There is nothing to be gained for your family and so much to lose if you throw away your lives unnecessarily. Remember, we want to try and capture weapons and if the opportunity arises, a vehicle. It won't be easy and will require much courage, but that's something I know you have plenty of. Good luck, and let's go."

They cheered as Teg jumped down, and they streamed through the barricade after him. The barrier was closed as soon as the last man was through, sealing the road between two high buildings. High-walled buildings stretched in both directions from the border, and the others like it were positioned to be the natural approach points for the enemy. They would be stoutly defended if the occasion arose.

The gunfire was loud and sporadic. Teg and six men crawled through the rough grassy ground between two heaps of rubble. Each of them was armed with a slim, very sharp throwing spear and a crude, but effective dagger. Two of the men had pistols, but these would only be used as a last resort due to the scarcity of ammunition.

Reaching the heap of rubble in front of them, the seven men spread out and inched their way to the top of the pile. At the left-hand end, Teg looked cautiously through a gap in a jumbled pile of bricks and rusted metal.

The ground sloped away from him for about a quarter of a mile before levelling out. There were many halves or entirely demolished buildings in the area and from where Teg lay, he could see a natural courtyard formed by three large buildings and two police vehicles. Between the cars and one of the buildings, policemen were moving about. From the third floor of what remained of the building, gunfire was being directed towards a rubble strewn hollow about a hundred yards away. Looking carefully, Teg could see at least three men pinned down by the gunfire and from the way the policeman behind the building was moving about, it seemed clear they were planning to encircle the beleaguered men.

"We've got to try and distract their attention from those men", he called to the others. "Ideally, we want to try and lead those police away from them towards the tunnels."

He and Marcus had discussed how the newly opened railway tunnels could be used. They had practiced various forms of ambush and escape tactics and felt that if they could lure the attackers to the tunnels, they had a good chance of springing a surprise.

To this end, it had been arranged that the moment a raid alarm was sounded, a reasonably large squad of men would go to the redoubts built around the tunnel entrances and wait there, hoping the raiders could be lured there. Various possible situations had been dreamed up, discussed, and rehearsed. From what had been learned, various bits and pieces of apparatus had been constructed and placed within easy reach of the defenders.

Anyone wandering innocently through the concealed entrance to the redoubt would have seen the tunnel entrance and no more. Attackers wouldn't have seen the men skillfully covered in artfully constructed hiding places on the inner walls of the redoubts. The gunfire from the building intensified.

"They're ensuring they stay down while the others move," shouted Teg.

Then, suddenly inspired, he called, "Can any of you drive one of those police vehicles?"

Two of the men put their hands up.

"Right, you two come with me. The rest of you, I want you to create a disturbance to attract the attention of the policemen over there. We're going to try and steal one of those vehicles, so wait until you see us close to it, then give them all you've got. They'll be more intent on chasing us if we succeed than worrying about you. As soon as you can, make sure those men down there are okay and then make your way to the tunnels, good luck!"

So, saying Teg was up and, running crouched over, doubled back around the pile of debris, the two other men following. They ran across an open space that had once been a road lined with houses, now resembling a vast row of broken teeth with scattered pieces. Feeling exposed as they dashed across the open space, they made it to the shelter of one of the destroyed houses. Running around to the back of the house, they continued from ruin to ruin, parallel with the road. As they reached the last place in the row, the sound of gunfire was deafening. Peering cautiously around the corner, Teg saw that the police vehicles were parked about fifty yards diagonally across from where he knelt. To approach directly would be suicidal; he looked around frantically for a means of approaching unseen. He was concerned that the policemen had started moving away from the vehicle's reparatory to encircle the trapped men. Whilst he wanted them away from the cars, he knew it wouldn't take them long to capture or kill the trapped men once they had surrounded them.

"We've got to move quickly," he said urgently to his companions. "We've got to make sure the others can see us as well, so they'll know to create a diversion". He looked around again. There was nothing for it but a frontal assault. He turned to the two men.

"We're going to have to make a direct run for it. One of you wait here in case something goes wrong. The other one comes with me."

They tensed like runners on a starting block, and then Teg yelled, "Now!"

They sprinted towards the nearest vehicle as fast as they could. The policemen near the other car seemed frighteningly close, and as they panted forward, they prayed silently none of them would turn.

They were about ten yards from the vehicle when the policeman nearest them began to turn. Seeing them, he spun about, raising his gun, his mouth opening to shout. At that instant, there were gunshots in the distance, and blood-curdling yells from the diversion squad. The policeman's companions ran forward, away from the vehicle, to see what the disturbance was, and his shout went unheard. Momentarily distracted, he had allowed Teg and the other man to get within a few feet of the vehicle, but now he spun around again and aimed his gun. At that moment, he staggered as a brick hit him on the side of the head. Stunned, he went down on one knee but still struggled to focus his aim as Teg scrambled into the vehicle. The policeman fired, and Teg's companion staggered, crying out in pain as a splash of red appeared on his upper arm. Turning around, Teg reached out and grabbed him, pulling him into the vehicle. Still on one knee but steadier now, the policeman aimed again. He whirled as there was a blur of movement to his left, but before he could react any further, the man Teg had left behind, stopped abruptly he then braced his feet as he had been taught and drove his spear straight through the other man's heart, killing him instantly. He had pulled the blood-stained spear free in one swift movement, stooped and gathered the gun, and was running towards the vehicle. A shout behind him told him he had been seen, and he doubled his pace, finally throwing himself bodily into the car.

The wounded man was in the driver's seat, forcing himself to ignore the pain and start the engine. As it whirred into life and began to whine with a surge of power as he swung it around, Teg snatched up the captured gun and, lying forward across his panting companion, fired a shot through the open door. He hit one of the policemen in the leg more by luck than judgment.

As he fell awkwardly, with a scream of pain, his companions instinctively ducked down, seeking cover. In the confusion, the vehicle roared out of the courtyard and, screeching around the corner, sped off along the rubble-strewn road. Its specially designed suspension only managed to cope with the jarring and bumping. Teg was crouched, looking through the back window. As the man was about two hundred yards up the road, he saw the second vehicle pulling out to pursue them.

"As fast as you can!" he yelled, grinning excitedly, the exhilaration of battle in his eyes.

They were thrown from side to side and bumped up and down as the chase continued. Speeding between two nearly intact concrete buildings, they had to swerve violently to the left as they came to a long, solid concrete wall. The force of the swerve and the effort required to execute it caused their driver to cry out in pain, and, for a moment, it seemed as though the vehicle would turn over. He gritted his teeth and fought with the controls and got it back on an even keel. Looking back, Teg yelled triumphantly as he saw the pursuing vehicle screech through the same opening and, in taking the same evasive action, clip the concrete wall with the rear end. There was a shower of sparks and dust, and the vehicle slewed across the road as Teg cheered.

For a moment, it looked as though it would come to grief on a massive pile of tumbled concrete, but Teg's cheers turned to groans as the driver of the pursuing vehicle fought skillfully to bring it back under control. The maneuver had allowed Teg's driver to widen the gap, and all three men cheered as they swung round a corner onto a long straight stretch of road at the end of which they knew was the second entrance to the tunnel. Teg silently prayed that the plan was going to work. Otherwise, he was leading his pursuers very close to the settlement. He looked back and saw them sliding around the corner about four hundred yards behind them.

"Bloody Hell!"

Teg whirled round at the driver's shout and saw, to his horror, another police vehicle pulling out of a side, turning in front of them.

"The radio," Teg groaned. "We should have thought of the radio."

Leaning forward, the third man switched the radio on. Immediately, the vehicle was filled with a babble of noise and excited shouting, foremost of which was a cry of, "We've got them. We're in front of them!"

The vehicle in front was turning to face across the road and blocked their way. In a moment of inspired bravery, the driver of Teg's vehicle pressed his foot down, giving full power, and the car hurtled at the closing gap. There was a splintering, crunching bang, and the whole vehicle vibrated, but the momentum carried them through, and to their relief, the engine and the wheels kept turning. The charge they had given the other vehicle had slewed it around at an angle, and as the driver fought to turn it, the first pursuing vehicle had to screech to a halt, unable to pass. The gap rapidly widened until Teg said, "Not too fast, slow down, slow down. We don't want them to lose us. They must see where we go. We want them to follow us."

They were now no more than two hundred yards from the redoubt and moved slowly forward as though their vehicle was severely damaged. Evidence of the success of the ploy came from the radio as a triumphant voice shrieked, "They're damaged. It looks like they're stopping. We've got the bastards!"

As they neared the entrance to the redoubt, Teg felt suddenly nervous, knowing the likely cost if things went wrong. Shaking himself mentally, he waited until the nearest pursuer was about two hundred yards away, then shouted.

The driver accelerated forward until he was level with the concealed entrance, spun the vehicle around through the first gap, braked violently, rounded the next hole, and shot into the walled-in clearing. Accelerating again, he sped into the tunnel entrance, the nose of the vehicle dropping alarmingly as it hit the ramp. Immediately, the driver switched on the headlights, and as they flashed into the tunnel, they caught glimpses of men on either side poised for action. The moment they had passed. The men they had seen went into action, pulling heavy pieces of wood, metal, and concrete across the tunnel. It was an eerie experience for Teg and his friends as they sped through the tunnel, the walls and roof seeming to rush at them as the headlights pierced the darkness, and then, in a surprisingly short time, the end of the tunnel appeared, and they flashed up the ramp into the open. Slowing drastically, the driver negotiated the concealed entrance, and, in a moment, they had cut across open ground and were back on the same road as earlier, only now they were behind the other vehicles.

As Teg's vehicle had disappeared, the nearest pursuing car had slowed almost to a stop, unable to see where they had gone. The puzzled voices on the radio became angrier as the occupants of the second vehicle blamed those in the first for losing their quarry. Suddenly, one of the more sharp-eyed policemen spotted the gap and pointed it out with a yell of triumph. Going slowly, the first car entered the hole and negotiated the entrance. The vehicle pulled into the clearing, and the driver shouted over the radio,"

"There's an escape tunnel. The bastards have got away. I'm going after them."

As he accelerated into the tunnel, the second vehicle entered the clearing. Almost immediately, there was a screeching of brakes, a loud discordant crash and a great cloud of dust blossoming out of the mouth of the tunnel. There was no movement from the second vehicle for a moment, but then the doors opened, and five policemen sprang out, guns in hand and rapidly deployed themselves around the entrance to the ramp. There was the crack of a pistol, and with a look of surprise, one of the policemen slumped forward, shot in the back. The others whirled around; guns held high but saw only the rubble walls.

The sounds of screams and curses came from inside the tunnel, and one of the policemen began to creep into the tunnel entrance. There was another gunshot, and he fell forward, half his head blown away. One of the remaining three policemen ran into the middle of the clearing, waving his gun frantically at the target. He just had time to see a man appear, as if by magic, halfway up one of the walls. Before he could aim his gun, the man's arm had flashed backwards and forwards, and the policeman fell to the ground, screaming in agony, a spear through his stomach. Panicking, the remaining two policemen ran for their vehicle. Before they had reached it, another one went down a pike through his neck. The remaining policeman ran for the entrance, looking wildly around, his gun held at his side. As he neared the door, he skidded to a halt as Teg stepped before him, the captured weapon in his hands. As the policeman raised his gun, Teg shot him.

It was all over. So fast, even the victors were stunned. As the last policemen dropped dead from Teg's shot, the men concealed on the redoubt's walls stood up, looking down in disbelief. Without a word, they began climbing down from their hiding places until ten stood in the clearing, staring around at the dead policemen and the captured vehicle. Teg felt a variety of emotions. He knew he should be feeling jubilant; the plan had worked far better than he had expected, but all he could see now was the look on the policeman's face as the shot had blasted him.

Suddenly, Teg and the other men whirled as a high-pitched yell issued from the mouth of the tunnel. A moment of tension dispersed almost at once as they saw Marcus, hands on hips, laughing joyously.

As the tension broke, the men around Teg began cheering. As their comrades began emerging from the tunnel, dusty, blinking in the bright light, clearly delighted with themselves, they were suddenly rushing at each other, patting each other on the back, hugging each other and chattering excitedly about their part in the victory.

During all the noise and jubilation, Marcus strolled towards Teg, beaming happily. They shook hands and, for a moment, remained staring at each other, hands linked before Marcus suddenly enveloped Teg in a hug.

"Perfect, it went perfectly!" he exclaimed. "The men were marvelous. Just think Teg, we had vague hopes of capturing a vehicle, and we've got three. It's unbelievable."

"The most important thing, Marcus, is how the men performed. The ones who were with me were great. My driver, in fact, is wounded. I want to get him back to the hospital."

"Yes, I've got a couple of wounded. Nothing serious, thankfully. Would you say something to the men, Teg? I think they'd appreciate it."

Nodding, Teg walked to the vehicle and climbed up on it. Seeing him there, the men cheered and gathered around, anticipating a speech.

"Men!" Teg began. "Today has been the proudest day of my life. Not just because we have won this battle, not just because we have gained vehicles and weapons that will be of inestimable value to us in the weeks and months ahead. My main reason for being proud is that I have been privileged to fight alongside men who have shown courage, initiative, and discipline. We must remember that this has been one battle of many that we will have to fight before final victory. Remember that what has happened here today will undoubtedly anger the rulers of the enemy, and they will be more determined than ever to destroy us. We must be alert to danger. What I have seen today gives me confidence, however, that no matter what they may throw against us, the final victory will be ours!"

The men cheered at this, and Teg let them go on for a while before raising his hands for silence again.

"We have much to do, men. We must get our wounded back to the hospital, remove and bury the dead, and move the vehicles and weapons to safekeeping. Before that, I'm sure you will want to join me in saluting those who, more than anyone else, made this victory possible. Gentleman, your commander Marcus!"

The cheers for Marcus that resounded off the walls of the redoubt were heartfelt and prolonged. Marcus was obviously moved and as the men began to disperse, he moved among them shaking their hands and murmuring words of congratulations.

Chapter 36

It was a strange procession heading down the road towards the barricade. The vehicle that had ploughed into the obstacles placed across the tunnel had been pulled out, its front badly damaged. It had been turned around and hooked up behind the undamaged vehicle, and it was pulled noisily along as pieces of damaged material dragged on the ground or rattled against each other.

The vehicle that Teg had captured was in the lead and fully serviceable despite the damaged bodywork. As they had come within sight of the barricade, they had seen the frantic bustle of activity on top of it. They knew that the defenders were preparing for an attack. Teg stopped the vehicles. He climbed out, followed by five other men packed tightly inside. Other men emerged and proceeded from the other cars, including one towed. Teg was walking in front, and a line of men was on either side of the vehicles, almost like an old-fashioned funeral.

The men grinned as they neared the barricade and saw the defenders' looks of astonishment. Suddenly, someone opened the barricade, and men came pouring through it, cheering, and shouting with delight as they realised what had happened.

As the vehicles entered, the excited men milled around. Someone climbed to the top of the barricade and, raising a horn to his lips, blew a long and piercing blast. Almost immediately, the sound was heard at different places, seeming to echo into the distance.

As the procession wound its way into the railyards, people began to appear, responding to the sound of the all-clear. They broke into a run when they saw the vehicles and the excited men around them.

The news spread fast, and soon, people were streaming to the scene from all over the settlement. Their happy faces and vibrant chatter gave the moment a carnival feel.

Teg climbed onto the top of one of the vehicles. The crowd responded with whoops of joy, clapping, and cheering until he held his hands in the air for silence.

"My friends, as you can see, we have won a remarkable victory today. Thanks to the leadership and training of our excellent Commander of Defence and the superb efforts of the men he has moulded into such a fine fighting force, we have seen the beginning of what I believe will be the fight for ultimate victory."

He paused while the crowd cheered, and some crowded around Marcus, patting him on the back and shaking his hand.

"Let there be no doubt, though; there is a long way to go. There will be setbacks; there will be times when we might wonder if we will succeed. One thing we can be sure of for now is that our enemies against whom we intend to pit ourselves have a mighty arsenal of weapons and equipment: they have reserves of highly trained men, and they will surely have a fierce determination to cling to the power they hold. These enemies of ours have no regard for human life or liberty. They care nothing for the sanctity of the human spirit; therefore, they will stop at nothing to defeat us. We must be on our guard and continue preparing for the fight ahead. Still, while we are determined to succeed, I believe we shall win".

As Teg climbed off of the vehicle, another burst of cheering came. Then, as the crowd dispersed, Marcus started moving the captured cars to the repair area, sorting, and checking the various captured weapons.

As Teg climbed into Mictors' vehicle, which had been left there earlier in the day, he found it hard to believe that it had only been a few hours ago that Jason and Margarita's wedding celebrations had come to such an abrupt end.

He decided to first see Mictor and apprise him of the day's events as a matter of courtesy and respect. Then, he would visit the hospital to see how the wounded men were faring and to see Jason, Margarita, and Elene.

At the thought of Elene, Teg felt a deep sense of warmth and realised just how much he had come to love her. He prayed that victory against The Forum would not be too long so that he and his loved one could begin to live an everyday life together. The thought made him smile, and when he stepped from the vehicle at Mictors house, he was still smiling.

"Well, well, there's a very happy-looking man!" Mictor exclaimed. He had found it easy to stop referring to Teg as a young man, it seemed unfitting.

"What a day we've had."

Mictor sat at the front of the house. Around him were several young people who arose when Teg approached. They started to move away, but holding up his hand, he told them to wait.

"Stay for a moment. You have as much right to hear about today's events as anyone. I trust that you will spread the word to all those who don't yet know, as you are all fleet-footed and talkative. Today, we were attacked by three police vehicles, each carrying several armed men."

The faces of the young people were alight with excitement and curiosity as Teg related the day's happenings. Nobody noticed that one of the young men, Daniel, seemed to be having to force his enthusiasm and when Teg finally dismissed them and, turning to Mictor, told him he wished to discuss something with him, they didn't notice Daniel, in the confusion, conceal himself behind a thick creeping wild rose that clung to the wall of the house at the right of the front door.

Once the need for pretence was gone, Daniels's face re-assumed its perpetual sneer, and there was hate in his eyes as he listened to Teg and Mictor.

"From what you say, Teg, it was a great victory today."

"It was Mictor, it was. What was most important about it was that Marcus and I felt that the time for making a move against The Forum was closer than we'd thought. I don't mean a final onslaught, of course, that will take much longer, but some way of sounding out their defences; I would like to go and have a look at The Forum, even from a distance, so that both Marcus and I have some idea of what we're up against. We have a series of exercises planned for the men over the next few days, and we also want to get the vehicles in shape, so we'll be making our trip in about a week or so.

"Well, Teg, I don't know about you, but I'm hungry. How about we continue our chat over a meal?"

Suddenly, Teg realised that he, too, was hungry; the day's excitement had driven all thoughts of food out of his mind. Helping the old man to his feet, he walked into the house with him, suddenly ravenous. Neither of them saw Daniel slip away.

When they were seated, enjoying the plain but wholesome food, Teg talked animatedly about how well things were shaping up.

"The men have taken to their training and seem to understand the importance of what we're aiming for. There were some remarkable displays of bravery out there today. We must keep the momentum going, and that's one of the reasons I have to go back to the town even though the idea doesn't exactly thrill me."

"Back to the town?"

"Yes, to get the lay of the land around The Forum. Only as I was coming here today did I realise I don't even know what part of town The Forum is in."

Mictor looked at Teg with an odd expression, then slowly nodded before saying, "Of course, I said many months ago that we must go on a journey. I think I might have a surprise for you, Teg."

Teg looked at Mictor in puzzlement as he saw the older man's secretive, almost mischievous smile.

"Teg, there you are, my boy; well, done, congratulations!"

Jason's effusive greeting rang through the hospital as Teg entered. Teg had already been feeling overjoyed by the day's victory, but seeing his grandfather heightened his jubilation. Jason and Margarita came down the ward arm in arm.

"Hello, Margarita," Teg said. "I am sorry that I never got a chance to congratulate you properly on your wedding, but, as you're only too aware, something came up."

They laughed at his understatement as they led him to where the day's casualties were sitting, either in or on a group of beds at the end of the ward. Despite his protests, they rose as Teg approached and only sat down when he formally requested it. It was odd for him to be among men much older than himself, men who had fought bravely in battle, suffered wounds in the struggle and yet looked up to him with such respect.

He chatted with them for a while and then returned to where Jason and Margarita were reviewing paperwork.

"Is Elene around?" he asked, disappointed that he hadn't seen her.

"Oh, she went for a walk," said Margarita. "I think she wanted to give us some time on our own. It's not easy when we've got a ward full of patients. Anyway, she should be back soon. It's getting towards evening, and the light will be fading. You might as well wait for her."

Although Elene had wanted to give Jason and Margarita some time alone, she had another good reason to go for a solitary walk: to think about Teg.

Elene had known for a long time that she loved Teg and believed that he loved her equally. Although they had agreed not to make firm commitments for now, she was sure Teg was considering the impact on her if he was to get killed. She wondered if Teg was trying to minimise the sense of loss she would undoubtedly feel. However, when she had watched him dashing off to fight that morning, she'd had an urgent conviction that it had been foolish to pretend things would be any different. She had walked deep in thought for a long time, leaving the hospital and the dwellings far behind. Elene resolved that upon Tegs return she would explain her thoughts. Teg was the only one for her, regardless of future outcomes, she could never love anyone else. She shivered with pleasure at the thought of a committed and happy life together.

Tired from her long walk, she rested against the tree trunk before she would return to the hospital. She was in an area that had probably once been a public garden, as ruined buildings surrounded it. Any formal layout had long since disappeared with the encroachment of weeds, creepers, and grasses. The profusion of wildflowers descended from what was once carefully tended flowerbeds. The warm evening air and the scent of flowers around her made her feel very tired and lazy, and she realised with a start that she was nearly falling asleep.

Climbing to her feet, she began to pick her way back through the trailing growth, heading toward the hospital. Suddenly she paused and cocked her head to one side. She nodded as though confirming to herself that she had heard something. It was a strange drumming noise but somewhat erratic. The sound was coming directly towards her, getting louder by the second. She stepped out from behind a brilliantly flowering bank of shrubbery. She stared in astonishment as she saw, galloping towards her, a horse with a young man clinging to its neck. Surprised but not anticipating any danger, she stood there watching as the horse thundered past her. She recognised the young man as Daniel and saw, as he flew past, that he had seen her. He frantically began to pull the horse to a stop. Still, it had travelled a hundred yards before he had it sufficiently under control to turn and head back to Elene. Had she sensed any danger, she would have had ample opportunity to flee, losing herself among the many broken-down buildings that bordered the park. Still, she waited, curious, as Daniel trotted the horse back to where she stood, pulled it to a halt, and jumped off its back. "Well, well, well, this is my lucky day."

"What on earth are you doing with that horse, Daniel? Roger will be furious with you."

Something in Daniels's face made her suddenly nervous, and she stepped backwards as he walked towards her. His face was a mask of hatred as he snarled at her, "I'll tell you what I'm doing, Miss High and Mighty. I'm going to put paid to that boyfriend of yours. He'll be sorry he ever set foot in this place!"

"Teg? You mean Teg?" she stammered. "I don't understand."

"I'll help you understand", he sneered unpleasantly. "Who the hell does he think he is, coming here and telling people what to do, trying to run the show, trying to make people think he's some kind of hero?"

"But he's trying to help you; he's trying to help you win your freedom!"

"Freedom, what's freedom? It's being able to do what you want, to have what you want. Well, I intend to have all that anyway, without the help of that jumped-up Wayperson!"

"What are you going to do?"

"I'm going to The Forum again. I'm going to…"

"Again?"

"Oh yes, again. I've reported Teg before. I've got friends there now, and when your lover boy gets his comeuppance, The Forum will take care of me."

"You rotten traitor!"

"Watch your mouth bitch", he snarled, and Elene reeled back as he slapped her across the face.

"Please, you mustn't harm Teg. He means well for the whole settlement, and you mustn't do anything to hurt him."

A cunning look crossed Daniel's face, and he stepped closer to Elene. "Well, there is one way you can save him."

"How…how is that?"

"Come with me. I've wanted you since I first saw you. The thought of that bastard having you makes me sick. You come with me, and I'll leave him alone. Not only that, but you'll also find I'm more of a man than he'll ever be."

Elene recoiled in disgust as she realised what he was proposing. She wanted to help Teg, but somehow, she knew that Daniel was too evil and hated Teg too much to keep his word. She guessed that as soon as she had given herself to him, he would delight in breaking his word. She straightened herself defiantly and said forcefully, "Go with you? You must be mad! Teg is a far better person than you'll ever be. I wouldn't give myself to you if you were the last person on earth. You disgust me, you traitorous pervert!"

Breathing heavily with anger, she stood there when she had finished, and then her spine tingled with fear at the distorted expression on his face.

"You bitch, you think you're too good for anyone else. Well, we'll see whether your wonderful boyfriend wants you when I've finished with you. You'll wish you'd given yourself freely because I will have you anyway!"

Saying this, he reached out to grab her. Jumping backwards, she eluded him and turned to run. She blundered into a thick growth of vines and bushes and, panicking, thrashed about, trying to fight her way through them. Elene screamed in pain as her hair pulled violently backwards.

Daniels's foot hooked around her ankle, and with a thud, she fell, winded, to the ground. Immediately, Daniel dove upon her, and she had to wrench her head aside as he tried to kiss her. Her heart was beating wildly, her head hurt where he had grabbed her hair, and her body trembled with pain as he rolled and fought on top of her. She stretched her arm out to her side and her hand grasped around wildly, finally she felt something rough and solid beneath her fingers. In one desperate effort she grabbed the rock and swung at Daniels head. Unfortunately Daniel had seen what was happening and at the last second was able to deflect the blow, preventing any serious injury.

Elene involuntarily whimpered with fear as he strengthened his hold on her.

He was silent as he fought, but his face was a mask of frustration and hatred. Her attempt to maim him only heightened his resolve, he eventually sprang up and sat heavily across her thighs.

"Right, you bitch, we'll see how he likes you with your eyes cut out."

Reaching under his tunic, he pulled a short, sharp knife from its sheath. For a moment, Elene was struck dumb with paralysing fear, but then, as he raised the dagger above her head, she screamed as loud as she could.

Her screams seemed to excite him, and he sneered as he plunged the knife downwards. There was a blur of movement, a snarl, a thump and more screams.

Elene stared in amazement as something knocked Daniel from on top of her, and he began to scream and wince in agony.

Elene rolled over and got to her knees to watch the violent struggle taking place. Suddenly, Daniel broke free and scrambled across the ground towards the horse. He reached out in blind panic trying to find the horse which was bucking and rearing in fright. The dark shape flashed across the ground once more, and with more screaming, Daniel rolled away. As he did so, the horse reared again in alarm, and as its hooves crashed back down, one of them smashed into the side of his head, silencing him immediately.

As if afraid of being punished for what it had done, the horse pranced backwards, whinnying in short, sharp bursts before turning and galloping away.

Elene stared in horror at Daniels' inert body. It was clear from the mess that had been his skull that he was dead. Suddenly, she sank to the ground, her face in her hands and sobbed from the shock of his attack.

She jumped as something cold and wet touched the side of her face, and as she turned her head, Tara licked urgently, ridding her of tears. Elene patted Tara in thanks, and as she lifted her hand to stroke Tara's back, she realised her hand had transferred blood onto the dog.

Chapter 37

There was complete silence as Aaron finished ranting. None of those assembled had witnessed him quite so angry before, and nobody moved or murmured for fear of attracting his ire. Even the second and Third Presidents were subdued as they sat quietly in the splendid ceremonial chairs for all The Forum sessions. Knowing that Aaron was in complete control for the moment and could put anyone to death at a whim if he so desired.

The session had started quietly enough, although the rumour had already circulated that there was trouble brewing. It had all boiled over when a messenger arrived and informed the President of the defeat of the raiding army sent to The Wastelands. It was the most severe reversal they had ever suffered, and it was clear that, behind his anger, Aaron was more than a little worried. He resumed his pacing and once more began shouting angrily.

"There are too many things going wrong. There is a slipshod attitude developing. In just a few months, there have been breaches of discipline, blatant defiance of The Way, and unexplained happenings right here in the heart of The Forum itself. There must be a traitor afoot. James resisted the temptation to look over to where Antony sat. They were both aware of the risks they had been running and expected that all hell would break loose one day. They had guessed that there hadn't been more of an outcry before now because The Supreme Council didn't want too many people knowing about the apparent breaches of forum security.

In his section as head of the supplies department, James was perfectly placed to hear much of the gossip circulating in The Forum. Antony was involved in various activities requiring his mathematical skills, which allowed him to overhear valuable conversation snippets.

The disappearance of policeman Tanner from the Interrogator's cells had not been discovered for two days. Recalling the condition the unfortunate man had been in when they had rescued him, James was convinced that, had they not done so, he would be dead by now anyway. The rage Aaron displayed before the whole Forum had, on that occasion, been reserved exclusively for Garon. For once, the evil torturer had known the taste of fear as the President had threatened him with some of his own treatment and, ultimately, death. Despite being not very bright, Garon had convinced the President that he had nothing to gain from the prisoner's disappearance.

Not daring to reveal that the heart of The Forums power had been penetrated, the President had instructed that whilst enquiries must be made into the policeman's escape, the actual reason must be concealed. The resulting investigation had become a bit of a farce and only James and Antony, among the Attendants, had known the true nature of the strangely worded questions being asked of them.

The rescue of Policeman Tanner had led to the subsequent serious breach of forum security when Policeman Valdor, in gratitude for the help extended to his friend, had agreed to help the Acolyte girl, Melinda, escape from The Forum and from the evil clutches of Delmo, the Second President. It was of policeman Valdor and the girl that James was thinking now. He knew that it would be a while before they reached The Wastelands as the policeman had said that he would not be able to leave his sick friend for the time the journey to and from The Wastelands would take and therefore was taking him along, moving slowly, and resting up as necessary.

Listening to the President's tirade, James silently prayed that the fugitives hadn't been accidentally caught up in the police operation against the settlement or that their arrival so close to the raid wouldn't cause problems. Knowing that worrying would achieve nothing, James forced himself to concentrate on the President's words.

"We must not allow ourselves to become complacent. We must always be alert for any signs of dissent or rebellion among the people and the slaves."

James felt like smiling ironically, wondering whether there was much difference between the people and the slaves.

"Security is to be tightened up," Aaron said. "There will be increased police patrols along our boundaries and more surveillance in the town to anticipate and weed out any signs of wrong thinking."

Silently, James wondered how many innocent unsuspecting people would fall prey to the whims of the secret police who would infiltrate them and, for a variety of reasons ranging from wishing to appear efficient to sheer sadism, arrest them and either slake their own perverted appetites by torturing them themselves or would hand them over for the Interrogator to wreak his evil upon them. James felt sick at heart at the thought of how long he had loyally supported the corrupt regime.

"Let there be no doubt in anyone's mind that anyone who is found to be working against us will be punished instantly and unmercifully; we will not tolerate it!"

As his last angry words echoed in the chamber, the President began to walk out, Delmo and David following. As the Attendants stood respectfully, Aaron glowered at the rows of faces as if wishing that he could, by divine means, tell what traitors, if any, were in their midst. James thought it was ironic that the last people suspected would be himself and Antony. Their loyalty and devotion to duty had been known for years, and no one would suspect them of treachery. At least, he hoped so.

Night had closed in, and Elene had not returned. Teg had become concerned and was considering organising a search party. He didn't want to appear unduly alarmist. Still, he felt sure Elene wouldn't have stayed out this late unless something untoward had happened. His anxiety turned to annoyance when Roger arrived in a foul temper, furious because somebody had made off with one of his horses. Teg felt irritated that Roger should expect him to be concerned about the horse when his immediate worry was Elene.

His attention was taken, however, when Roger mentioned the name Daniel. Teg instantly remembered the sneering, unpleasant boy who had accompanied him and Zack on the herb-gathering expedition, and instinctively, his interest was aroused.

"What was that you said about Daniel?" he interrupted Roger.

"I said it appears he's the one who took the horse. He, or somebody like him, was seen riding it down towards here a couple of hours ago. I've been waiting for him to bring it back so I can tell him exactly what I think of him".

Teg felt a shudder of premonition at the thought of Daniel. He recalled how the same boy had eavesdropped on his conversations with Zack and reported them back to Marcus. Had things turned out differently, he could have been the cause of Teg's death, as well as Jason and Elene's.

Thinking of Elene again, in the same context as Daniel, made Teg suddenly nervous, and he said, urgently, to Roger, "I've got a feeling that Daniel's up to no good, not just out joyriding. Will you gather some men and organise a search party. Elene's out there somewhere. She should have been back hours ago. I don't like the feeling of this at all."

At the mention of Elene's name, Roger sprang into action. He had grown to respect Teg enormously, and knowing how fond he was of the girl, he was determined to find her.

Within minutes, he had returned with a group of men and an armful of torches, which they lit before setting off in the general direction Daniel had been seen heading in. As they proceeded, they broke into groups of two, moving out sideways until they were travelling on a broad front, occasionally losing sight of each other between the ruined houses and tumbled debris. Teg was nervous; his concern for Elene was paramount in his mind, and therefore, he was in no mood to be playful when Zack's dog suddenly came running along the road and pranced around in front of him, barking a greeting.

"Not now, Tara", he protested as the dog ran away a few paces, looked back and barked, and ran away a few more paces. When the men ignored her, she ran up to Teg again, whimpering and pawing at him. Irritated, Teg reached down and pushed the dog away, then stared at his hand in horror. Tara's coat was matted with blood. With a sinking feeling, he knelt and examined the dog. As he had feared the dog was uninjured, and the blood was from some other animal or person.

"What is it, Teg? What's wrong with the dog?" asked Roger, surprised that Teg's immediate concern for Elene had been apparently outweighed. Teg, suspecting that the dog's peculiar behaviour was more than just playful, rose to his feet and said, "There's blood on the dog, and it's not hers. It may just be from another animal, but I've got a feeling that Tara wants us to follow her. Let's see."

Standing, he pointed back in Tara's direction and shouted, "Go, girl!" Immediately, Tara ran off, stopping after a few yards to look back.

Satisfied that the men were following her, she continued but checked every so often that they were still there. After a while, Teg began to wonder whether he had made a mistake and whether it was just a game for the dog. And then he pointed and called, "The horse Roger - look!"

They had come to an area with more trees and grass than ruins, and the horse was standing quietly grazing near a large clump of flowering creepers. The dog, meanwhile, had run off to the left and was standing, barking near a dark shape in the grass. His heart thudded; Teg ran to the dark shape and stared in horror at his beloved Elene. Her face was white in the darkness, her hair sprawled out to one side. She lay on her back, one leg drawn up, her arms crossed on her chest. His eyes filling with tears, Teg fell to his knees beside her and gently took hold of one of her hands.

"Oh, my love", he whispered fearfully, "please, please be alright?" When she didn't stir, he closed his eyes, feeling the hot tears squeezing through the lids and running down his face.

"Teg?" The voice was weak, and at first, he thought he had imagined it, but when he felt her hand tighten on his, he looked down with a sudden rush of relief to see Elene smiling weakly up at him.

"Oh, Elene", he murmured, "I thought, oh, I thought..."

Lost for words, he reached down and, putting his arms around her, cradled her protectively against his chest.

"What happened" he murmured; his voice muffled by her hair where his face rested against the top of her head. She stirred in his arms, then shuddered as she recalled what had happened.

"It was Daniel. He was on the horse. He stopped when he saw me and...and..."

She sobbed quietly, the memory of the attack distressing her, and Teg told her to forget it for the moment, but she went on, "He's a traitor, Teg; he was a traitor", she amended, recalling what had happened. "He was going to betray you; he hated you. He said he had been to The Forum before and had friends there who were going to help him. He wanted me to go with him, oh Teg." Now she sobbed bitterly, her whole body shaking, her tears soaking his tunic. Teg was furious at what he thought had happened but also felt deep compassion and love, knowing it would not alter how he felt for Elene. He felt a sense of relief, however, when she controlled her sobbing and told him of how Daniel had attacked her and how she'd fought with all her might and that Tara had been such a smart dog, she seemed to understand that she needed help and had tried to rescue her. She shuddered again as she described how the horse had stomped Daniels's head, killing him instantly.

"I started to try and make my way back, but it was getting dark, and I was shaken, and in the end, I just sort of passed out."

Relieved that she was not hurt, Teg helped Elene get to her feet. He stood holding her for a while and asked, puzzled. "What on earth were you doing all the way out here anyway? We've been worried sick about you."

"Teg", she whispered shyly, "I wanted to think of how I was going to tell you that well, that I didn't want to wait to let you know that I'll never want anyone else. I know we agreed that we would leave each other free for the moment, but I'm sorry, Teg, but I don't want to; please don't be angry."

"Angry? Just listen to me. From now on, you're mine, forever. I think even if you hadn't said what you've just said, I wouldn't let you be anyone else's anyway."

Happily, Elene raised her face to his, and their lips met in a long, lingering kiss. As they drew apart, smiling broadly, they became aware that the night around them was flickering strangely and turning; they saw Roger standing with the men who had been searching, flaming torches held high and huge grins on their faces.

"I think we'd better get going", Teg said, and they walked away, their arms around each other.

Chapter 38

There was a conspiratorial air, Teg felt, among the others who were to accompany him on his trip. He had seen Roger and Marcus in conversation with Mictor, looking over at him once or twice as though they were sharing some private joke. When he had tried to find out what it was about, Marcus had just laughed and said, "We don't want to spoil Mictor's surprise.".

Teg, Mictor and Roger were to travel in the leading vehicle. Marcus, with four handpicked men, would follow at a distance in one of the recently captured vehicles.

Apart from overnight camps or stops for discussions, they would remain apart so that in the event of any trouble, one vehicle could assist the other. It had been agreed that two weapons per vehicle would be taken from the recent haul to ensure sufficient protection was available for the settlement in the event of a raid. It was hoped that the precautions for the journey would prove unnecessary, but Teg wanted to take no chances.

They had said their goodbyes the previous night as their departure was scheduled for the first hint of light. Still, as the vehicles began to move in the gloomy, misty dawn, Teg glanced back and saw Elene standing just inside the house door, her expression forlorn. Like her, he did not like the thought of being apart for several days, but as they turned the first corner, leaving the house behind, he strove to put all thoughts of the settlement out of his mind and concentrate on the task ahead.

The hour's earliness and lack of sleep created a solemn atmosphere, and they didn't speak or move for the first hour. With the settlement's boundary behind them about ten minutes before they crossed a river by a bridge that Teg didn't recognize, he finally broke the silence.

"We seem to be going the wrong way," he said, puzzled, "I thought we'd have to head west to the town."

"No, we're going in the right direction," Mictor said, and Teg was sure he detected the old man and Roger sharing the same conspiratorial smirk.

He shrugged and sat back, letting his thoughts wander as the vehicle moved smoothly. The sun was dispersing the mist as they passed a few tattered remains of what country cottages had once been. The gardens that had once been tidy and well-kept were now a continuous wilderness of dogroses, vines, and brambles and creepers. What had once been a narrow country road still showed, vaguely shaped by the sloping verges and straight lines of trees marching down either side. However, the surface of the road had long been reclaimed by nature, and wild grasses and creepers made the way bumpy. Occasionally, the men would have to disembark to remove small trees that had fallen across their path. The trees formed an almost continual tunnel of green over their heads, and except for occasional sharp beams of sunlight dappling the trail ahead, the light was pleasantly subdued.

When they finally emerged from the tunnel of trees, the brightness of the sunlight was almost painful by contrast, and, for a while, they had to squint their eyes to see anything. After a further half mile or so, the road they had been following dropped away abruptly where the untended banks of a dam had collapsed, and over the years, water had eroded the hillside far below until the weight of the ground above had pressed down once too often. A large part of the hillside had slid away.

They waited for the following vehicle to catch them up and agreed on the route they would follow across the country. Teg didn't participate in the logistical discussions. He took the time to enjoy the clean country air and the beauty of the green rolling hills and plenteous trees. Climbing back into the vehicle seemed a shame, but they had to keep moving. So, Teg silently promised himself that one day, when it was safe, he would return here with Elene and explore the beautiful countryside.

At the thought of Elene, he became introspective again and hardly noticed the passing of time as he mused on how much he had come to love her. He was surprised at how quickly time had passed when they stopped for a meal, and he realised that the sun had already passed overhead and had begun its slow passage down the sky to the west. Teg was puzzled when, during the meal, Mictor mentioned that he expected to reach their objective by mid-morning the following day. Teg had expected the journey to town to take much longer. Still, he made no comment, admitting that he was utterly lost anyway. The temperature had climbed when they resumed their journey, and it became uncomfortable in the heat. They were passing across the face of substantial grassy hills that rose above a narrow verdant valley through which a sparkling ribbon of river flowed. Teg found himself imagining walking along the banks of the river with Elene, hand in hand, stopping occasionally to kiss or to sit on the grass and dangle their feet in the cold water.

"Teg, Teg!" He started to realise that his name was being called. Then, with astonishment, he saw that the vehicle was stopped under the shelter of a group of stout trees and that the daylight had gone to be replaced by the darkness of night. Befuddled, he stared in confusion until Roger's laugh intruded into his foggy mind.

Roger chortled, "You were sleeping, Teg, like a baby. We didn't have the heart to wake you."

There was a sudden rush of cold air as the vehicle's door opened, and Marcus's grinning face appeared.

"Hello Teg, I hear you've had quite a deep sleep. Well, if you want something to eat, it's about ready."

He felt embarrassed as he stepped into the cold night air to see that while he'd slept, the camp had been set up, firewood collected, a fire lit, and food had been prepared and cooked. He shivered with a combination of waking chill and the drop in temperature that had come with the darkness.

Mictor was seated by the fire, already eating, and smiled as Teg sat beside him, holding his hands out gratefully to the warmth.

"You certainly needed some sleep, Teg," Mictor said. "It will have done you the world of good. You've hardly stopped since you arrived at the settlement; taking a breather is not bad."

"I'm surprised I slept so well." A plate of food was handed to him, and he realised how hungry he was. When the meal was finished, there was some desultory talk. Still, the day's journey had clearly taken its toll and one by one, the men drifted away from the fire and were soon rolled up in bedding and fast asleep. Soon, only Teg and Mictor were left, and Teg, refreshed from his long sleep, excused himself and strolled through the trees. They were camped in a hollow with the trees uphill from them, and as he emerged, he could see the crest of the hill outlined against the clear night sky. The moon was nearly complete, and the sky was peppered with stars. As he came onto the crest of the hill, he stared in wonder at the moonlit landscape before him. The mountain sloped away beneath him long before it was crossed by a dark belt of trees. Beyond the trees, the ground continued to fall at another excellent distance before levelling into a flat-bottomed valley. Even with only the moonlight for illumination, it was clear that at some time in the distant past, the land had been cultivated as vast tracts of wild cereals held the darker colours of the grasses and weeds at bay.

On the valley's far side, the ground rose again in a series of great hilly ridges, and beyond them, it climbed higher and higher until sharply delineated by the moonlight, rocky peaks soared into the sky. Sitting atop the hill, Teg felt he could almost reach out and touch the stars and the moon. He sighed profoundly, thinking of all the life that had once teemed across it until the abuses of humanity led to the changes that had, all these generations later, led Teg to this hillside.

"It's a beautiful night, Teg, isn't it?"

The gentle voice didn't even startle Teg; it seemed to fit perfectly with the night. Mictor came and sat beside him, and for a while, he looked out over the valley and up into the star-spangled sky.

"I thought you would be asleep by now."

"Oh, when you're as old as me, Teg, you find that sleep comes when it's ready rather than when you tell it to. It won't be long before this old body of mine gets all the sleep it could ever want; I feel happier, not wasting too many hours left in me."

"Oh, don't talk like that."

"Would you miss me, do you think?" the old man asked, and there seemed to be a note of gentle pleading in his voice.

"Of course I would, I'd miss you very much."

If it was possible to look sad and happy at the same time, Mictor managed it as he sighed and said, "Thank you. That means a lot to me.

How I wish I had known you long ago when I still had the fire in me. I would have been happy to march with you, Teg."

"I still find it hard to accept that people can so readily put their trust in someone as young as me, Mictor. It's quite frightening sometimes."

"I can imagine how you feel, Teg, but as I have said before, your youth should not be used as a yardstick purely on its own. I know many foolish old men and many clever young men, so age does not always dictate the degree of wisdom. Even so, it is not just a question of cleverness or wisdom, of age or youth; it is something else altogether. Throughout history, there have been people who have stood out from others. However, a select few simply have some other special quality that sets them apart as leaders."

"What exactly are these qualities, Mictor?"

"Ah, and therein lies the question, Teg. One of the odd things about the qualities that make a leader is that many of the same qualities appear in both good and bad people. There must be intelligence, drive, determination, and a goal to aim toward. There is also a unique charisma, an air of leadership."

"If so many of these qualities are the same, how is it that some leaders are bad, and some are good?"

"Motivation more than anything, I suppose."

"Motivation?"

"Yes. A man can be motivated by many things, such as love, hate, greed, and a lust for power. Suppose his motivation is strong enough and he has the necessary qualities. In that case, it's surprising how easy it is for him to persuade people to follow him."

"Have you known many leaders, Mictor?"

"No, not personally."

"I didn't mean personally; I meant in what you've learned of history. It's just that we were taught practically nothing about the leaders of history in school. Only recently, Grandad told me about some of the great religions we'd been told nothing about during school."

Mictor looked at Teg with a strange expression, half regretful, half shameful.

"I fear I may have been responsible for some of that, Teg."

"How so?"

"When I tried to persuade the people of the town to overthrow The Forum, a lot of what I told them was based on history I'd learnt at school. I..."

"At school?" Teg interrupted," You had schools in the settlement?"

"No, Teg, you see, when I was your age, I lived in the town too."

"Really?" Teg asked, stunned by the revelation.

"Yes, Teg, you're the first person I've told that to. When I was a couple of years older than you are now, I made up my mind that the system under which I lived was evil and unjust. I wandered the country for two years before I stumbled across the settlement. It was in a different place then; we've had to move a couple of times because of increasing police raids. Anyway, the thing is, by the time I found the settlement, all the polish of being a Wayperson had worn off me. It was just as well because the feeling against the Waypeople was even worse back then."

"That explains a lot; it's often puzzled me."

"What's that?"

"I've often wondered how you took such an active part in the fight against The Forum if you didn't know what it was like to live under their rule."

"Well, now you know. Anyway, as I was saying, the things I tried to teach the people in the town were based very much on what I'd learned from the history books and what I'd seen happening in the cities. I'd been in the settlement for a few years then, so I'd had time to formulate ideas about freedom and life. The problem was, when my little revolution fell through, and I fled back to the settlement, one of the first things The Forum did was ban the teaching of history."

"How important is history, Mictor?"

"Very, very important. History is the record book of our world. It lets us see the good things that have happened, and it provides society with an opportunity to learn from the bad things that took place in the past. In an ideal world, we would learn much from history and avoid the mistakes of the past. Unfortunately, there'll always be those who think that they know better and feel they can avoid repeating the mistakes of the past even though they follow similar disastrous paths as the ones they attempt to emulate. Fortunately, many have learned from history, seen the good things, studied the excellent men, and sought to build upon them. Taken on balance, the propagation of the good stuff is in history's favour."

"What has history got to teach us, Mictor?"

"As I've said, there are those who will learn from history and those who will try to follow the historical lessons. There is also a class of people who would willfully misuse the lessons of history and, in doing so, commit many of the evils and repressions against the people that the same history will teach us must inevitably fail as long as the human mind and spirit live."

"You're saying that The Forum has distorted history, misused it?"

"Surely! Let there be no doubt in your mind, Teg, that the dreadful events of The Bad Times were inexcusable, catastrophic, and must never be repeated. There must have seemed much merit to the survivors of that awful time when men came forth preaching the doctrines that they did. They knew there had been overpopulation; they knew there had been a breakdown in law and order. There was evidence of environmental pollution all around them. It must have seemed so right when the new leaders proclaimed The Way to them.

The Way Teg. The way to a new life, the way to a clean new world, the way to lawfulness and moral righteousness. We should never judge our ancestors harshly for how they embraced the new creed. The horrors they had come through made them receptive to the leaders who showed them The Way to Salvation!"

"Then what went wrong?"

"It didn't go wrong, Teg; it was terrible. The new leaders who appeared were opportunists. They saw their chance to dominate and control people, to dictate the course of their lives, to use them by the exercise of their will. They saw the opportunity for power. Power Teg is history's greatest curse, the lust for power. A man who lusts for power soon loses his moral judgement, Teg. No matter the reason for his seeking power, once the lust is upon him, the power becomes all. Any means justify the end. The desire for power becomes a need, the need becomes an irresistible urge, the urge becomes lust, and the lust becomes uncontrollable.

Many men have sought power for many good reasons. However, when power, having been attained, becomes its own reason for existence, ideals fly out the window, good intentions crumble, and evil results. A wise man, Teg, said many years ago that power corrupts, and absolute power corrupts absolutely.

That is where The Way was doomed from the outset. The men of The Supreme Council, who truly dictate the ways of The Forum, devised The Way to attain and to hold on to power. They have managed it for many generations, but the lessons of history, Teg, teach us that the spirit of man, the inner need for freedom that lies deep within us all, whether we know it or not, must one day surface and the tyrants, the dictators the robbers of liberty will be overthrown. One day long ago, I thought I was the man who brought freedom to the town and, through that, to the people of the settlement. I was wrong, Teg; the time had not arrived then; I was not to be the one. I can only thank whatever fates control my destiny that I was still here to see your arrival because I believe that you, indeed, are the one who will bring the freedoms I failed to do."

Chapter 39

The old man sat silent as if exhausted from talking.

Teg felt embarrassed afresh by Mictor's laudatory words about him. What the old man had said had sent many thoughts flying around in Teg's mind, and he sought to pluck one out of the maelstrom.

"Have you ever tried to teach what history you know to the people of the settlement?"

Mictor looked at him in surprise, and then his brow wrinkled before he turned and confessed,

"No, Teg, I never have. When you ask me a question like that, it seems so obvious, yet I have never thought to do it. What a fool I have been."

Embarrassed at making the old man feel bad, Teg hastened to reassure him, "Oh, don't say it like that, Mictor; after all, you have given much of yourself to the people of the settlement, and in any case, surely it's not too late?"

"I am too old to teach Teg. The young are boisterous and demanding, and I tire easily. I fear I don't have the capacity anymore. How I regret that I did not do something about it before."

Anxious to divert his friend from his self-criticism, Teg asked him about the events he had set in motion all those years before.

"How did you set about infiltrating the town," he asked.

"I was so sure that the words I wished to convey to the people of the town would be received openly, and understood, that I had just begun going into the town and talking to them in the places where they gathered. I felt so sure I could convince them of the evil of the system under which they lived that I never thought of trying to be secretive. I was convinced that if the need arose, the people of the town who had heard what I had to say would rise in my defence. I was so naive; I find it hard to believe now. It was amazing that I wasn't turned into the police immediately. I really thought I would succeed when one of the townspeople involved in the communications service obtained some film of the great cities before The Bad Times and helped me to transmit it to the people of the town by feeding it into one of the relay stations."

"Grandad told me about that when I first heard your name! He said that such films were banned after that. I never realised that you were still alive or that I'd ever get to meet you. One thing has always puzzled me about that. Grandad said that the film showed just how crowded the cities were, how many people there were, and the incredible number of cars and other things that made it so hectic. Grandad also said that it was banned straight after you showed that film, which puzzled me. Surely the film showed just how bad the cities had got - why should they have banned them?"

"It's a good question, Teg, but strangely enough, The Forum was afraid of the very crowded nature of that city in the film. You see, despite the crowding, the people were happy. Some very old people were seen as being happy and active and accepted by the community, there were crippled people and retarded people, but they were all shown as having their place in the order of things. That is what The Supreme Council didn't want people to see. They feared that people might begin to question the extremism of The Way. That is why they started the purge. I had already left the town, but they feared I might have sown seeds in people's minds. Utilising the purge, they created fear throughout the town; they sowed mistrust, hatred, and uncertainty. They created evil, and then they purged the town of evil. By the time they had finished, all the townspeople could think was that The Forum had delivered them from evil.

It was vile Teg, it was insanity, it was murder, and I caused it."

Teg felt uncomfortable as he always did when Mictor suffered from the belief that he had been responsible for the tragic events that had followed his efforts. He tried to distract him,

"What happened to the men who went with you, Mictor?"

The old man looked at him for a long while, a strange expression on his face, and then he shook his head as though hardly able to believe what he was about to say, "There were no men Teg - I went alone."

"Alone? Do you mean you were the only one with no followers? That's incredible!"

"There were those in the settlement who listened to my words, but I don't believe they really understood my concept of freedom. Certainly, they merely thought I was mad when I suggested we go to the town. Perhaps that's why they've respected me so much ever since. I believe some ancient religion saw madness as a sign of divine intervention, and perhaps that's how the people of the settlement saw me."

Teg was lost for words; he found it hard to believe that what he had just heard was true, but the quiet, matter-of-fact way Mictor had told his story was more convincing than anything else. After a while, he said, "I had imagined that you had a band of men, that you would attack The Forum and take over by force if necessary."

"I must admit that I was thinking of taking a look at The Forum's defences with a view to possible future action should the need arise. What I found out was enough to convince me of the futility of my efforts and make me feel like an incompetent fool."

"What did you find out that was so dramatic?"

The old man turned to him and smiled his enigmatic smile.

"You will soon find out, Teg. At least you will avoid the fundamental error that I made. From the look of that sky, it won't be long before I can show you what I mean."

Teg turned to look in the direction the old man had indicated. It was surprising that the horizon was already growing light. Turning to Mictor, he said, "After what you've told me tonight, Mictor, promise me one thing."

"Ah, what's that Teg?"

"Whenever you talk of your future efforts against The Forum, please don't ever be ashamed that you failed."

The hospital was quieter than it had been since their arrival, and Jason and Elene had found plenty of time to sit in the sun and just talk. Many of the beds in the ward were empty now, and even the most seriously wounded had recovered sufficiently and been moved into minimum care. Elene missed Teg greatly, although he had only been gone since the previous morning. She was glad to have Jason to talk to and was particularly happy because he had made it clear how delighted he was that she and Teg were so close.

"Do you remember the days before you came here, Jason?"

"Often, my dear, often. Even now, I find it hard to believe such a life existed. I've become so used to being the master of my destiny, not serving some despotic ruler. It seems impossible to think that once upon a time, I would gladly have given up my life for no better reason than they told me to. How easily the human mind can be conditioned to unquestioning obedience."

"So, you've no regrets about coming here?"

"Regrets? My goodness, no! I have found such happiness here. How could I have regrets? Had I stayed in the town, I would be no more than a memory now. No, I bless the day or night that Teg came to me and told me of his thoughts. In any case, my dear girl, I must be glad we ran away. Otherwise, I would not have met my darling Margarita, and Teg would not have met you. I do not doubt that if he had not met you, Teg's life would have been much poorer, even if he hadn't known it."

He sighed with satisfaction, looking over his shoulder at the hospital behind him.

"I thought my life was finished before Teg convinced me otherwise, and now look at me. I'm working harder than ever, loving every minute of it, and I hope I'm doing some good work."

"You certainly are. You and Margarita have transformed this place."

"Hello, did I hear my name being taken in vain?"

They turned as Margarita approached, smiling. Elene was conscious of the immediate feeling of affection that flowed between the other two.

Grinning, she arose and said cheekily, "I'll leave you two lovebirds alone; who knows what mischief I might learn if I stay?

They laughed, standing hand in hand; they watched her walk away. But before she got too far, Jason called out, "Don't stray too far, Elene!"

He didn't have to explain his fears; she immediately understood what he meant, and a picture of a horse rearing flashed into her mind.

She waved to let him know she had heard him and wandered on. Her thoughts were of Teg, and she sighed as she wondered where he was right at that moment. She sat on a wall and daydreamed about what being Teg's wife would be like. She had seen Jason and Margarita's happiness and knew that she and Teg would be equally delighted. She was fearful of trying to hurry Teg, not wanting to spoil things by putting him under pressure. Still, at times like these, Elene wished he would ask her to marry him immediately, even if they were very young. She smiled and shook her head, telling herself not to be so foolish, and then tried to scream in alarm as suddenly a firm hand was clamped over her mouth. For a moment, she thought it must be a joke. Still, as she was lifted bodily by a strong arm that encircled her body, trapping her arms at her side, she was carried into the ruined houses. She knew for sure it was no joke now.

The man hurried, anxious to be away from the hospital area. Elene's heart was beating wildly, and her chest and throat hurt from not being able to breathe properly due to the hand that was still clamped over her mouth. It was a nightmarish journey as she was half-dragged, half-carried for what seemed an interminable time and then suddenly, she was dropped to the ground, and the man knelt, puffing, and panting from his exertions. She fought frantically to breathe and was only too happy to nod vigorously when he said, breathing heavily, "If you promise not to scream, I'll let go of your mouth."

As the hand was removed, she gulped in great gasping breaths of air into her lungs. She was trembling with the fear and shock of her abduction, and when the man dragged her to her feet and told her to get moving, she tottered forward on legs that trembled violently.

There was no respite for what seemed a very long time. Elene was pushed or pulled on a zig-zag route through streets and buildings she had never seen before, and she knew that even if she could break away, she would have no idea in what direction she should run. Then, suddenly, abruptly, they turned a corner and stopped. They were between two concrete structures that had withstood the ravages of time and provided a solid, well-concealed hiding place. Elenes's heart sank as she took in the lines of the police vehicle before being bundled inside.

As she lay breathing heavily and painfully on the floor of the vehicle, which shuddered as it began moving, she began to cry hot, bitter tears, and she whispered to herself, repeatedly,

"Goodbye Teg, goodbye, my love."

"We should be on the lookout from here," Mictor said.

"What exactly are we looking for?" Teg queried.

"A rock formation that resembles a group of birds sitting together. We'll have to leave the vehicle and walk around it."

It was fifteen minutes later that Roger suddenly pointed ahead and to the left. The hills rose sharply on this side, and about a mile ahead, a cluster of dark, smoothly rounded rocks stood out against the skyline. Teg smiled as he saw the resemblance to a group of plump birds clustered in conversation. Still, his smile faded as he looked around him and realised that although he was familiar with the hills around the town, none of the terrain here seemed familiar.

They parked in the shelter of a group of raggedy trees whose leafy branches dropped to the ground. Concealed thus, their vehicle was only visible if viewed very close up. As they walked out of the shelter of the trees, they could see their support vehicle being driven into a cluster of rocks lower down the hill and about a quarter of a mile back. Cautioning them to be alert, Mictor led Teg and Roger up the mountain, leaving the driver with the vehicle. The more Teg thought about it, the more he felt sure a mistake had been made. He was convinced that these hills were far from the town.

As they neared the cluster of rocks, Mictor cautioned them to keep below the skyline. He led them past the first two of the large, almost black stones and then stopped. Teg came to a halt beside him and looked between two rocks. The view was so unexpected that he blinked as if doubting his vision.

Below him, the hill swept down to yet more hills, which gradually bottomed out into a vast, flat valley. The valley stretched into the distance in either direction. It was extensive, the ground not beginning to slope again for about two miles. The land was obviously wealthy, as testified to by the variety and profusion of crops that grew in well-tended geometric patches throughout the valley. Beautiful, sumptuous-looking homes spoke of luxury and opulence even at a distance. There were superb gardens, miniature lakes, swimming pools, and sheltered pagodas set amongst ornamental trees. About a mile away, to the right, was a large lake on which small sailing craft bobbed indolently in the breeze. What caught Teg's attention most was half a mile to the left of the lake. A huge white building, its many faces and towers shimmering in the sunlight, dominated the valley. It reminded Teg of a fairy princess's palace he had seen in a book once. The land around the building looked superbly kept; even from this distance, it was immaculate.

The whole valley was luxurious and so magnificent that Teg found it hard to believe.

"What is it? What is this place?" he asked, stunned.

Mictor smiled, seeming to enjoy Teg's surprise, but his mouth had a bitter twist when he replied.

"The large white building you see there is The Forum."

"The Forum, but surely The Forum's in Town?"

"No, Teg. That's the very same mistake I made. I had always believed that the town was the whole thing, that it was not only ruled by The Forum but shared by them. How very wrong I was."

"But why, what does it all mean?"

"It's quite simple, really, Teg. What you see before us is the ultimate in elitism. When the new leaders emerged after The Bad Times and showed the people The Way, they were, in fact, setting themselves up as kings of a very select Kingdom."

"But how have they got away with it for so long? Surely, someone, somewhere, must have suspected what was going on or been disillusioned by such corruption. It seems unbelievable that it could have gone on for so long."

"Remember what I told you, Teg, about power corrupting. The people selected for The Forum, whether Acolytes or Attendees, are immediately in a privileged position. They have a lifestyle that is far more comfortable and far more sumptuous than the people of the town. They are close to the seat of power and may aspire to share that power. Ultimately, they are allowed to live the term of their natural lives. Few would be prepared to give all this up for the sake of an ideal that is not a part of their everyday thinking processes anyway. Generations of indoctrination have led the townspeople to believe in a certain way.

Those who aspire to become Forum see it as an elevation to a higher plane, and those who achieve it must naturally accept the advantages that accompany it as their due.

"But surely there must have been some who saw the evils in the system?"

"No doubt, Teg. You must remember, though, and this is something else that history teaches us: Any dictatorship that is not benevolent must, of necessity, maintain the means of ensuring that should any dissenters appear in their ranks, they can be quickly disposed of!"

"The police?"

"The police mainly, in the case of The Forum, yes. In generations past, it would have been armies or secret police. The sad thing is, Teg, that the very nature of the police in history has been a benevolent force for the protection of the people and the administration of the law. Since The Way was foisted on these unsuspecting people, the police have become an instrument of repression wielded by The Supreme Council in whatever way they choose."

"But why the town, Mictor? Why do they keep the town as it is? It's obviously a long way from here and where the council members live themselves. What is the benefit of continuing to rule the people so harshly?"

"They have the perfect system, Teg. By an ongoing system of misinformation and repression, they have created a place where the needs of The Forum can be met by unsuspecting people. By leading the people to believe that the lands beyond the town, The Wastelands as they are called, are still poisoned and poisonous, they remove any desire on the part of the people to move beyond the approved boundaries of the town. Should any more adventurous or intellectually aware citizen decide to make a move, then the full weight of the system is brought to bear to either capture or destroy the offenders; just witness what happened to you and your grandfather. In any case, the result for the offender will be death unless they are fortunate enough to escape. Rest assured, Teg, if either you, Jason or Elene had been captured, you would certainly have ended up dead."

"But why should they continue to restrict the population so much? Surely, there is ample space now for everyone. There would be no danger of overpopulation for hundreds of years, and with the lessons of The Bad Times, there could be much better environmental controls. It surely can't be necessary to kill people when they're sixty-five or restrict families to one child. I can't imagine that that has been necessary for many years."

"Teg," said Mictor sadly, "I doubt it was ever necessary, as you put it. Can't you see, though, that it was the perfect means by which The Forum retained its power? The town gave them the manufactured goods needed to maintain their luxurious lifestyle. The town provides them with the latest research benefits and the by-products. The town's children provide a pool from which they can select the most likely candidates to continue their dynasty. The use of the age restrictions, the family restrictions, and the use of the death penalty for criminals and cripples ensure that there will never be overpopulation in the town and therefore no need for a move outwards whereby the truth about the so-called Wastelands might be discovered."

The concept was so vast and audacious that Teg found it hard to visualise how the huge confidence trick could have gone on and on, unchallenged for generations. Then he thought of Jason, and he realised that if an intelligent, sensitive man like him could be fooled, what chance was there for a more ordinary person?

"The land down there," he said to Mictor, pointing to the cultivated crop interspersed among the luxury estates and homes littering the valley. "Who cultivates that? It must take a great deal of labour."

Mictor looked angry, the first time Teg had seen him so.

"The slaves Teg! the people of the settlement, captured by the police on numerous raids. They are our people down there, our people even up to third and fourth generations, and they are slaves."

"Third and fourth generations?"

"Yes, Teg, it's not a new phenomenon. The history I keep telling you about has many parallels to this. The nearest I could think of would be back in the eighteenth and nineteenth centuries when the negroes were brought from Africa to America and used as plantation slaves. They were bred like animals, and their children and their children's children were born into slavery. So, it is with the slaves down there, Teg. They have no rights at all, and they live the lives of animals."

"Do they never try to escape?"

"Oh, yes. In fact, there is one old man in the settlement who escaped many years ago but escape is rare. Look closely Teg. Look at the trees to the right of that lake."

Following Mictor's pointing finger, Teg could just discern the thin outline of a wire fence that ran behind the trees at the side of the lake. Now that he had located a part of the fence, he could follow its route along the valley as far as he could see. He could see it was high even though they were a long way from the wall. Even as he looked, he saw, emerging from behind, a slight rise in the ground, a patrol of three-armed policemen. Concentrating hard, he followed the fence line up and down for as long as he could see and picked out two other similar patrols.

"It would be interesting to know how many policemen they have altogether" Teg said, continuing to scan the valley. Finally, he shook his head in puzzlement and asked Mictor.

"There must be many slaves somewhere; where do they live?"

"You can't see from here, but if you look over there beyond those three big houses, you'll see how the ground rises, where those trees are. Well, behind those trees is the police complex, and beyond that are the slave quarters."

"How many slaves are there?"

"Who knows? This is the first time I've looked at this place for years. The last time I looked was at the beginning of the farming season, and at least two hundred people were working on the land. When you take into account the number of other things they probably have to do, you could almost certainly double that number."

"Um. It would help if we could get someone on the inside."

"On the inside?" Mictor asked, startled, "If anyone went in there and was caught, it would mean death for sure, and probably not a very pleasant death."

When Teg looked at him curiously, he went on.

"They have a man they call the Interrogator. His function supposedly is to question people suspected of crimes or working against The Forum. The truth of the matter is that he is, or at least he used to be, nothing more than a torturer. I assume he'd still be much the same; it would fit the pattern of terror and repression."

"It seems that the more I learn about this Forum, the eviler it becomes. The sooner it is overthrown, the better."

"So, you still intend to fight them, even after what you've learned today?"

"Even more so, what I've seen and heard today only makes me more determined. Good grief, Mictor, repression, torture, slavery, what more reason need there be?"

"Well, at least you have the advantage of knowing where The Forum is. Although I didn't know it at the time, my little foray into the town was doomed from the start. The seat of power was miles away."

"Yes, I can see that whatever happens in the town cannot be effective unless this place is taken. One other question, Mictor. There are obviously far more homes and facilities in this valley than The Forum would need. Who occupies the others?

"Family and friends, former members of The Forum, all sorts. It amounts to a very privileged elite who are quite content to live a life of luxury and idleness and to allow any amount of evil and repression to be practised by the rulers, provided their way of life is maintained. Why, there are children there who will never work a day in their lives and who regard slaves as mere animals; it's obscene."

"Well, you've certainly surprised me today. I can now see why you acted so funny before we started. It's given me a lot to think about. It's funny how little things start to fall into place. I can now understand why Elene was made to sleep throughout her journey to and from The Forum. They obviously don't want the location to become known in the town. Can you imagine what the townspeople would think if they could see this place?"

They remained for a while longer, looking at the paradise spread below them. His mention of Elene had restored Teg's longing to see her again, and finally, he turned away, saying to Mictor and Roger, "I'm glad I've seen this place and learned so much; now I know what we face. When we get back to the settlement, we've got a lot to do and talk about, so the sooner we get started, the better."

Taking one last look at the valley, they began to move away from the cluster of rocks and down the hill.

Chapter 40

Now that they were moving, Teg was anxious to return to the vehicle and be on his way home. He moved briskly across the face of the hill and had gone several yards before he realised he was leaving Mictor and Roger behind.

Embarrassed, he turned and started back towards them. Just as he neared them, he heard a shout of "look out" from above them. Spinning round, Teg saw a thin, scruffy man at the top of the hill running towards them. At the same time, he saw, behind and above the man, a policeman with his gun aimed towards Mictor. It all happened so quickly that Teg hardly had time to think. He heard the shout, saw the running man and the policeman and launched himself at Mictor and Roger all in the space of a second, and as he crashed to the ground, taking the other two with him, he heard the distinct whine of a bullet passing over them and the powerful crack as it thudded in the rock-strewn ground beyond them.

Rolling over, Teg had time to see the policeman turn his gun on the running man. A bullet hit him, and with a shriek of pain, he staggered, fell, and rolled to a stop against a tangled growth of brambles. Another policeman appeared over the hill behind the first one, and both were about to turn their attention back to Teg and his companions when one of the policemen suddenly staggered sideways and fell. The crack of the shot that had felled him seemed to come afterwards, but it was enough for the second policeman to dive to the ground.

Taking advantage of the diversion, Teg and Roger helped Mictor to his feet and began running for their vehicle's cover. Diving through sheltering trees, they bundled Mictor inside the car and slammed the door. Running back to the trees and sheltering behind their trunks, Teg and Roger watched with appreciation as Marcus and his men moved with discipline, spreading out and surrounding the policeman who had dived to the ground and a third one who had joined him. It was all over, surprisingly quickly.

Realising they were surrounded, the two policemen tried to make a run for it. A well-aimed shot brought the first one down, and the other one threw down his gun and held his hands in the air. Teg turned his head away as Marcus walked to within four paces of the policeman and shot him dead. The men with Marcus quickly gathered the weapons from the dead men and loped down the hill to where Teg and Roger had emerged from the trees. Marcus, as if sensing Teg's possible disapproval of his action in executing the policeman, said simply, "It's the only way, Teg; we mustn't jeopardise ourselves now. If the positions had been reversed, he would have thought nothing of killing us or handing us over to the torturer, so don't waste any sympathy on him."

Teg nodded his head slowly, seeing the other man's logic, "I understand, Marcus," he said, "You and your men did marvelously; your training has made soldiers of them".

"Thanks Teg. We ought to be going, don't you think?"

"What about the man who warned us? Where did he come from?"

"I haven't a clue, Teg; I'm just glad he did. The poor fellow paid dearly for helping us."

"Is he definitely dead?"

"I'm not sure, although I would have thought that he would have been unlikely to survive at that range."

"Well, I'd like to find out. If he should still be alive, I'd hate to think we'd just left him."

"Fair enough, but we'd better hurry."

They loped across the hill and up to where the man had fallen. To their surprise, he was on his hands and knees and, although badly wounded in the shoulder, was trying to crawl into the shelter of the brambles, probably trying to hide before any more police came. He was startled when Marcus fell to his knees beside him and took hold of his uninjured shoulder. The man's face was gaunt, almost starved. His clothes were dirty and unkempt, and his beard was matted and rough. His pain-filled eyes showed fear as Marcus gently turned him around and then filled with tears of relief when he saw that they were not the police.

"Take it easy", said Marcus. "We'll bring a vehicle over."

"Bring mine" commanded Teg, staring down at the man "I want him to travel with me."

Hearing Teg's voice, the man blinked and raised his head, focusing on Teg's face. He grinned weakly and said, in a tired voice, "Hello Teg, I wondered if I'd ever see you again."

"I'm glad you did, Teacher Johansen; you probably saved our lives."

"Well, I'm glad that I've made some amends for the past. I can die a bit happier now."

"Who says you're going to die" Teg began but stopped when he saw that the teacher had fainted.

The return journey was slow as the driver carefully took the vehicle over any obstacles or uneven ground. Nonetheless, it was clear that the teacher was suffering greatly. They had managed to staunch the bleeding from his badly damaged shoulder, but his blood loss, combined with his already weak state, had left him in a severe condition.

Teg, having overcome his astonishment at discovering this unexpected link with his past, told Mictor and Roger all about the teacher, and Mictor seemed to have taken it upon himself to nurse the wounded man.

When they made camp for the night, they chose a spot well sheltered from the cool night air and close to a clear, fast stream that flashed around and across rocks and sand with an almost musical tinkling.

The cessation of movement benefitted the teacher, and he soon fell into a deep sleep. At first, he moaned and shivered feverishly, but Mictor patiently moved back and forth with cool water from the stream and bathed his wounds and his forehead until, gradually, he quietened down and slept quite peacefully.

Teg only dozed fitfully through the night, and by the time the sky was lightening, he had already risen and gone to the stream to wash in the cold, refreshing water. Turning away, he saw that Mictor had sat up and was adjusting the temporary dressing on the teacher's wound. Teg moved over to sit beside Mictor and was welcomed with a weak smile by the teacher. He was pale and clearly still weak, but he seemed in better spirits than the previous night. Seeing that he was awake, Teg asked him how he felt.

"It's dreadful, but at least I'm alive. How long that will be, though, I don't know."

"You'll be alright. Don't worry; we'll get you back to the settlement and get you some proper treatment."

"The settlement?"

Teg briefly outlined the events that had occurred since he and Jason fled the town. He described how they had found the settlement and were now part of it.

"How I envy you", Teacher Johansen sighed. "Since I fled the town, I have been so lonely, I have often wondered why I've kept going. More than once, I've felt like surrendering to the police, just walking out of hiding and giving myself up. Somehow, though, I just felt that I must go on."

"And how right you were," said Mictor, clearly moved by the teacher's story.

"You're among friends now, and you'll find that life is still worth living. Teg is our leader now, and he has already created a new spirit in the settlement. He has raised an army, and it won't be long before they are ready to strike against the evil Forum. You have arrived among us in good time, my friend."

Teacher Johansen looked up at the old man, and there were tears in his eyes as he shook his head and spoke sadly, "How good it is to have someone call me friend, but I fear you wasting your time with me. I have never been a man who would be able to fight, and he looked down at his shattered shoulder, "I am even less able now. I fear I am of no use to you."

He turned his head to the side, away from Teg and Mictor, but they could still see the tears welling out of his eyes. Mictor shook his head in pity, and then, glancing at Teg and then back to the teacher, he smiled and, leaning over, gently patting the crying man on the shoulder, he said,

"You are wrong, my friend; we have much use for you. I begin to see how fortuitous your arrival really is. What do you think, Teg?"

Teg stared at the old man, puzzled, and suddenly, it dawned on him. He grinned and nodded.

"Yes, I see it now. If you are willing, Teacher Johansen, I think you and Mictor will spend a lot of time together. When he has told you all he knows, we will finally have someone to teach our children the true history of our world. We will even build you a school. How does that appeal to you?"

Too moved to say anything, the teacher merely smiled and nodded.

When they arrived back at the settlement, Teg and his party drove immediately to the hospital to deliver Teacher Johansen into Jason's care. The moment he stepped out of the vehicle and turned to greet Jason and Margarita, who came hurrying out of the hospital, Teg knew something was very wrong.

Margarita was obviously crying, and Jason looked haggard and drawn as though he hadn't slept for days. Immediately, Teg noticed that Elene wasn't with them and felt the icy clutch of fear in his heart, as he instinctively knew something had happened to her.

"What is it? Where's Elene? Something happened to her, hasn't it."

Jason nodded miserably.

"Teg, she's been kidnapped."

"Kidnapped, by who?"

"There's a message for you in Margarita's office. We didn't see anything; all we knew was that when Elene failed to return, we looked for her and found a message addressed to you, Teg."

"Addressed to me?"

"Yes, Teg, they know you're here."

"They?"

"The police Teg. One of the men reported seeing a police vehicle near the outskirts of the settlement about an hour after Elene disappeared."

"Can you be sure there's a connection?"

"The note, Teg, is written on the same type of paper the police use."

"I must see it right away" He began to move away then, remembering, stopped abruptly and, gesturing to the vehicle, said, "The day is full of surprises, Grandad. Do you remember me talking about Teacher Johansen? He's in there; he's quite badly hurt. Could you give him your best care? He saved our lives yesterday."

With that, Teg strode into the hospital. The few patients in the ward who would normally have greeted him cheerfully merely looked sympathetic as he strode worriedly past.

The message was on a rolled sheet of paper tied with a flat strip of bright yellow material that had been nailed to a tree near the hospital. The paper lay in the middle of the desk, and Teg sat down and stared at it for a while as if expecting it to burst into flames.

Finally, he slowly reached out and unrolled it. The message was straightforward and to the point.

Teg,

We have the girl; we know what she means to you. We do not wish to harm her. You must come alone, unarmed. You will light a fire on top of the hospital. When we see the smoke, we will light a fire to show you where to come. Remember, you must come alone.

As he stared at the note, Teg realised Jason was standing at the small office door.

"Come in, Grandad"

"I'm so sorry, Teg. I wouldn't have had this happen for the world. I love that girl as though she were my own daughter, and I know how much she means to you. I've taken no action for fear that we could end up jeopardising her life."

"I'm glad, grandad. That was right. Of course, I'll have to go."

"I understand how you feel, Teg, but you realise that all you may achieve is to put yourself and Elene in their hands. Once they have you both, it would be simple enough for them to lure me into their clutches by threatening you both."

"But I must go to her grandad" Teg protested, even though he saw the logic of what Jason said.

"I understand, Teg; when will you go?"

"Right away, there are still several hours of daylight left; it has to be right away."

He arose and almost ran out of the hospital. He summoned a concerned Roger and instructed him to light a fire on the hospital's roof. Immediately Roger gave the word, half a dozen men began frantically preparing the fire. They dragged a sheet of broken concrete, cracked and held together by the rusting reinforcing steel, to the roof. Hauling this to the roof, they built a fire upon it, not wanting to risk damaging the roof itself.

Once enough material had been piled, they set light to it. Once it was burning well, they began to add grass, green twigs, and leaves so that it began to smoke fiercely. At first, a grey canopy of smoke hovered over the fire and then began to spread across the roof, but then a sudden updraught caught at the fire, and a thin spiral of smoke coiled into the air.

As if tied to it by invisible strings, more smoke began to eddy around the fire, then leap up to thicken the grey stream that trickled into the air. To the watchers, it seemed maddeningly slow. Still, the smoke gradually thickened and began to push into the air more urgently. When the column of smoke was well established, soaring into the sky above their heads, the men on the roof began to scan the horizon in all directions. Five, ten, fifteen minutes passed with no sign, and then suddenly, one of the men shouted and pointed.

Across the derelict city, about a mile away in a straight line, stood the pretty intact remains of what had once been a seven-story office block. From the roof of the building, a barely discernible wisp of grey smoke curled into the air. They weren't sure if they imagined things at that distance as the smoke seemed to come and go against the cloud-speckled sky. And then, suddenly, the smoke-blackened and belched high into the sky as something was added to the fire. The two columns of smoke streamed into the air as the watchers stood on the roof. Still, Teg was already running along the street below, his form diminishing as he raced into the distance. Teg cursed at every change of direction he had to make, wanting to fly straight to where Elene was. Each time he turned a corner, he feared he would not regain sight of the deserted building and its plume of smoke. And then Teg turned a corner, and straight ahead was the building. He stopped, breathing heavily from his non-stop run. He stared up at the building directly at the end of the road on which he stood. Looking up, he could not see the more intense lower part of the column of smoke; from where he stood, it looked almost as though the whole roof was giving off a blanket of smoke.

Slowly, he began to walk down the quiet rubble-strewn street. As his breathing slowed, he became aware of his heart beating furiously, and he knew it was not just from his exertions. He was desperately afraid for Elene, and he knew, with certainty, that if he had lost her, his life would mean nothing to him anymore.

Chapter 41

Suddenly, he froze. From behind him, on the left side of the street, he had heard the crunch of broken glass underfoot. He stood still, his spine-tingling, and clenched his teeth as clearly across the road came the sound of glass being walked upon. Then, the footsteps were on the pavement, and he knew someone was there.

"Teg?"

He whirled and stared, unbelieving, as Elene walked slowly towards him. Confused and suspicious, he looked around frantically, but suddenly, Elene was running and was in his arms crying as he hugged her and murmured over and over, "Oh Elene, my love, my love."

They kissed, happily though tearfully and then he hugged her again, shaking with relief.

"It's alright, Teg. It's alright," she murmured. "It had to be this way; you'll see."

Remembering where and why he was there, he looked around curiously but saw no one. "What do you mean? What had to be this way? What's going on?"

"They are friends, Teg, and they've brought another girl with them, who was in the same trouble as me."

"Who are they?"

"Come with me, Teg, and I'll show you, but promise me, you won't harm them."

"But these are people who kidnapped you."

Elene took Tegs hands. "Do you trust me, Teg?"

"Of course I do."

"Good; all I ask is that you take the time to listen and understand everything that has happened. Follow me."

Elene led him to the opening from which she had appeared. They passed through the opening into a large square that had once been grassed and planted with shrubs and trees but was now an overgrown wilderness. She led him through a greenery tunnel and into the square's centre. They walked between shrubs and trees and came to a clearing. Teg stopped abruptly as he saw the police vehicle parked under a tree. He turned, startled, as a policeman stepped from behind a bush, holding a young girl by the hand. The girl smiled happily when she saw Elene and ran to her, clasping her hand as she looked curiously up at Teg.

"Teg, this is policeman Valdor, and this is Melinda."

As policeman Valdor approached and held out his hand, Teg glanced at Elene, but she just smiled encouragingly. Slowly, he held his hand out and shook the officers' hand.

"I'm honoured to meet you. I bring you greetings from your friends in The Forum."

"My friends in The Forum?" Teg said, astounded, dropping the policeman's hand and stepping back quickly.

"Teg, don't you see how marvellous it is. You've got friends inside The Forum who will help you."

"Why should you want to help me? How do I know this isn't some kind of trick?"

The policeman looked at Teg with an expression that suddenly made him uncomfortable.

"Come with me, Teg, and I'll show you."

Teg knelt white-faced beside policeman Tanner. He was lying under the shelter of a wild rose bush that filled the air with its sweet scent. When policeman Valdor introduced his friend and explained his condition, Teg could only stare at him for a long while before he dared speak. Still, when he did try, he found it challenging.

"How could anyone do such a thing... ? his voice broke as he imagined the suffering that the policeman had endured at the hands of Garon. Without warning, a tear slid down Teg's cheek and dropped onto the man's hand.

"1... I'm sorry," Teg stammered, turning his head away. Then he looked back down at the sick man.

"I find it hard to believe that you can feel such compassion for a man you don't even know and one who has been your enemy. I feel shame now to think I ever served those heartless evil men of The Forum; I don't deserve your pity."

Teg stood up suddenly and, turning to the policeman, Valdor commanded, "Get him into the vehicle; we must immediately return him to the hospital. He'll be in the best possible care there, and you can tell us all about yourself."

Teg saw Elene grinning as the policeman rushed to obey his command. He smiled wryly as he realised he could already issue orders as though he'd been doing it all his life.

The journey back to the hospital was slow because of the sick man's fragility and because Teg and Elene rode back on top of the vehicle. Teg is anxious that his men should be able to see that he was unharmed and that they shouldn't open fire on them.

There were cheers as they turned the corner by the hospital. Teg saw that the men he had left behind had been joined by others ready to sally forth in defence of their leader. He grinned and waved at them as he helped Elene down and then turned as cheers faded and ugly murmurings took their place. A very apprehensive-looking policeman, Valdor, had climbed out of the vehicle. At the sight of his uniform, the men began to close in, their faces hostile and weapons drawn.

"That's enough!" Teg snapped out angrily and was gratified when the men immediately came to a stop.

"Do you believe this man would be here if he was our enemy? He is here to help us. His coming here is our best hope of successfully defeating our enemies."

The men were curious now and were looking at the policeman with interest.

Teg whispered something to him, and when he nodded, he turned back to the assembled men.

"It's not my wish to make a sideshow out of anybody, but I want you to see something. This gentleman is policeman Valdor, and the reason he is willing to help us is inside this vehicle. Not long ago, policeman Valdor's friend was a fit and healthy man. For no other reason than that he had information that one of The Supreme Council members wanted, he was tortured. Tortured badly.

When you consider this policeman, think about his willingness to provide freely what information he had and how unnecessary the ensuing torture upon him was. Then, my friends, you will know the depths to which The Forum has sunk. When you see Policeman Tanner, you will understand why we must fight the evil system that acts inhumanly. Whatever help we can obtain from the heart of The Forum will be of inestimable value, and I ask you to remember here: that these two men are our allies."

Signalling to one of the watching men to assist Policeman Valdor, Teg stood back whilst they gently lifted Policeman Tanner from the vehicle. There wasn't a sound from the men as the sick man was carried past. As Teg scanned the men's faces, he could see how deeply they had been affected. As the trio disappeared into the hospital, the men looked at each other mutely, their eyes reflecting their horror at the thoughts of the agony that Tanner must have undergone.

Their attention was diverted when Elene approached the vehicle and called Melinda, who had stayed with the sick man, to come out. Although only two years younger than Elene, Melinda appeared younger. As she stood there shyly, the men responded to her with smiles, happy to have something to take their minds off the horror they had just witnessed. When she smiled shyly back at them, her eyes big and brown, Teg understood Melinda had already been accepted into the community.

He caught their attention as he said, "This is Melinda. Melinda is thirteen years old and was an Acolyte at The Forum. The reason she is here now is that she fled to avoid the unwelcome attentions of a member of The Supreme Council."

"You don't mean…" asked one of the men incredulously.

"Yes, that's exactly what I mean. Here, gentlemen is another reason why we must be determined to fight for ultimate victory!"

The men were clearly angry at what Teg had told them and looked with sympathy at Melinda. One of the men, Thomas, a big, gentle bearded man known to them all for his happy family and his love of children, stepped forward and said to Teg, "The child will need somewhere to stay; I have three daughters and two sons, but we can make room for another if she wants to live with us. She won't lack company in our home."

Before Teg could say anything, Melinda stepped forward and looked up at the big man in amazement.

"Did you say you had three daughters and two sons?"

Not understanding her confusion, the big man nodded happily, "Yes, yes, but don't worry, there'll be plenty of room for a little girl like you."

"I don't think that's quite what Melinda is questioning, Thomas," said Teg, moving forward and kneeling beside Melinda.

"It is different here. There is no one to say you can have only one child in a family. Many families have more than one child. When they are boys, they are called brothers; when they are girls, they are called sisters."

The big man now understood Melinda's confusion, and there was compassion in his eyes as he held out his hand and said, "Come with me, Melinda, and you'll find out what it's like to have your own brothers and sisters."

They all watched as the big man and the young girl walked away hand in hand. One of the men said quietly, "How many more there are like her?"

"The sooner we find out and set them free, the better!" said another.

The men dispersed with renewed determination on their faces.

When Teg and Elene entered the hospital, they found Policeman Tanner in bed. Policeman Valdor was sitting and talking to him. Jason and Margarita, having welcomed their newest patient, were back at the bed in which Teacher Johansen lay. As the young couple approached, they straightened their stance with smiles on their tired faces, and their hugs were compounded of both affection and relief.

"Thank God. you're safe!" Jason said, "Your policeman friend has told us about your adventure. I understand we have another girl recruited for the settlement."

"Yes, the poor girl's bewildered, but I think she'll be happy. She's gone with Thomas to his home. With his brood, she'll soon settle in." He lowered his voice now and asked, "How's Johansen?"

"Very weak and undernourished but surprisingly tough; I think he'll be fine given time."

"That's good. I haven't had a chance yet to ask him how he got where he was, but thank heavens for him!"

"That's for sure. What do you think having an insider at The Forum will mean?" Jason nodded towards the policemen.

"If what Valdor says is true, it's not just him. He tells me that two senior Attendants are just waiting for a chance to overthrow The Supreme Council. Not because they want to take their place but simply because they're sick of the system. I'll be having a long chat with Valdor then I will call a meeting so we can decide on the best approach. I'd like you to attend the meeting, Grandad, if you don't mind."

"Mind? Of course, I don't mind. Like this community, I completely support your direction, Teg and will be wherever you tell me to be."

Jason smiled as he said it, but Teg felt odd at the knowledge that his grandfather genuinely meant what he said.

Policeman Valdor needed to return to his duties as soon as possible, so after spending a couple of hours talking to him, Teg left him to rest. He asked Roger to summon select people to attend the meeting at Mictor's house that night. Having organised this, Teg wandered back to the hospital, and his face broke into a broad smile as Elene came running out the door to greet him. He held her close for a moment, feeling deep contentment.

"Can you get away for a while?"

"Yes. They're not expecting me back for ages."

They walked hand in hand, not speaking. Occasionally, they would look at each other and smile or stop and kiss. They came to what had once been a patio at the rear of a tall building. The concrete was now pitted and cracked; grass and weeds had made their homes all over it. Teg and Elene sat on a thick patch of grass at the very edge of the patio with their legs dangling over the five-foot drop to a sloping grassy bank that gave way to a rubble-strewn hill. From where they sat, they looked out over the roofs of hundreds of low buildings of varying heights and sizes interspersed with many much taller buildings, some looking as though they were about to fall. Other buildings looked like they needed only glass in the windows to prepare them for occupation. After a certain distance, the damaged condition of many of the buildings was difficult to discern. The city in the vast valley of buildings spread out below them, looking as though it needed only traffic and people to make it as it was long ago. It was an eerie sight, and Elene shuddered as she tried to imagine how it had been in the last days of The Bad Times.

Seeing her shiver, Teg put his arm around her shoulders and pulled her close. She laid her head against him and asked softly, "Do you think it will ever come alive again, Teg?"

"If it does, it will be a long time from now, and one thing is sure: we won't be around to see this city returned to what it once was. When you think of how long it took man to reach the development stage necessary to build cities like this one and the machines and equipment that became commonplace, you wonder how it was ever allowed to come to this. Mictor summed it up best. He says it was mainly due to greed. The greed that was so intense it drove out any consideration for others. He says that greed fed on itself until it dominated the people who practised it, and then they became blind to what they were doing. We can only hope that the same mistakes are never repeated."

"Doesn't it make you feel creepy to think that you could be the one to start its life once again?"

"I'd never really thought of it like that; all I've considered is getting rid of a corrupt system."

"There must be some way of ensuring it doesn't happen again."

"The only way to ensure this would be through coercion, whether through law or by other means. The danger is that it can get out of hand, and the cure becomes worse than the disease. The crazy thing is that if you didn't know how bad and evil The Forum is, you'd think it was marvellous if you only knew what its apparent aims are."

"The answer must be education; that's the only way, Teg."

"Yes, but one of the great problems we currently have is that educational material is not permitted in town schools, and teachers are not allowed to discuss history in the classroom. Society needs to learn from the mistakes of the past, and tearing down this barrier to history lessons is the only way to avoid mistakes continuing or repeating. Unfortunately, The Supreme Council strictly controls and enforces the current rules.

When we've managed to get rid of them, I'm hoping one of the first things we can do is start teaching the true history of the world so that we can begin to make people understand the value of learning the lessons from history. I remember how teacher Johansen reacted when I asked him awkward questions. I always sensed he wanted to tell me some of the truths he was aware of, but like everybody else, he was too scared. Despite everything, he was a good teacher, and it's terrific that he has turned up. When he's finished learning all he can from Mictor, he'll be able to pass the history lessons on to interested others, and they can spread them on and on."

"Like throwing a stone in the water and seeing the outward flowing ripples, right?"

"Exactly."

"Do you ever feel frightened that you seem to have been chosen as the one to throw that stone, Teg?"

"Frightened? No, not frightened. I am trying to figure out what the right word is. Surprised? Humbled? I don't know. One thing I can say, though, is that if I am to be the one to lead, then I intend to do my best."

"I know you will, Teg. What about us?"

She said this last quickly as though hoping to slip it in unseen, uncertain of his reaction. The sudden change of direction took Teg by surprise, and he stared at her for a moment before asking, "Us? What about us?"

"What happens to us, Teg, you and me? I know we said we wouldn't firmly commit yet, but after the last few days, I don't want it to be this way anymore. As far as I'm concerned, you're the only one I'll ever love. I'm not asking you to commit to me Teg, I just want you to know how I feel."

Elene finished in a shaky voice and, in the ensuing silence, looked down at her feet as she swung them backwards and forwards. Teg glanced sideways at her and grinned slightly, then trying to sound off-hand and casual, but spoiling the effect with a tremor in his voice, he said, "Well, I guess we'll have to get married then."

Still looking down, Elene nodded absently, still swinging her feet. Teg frowned with mixed disappointment and surprise at her reaction but then grinned. Suddenly, her feet clattered to a stop against the concrete, and she turned her head, looking up at him.

"What did you say?"

"I said we ought to be getting back."

"That's not what you said, is it?"

"What else?" said Teg, struggling not to laugh, but then he saw that she believed him and was near to tears, so reaching for her hand, he said softly, "I said, will you marry me?"

"Oh Teg, oh Teg" She was crying now, tears of happiness sparkling on her cheeks like jewels as she threw herself into his arms. Elene dried her tears, but she couldn't stop grinning. Teg grinned back, and as their grins met, they became more enormous grins that grew into laughter. Teg jumped up and pulled her to her feet. They began to run and skip along the road, laughing madly. Finally, out of breath, they stopped and stared at each other; suddenly, serious Teg pulled her close and kissed her.

"I love you, Elene, I really do."

"Oh Teg, I do love you too."

Suddenly, she looked concerned and asked worriedly, "Will we be able to get married, Teg? After all, we are very young?"

"You have to remember, there are no rules, my love. In any case, I don't think we're too young. If we're realistic, we must face the fact that things could go wrong, and I could end up getting killed. If I'm old enough to get killed, then I'm old enough to get married."

"Oh, don't talk about getting killed, Teg; I couldn't bear it; I just couldn't."

"I certainly don't intend to get killed. However, the thing to remember is that at least we will have known true love, which must be worth something. I'm sure that, whether now or in fifty years, if one of us loses the other, we will be sad and miss them. That is so much better than the cold way people of the town accept the deliberate death of their partners; it's almost as though a familiar piece of furniture has been thrown out because it's no longer fashionable."

"You have a marvellous way of putting things, Teg. I might enjoy being married to you."

"You think you might? Well, that's lucky, he broke off, laughing, as she grinned impishly up at him. He put his arm around her, and they returned to the hospital. Looking down affectionately at her, he said, "There's another good reason why we can get married, of course."

"What's that?"

"I'm the leader; who can stop me?"

Chapter 42

"I haven't seen you for a while, Antony; I'm disappointed you've had nothing to tell me."

"I wish I had something, Second President. I would be only too pleased to serve you."

"Well, I think I know of a way you can."

"You do, sir?"

"Yes, you could find out from one of the other Attendants about his trip to the town. Do you remember that? The Third President had sent him there."

"Yes, Second President, I remember. His name was James, the head of the supplies department."

"That's the one. Now, we can get at the Third President through this man."

"You can, sir?"

"Yes, I'm pretty sure that the Third President has some hold over this Attendant, James, and I want you to find out what it is. If David can apply pressure to this man, I most certainly will be able to use my own."

"Yes, Second President. With respect, sir, may I ask how that will help you?"

"James is a very respected Attendant. When he testifies against the Third President, his testimony will carry a lot of weight."

"Testifies about what, Second President?"

"Oh, we'll think of something, never fear."

"What if he refuses to cooperate?"

"Then he'll have to be persuaded; I'm sure the Interrogator would find some means of making him testify."

"What if I can't find out what the Third President has as a hold over James, sir?"

"Then I would have to inform the Third President about you and the delectable Carla, Antony. I'm sure you wouldn't want that, now, would you?"

It was much later that day before Antony managed to spend time with James and apprise him of his conversation with Delmo. They had become so used to their idea of planning to overthrow The Forum that all thoughts of their earlier involvement with the two Supreme Council members had been pushed far back in their minds, even though it had triggered their rebellion. They had felt great triumph at spiriting away both policeman Tanner and the girl, Melinda. Having the assistance of another policeman was of inestimable value, and they had the makings of a revolutionary team, particularly since learning about the settlement in The Wastelands from the boy Daniel.

"What on earth are we going to do, James?" asked Antony worriedly.

"At this time, I haven't a clue. We must try and think of some way of at least stalling matters."

"I'm afraid that Delmo will not be all that patient James. He hoped to get rid of David months ago and wasn't happy when that fizzled out."

"Yes, the Third Presidents the same. When he got the information that I'd brought him from town and that Garon extracted from that poor wretch Tanner, he was hoping to find some way of using it to get rid of the Second President. The trouble was he waited so long, trying to work out the best way of approaching the matter, that his star witnesses upped and disappeared."

They both grinned as they recalled the consternation in The Forum when Tanner's disappearance had been known. It had been amusing to watch Delmo, who knew nothing of the prisoner, trying to find out who he was. Seeing David trying to act as though he knew nothing of the prisoner had been dually amusing. The only saving grace that Garon had was that he gave equal loyalty to all members of The Supreme Council, even the President, and would not reveal how the policeman had come to be in his cells except to say he was an enemy of The Forum. In this way, Garon assured himself of the patronage of all the Presidents, no matter which way any power struggle might sway.

"We're going to have to think of some way of accelerating the fight," said James.

"That's easier said than done. Sometimes, I worry we are in over our heads. We're hardly the stuff of revolutionaries, are we?"

"I don't mind admitting I get scared sometimes thinking about what we've done and what we're planning to do."

"You're not alone there, Antony. I get scared as well, you know. All I need to do is remember Tanner's condition and the fear in little Melinda's eyes. I think about the way innocent people were killed just to mislead the President, and I remember yet another girl who fled because of the corruptness of one of The Supreme Council. I don't know what the stuff that revolutionaries are made of is, but I do know that I would rather die now than just walk away from what I've learned. We must also remember that if this power struggle between Delmo and David really boils up, we may not be safe anyway."

"I don't want you to think I'm giving up, James; it's just that when you think we're hoping to overthrow a system that's existed for many generations, it seems, I don't know... presumptious somehow. I suppose what hasn't helped is how security has stepped up since the President blew his top. You get that feeling that you could be arrested anytime for no reason."

"That's part of why The Forum has ruled for so long. Fear is one of the main weapons in The Supreme Council's arsenal. We just have to keep our cool and hope."

They spun around and stared at the door as it reverberated to loud, urgent knocking. Since security had been stepped up and suspicion had become rife, they had locked the door whenever they met to discuss their plans.

The knocking came again, more urgent. James looked at Antony with a sudden look of hopelessness and saw the same expression on his companion's face. As the knocking came again, he shrugged and sauntered to the door. Unlocking it, he turned the handle and opened it. Immediately, the door was pushed inwards, and he reeled back, the policeman's uniform registering on his mind as he sought not to fall over anything. There were two of them, and as the door was slammed shut, they stood with their backs against the wall, breathing heavily. Antony, as if seeking to reassure his friend, had rushed to James' side, and they stood together as the policemen removed their helmets. The first one was very young, with a robust and pleasant face. They stared incredulously as the second policeman removed his helmet, revealing himself as policeman Valdor.

Stunned, they turned to the first man as he said.

"Good evening, my name is Teg."

"Married? But you're so young!"

Jason had exclaimed when Teg and Elene had returned to the hospital and happily told them of their decision.

"Jason," Margarita said, smiling wryly. "In a few hours, this young man will be chairing a meeting to plot the overthrow of The Forum. He'll be doing it in his capacity as leader of this settlement. Since he was here, he has raised an army, fought in battle, inspired the people to have a sense of confidence and unity I wouldn't have thought possible and displayed maturity and wisdom that even the master acknowledges. Elene has stood by his side and has been through adventures that would have unhinged the mind of a lesser person. She has worked in this hospital with dedication and the capacity to learn, which has endeared her to all the patients who have been through here. Now, I would hardly call these two a couple of innocent kids, would you?"

Teg and Elene listened to the exchange with amusement, knowing that they would marry regardless of the outcome. They grinned when Jason raised his hands in mock terror at Margarita's words and cringed back, saying. "I surrender, I surrender, anything you say, my love."

He turned to the young couple, nodding his head, "Margarita is quite right, of course. I'd forgotten for a moment what's happened in the past year. You must forgive an old man for being so silly. I know you were made for each other; you'll be happy together. Bless you both."

Later, a much more subdued group sat around the room in Mictor's house. There was no formal arrangement, but by unspoken agreement, all the chairs had been turned at an angle so that their occupants faced Teg. He sat with Marcus on his left and Roger on his right.

Jason sat with policeman Valdor on one side and Mictor on the other. Four other men were in the room, each hand-picked by Marcus as squad leaders and chosen for their intelligence as much as their fighting skills. Teg began the meeting by recalling how he had come to the settlement in the first place and summarising the facts as he knew them.

"I had begun questioning some of The Forum's rulings long before I finally fled the town. I couldn't accept the idea that people should be made to die just because they had reached a certain age. One man who, more than any other I knew, had much to offer and good reasons for remaining alive, was my grandfather."

Jason looked slightly embarrassed at Teg's words, knowing what was coming. Still, he smiled encouragingly at Teg to show he didn't object.

"Apart from any other reason he was critical to me, I greatly love him. I just couldn't understand why he should be taken away just because he was at the end of his sixty-fifth year. The incredible thing is that, at first, he was angry with me when I suggested that it was wrong for him to have to die. Despite being an intelligent, thinking man, he, like all the other inhabitants of the town, had been conditioned to accept that it was essential for the survival of humans to have a limit set on the number of years a person should live. It's a measure of how brainwashed people have become that it came as something of a shock to my grandfather when I pointed out that the three men who make up The Supreme Council and impose the Dying Day rule are all much older than sixty-five. Subsequently, on my trip to the hills overlooking The Forum, I learned from Mictor that the members of The Supreme Council, their families, privileged friends, and predecessors, who have voluntarily given up their power rather than being deposed, all live a life of luxury in a closely guarded, carefully preserved valley and that they are free of all the repressive measures that they impose on the town. I have also learned of slavery, torture, and corruption so evil there can be no doubt in the mind of any right-thinking person that it should be challenged and, hopefully, overturned. When I came here, I had no idea that things would develop as they have or that I would be chosen as your leader. I am aware of how young I am, but I assure you that having been chosen, I will do my best to achieve our aims. I have been told by my friend Valdor here that since policeman Tanner and the young girl Melinda have been rescued from The Forum, there is a severe security purge, which has heightened tension and made life more dangerous for the people who carried out these acts. I was told that their names are James and Antony, and they are Forum Attendees. The existence of two such people within the enemy camp, as it were, and our new friend Valdor's availability are of the utmost importance to our fight. The fact that their continued existence is threatened means that the situation's urgency has increased. We are going to have to strike soon."

There was a stirring among the listeners as they sensed, from the way Teg spoke, that the objective they had been preparing for was suddenly not far away. This was confirmed as Teg went on, and his following words caused consternation around the room.

"At first light tomorrow, I shall leave with Valdor for The Forum. All being well, he will be able to smuggle me inside, and I will meet James and Antony. I know this is a big risk, but I'm convinced we can only hope to win if we coordinate our efforts. While I'm gone, several things need to be done, and I'd like to outline them for you now."

There was a general shuffling as people moved to more comfortable positions. Jason looked at Teg as though he wanted to dissuade him from his proposed visit to The Forum, but he finally shrugged and settled back as he went on.

"Valdor here will, immediately after this meeting, spend a few hours with you, Marcus, and your squad leaders. I've also arranged for Elene and Melinda to be available. In the time that you have before Valdor and I leave in the morning, you must learn all you can from him and the girls about the layout of The Forum and its internal workings. Mictor, you've seen the valley from several points; I'd appreciate it if you'd join Marcus for a while. It would be a good idea to develop a map or model of the place to give all the men an idea of navigating it. Afterwards, Marcus, I'd like you and your men to work on ideas for breaking through or getting over the fence around that valley. We need an element of surprise, but I suspect they'll soon rally their forces once they know they're under attack, so the quicker we can get our forces on the other side of that fence, the better. Roger, I'd like you to work together and begin stockpiling supplies. We will have to move the men on foot, and they'll need feeding."

"If we're fortunate and have a quick win, we'll be able to find all the supplies we'll need, but we must be prepared to feed a lot of men for some considerable time if the worst comes to the worst. Marcus, you'll have to delegate people to gather all the weapons we can muster. They'll have to be checked and overhauled where necessary, the ammunition must be counted and allotted the best you can, and you'll have to set some of the men to make spears, knives, and any other simple weapons you can muster. Jason, I'd like you to organise the stockpiling of medicines and materials for some field hospitals. We'll be moving a lot of men a long distance. We may have accidents or skirmishes. Some'll get sick, and when we go into battle, there will be wounded. I suggest you rope in Zack to help as he knows where many of the herbs and roots, you'll need are, and he's popular with the other boys, so he'll draw in plenty of help. As soon as we've got the first batch of food, weapons and medical supplies ready, we'll transport them by vehicle to a hidden location near The Forum. We'll reserve the vehicles for final supplies and transporting those who will find the journey on foot too arduous. Jason, for one, will need to be fit and refreshed to set up the hospital facilities. Right then, I think that's covered the main points; there'll obviously be a lot of detail to work out, starting right after this meeting, but in the meantime has anyone anything they'd like to add or any questions they'd like to ask?"

There was silence as Teg finished, and the looks on the faces around him showed clearly how impressed they were by the way he had outlined his initial strategy. It was Marcus who voiced his thoughts, "At this stage, Teg, I don't think you've left much out; you've obviously given this much thought. The only points I'd like to clarify are the planned points of attack and the movement of troops. We should move men via multiple routes and attack from more than one point. Both these things will require pre-planning, and if you are going to The Forum alone, a couple of men should travel with you to reconnoitre the valley. Because of time constraints, we will have to use one of the vehicles for this, but it'll be well worth it."

"All good points, Marcus, and I'm confident leaving you to plan the routes while I'm gone. Before then, if you'd like to select a couple of men to travel with Valdor and me, you can brief them on what you want and make sure they're fitted out with what they'll need. I am still determining how long I'll be able to stay in The Forum, but I'm assuming I will get in safely. We must prearrange a pickup point for your two men later. They'll obviously need far more time than they'd have if they came back with me. Right! Anything else? No? Okay then, if you and Valdor will get your session organised, Marcus, I want to chat with Roger and Jason before I sleep."

The meeting broke into groups as Teg finished talking and walked over to Jason. Mictor came and stood with them and nodded his head as he looked into Teg's face. "I knew you were the right one, Teg. Just look at them! Everyone here really believes they can do it. Well done!"

There was indeed an air of confidence in the room, and as Marcus began to lead his group from the room, most of them looked back at Teg with admiring glances.

"Let's just hope that everything works out alright. So much hinges on my meeting with the men inside The Forum. They must be taking an awful risk. If that indicates the kind of men they are, they should be worthwhile allies."

"You'll be taking a considerable risk yourself, Teg." said Jason. "I know you've made up your mind, but I can't help feeling your entry into The Forum is too risky."

"It's the only way, Grandad. If we try to attack the place without coordinating our plans with those inside, it could be disastrous."

"Well, take care of yourself, do you hear? More than one person here will be anxious for you to get back safely. I know you're the leader here, and you could tell me to mind my own business, but you're still my grandson, and you mean a great deal to me."

"Thanks, grandad. Please promise me that you will take care of Elene if I don't return."

"I'd rather not think about it, Teg, but you know you've got nothing to worry about on that score."

"Teg - Teg, it's time to get ready."

He felt as though he had just fallen asleep but forced his eyes open to the grey light of early dawn already rising outside the window. He looked groggily at Mictor as the old man bustled about the room, gathering Teg's clothes and throwing them onto the bed. Having ensured Teg wouldn't go back to sleep, Mictor left the room. All at once, Teg realised the day's importance and began to dress. As he readied himself, he shook his head sadly, recalling Elene's upset when she learned of his plans to go into The Forum. He had finally managed to calm her down, but her distress had been so intense that the thought of it had prevented him from falling asleep for a long time. As a result, he felt thick-headed, his mind sluggish, and he had to make a determined effort to organise his thoughts. After a quick meal and a cold brisk wash, he was ready.

He stood for a moment with Valdor whilst Mictor stowed food and drink in the vehicle, and then they climbed inside, shivering in the early morning chill. The briefest of waves went to Mictor, and they were off, their minds now concentrated on the dangers ahead. A short stop was made to pick up the two men Marcus had assigned to accompany them, and then they headed out of the settlement.

At first, there was a strained silence in the vehicle as the two men in the back reacted uncomfortably to the experience of travelling in a police vehicle driven by a policeman. Sensing their discomfort, Teg set out to ease the atmosphere. Turning to Valdor, he said. "As we're all going to be together for a while, you might as well know who your passengers are. The man sitting directly behind you is Peter. Marcus speaks very highly of him and tells me he will play a big part in the attack on The Forum when it takes place. The other man is Hal, he's apparently quite a strategist and will probably have a lot to say about where the actual assaults on The Forum occur. Gentlemen, you have already been introduced to our friend Valdor here. I know that you must still harbour some suspicion about him. Still, if we are to succeed, we may end up relying very heavily upon him."

The two men looked uncomfortably at each other, but the policeman spoke up before either could say anything. "I can quite understand your suspicion, my friends. There's no way I can force you to accept me, but I will say this: what happened to my friend so sickened me that I felt I wanted to rush straight in and try and kill The Supreme Council single-handedly. It would have been futile, of course, and I would most certainly have ended up dead. I'm only too glad now that I waited because I believe I have a chance to play a part in the downfall of those hateful bastards. Whatever you may think of me, I swear to you that even if I should die in the attempt on The Forum, you have my word as a human being that I am one hundred per cent on your side."

There was so much sincerity in his voice the two men looked at each other almost guiltily, then Peter leaned forward and touched Valdor on the shoulder, "That's good enough for me, friend; welcome aboard."

The atmosphere in the vehicle lightened perceptibly, and the rest of the day passed companionably. Peter and Hal took the opportunity to ask Valdor questions about the valley and its layout. Although he wasn't familiar with the whole complex, he knew enough to suggest that the most likely places for launching an assault were on the far side of the slave's enclosure and at the top end of the main lake. The two men agreed they would concentrate their efforts in these two areas, thus making the most of their time in the valley. They pushed on until late evening, hoping to reach the valley early the next day. Valdor's opinion was that the best chance of getting past the guards at the main entrance to The Forum complex would be in the early morning before the rest of the valley had stirred.

It was almost pitch dark when they finally camped for the night; the sky had clouded over during the evening. They made camp by the light of the vehicle headlamps and ate a quick meal before turning in to get a few hours of sleep. Teg was unable to sleep at first and was turning restlessly when he noticed Valdor, who was just a couple of feet away, watching him. When he saw that Teg had caught him, he said quietly, "You do realise how much of a risk you'll be taking, Teg, don't you?"

"We'll both be taking a risk, and you must be taking the bigger risk, seeing as you are one of them. They won't take too kindly to being betrayed."

"I can accept that risk, Teg; if need be, I can put an end to my own life. I've lived many years more than you, and I'm ashamed of the fact that for a lot of those years, I've been the tool of an evil system. With all due respect, though, Teg, you're very young. I know how mature you are for your age, I can see how good a leader you are, but I still can't forget how few years you've lived."

"Don't let it worry you. Just remember that the way I feel, I wouldn't want to live much longer anyway if I didn't at least try and do something about the world I live in."

They were silent for a while, but still, Teg couldn't sleep. Looking across at Valdor, he saw that he, too, had his eyes open, so he asked him, "What exactly is the security like at The Forum?"

"Well, starting right at the beginning, you have the main entrance. That's a guarded double set of electronic gates."

"How many are on guard at the gates?"

"Usually, there are six men, but during the night and early morning, a couple of the men will stand guard while the others either sleep or play cards."

"Do the actual guards have much to do?"

"Oh no, very little. The main traffic through the gates is police traffic. Some of us have free access as we have a roving function. We're not always tied down to any one group or area. It's ironic to think that it's because Tanner and I were seconded temporarily to the group searching for you and your grandfather that I've ended up here with you, trying to smuggle you into The Forum."

"Yes, whilst I regret what happened to your friend, I can't help thinking that it must have been fated, I don't think we could be as near to our objective as we are now, without your help."

"Anyway, to get back to security, there are facilities in the gatehouse to summon help from the main barracks. The barracks is only about half a mile away, so it wouldn't take long for help to arrive."

"How is that signal given?"

"They just push a button."

"No-sorry. What I meant was how the signal is conveyed. Is it by a siren or something? Is it by radio, underground cable or what?"

"Oh, I see. Well, I can tell you it is by underground cable. I remember the time one of the slaves was preparing the ground for a new storehouse and dug up the cable."

"What happened?"

"Oh, he was executed; they called it carelessness."

Valdor suddenly looked embarrassed at the off-hand way in which he'd referred to the slave's death. He frowned as he went on, "It seems hard to believe that anybody can treat such a thing so lightly, but that's how we were. I feel ashamed to think of it now."

"Well, let's hope we can stop it. Anyway, what I really meant was, what happened when the cable was dug up? Was there a general alarm or something?"

"No, but I don't quite understand the question."

"The cable was actually broken, I take it?"

"Yes."

"What I'm getting at is that if the cable was broken, but no alarm was triggered, then there would appear to be no safety backup or call system."

"Oh, I see, you mean that the guards at the barracks would have been alerted that their link with the gatehouse was broken."

"Exactly; after all, who's to know how it got broken?"

"But they know how it oh, I think I'm beginning to see what you mean; you're thinking of sabotage."

"Right. If we could isolate that alarm and surround the barracks before the police know it, we could effectively isolate quite a number of the enemy."

"Yes, but you still have to get past the gatehouse."

"We can work on that; I want to consider all the possibilities. What about the rest of the security in the complex?"

"Before I go onto that, Teg, I really think I should emphasise the nature of the enemy you're up against. In my own defence, I will say that I was never cruel or vicious just for the sake of it. Still, the average policeman in that place will show you absolutely no mercy. They're hand-picked for a variety of qualities. Still, many of them are picked simply because they can be easily controlled and are naturally brutish. They like nothing more than to be given the freedom to kill, maim, and torture; anything goes as far as they're concerned. Unless you can get that right in your mind, you haven't got a chance, Teg. I don't think you'll find it easy, but you'll have to fight really dirty."

Teg stared at the sky while thinking about what Valdor had said.

Broken clouds scudded across his field of view, and every so often, he would see the moon or stars in the gaps. He looked up for a long time before he finally turned and looked at his companion.

"I know what you're saying is true. I know you're right when you say it won't be easy for me, but you can be sure that this fight is too important for me to allow squeamishness to get in the way. I'll do what must be done because this is one time when, however inhuman our measures may have to be, the end justifies the means. What else can you tell me about security?"

"The patrols you already know about. There are, or at least there were twenty patrols. That number has probably increased by now because of the increased security. There are fewer patrols at the bottom of the valley, and they use vehicles. At the top end, nearer to The Forum, there are more patrols, generally on foot. In addition, teams of officers drive around, making spot inspections. All the patrols carry electronic sounders that activate an alarm at the barracks and a separate police depot on the far side of The Forum. The Forum area is the most closely guarded, naturally. They have a force of about forty men stationed permanently there, of whom a dozen or so at any one time will be patrolling within the building itself."

"It doesn't sound all that massive a security force when you consider the size of the valley and how the homes are all spread out."

"That's where The Supreme Council have a problem. They're afraid that if they make the police force too big and unified, they'll create a force that could stage a takeover. That's why The Forum police are a select breed with special privileges. They also happen to be the most vicious. They are virtually a separate force from the general police, and there's quite a bit of rivalry between the two groups. Anyway, Teg, be aware of the limited numbers. You've got to remember that they're all armed with the latest weapons, they have many vehicles, making them fast and mobile, and there are reserves in the town. If required, they can be here within twelve hours."

"Twelve hours, is that all?"

"That's right. You must remember that we've come here from the settlement by a route that takes us nearer the town. From what I can tell, how you and your grandfather travelled to the settlement was a roundabout route. You must remember that twelve hours in a fast vehicle still represents a pretty good distance; I imagine you're looking at something like four hundred miles. It would take a lot less time to get here if all the roads were good, of course, but as it is, twelve hours isn't bad."

"So, we'll have to assume that in an attack on the valley, a signal will be sent to the town once they know it's a significant attack. Let's take two or three hours for them to muster their forces, about fifteen hours before they reach the valley.

"Perhaps you could arrange some kind of ambush or delaying tactics on their route."

"No, I don't think so. We'll need all our strength at the valley, and in any case, I'd rather see the police reserves get there."

"You would?"

"Yes, because I'd sooner have all the enemy in one place. I want to avoid going to the town afterwards and fighting another battle with a force that would have received plenty of warning by then. Let's get them to the valley and deal with them there. We must make sure we're ready for them in the fifteen hours or so that it will take them to get there."

Teg could feel tiredness creeping over him now, and he could tell that Valdor, too, was getting sleepy.

"I'm sorry to have kept you awake so long. I'm glad we've had this chance to chat, though. It's given me a much better idea of what we're up against. Tell me, how much of this have you discussed with Marcus?"

"All of it virtually; the only thing that he didn't pick up on was the possibility of disabling the gate alarm."

"Well, whilst I'm sorry to have dragged you over all the same ground again, it's been well worth it. All we've got to concentrate on now is getting into The Forum tomorrow."

"Oh, is that all? And here I was thinking it would be a difficult day."

They were both grinning as they settled down and, within minutes, were fast asleep.

Chapter 43

The two men faded into the early morning mist. It closed around them like they'd never been there, and all was still again.

Having watched the two men until they were out of sight, Teg and Valdor returned to the vehicle, which was well concealed behind a thick stand of bushes. From the time they had woken, it had taken only two hours to get to this point, which, according to Valdor, was about a mile from the main entrance to The Forum complex.

At the vehicle, Teg stripped off his outer clothes. He quickly donned a spare uniform provided by Valdor and adapted by a woman in the settlement to fit Teg. It had been agreed that it would be safer for Teg to remain concealed until they were inside the fence. So he crawled under the front seats, usually reserved for tools and equipment. It had been emptied and lined with cloth to protect him from the dirt and grease. Holes for breathing had been drilled into the sides of the compartment, and as the lid was lowered on him, Teg turned his face to the holes in the front wall. As the darkness descended, he had to fight claustrophobic sensations and, for one moment, nearly panicked and wanted to thrust upwards at the top of the coffin-like enclosure. Breathing deeply, he managed to calm himself, and when he turned his face to the breathing holes and could see fragments of daylight, he felt much better. He flinched as the engine whirred to life, sounding incredibly loud. The noise vibrated through the enclosure and then through his whole body. The noise and the vibrations lessened as the vehicle moved, but it was still noisy.

The floor of the compartment was slightly lower than the main floor of the vehicle, and by laying his head flat against the base, Teg was able to see through the breathing holes. Being so close to the ground was a strange, unsettling sensation.

The grassy slopes seemed to rush past at fantastic speed, and the trees and shrubs that Teg could glimpse through the gaps appeared to jump past the vehicle rather than the other way around. The vehicle slowed as it neared the bottom of a slope, and Teg guessed that they were nearly at their destination. He concentrated hard on what little he could see as the vehicle was turned around behind a small group of trees and then driven up a slight incline. Then they were on a level stretch of ground that may once have been a narrow road, but nature had reclaimed and was now grassed over. As they followed this pathway around a tight bend, the ground began to rise on either side, so they were soon travelling along a narrow space between two steep hills. About two hundred yards ahead, the path ended abruptly at the edge of what looked like the beginning of a forest. The vehicle drove straight into the green blanket of leaves that hung down to the ground, and for a while, all Teg could see was a mixture of shadows and light. Then they came through the belt of trees and bushes into the open, and the fence was about ten feet ahead. From his viewpoint, Teg could not see the top of the fence, but he could see enough to know that it was very high. The ground on either side of the wall was flat, and the wire mesh appeared to go straight down into the ground. The vehicle turned right, moved parallel to the fence for about fifty feet, and stopped outside a pair of gates. The wall here had been formed into a large cage inside the complex with a second set of gates at the other end of the cage. As Teg watched, he saw the portion of the gate that he could see swing inwards. The vehicle moved a few yards and stopped inside the cage. From here, Teg could just see, beyond the next set of gates, the bottom corner of a white structure, which he assumed to be the gatehouse. To his surprise, the inner gates opened almost immediately, with no challenge from the guards, and the vehicle moved forward again. He heard the rattle of the gates as they swung closed behind them. They were inside the complex. Now, all Teg could do was listen, his vision restricted to the white wall of the gatehouse. The exchange between Valdor and his colleagues was so every day that Teg found it hard to believe that his life would be forfeited should they suddenly decide to search inside the vehicle. He was relieved when Valdor finally climbed back into the car and, driving past the gatehouse, began following a well-made uphill road. All Teg could see for a while was the grey-black surface of the road until the vehicle crested the hill, and he could see a series of tiny houses set, apparently randomly, among small trees and flower beds. They continued past several houses and turned down a small side road. The vehicle was driven behind a screen of climbing roses and abruptly stopped. The darkness beyond the front of the vehicle and the complete silence as the engine was switched off left Teg feeling claustrophobic again.

He heard Valdor moving above him and climbing to the ground. He waited impatiently for the lid of the compartment to be lifted. Still, nothing happened. Feeling even more closed, he fought not to panic. Still, almost without realising it, he had put his hands against the top of the compartment and pressed upwards. His heartbeat wildly as he felt the weight of the seats bearing down on the lid, and he knew he couldn't move it. He was sweating now, feeling his control slipping, and he opened his mouth to shout. Abruptly, he closed his mouth again as he heard, right next to the vehicle, a voice addressing Valdor.

"You did the right thing getting away, didn't you."

"How do you mean?"

"It's been murder here the last few days. The President's got some bees in his bonnet about security, and he's been doing spot checks and snap searches everywhere."

"It was like that before I went away."

"Oh no, it wasn't! This is worse. The way they're going on up there, you'd think there was a revolution brewing or something."

"That'll be the day! Who on earth's going to organise a revolution anyway?"

"As I said, the President is very touchy at the moment. He says there are too many things going wrong, and it's a bad omen."

"All it'll mean in the end will be more work for everybody, you'll see."

"That's for sure! As a matter of fact, that's what I'm here for; I'm supposed to search your vehicle."

"You're supposed to do what?"

"I know, it's stupid, but that's my instructions. I'm supposed to check every vehicle in the place."

"What on earth for?"

"Would you believe concealed weapons and radios?"

"You're joking!"

"The President is quite paranoid about trouble coming from those bastards in The Wastelands. He thinks they'll get some help from the inside, and the things they'll need most will be weapons and radios."

"Tell me something, my friend."

"What's that?"

"I've just returned after several days outside. I've just got up here at this minute. Now you tell me that you've got to search my vehicle. Why would I be smuggling weapons and radios into this place?"

"What do you - oh, I see. It is a bit stupid. See how they get you with all this security business? I must be going senile. You look shattered. I'm sorry to have held you up. I'll see you around."

"Yeh, see you around!"

Seconds later, the thump of the seats shoved back sounded in the stifling compartment. Suddenly, the lid was thrown back, and even the subdued light hurt Teg's eyes. He barely had time to blink before Valdor had hustled him out of the vehicle and, pressing the cloth that had lined the compartment into his arms, said urgently, "Quickly enter the house and take that with you. In the second room, there's a clothes closet. Hide in there, hurry!"

Sensing the almost desperate urgency of the other man's words, Teg hastened to obey. As he ducked around the vehicle, he saw Valdor frantically grabbing the tools from behind the seat and dumping them in the compartment. The car was parked in a covered entrance area at the side of the house. The side and back of the structure were covered with climbing roses, forming an effective screen against casual observation. The front of the vehicle was almost touching two stone steps which led up to a door. The door opened at Teg's touch, and he ducked inside. He was in a combined dining and kitchen area, and an opening on the far side led to a lounge area. The large room had a pair of timber doors closing off what proved to be a large clothes closet. Pushing between the many garments hanging there, Teg stood against the back of the closet, the cloth still bundled in his arms.

He could see a sliver of light where he hadn't entirely closed the doors, and just as he reached out to pull them closed, they were suddenly pushed shut from the outside. He heard the muffled thump of a bag being dropped on the floor and then, almost immediately, muffled but clear enough for him to know it was the same man he had heard talking to Valdor, he heard, "I hope you don't mind, but I should go through the routine even if you have just returned. It'll be just my luck if I say I've searched every vehicle, and they find out somehow that I didn't search yours."

The voice faded as Valdor left the house with the other policeman, but not before Teg heard the other man say, "You'll probably find out sometime anyway, but they've already searched your house. Oh, not just yours, of course, but everybody's. Yesterday it was, right about this time it was, funnily enough"… Then Teg could hear no more. By this time, his shaking legs had given out, and he had slid to the floor where he sat surrounded by shoes, his head draped with Valdors clothes.

It seemed an awful long time before Valdor opened the closet doors. Teg pushed his face out between two pairs of trousers and breathed deeply, feeling the effects of too much confinement.

"Sorry about that, I've never known a man talk so much. Anyway, he's gone now."

"Thank heavens you got me out of there as quick as you did."

"I had a feeling about him. He's one of those goody-goody men who like to work to the letter of the law. I was sweating on him, wanting to search immediately, as it was we were only just in time."

"That would have been the game finished before it had begun if he'd found me."

"Oh no, it wouldn't. I'd already made up my mind that I'd have to kill him if need be. I'm glad I didn't have to, not because I wouldn't like to see him dead, but more because I wouldn't want to create any unnecessary problems at this stage."

"Why do you say it's not because you wouldn't want to see him dead?"

"If you'd been able to see him, you'd think he was one of the nicest-looking guys in the world. Listening to him, you must have thought he sounded light and inoffensive."

"That's right; he didn't sound like anything unusual."

"That's part of what I told you about when I said you've got to be prepared to fight dirty. If you came up against him without knowing about him, you'd likely think he was quite harmless and want to spare him. Well, let me tell you, I've seen him beat two slaves to death for misbehaving."

"Beat them to death?"

"Yes, quite cold-bloodedly. It was a male slave of, I suppose, eighteen and a female slave who was probably just a bit younger. They were a pleasant couple, did as they were told, had no trouble, worked hard, and didn't know any difference anyway."

"So, what was the misbehaviour that warranted being beaten to death?"

"Well, they were in love. One day, he caught them kissing and said that they were animals who had no right to do the sort of things that people did."

Teg didn't say anything; his expression said it all. Valdor stared at him for a moment and then shook his head. "I meant it, Teg. It'll have to be a dirty fight; there can be no quarter given."

"How much of that sort of thing goes on?"

Valdors eyes were bleak as he looked at Teg's stricken face, "A great deal, Teg, a very great deal. This is indeed an evil place."

There was space beneath the roof for Teg to hide until the evening, Valdor considered this the safest time to move to The Forum building. The provision of a few blankets and pillows and Teg was surprisingly comfortable. However, he felt a twinge of discomfort as the access hatch to the roof was pulled back into place, and once more, he was in darkness. He stretched out on his makeshift bed, closed his eyes, determined to try, and relax and rest before the evening. It was warm in the darkness of the roof space, and at first, it seemed he would fall asleep quite quickly. He began to doze, but then, as his mind and body relaxed, he became aware of the sounds that drifted in from outside, some surprisingly loud. In the distance, he could hear shouts, some of them seemingly angry, and his hope of sleeping fast vanishing; he opened his eyes. The roof space wasn't as dark as it had first seemed, with numerous small gaps between the tiles allowing light in, and most of the sounds were coming through these gaps. Curious, Teg carefully moved through the semi-darkness until the roof's slope prevented him from going further. Lying flat, he eased forward as far as he could until his head was almost wedged in the angle of the roof. Being this close to one of the gaps, he had a surprisingly good view. He was at the back of Valdors house, and directly below was a small garden. Beyond the garden was a grassed area across which a narrow road cut. The ground rose sharply a few feet just beyond the road, and then it levelled out. The ground became rough and uncultivated beyond this point, and about fifty yards away, there was a wire fence. Beyond the wall was the first of a long row of tiny, basic houses, more like huts. A bit further on, the huts were spread out with dirt paths between them.

More shouting attracted Teg's attention to the left, and he saw that where the road curved away on the left, about a hundred yards from the house, a gate was set into the fence. Several policemen stood near the open gates, and several more were approaching the gates, escorting a ragged column of people. The poor quality and condition of their clothes and their somewhat submissive attitudes immediately marked them down as slaves, and Teg studied them intently as they filed through the gates. The slaves were a mixture of men, women, and children. The men and women ranged from young to old. The children were generally boys whose ages were around nine and upwards. Teg was disgusted to see that several policemen would lash out at random with fists or boots for no apparent reason, sending the recipient of the blow reeling and even, in some cases, falling to the ground. He was astonished to see that the slaves made no effort to defend themselves or to avoid the blows. A few moments later, he saw why when, as he was suddenly struck on the shoulder by one of the policemen, a young man of about eighteen attempted to duck out of the way of a second blow. He glowered angrily at the policeman who had hit him. The policeman immediately grinned and, saying something to his companions, walked up to the young man and shoved him, making him fall.

The policeman then began kicking him, slowly and deliberately, while the other policemen laughed and jeered. Teg's face was tense with anger and disgust at what was happening, and he had to restrain himself from shouting out. However, he thought he would have been heard only by Valdor in the house below. Fortunately, the line of slaves that continued to pour through the gate was beginning to back up and seeing this, the policeman gave the young man a last contemptuous kick and walked back to his colleagues, grinning hugely. Teg watched helplessly as the young man crawled away, and he suspected that the only reason some of the other slaves did not help him was fear. Teg watched until the last of the slaves had been shepherded through the gate and had dispersed to their own huts. He estimated that there had been about two hundred people in the column. He noticed that they had all disappeared inside their huts within a few minutes of passing through the gate, and it was as though they'd never been there. The policemen wandered away from the gate and followed the narrow road past Valdor's house. They were within twenty feet of Teg at their nearest point. He concentrated on their faces, vowing to himself that he would show no mercy if he ever came face to face with any of them.

The exhibition of brutality he had seen had unsettled Teg, and he found it difficult to relax. So, when, after several interminable hours, Valdor opened the roof hatch and beckoned him down, he was very edgy and angry. Sensing his mood, Valdor queried the reason for it, and when Teg had explained, Valdor said sadly, "That's nothing, Teg. Oh, I don't mean that the way it sounds; I mean it's nothing in terms of some of the things that happen here."

"What staggered me was the way they just took it. They just allowed themselves to be treated like dirt. Only one lad resisted at all, and he was nearly kicked to death for it!"

"That's exactly why they just put up with it. Any resistance will result in even worse treatment."

"It still seems incredible, though, seeing a couple of hundred people meekly allowing themselves to be mishandled by a handful of thugs; why don't they gang up on them?"

"Come on, Teg, surely that's obvious. Those slaves out there are mainly descended from other slaves. They were born to it; they are conditioned to accept it. Their own parents conditioned them because they knew that any stepping out of line by their children meant trouble for them."

"But surely they're not all born to it. What about the people who've been captured?"

"That's true, Teg, but look what they're up against. You know full well that those policemen at the gate are only a tiny part of the force available; gang up on them, and they bring down the wrath of the rest of them, and they've got the weapons, don't forget."

"I'm still surprised no one feels like fighting back."

"I didn't say that."

Valdor stopped abruptly as if regretting what he'd said, "What do you mean? You're saying there is someone?"

"I shouldn't have said anything, Teg. I just have a feeling it will only lead to trouble."

"Tell me."

"Very well. There is one slave: he's about twenty years old, and he's very bright. His big problem is he's likely to find himself in big trouble one day for trying to stir the others up".

Teg's face was suddenly animated, and he asked excitedly, "How do you know about him?"

"It's pretty amusing in a twisted way. I was in the fields at the bottom of the valley; I'd been down to deliver a new gun to one of the patrols there. Anyway, on the way back, I had to stop, the call of nature. I'd just finished and was about to walk back to my vehicle when I heard voices, or should I say a voice. There was something… I don't know… compelling about the voice, I suppose. It was full of passion and was going on about freedom and justice.

I was standing, and around a bend came this group of about seven or eight slaves. Right in the middle was this fellow. When they saw me, they stopped dead. They all looked petrified, except for him. He looked defiant and proud as well. I don't know why; I should have arrested him there and then, but there was something about him. I just turned and walked away. I suppose it's not funny, but I've often wondered what they must have thought. They must have been expecting all sorts of dreadful things to happen. It must have been very confusing for them when nothing happened."

Teg had listened with growing excitement to Valdor's story, and when he had finished, there was a gleam in the young man's eye. "Do you know this slave's name?"

"Name! They don't have names, they have numbers."

"Numbers? You're joking, surely."

"It's part of the dehumanising process, Teg."

They are numbered based on the quarters they live in. If they move to different quarters, their numbers will change.

"What about your man? Do you know his number? Is it the same as it was?"

"Oh, yes, it was only a couple of months ago, and there have been no major changes since then. For what it's worth, his number is 4 8 1 4."

"So, if his number hasn't changed, you'll know where to find him?"

"Yes, of course. Why do… oh no, Teg. You're taking too much of a risk as it is, and you're surely not going to ask me to take you to him."

"That's exactly what I am going to do."

Valdor sighed as he looked at the determined young man who seemed to grow in stature constantly; he could see no point in arguing with him. Nonetheless, he tried.

"You certainly don't shrink from taking risks, Teg, I'll give you that, but do you think the risk is justified in this case?"

"I won't know that until I meet this man, but I won't be happy until I do."

"Well, can we concentrate on one thing at a time? It's going to be nerve-racking enough trying to get you into The Forum as it is."

Now that he had embarked on his dangerous venture, Teg found that while he was tense and keyed up, he no longer felt any fear. It was as though, having committed himself, he was prepared to accept whatever might happen. So, he continued to surprise Valdor with his cheerful manner and apparently relaxed attitude as they prepared to move to The Forum building.

From the clothes closet Teg had first hidden, Valdor produced two policeman's helmets. The one Teg put on was slightly too big and sat uncomfortably low on his head, but it effectively disguised him with the visor down. Valdor left the house first, and when he was sure the coast was clear, he started the vehicle's engine while Teg hurried out and climbed into the passenger seat. He ducked low as the car backed out and turned onto the road. He remained below the window level until they cleared the police houses.

When Teg finally sat up, he got his first good view of the part of the valley where the police and slaves' quarters were. Looking back, he could see the gates at the main entrance to the complex already diminishing as the vehicle picked up speed. They were on a road almost parallel to the fence at about a hundred yards. For the first time, he could appreciate just how high the wall was and how exposed anybody would be trying to climb it. The top of the fenceposts bent outwards at an angle and were linked with strands of a vicious-looking barbed wire. Teg noticed sufficient space between the top of the fence and the lowest strand of barbed wire for a child to just about squeeze through. The thought brought to his mind young Daniel. He realised that this was how he must have entered the complex and how fortunate he must have been not to have been spotted. Teg's blood ran cold at the thought of what might have happened if Daniel approached any forum member other than Antony.

The thought of Antony and the other Attendant, James, brought Teg's mind back to the present. He became aware that the road was further away from the fence, and they were moving towards the valley's center. They drove up a long, gentle slope and then suddenly were on level ground and moving between small fields of different types of crops. Where the crops were young or low-growing, Teg could see the valley stretching out on either side with the hills in the distance. The sun was low in the sky ahead of them, and the mountains on either side began to grey as they lost the light. The floor of the valley had appeared flat from up on the mountain, but it was a series of gently rolling low hills with shallow valleys in between. At times, they were surrounded by crops and could see no further than the next bend in the road; other times, they could see for long distances, although it became progressively more difficult as the sun finally lost its grip on the distant hills and slipped over the edge. Teg stared in amazement as suddenly they flashed past a large white house.

It was superbly built and featured tall cylindrical columns supporting an upper level, with the ground floor set back so that the columns formed an arcade for a large, covered terrace. The size of the house staggered Teg, and he gaped in awe as he caught glimpses of the luxurious interiors of the brightly lit rooms. Even the grandest buildings in the town hadn't prepared Teg for this. Still, as they passed another and then yet another equally grand house, he found himself comparing them to the miserable huts in the slave quarters.

The light was almost gone now, and the vehicle headlights made a bright diminishing cone ahead of them. They passed several more houses, only dimly seen in the darkness. However, the occasional undarkened window permitted glimpses of the same sumptuous luxury he had seen before.

They approached a four-way road junction, and Valdor turned the vehicle to the right. As they came up onto the top of a rise, Teg sensed, rather than saw, that they were heading directly towards the fence, although it was at least half a mile ahead of them. The light had improved slightly as cloud cover had broken up, and the moon shone through. The hills at the valley's far side loomed against the sky, and Teg guessed that if it had been light enough, he would have been able to see the fence ahead of them. Then, suddenly, they turned left and moved parallel to the wall again.

They came up slightly, and Teg could see the moonlight glinting on the lake, which he had seen from up on the hills. Knowing what he would see, he looked to the left and gasped. From the mountain, it was clear that The Forum building was large and magnificent. Nothing had prepared Teg, though, for just how huge it was, and they were still half a mile away. The beautiful architecture was brilliantly lit and stretched a great distance. The whole perimeter of the building was a series of columns and arches that created an almost grotto-like effect so that Teg could practically imagine the elves and pixies of his childhood stories popping their heads out to greet him.

Abruptly, Valdor switched off the headlights and reduced speed until they moved slowly to the right, leaving the road and passing between randomly spaced trees. They drew level with The Forum building, and Teg could now see that it was almost as vast from front to back as from side to side.

The vehicle was almost level with the rear of the building when Valdor drove it into a clump of trees and bushes and switched off the engine. They sat there in silence, the only sound of the hot engine ticking in the cool night air. Leaves and branches hung around them, giving only glimpses of the brightly lit building on their left. To their right was only darkness. They alighted from the vehicle, moving as quietly as possible, and moved to the edge of the overhanging leaves.

"This is how we'll do it," whispered Valdor. "Those three columns on the far right are at the end of a courtyard, which leads to the chambers of The Forum members who live in the unserviced quarters."

"What do you mean by un-serviced?"

"They're for the Attendants who prefer to live independently, without servants. There aren't many of them, and James and Antony happen to be two of them, which works to our advantage. The disadvantage is that Garon is another who prefers to live alone." Valdor shuddered as he went on,

"Not that he usually lacks for the kind of company he prefers."

"He's the one you call the Interrogator?"

"Right. Anyway, we'll stay inconspicuous until we cross that open ground there and start praying."

"If we see another policeman, is there any special way I should behave?"

"Yes, run so fast your kneecaps threaten to shatter!"

When they reached the last of the trees, they stood there for a while, looking around carefully. The stretch of ground between them and the columns of The Forum building looked incredibly wide to Teg. Where the light was brightest, close to the building, he imagined that a thousand pairs of eyes were watching, waiting for someone like him to walk into the spotlight.

Then they were moving, walking as quickly as they dared without seeming hasty. To Teg, they were on a moving surface that ran backwards, keeping them at a constant distance from the building. He looked down and reassured himself that the ground was moving backwards beneath his feet, and when he looked up again, the building was rushing towards them. As he looked at the spaces between the approaching columns, he knew that somebody was waiting there, and his chest prickled with imagined bullets. They passed the nearest column and entered the courtyard.

There was nobody there. The courtyard was bounded on two sides by solid walls. Still, the end of the rectangle towards which they moved was mainly dark, smoky glass, and to the right-hand side was a door, just one ordinary-sized door, and Teg knew it would be locked. They reached the door, Valdor pushed against it, and it moved noiselessly inward. Then they were inside. Quickly, Valdor led Teg to the right until they were clear of the glass, and there they leaned against the wall and relaxed for a moment. Teg was surprised to find his legs trembling violently and his hands tightly clenched. He consciously tried to calm his hands and then concentrated on relaxing the rest of his body. He looked around him. They were in a long, dark corridor with other corridors going off at right angles at irregular intervals. Some of these corridors were lit, and splashes of light were thrown onto the floor. Teg jumped as Valdor touched him on the shoulder. "We've got to get moving. Same thing as before, quick but not too quick."

They walked side by side along the corridor, passing across the ends of the brightly lit passages leading to the left. The third passage was unlit, and they turned down it. Further on, there was a brightly lit intersection, and it was about halfway to this that Valdor stopped at a door that had been almost invisible to Teg.

"I hope he's in," Valdor whispered. He raised his hand to knock and, at that moment, clearly heard feet marching down the intersecting corridor.

"Patrol!"

Valdor began urgently knocking on the door. They were poised, ready to push into the room as soon as the door opened. Nothing happened. The marching feet drew nearer. Valdor knocked again urgently. The feet were almost at the corner. Suddenly, the door opened, and they were thrusting inside, slamming the door behind them.

It was James who recovered first. Smiling broadly, his relief evident, he stepped forward, hand outstretched.

"So, you're Teg! This is most unexpected, but I can tell you that we are delighted to meet you at last."

"This is Antony, who I'm sure you've heard of."

As he shook Antony's hand, Teg was struck by the fact that these two men were the most unlikely-looking revolutionaries one could hope to see. Then he smiled wryly as he considered what impression he must make on them. Whatever their thoughts about his age, they obviously recognised his air of command because their expressions and voices were respectful.

"I hope we haven't put you at too much risk by coming here," Teg said as he gratefully sank into a comfortable chair. Don't you worry about us," said James. "It's you who's taken the greatest risk. How on earth did you manage it?"

They listened spellbound as he described their journey and the near disaster when they reached the door. When he had finished, there was an awkward silence until Antony broke it.

"I suppose you've come to find out what help we can give you, Teg. I'm afraid our options are limited, but whatever you ask, we'll do our best."

Teg was surprised and gratified at how easily they had put themselves under his command. Anxious to know more about them, he asked how they had come to be involved in working for the downfall of The Forum. It was James who told the story.

"It should end with you because it began with you. When you and Jason ran away, it caused quite an upset. Jason was a prominent citizen and was honoured by The Supreme Council, but on the same night, he fled, as you know. It's not the first time it's happened, but usually, there is a quick, intense police hunt, and the offenders are caught and forced through their Final Walk, only this time in disgrace. The President must be shrewd because all hell broke loose when you and Jason disappeared. He suspected someone as intelligent as Jason could be a threat. Just how shrewd Aaron is, though, was shown when he found out you were also missing. That's when he went over the top. He instinctively guessed that you might be an even bigger threat than Jason. How right he was!"

There was a break in the narrative as Antony appeared with drinks, which were welcomed by all. Teg suddenly realized that the tension had left him feeling dehydrated and drank deeply and gratefully of the cool juice as James went on.

"When your disappearance was announced, the Justice Session was on, and Delmo, the Second President, was sitting. It's ironic because he had just sentenced the Acolyte Elene to death. I understand she's now with you?"

"That's right, as a matter of fact, we're going to be married."

"Really? Well, congratulations! If all goes well, we might even be there for the marriage. Anyway, to get back to the story. Delmo was put in charge of searching for you but was unsuccessful. He was given an ultimatum by the President to have you either killed or captured by the next full session of The Forum. What we now know is that Delmo arranged for one of the Acolytes here, a lad about your age, and an old man who was kidnapped from the town, to be dropped somewhere near to where the search for you was going on and, by arrangement with one of the officers, they were shot dead and buried. It was announced that it had been you and Jason."

Teg was appalled at the cold-blooded actions of the Second President. "This Delmo fellow sounds like a dangerous piece of work."

"He certainly is, but he's not alone. There's great rivalry between the Second and Third Presidents. When your deaths were announced, David, the Third President, was suspicious and persuaded me to go to town and investigate. He also arranged for two of the policemen who had been on the search party that carried out the killings to be brought here and questioned by Garon, the Interrogator. You'll see the results of his handiwork if you ever meet Valdor's friend, policeman Tanner."

"I already have, and I know what you mean. You said something about two policemen?"

"Yes, the other one didn't survive."

"This Garon seems reason enough to overthrow this regime without considering additional factors. Anyway, go on."

"Well, to cut a long story short, Delmo was trying to use Antony in the same way David was using me. Knowing that I was involved, Delmo set Antony to try to incriminate David through me. It was when we got to talking that we both realised exactly what kind of people we worked for and how much it sickened us.

So far, we've managed to stall, but I was here tonight to tell Antony that Delmo is trying to bring things to a head; I'm afraid time is running out.

"Well, if you can manage to stall things for a bit longer, I hope we'll soon be moving."

"How soon, do you think?"

"Well, by the time we get back to the settlement and coordinate what I've found out and what Peter and Hal have found out, and by the time we get ourselves organised, I would hope no more than a couple of weeks."

"A couple of weeks! You think you can be ready that soon?"

"Our men are reaching a peak. The preparations for supplies and medical services are well underway by now, so there's no benefit in delaying any longer than necessary."

"Well, I'm sure we can stall things that long. Now, how about you tell us how best we can help you?"

"Mainly by providing some means of inside information. Having you two inside The Forum is invaluable to us. With our limited number of weapons, we need all the inside intelligence we can get. Our big problems are going to be getting messages to and from each other. We'll also need to make sure that you're forewarned when the attacks are about to take place. We don't want you two ending up killed by our own."

"I've got it!" Antony exclaimed before Teg had finished. They looked at him curiously, puzzled by his sudden excitement.

"It just struck me. When attempting to blackmail James into helping Delmo, I threatened to tamper with the computers to make it appear that he'd been misappropriating stores from the supplies department. Well, don't you see? I can falsify the computer records to show that we should have fewer weapons and radios in stock, and we can transfer them to you, Teg."

They stared at him with dawning comprehension. Teg looked at James and sought his views, "Do you think it could work?"

James was smiling now, looking at Antony admiringly. "Of course, it's so simple. The things that are checked most often are the police supplies, such as guns, ammunition, radios, and vehicle spare parts. They only obtain a computer stock sheet print-out and check the stores against that. They do not know that the stock sheets are wrong. It's brilliant, Antony, brilliant." Teg was secretly thrilled at the idea but felt it was wise to be cautious.

"Are you sure they won't realise that there has been a change? After all, they'd know if a large issue of weapons had taken place, for instance."

"You don't realise just how much of an arsenal we have in the supplies department. The other thing in our favour is that these checks have been taking place for years and years, and there's never been any cause for suspicion. They're not likely to think anything's wrong now."

"I hope you're right; it's certainly an exciting prospect. How can it be done?"

"That's something we'll have to work on. Most importantly, we need to let you know what's happening. I can get you some pocket radios to take with you. Antony and I will each keep a radio hidden in our chambers. When we have something to report, we can call you. If you have something to relay to us, it must be in the evening when we're alone in our chambers."

"What range do these radios have?"

"It's adjustable. The longer the range, the less time the power pack will last. They're normally set for a range of about ten miles, but they can be adjusted for up to fifty miles or down to half a mile."

"We'd need quite a few then to set up a relay system from here to the settlement. How many can you get for us?"

"As many as you need, the problem will be getting them out."

Valdor had been sitting quietly listening to the others, but now, glad of the chance to be involved, he reassured them. "Leave that to me. Let me have the radios, and I'll smuggle them out."

"You'll be taking a hell of a risk", said Teg. "They're some of the things they're looking for in their vehicle searches."

"We've got to take risks, Teg; there's no other way."

After further discussion, it was agreed that Valdor would pick up the radios in the morning before the rest of the Supplies Department staff arrived. With the patrols in the building during the night, they considered it too risky to open the department especially.

They discussed the possibilities of victory in the coming fight, and by the time they'd finished, there was an air of quiet optimism among them. Finally, Teg asked about the radios. "What are the dangers of conversations being overheard. That could be a great danger to you, couldn't it?"

"That's a good point. We'll agree on a specific channel and hope nobody else uses it. The police normally work on an open channel, so the chances of being overheard on any channel are fairly remote."

"Is there no way you could always carry a radio so we can contact you during the day?"

"I don't think so, Teg. Can you imagine a forum meeting being interrupted by a radio beeping or me serving a policeman in the department and he hears a radio beeping inside my tunic? I think it would create quite some interest, don't you?"

"Point taken", said Teg, abashed. "I'm just thankful we'll have some form of contact anyway."

It was with heartfelt gratitude that Teg thanked the two men for their efforts, and they, in turn, were clearly impressed and excited by Teg and his plans. James ascertained that the corridor was clear, Teg and Valdor donned their helmets and slipped quickly through the door. They didn't speak as they moved swiftly through the building and seemed to reach the door to the courtyard very quickly. They crossed the courtyard, paused by the pillar, and were about to start moving across the open ground when the whine of a vehicle rounding the corner of the building shattered the silence.

Valdor had already stepped forward and must have been seen. Thinking quickly, he continued walking, hoping Teg would have the good sense to stay back. He needn't have worried, as Teg had immediately ducked down behind the nearest column, making himself as small as possible.

The driver had obviously spotted Valdor, as evidenced by the slowing of the vehicle. Appearing much calmer than he felt, Valdor stopped and removed his helmet, wiping his brow as though he was warm. Seeing his face and the friendly wave he gave, the driver sped up again, and the vehicle moved away. Knowing they would likely be looking back at him, Valdor casually strolled towards the trees. He prayed that Teg would only move once the vehicle had turned the far corner of the building. To his horror, the car stopped just before reaching the far corner.

The passenger door opened, and a policeman stepped out. Valdors hands were clenched now as he wondered what had gone wrong. Still, they slowly relaxed as he saw the policeman close the vehicle door, wave, and walk into The Forum building. Immediately, the vehicle moved and turned the corner. Still worried, Valdor continued his casual pace, even when he heard the frantic pounding of Teg's feet as he raced for shelter in the trees. Risking a quick glance over his shoulder, Valdor saw the young man's flying form disappear into the darkness of the trees. Then, as he looked to the front again, he thanked the intuition, preventing him from immediately heading into the trees. The vehicle had come back around the corner and was heading towards him. Heart beating wildly, legs trembling slightly, he tried to remain composed as the car approached. Suddenly, it was alongside; the driver smiled and waved, roaring away, back the way it had first come, and rounded the corner, the whine of its engine gradually fading to nothing. Now, Valdor darted into the darkness of the trees and ran back the way he had come. He realised how far he had been forced to walk when he found that the vehicle was much further on than he'd thought. When he reached it, he was perturbed that Teg wasn't there. He was about to go and search for him when the young man's helmeted head appeared in the side window of the vehicle. He was grinning.

"I'm glad you think it's funny", Valdor grumbled as he climbed into the driver's seat; then suddenly, he, too, was grinning with relief. When they returned to Valdor's house, Teg insisted on changing his clothes before visiting the slaves' quarters. He reasoned that if he was in police uniform, the slaves would be less likely to talk to him. He also suggested that if he and Valdor were intercepted by other policemen, then Valdor could pretend to have captured Teg, and they might be able to extricate themselves. Although still unhappy with the idea of visiting the slaves, Valdor nonetheless conceded. Soon, they were moving swiftly through the shadows away from Valdor's house, which was also in the opposite direction from the main gate of the slave compound. The policeman explained that other smaller gates were set into the fence at intervals, and they would use one of these.

The grass was wet under their feet as they moved through a low-lying mist that clung to the grass, making it look almost as though they were walking through water. It was completely still and quiet when they reached a small gate into the wire fence. They crouched down against a bush while they strained their ears and eyes for signs of anyone else. It was Teg who spotted the shiny tracks leading up to and beyond the gate.

"Someone's been through here recently", he whispered, pointing to the trail marks.

"Perhaps we should abandon this Teg; that tells me there are policemen in there."

"How can you be sure they're policemen, and what would they be doing here this time of night anyway?"

"The police are the only ones who have keys to these gates. It's too risky, Teg. Let's leave it."

"You didn't answer the rest of my question."

"They come here for the girls", Valdor answered uncomfortably, "The slave girls, they come here to - to use them."

"You mean the slaves allow their girls to cohabit with the police?" Teg asked incredulously.

"They don't allow anything, Teg. They have no say in the matter. Remember what I said? They're not even regarded as human."

Teg was appalled and stared into the darkness beyond the fence as though able to see within.

"I'm still going in," he said determinedly. "You can see by the tracks that there can't be too many. Anyway, the chances of them spotting us must be pretty remote."

Valdor shrugged and moved to the gate. When he unlocked it and held it open, Teg hurried from the shadow of the bush into the compound. Relocking the gate, Valdor signalled to him to follow, and they moved off through the darkness, only the dark shapes of bushes and trees keeping them company.

They moved silently for about ten minutes, and then, as they rounded a large bush, they could see huts silhouetted against the faint glow of a fire. As they approached the huts, they began to hear the occasional murmur of voices or a cough. Moving from shadow to shadow, they came to a large barn-like structure open on two sides. Row upon row of spades, forks, pitchforks, and other agricultural implements cluttered the barn's interior.

"The slaves in this section work the fields and gardens", Valdor explained, "This is their main tool store; we have to go there, where that large tee is."

He pointed to the right, where the flickering of the fire was visible over the dark shapes of the huts.

They moved on, using the deep shadows at the backs of the huts as cover. With each hut they passed, they moved nearer to the fire and were about to cross another gap when an angry voice stopped them.

"Get out of the way, damn you!"

The voice was brutal and seemed familiar to Teg. For one awful moment, he thought the voice was directed at him but then realised it came from the other side of the hut. Then he heard the scared, pleading voice of a young man.

"Please no, please leave her, she's mine, please don't touch her."

His curiosity aroused Teg crept along the side of the hut and peered around the corner.

The hut was on one side of a clearing in the centre of which an open fire burned. Pots and cooking implements were scattered about, and somehow Teg knew instantly that they had been deliberately scattered. A group of slaves of varying ages and sexes were gathered on one side of the fire. On the other stood the policeman that Teg now recognised from his voice as having been the one who had searched Valdors car. He had obviously been drinking, although he wasn't quite drunk. He looked angry, his rage making his unpleasant face even uglier. A short distance before him, a young man of about seventeen cowered. Although he looked petrified, he was defiantly trying to shield a girl, perhaps a year younger than himself, who was clearly even more frightened.

"I'll kill you, you interfering bastard", the policeman growled and, pulling out his gun, pointed it straight at the young man's head, his finger tightening on the trigger. Without realising he was doing it, Teg had launched himself forward and, in four swift paces, was close enough to hurl himself at the policeman. As they slammed to the ground, the gun fired aimlessly into the air. Surprised, Valdor had run forward and shouted, "Teg, no Teg!"

Teg continued to wrestle with the policeman. When he managed to force him to drop the gun, he suddenly rolled away from him and, jumping to his feet, kicked the gun away. Turning back, he moved in on the policeman, who had also scrambled to his feet. Just as they were about to clash, there was a commanding shout: "That's enough; hold it right there!"

'Teg's heart sank as he realised that there had been another policeman in one of the huts. He now had them covered with an automatic weapon aimed equally between Teg and Valdor. The slightest movement either way would be sufficient to kill them both if the gun was fired. The policeman Teg wrestled with had moved out of the line of fire as his colleague moved forward. "Well, well," the policeman with the gun said, "so you're not dead after all."

The man Teg had wrestled with looked puzzled as he picked up his gun and holstered it. His colleague enlightened him, "We're in real luck here; we've got ourselves first prize. This is the young rebel that Aaron has been getting so uptight about. We've done ourselves a bit of good here."

He looked at Valdor with a sneer and said insultingly, "We got ourselves a traitor as well; this is our lucky day."

Valdor tried to bluster his way out, feeling angry with himself for having reacted the way he had and jeopardising everything.

"I don't know what you're on about here, but this man is my prisoner; I'm taking him back to the cells now."

The other man laughed derisively.

"Forget it, Valdor. I heard you call his name, and you weren't talking to any prisoner."

He waved the gun at them and grinned.

"Right then, let's get going, I'm looking forward to…"

The words were choked off abruptly by a strangled, agonised scream. His gun dropped to the ground, and he fell forward, eyes staring, mouth open as his scream died to a death rattle. The tableau remained motionless for a moment as they stared at the pitchfork that protruded from the policeman's back and the slave who crouched there, scared but defiant at what he had done.

Suddenly, the other policeman was reaching for his gun, his face a mask of astonished fury. There was a flash of movement above his shoulder, a solid-sounding blow and, without a sound, he fell forward to the ground, blood pumping from his neck where his head had been almost completely severed. The slave who had killed him threw aside the spade he had used and stood there as if expecting to be punished for what he had done. Other slaves had begun to appear from the shadows, most of them carrying pitchforks, spades or other tools that were clearly intended as weapons. One of the men sidled into the clearing and stood looking down at the body of one of the policemen. Looking up, he saw Valdor, snarling he began to move towards him, swinging from side to side. Valdor's hand moved towards his gun, then stopped and fell to his side. Teg seemed unable to move as he watched Valdor standing there, apparently unwilling to resist as the slave advanced. It was clear that at any moment, the spade would be within range of Valdors head, and Teg had just tensed to spring forward when a voice rang out the command, "No."

The man with the spade stopped the blade glinting from the dancing flames of the fire above his head. He looked round in surprise and frustration at a young man who had walked into the clearing and who said, "Don't be a fool; he's obviously with this other one; he means no harm to us."

The young man moved forward and looked at Valdor closely, smiling slightly.

"I'm sure if you had meant us harm, you would have had ample opportunity before now. I've often wondered why you acted the way you did".

Valdor, obviously shaken by his near encounter with the slave with the spade, licked his lips before replying.

"Whatever my reasons were, I'm glad I did what I did; perhaps I might not be standing here otherwise."

The young man moved forward and stood before Teg, staring at him curiously. Teg returned his scrutiny and was impressed by what he saw.

The young man was stocky, dark-haired, and had an air of dignity about him, as though he refused to be bowed by his low status. Teg held out his hand. "I am Teg, I'm pleased to meet you."

The slave stared at the outstretched hand in surprise, and Teg realised it was probably unknown for a slave to shake hands, at least with a non-slave.

"I would like to shake your hand," Teg said.

"Why would you want to do that?"

His voice was strong and pleasant, and his query was obviously genuine.

"Because of what you did, the way you think."

"What do you know about how I think?"

"I take it you are the one known as four eight one four?"

"That's right."

"Then I know that you believe in freedom and justice, and that is the reason enough for me to want to shake your hand."

The slave stared at Teg for a long while and then slowly raised his hand, recognising the sincerity in his voice and expression. As they clasped hands, there was a murmur among the other slaves, and suddenly, the young man's face was lit by a broad grin.

"I don't know who you are," he said to Teg, "but I am pleased to meet you."

"I would like to tell you about myself," said Teg, then gestured towards the dead policeman, "but what will you do about these?"

The slave grinned. "The tools we use are not really designed for killing. We will put them to their proper use. They will be buried so deep they will never be found."

He signalled to some of the other slaves, who immediately picked up the bodies and carried them from the clearing. As Teg and Valdor were led to one of the huts, Teg felt a tug on his sleeve. Turning, he saw the young man who had defended his girl - she was now holding his hand. The young man looked nervous and said quietly to Teg, "I would like to thank you for what you did. You may get into a great deal of trouble, though. You really shouldn't have taken the chance."

Teg looked at the young couple and was reminded of himself and Elene. His voice when he replied was warm and sincere, and the young man looked surprised when Teg spoke.

"My friend, you showed great courage tonight. There is no way I could have refused to help you. I hope the fear you speak of will soon be a thing of the past."

The hut was simple, divided into two by a thin partition. The lighting was from a small oil lamp, which made the air musty while only providing a poor light. Four other young men came into the hut and sat against the walls, and it was clear they regarded the other man as their leader. When they were all seated, Teg spoke to the young man first.

"I'm afraid I cannot think of any human being as just a number. Do you have a name by which you are known among yourselves?"

The young man stared at Teg in amazement.

"A name? We are not allowed names".

"I would like to address you by a name. Would you mind if I chose one for you?"

"A name - for me?"

"Yes. I once had a good friend; it seems a long time ago. I would like to call you by his name - Jon."

"Jon? You want to call me Jon."

The young man was clearly intrigued by the thought of having a name and spoke it almost as though tasting it. He smiled and nodded. "Why you should want to give me a name, I don't know, but if it makes you happy, then I agree. In any case, I must admit it also makes me happy".

They talked long into the night. Teg and Jon immediately established a rapport. Despite their disparate backgrounds, it soon became clear they had much in common intellectually. Jon and the other slaves listened in awe as Teg recounted his adventures from the very beginning. He had to stop often to give more detailed explanations of some parts of his story. He soon realised that the concept of the town, The Wastelands, or how the world had been before The Bad Times was utterly alien to them. When he had brought them up to date, he remarked to Jon, "When we have achieved our victory, we will be able to arrange for you all to learn about the whole history of our world. I'm sure Teacher Johansen will find many fertile minds here."

Jon had trouble coping with the incredible range of thoughts and ideas he had been regaled with. He shook his head in despair. "You talk of so many things beyond our understanding, Teg. You speak of us slaves being free to learn from a real teacher. By the very nature of your words, you invest in us with a dignity and importance we don't possess. I'm touched by your attitude, but I must be honest, I can't help but believe it will all remain a dream. A wonderful dream, but still a dream."

"You disappoint me, Jon. I thought you believed in freedom and justice."

"I am, but believing in it doesn't make it happen."

"So, you're prepared to just forget the whole idea without trying to do anything about it?"

"It's not that simple, Teg. I personally would do anything, even die, if necessary, to fight for freedom, but what could I do on my own or with the few here who would back me? The majority, the large majority of slaves here, wouldn't even admit to the idea of freedom, let alone fight for it."

"That's where someone like you is so important. You are intelligent and obviously have reasoning powers. At least some people here regard you as a leader. Now that you know that we will try and fight the system, surely you can persuade some of your people to be ready to join in."

"You mean you want us to fight with you? Indeed, you're joking? What do we know about fighting? What weapons do we have that could stand up against the guns of the police? I'm sorry, Teg. I admire what you're doing, and I would be honoured to be a part of it, but I have to say, in all honesty, that your hopes for us are too high."

"I don't think so Jon, with someone like you to lead them, I think you'll find that your fellow slaves will turn out to be a lot different from what you might expect. After all, they are people - human beings, and all they need is motivation. You're the one to do that. Will you at least try?"

Jon stared at Teg, his face mirroring his conflicting emotions. He sighed, then shrugged, smiling wryly. "I'll try Teg, I'll really try."

"Good, Jon. What you must remember is that whether your people choose to fight for themselves or not, if we succeed, they will become free people anyway. They're going to have to come to terms with that one day." Jon looked away, but not before Teg had seen the glint of sudden tears in his eyes. There was a catch in his voice as he said, "Free? If only it could be."

There was a suspicion of dawn in the sky as they emerged from the hut. Teg and Valdor said their goodbyes to the other slaves in the hut with them and took great delight in emulating Jon by shaking hands with the visitors. Jon accompanied them back to the gate, and they solemnly shook hands before slipping through the gate. Having locked the gate, Valdor looked at the key momentarily and then pushed it through the fence. After hesitating for a moment, Jon reached out and took it.

"I don't know if you'll ever use it," Valdor said, "but I'd like you to have it as a symbol of the freedom that may one day be yours."

Quickly, Teg and Valdor crossed to the shelter of the bushes and began returning to the house. They had covered about a hundred yards when Teg looked back through a tree gap. Centrally in the gap at the gate was Jon still standing there, looking towards where they had gone.

Once more, Teg sat in the roof space, listened to the increasing sounds of the day beginning, and wondered what would happen to him in the next few hours. Valdor had gone to The Forum building to requisition supplies for the police headquarters. James would provide him with papers when he collected the radios so that he could explain his possession of them if he was stopped on the way back to the house. Although tired from his night in the slaves' compound, Teg was too keyed up to sleep and spent endless hours just sitting in the gloom of the roof space. He tensed every time he heard a vehicle approaching the house. Still, there were quite a few false alarms before. Finally, the sound of one vehicle came closer and closer and stopped beside the house. When Teg had climbed down from the roof, he could see immediately that Valdor was troubled. "Something wrong?" 'Teg asked.'

"I'm worried about the way the security's been stepped up. I've seen several vehicles stopped at random and searched. I understand every vehicle leaving through the main gate is being thoroughly searched. We have got a problem." They both agreed that the sooner they could leave the valley, the better. After securing the house to avoid accidental discovery, they ate a substantial meal to fortify themselves for their journey. They discussed various ways to avoid having the vehicle searched, but each one had patent shortcomings. Finally, Valdor sighed,

"I'm afraid that we're likely to end up being searched one way or another.

"That's it!" Teg interrupted him, "That's where we're going wrong. We shouldn't be trying to avoid a search at all!"

He thought about it for a moment and then nodded. "It's risky, but it just might work."

Determined not to be taken without a fight if he was discovered, Teg held Valdor's gun in his hands as he crouched down below the level of the window in the passenger side of the vehicle. Valdor's hands were white, and there was tension on the steering wheel as he drove toward the main gate, praying they wouldn't be seen or intercepted. He was still tense as he glided the vehicle to a halt at the side of the road just before the bend that led onto the last short stretch before the gates came into sight.

As the vehicle stopped, Teg, now once more in police uniform, opened the door and jumped out, disappearing into the bushes. Valdor waited a few minutes and then moved the vehicle slowly forward. He could see the gates at the bottom of the long, gentle slope as he rounded the bend. Several policemen were standing around. A couple of them looked in his direction as he stopped at the command of the policeman who stepped from the bushes before him. Praying that the distance was enough for the policeman at the gate not to recognise Teg as an imposter but not too great that they wouldn't be able to tell what was going on, Teg and Valdor went through the pantomime of searching the vehicle. They didn't want to hang about for too long in case another police vehicle should come along. Still, they needed to make it appear that a thorough search was occurring. They were both sweating with tension when Teg finally stood behind the open passenger door. The seats were tilted back, and the cover off the tool compartment. As Valdor moved around the front of the vehicle and approached the passenger door, screening it from the men at the gate, Teg ducked into the car and slid into the tool compartment. Trying to appear casual, Valdor slammed the door and strolled to the driver's side. Leaning in, he closed the compartment lid and pushed the seats back into place before climbing in and shutting his door. Breathing deeply to try and settle his nerves, he set the vehicle in motion and slowly moved down the slope towards the gates. The inner gates opened as he approached, and he was waved into the cage-like structure. Stopping the vehicle, he climbed out, smiling as naturally as he could as he turned to the other policeman. "Half the day will be gone before I get through being searched," he said resignedly.

The senior man there laughed and pointed back up the slope, "I doubt very much that that search could have missed anything. It's any wonder he didn't ask you to strip your engine down. I'd also be very surprised if you'd managed to smuggle anything aboard between there and here unless you're some kind of magician. No, I don't think we'll waste our time. We've got more important things to do. Mind how you go. Open the gates!"

Trying not to laugh with relief, Valdor climbed back into the vehicle and moved it forward as the gates opened. It wasn't until he had travelled along the grass and turned into the abrupt shelter of the trees that he realised he had been holding his breath.

Chapter 44

"Do you believe in the sanctity of life?"

"I do."

"Do you believe in the sanctity of the mind?"

"I do"

The vast crowd was silent as Mictor asked questions, and the responses drifted over their heads. Almost everybody in the settlement had turned up for Teg and Elene's wedding, and there was an air of expectancy and happiness among the crowd.

Since Teg's return, the activity had been feverish, and he had been staggered at how much had been achieved during his absence. Within hours of his return, he had seen vast stockpiles of food and other supplies stored in the underground railway tunnels. Roger had demonstrated remarkable organisational abilities and had formed a well-organised team that had begged, borrowed, and possibly even stolen supplies necessary for the coming campaign. Marcus, too, had been busy. Soon after Teg had left the settlement, another vehicle set out and, acting upon the information supplied by Valdor, worked out three alternative routes to The Forum. He had explained the strategy to Teg a few hours after his triumphant return.

"Our force will be split into three equal groups. They'll follow a common route, although the groups will leave at two or three hour intervals until they're about twenty miles from the valley. At that point, they'll head in different directions. The first group will skirt the valley's eastern end and come up on the general area of The Forum building from that side. Another group will head for the main entrance to the complex, and the third group will approach in the direction of the lake."

"How do you propose to get over the fence?"

"He doesn't."

Marcus grinned at Teg's puzzlement and then explained, looking pleased with himself.

"We'd agreed on a possible way of getting in, but we needed Peter and Hals report before we could be sure. From what they tell us, we think that'll work."

He led Teg to a table on which a crude, but none-the-less representative model of the valley had been prepared. Most of it had been based on Valdor's information, and Teg was surprised at how easy it was for him to identify the main features.

Marcus pointed to places in the areas he had designated as attack points. "We had guessed that there would be suitable places, and Peter and Hals's report confirms this, where we could dig our way under the fence."

"Under it? You're not serious, surely? That means you're almost certain to be seen before entering the fence."

"Not necessarily. What we need, and what we understand is available, is a clump of trees or bushes just a short distance from the fence and in an uneven area. If we start digging in the shelter of the trees or bushes, we can gradually dig forward without being on top of the ground."

"You mean tunnel? But that's far too involved!"

"Not a tunnel, no. As you say, that would take far too long and require special materials. No, what we do is trench towards the fence. If we choose a place where the ground slopes up slightly towards the fence, there's little chance of being seen by anyone inside unless they come right up to the perimeter."

Teg considered it for a while and then said, "It might just work at that. What are the chances of fixing up some kind of trial here?"

Marcus looked very pleased with himself. "I'm ahead of you. Come with me." They walked through the settlement to a space that had been cleared in one of the overgrown grassy squares between derelict houses. The ground sloped slightly upwards from where they stood, and a short length of rusty wire fence had been erected at the top of the slope.

"Imagine that is the fence around The Forum," said Marcus. "We're on the inside, and this is about the distance from the fence where the police patrol. Now come and look at this."

He led Teg up the slope. They had almost reached the rusty wire before Teg became aware of the dark gash in the trench running away at right angles from the wire and disappearing into a clump of wild roses at the bottom of a similar slope. The trench was wide enough for a laden man to pass through easily and deep enough for a tall man to run through at a crouch.

"I'm impressed, Marcus, you've solved one of our biggest problems. How long did this take?"

"Just over six hours. We used several men in short bursts. That way, they could go hell for leather and not worry about running out of steam. The moment one of them showed signs of slowing, another one would take his place."

"It still seems an awful long time to be out there."

"It's not really. We must get into position before nightfall, wait overnight, and start digging the moment it's light enough to see the front of your face. At this time of year, we can be halfway to the fence before The Forum's even stirring."

"Well, I can't think of a better alternative; all I can suggest, if you haven't already thought of it, is that you see if you can improve your digging implements and make sure you've got enough sharp ones on hand. Right then, what about our radio men?"

"It's all taken care of. They should be leaving within the next hour or so. Rogers arranged supplies and equipment for them, and I've given orders for them to be supplied with a gun each. They'll be on their own out there for quite some time. If we lose one, it could make the whole exercise pointless."

They had returned to Mictors' house then, and as they approached the door, the old man appeared and gestured to Teg.

"There's something here. I think you should see Teg." Curious, Teg entered the house, surprised when Mictor continued up the path to meet Marcus.

"Hello Teg."

Her voice made him spin around. She stood by the window, grinning at him, and then launched herself across the room into his arms.

"Elene", he murmured, having kissed her ", I wondered where you were when I got back. Margarita tells me you've been visiting."

"Yes, Teg", she said shyly, "I've been to see Melinda and her sisters."

"Her sisters?"

"Oh yes, they insist she's now one of their sisters, and she's thrilled."

"I should think so. Did you go there for any reason?"

"I wanted to know if one of Thomas's daughters would like to er well if one of them would like to carry the birds for me. They said Melinda should do it."

"Carry the birds; what on earth is that about."

Elene looked disappointed and somewhat apprehensive as she answered. "At our wedding. You know, like Margarita and Jason had."

"Don't you think it's a bit early for that?"

"Oh, why Teg, why? There's no reason to wait now, is there?"

She looked at him doubtfully.

"Have you changed your mind about wanting to get married?"

"No, of course not; it's just that I don't think we should get married until after the attack."

"Oh no, Teg, I don't want to wait until then. I thought we'd agreed. Oh, Teg I'm" suddenly, she was crying, her shoulders shaking violently with the force of her sobbing.

Helpless, not sure what to do, Teg just hugged her. Finally, her sobbing subsided, and she mumbled against his chest, "I'm sorry, Teg, that was childish of me. I won't do that again; we'll wait until you're ready. He was deeply moved by the sadness in her voice as she tried to pretend that his words hadn't hurt her badly.

"I've got to go, my love," he said.

She kept her head bowed as she shrugged and stepped away from him. She said nothing as he walked to the door, but he saw a tear slide down her cheek. He wasn't sure whether to laugh or cry as he stood in the doorway and said, "Yes, I've got to go. I've got to catch a couple of birds. Otherwise, Melinda won't have anything to carry tomorrow."

The birds flew upwards, circled, and sped away, their wings fluttering violently. The crowd cheered and cheered as Teg and Elene hugged and kissed as husband and wife. They were congratulated by the others on the platform, and then Teg was just about to step forward in response to the crowd's chant of Teg, Teg, Teg," when Marcus stopped him with a gesture and stepped to the edge of the platform. He stood facing the crowd as some of his men moved along the fringes, and suddenly, there was movement as the people on the flanks began to edge sideways. Teg could now see what he hadn't noticed before, that the tightly packed centre portion of the crowd was made up entirely of men Marcus had been training for the previous months. There were at least four hundred of them, and they stood there expectantly as the crowd fell silent. Marcus looked at Teg, licked his lips nervously, and then turned back to face the massed group of men.

"Men!" his voice roared out. There was a perceptible tension among the men, and then, as Marcus roared "Form Squads", they began to shuffle and rush. The only sound was the rattle of booted feet moving. Teg stared in astonishment as the whole mass of men had resolved itself into twelve neatly squared-off blocks in less than two minutes.

"Attention!" roared Marcus, and with almost one sound, feet were raised, stamped down, and the whole army snapped to attention. It had all been done with such discipline, skill, and perfect timing that Teg could hardly believe what he'd seen. He stared out at the perfectly formed groups of men, all standing rigidly at attention, and he shook his head in disbelief. A pleased smile played at the corner of Marcus' mouth as, turning, he saw Tegs gesture. Teg was even more astonished when Marcus came to attention in front of him, saluted and said proudly, "Teg, your army is ready."

It was as though time had been reeled back, so clearly did she recall another place, another dawn, and another bird singing. She peered into the trees, wondering foolishly whether this might be the same bird whose song matched her joy. She remembered how, in her happiness, she had wanted to fly to the tops of the trees with the birds and proclaim her love to the world.

The scent of roses and lemon balm matched her sweet mood as she crouched there and stared at Teg's sleeping face. Her heart swelled with love, and momentarily, she felt an irrational fear that it might burst and spoil everything. Then she giggled, almost childishly, although she was no longer a child. Even in repose, Teg's face showed strength and maturity far beyond his years, and Elene felt a sense of awe at the knowledge that she was his and he was hers. She reached out, wanting to wake him and have his love for her reaffirmed and to reaffirm her love for him. Instead, she slowly traced his face's outline with her fingers just clear of his skin. She felt sure he must have the most perfect features in the world and prayed silently that nothing would ever take him away from her.

She shivered as she thought of what tomorrow would bring. Standing, she slowly moved to stand by the overhanging roses that had shielded them from the night. The bird flew into the sky at her movement, still trilling its song. For a moment, she wished that she and Teg could fly thus, high into the sky, out over The Wastelands and into the green and beautiful hills that Teg had described to her. Her fear made her want to run and wake Teg and beg him to take her away, now, right now, this very minute. Then she sighed and looked back to where her young husband slept so peacefully. She knew that the fates that had brought them together must also determine what the future would bring them. Looking at him, she could see him again as he had stood there on their wedding day. She could hear again his voice ringing out over the heads of the crowd and, in particular, the heads of the massed ranks of Marcus' men, who even now were well on their way through the countryside to the valley where the fates would decide what their world would be.

"Men, as I stand here, on what I already knew was going to be the happiest and proudest day of my life," he turned and looked at Elene, who blushed prettily, and a cheer began in the throats of the crowd, but died away as he turned back and went on, solemnly, "I hadn't realised just how proud and happy I was going to be; I don't have to tell you that we are on the brink of possibly the most incredible adventure the world has ever seen, at least the world as we know it. It has been my dream, my burning ambition, to see the day when we might go forth and smite the evil beings who masquerade under the name of leaders and who, through their corrupt and repressive system, deny to so many the rights and privileges that should be theirs without question. I have lived in the town, and I have seen control exercised over the minds and bodies of the people. I have seen the so-called Sanctum of Well-Being, which is no more than an execution chamber for the weak, the defenceless, the ones who might question the philosophy that allows such a place to exist. I have seen men and women who walk proudly into that Sanctum to surrender their lives to the State. Men and women whose only crime, whose only qualification for death, was what?!

They had lived for sixty-five years. Consider, my friends, how you would feel if one of your loved ones was made to rise one morning, to walk from your house and be put to death simply because some corrupt and self-serving leader had proclaimed it must be so" The crowd was hushed, the silence almost palpable. Young people looked at elderly parents or grandparents and moved closer to them. Old people looked at babies and young children who crawled at their feet, and when they looked back at their young leader, there were tears in their eyes.

"Thoughts of these things happening are bad enough. What is the real evil of the system, though, is that the people go to their deaths happily, proudly, with what they would claim is dignity. That is the evil that we face: a system that takes away the minds of the people, a system that represses them and conditions them to believe that in succumbing to the foul and evil laws of their rulers, they are serving their fellow men."

For a moment, Teg paused, breathing heavily, the adrenaline flowing as he sensed the unity of the crowd and the intensity with which they received his words. When he resumed, his tone was almost conversational at first but began to harden as he recalled the injustices he had seen.

"It is an evil system that keeps the people of the town so repressed, repression that they are really not aware of, but I have been somewhere else that makes the lives of the people in the town, the people as you know them, seem like paradise. There are those among you who have lost loved ones and friends during the raids that the police have, on occasion, made against this settlement. You will know that those who were captured were taken to serve The Forum as slaves. My friends, I have been among those slaves; I have seen the hovels in which they live, the conditions in which they work, and the violence and cruelty with which they are treated. Worst of all, I have seen that they are not even granted the dignity of the status of human beings. They are regarded as animals. I have seen a young man on the very point of being killed because he wished to protect his loved one. Protect her from being used as a vessel of lust by the cruel, evil men whose very existence is a blight on our world. I have sat with these slaves, I have talked with them, and I have learned that they are far from being animals. They are as human as the rest of us. For some, those who have been born into slavery, as most of them have, the concept of humanity and freedom is too hard to grasp. Another sign, my friends, of the evil practised by The Forum. People who cannot accept the idea that they are human."

As Teg paused, a small child suddenly burst into chatter. Many people looked as though they might have laughed, but the weight of Teg's words was still heavy on them, and their smiles were brief.

"I have told you of the town, I have told you of the slaves, and you are only too aware of your own existence. My friends, the ultimate evil I have seen is in the valley where The Forum lies. I have seen the homes of the families and friends of the rulers. I have seen their magnificent houses and glimpsed the unbelievable luxury in which they live. I have learned that they are free from other people's restrictions. They are served and pampered by slaves and servants; they want nothing and give nothing. Consider my friends. The people of the town, the hundreds of slaves in the valley, are subject to all the forms of repression I have spoken of; the people of this settlement, you - my people, live in fear and uncertainty, never knowing when the forces of The Forum may once more seek to wipe you out or to enslave you. Consider my friends that all this permits a select few to live a life of privilege, luxury, and idleness. I have told you of my dream, my burning ambition to see an end to this evil.

When I first came here, the dream might not have been realistic. I saw the willingness to learn to grow among you and sensed the rising belief in your capabilities. I began to hear you talk of freedom and justice, not as abstract theories but as attainable objects. I saw your growing willingness to fight for liberty and justice, which is rightly yours. Today, my friends, I have stood here, and I noticed that our dream was within reach. Today, I have seen the beginning of the realisation of all our hopes. Look with pride upon these men, for they are ready and willing to fight, and I know that they will win!"

Now they cheered, not just the cheering that might greet a parade but a heartfelt outpouring of emotion that signified their belief in themselves. Marcus turned to Teg and held out his hand. As they shook hands, their eyes met, and they stared at each other solemnly. Then, as if by prearrangement, they both nodded. "I think it's time," said Teg. "Boo."

Elene jumped, startled, even though the word had been said quietly. She turned to face a grinning Teg. His grin faded to a soft, gentle smile as she slipped into his arms. They kissed gently, exchanging a thousand words without speaking one. Contented, she laid her head on his shoulder, her arms around him, his arms holding her protectively. "You were miles away", he murmured.

"I was thinking about you leaving tomorrow. It isn't possible that it's going to happen."

"It's already happening. That's what's hard to believe, the fact that we've got hundreds of men out there. We've got supplies stored in all sorts of places, medical supplies and equipment already stored within a mile of the valley and established the radio link with James and Antony." Teg glanced at where his radio lay on top of his pack and where they had slept. He had relayed messages twice to The Forum. Brief, careful messages, letting James and Antony know what was happening. In turn, he had received a message from James only the day before, letting him know that, with Valdor's help, they had smuggled weapons out of the supplies department and concealed them in dense growth near the places where the breakthroughs were planned.

"I still feel that I should have gone with the men," Teg said now, sitting down on a low, moss-covered wall.

"Well, I'm glad you didn't," Elene said, sitting beside him, "this could be our last time together for a long time."

She fell silent as the thought depressed her, and Teg reached out and pulled her close to him.

"It's going to be alright. When I look at what we've achieved, I can't help but feel confident. More needs to be done before it can all be used. I'm astonished at what Marcus has done; he's created a superb army in less than a year. You saw them at the wedding, they were magnificent. We've also got the element of surprise, plus inside help. Believe me, my love, we're going to win."

Although she was dreading Teg's departure. Elene knew she had found a kind of happiness that she would never have dreamed possible. She remembered the dreadful day at The Sanctum, her headlong flight, capture, and rescue. She thought of how her love for Teg had blossomed, of how she had dared to hope that he might love her too. She smiled and snuggled closer to him as she remembered the little signs, the magic moments when her heart had leapt with happiness at some word or gesture from him that seemed to indicate that he had returned her love. She remembered clearly when he had first declared his love, and she felt almost shocked at the realisation that they were now man and wife. She dreaded his departure tomorrow. But she knew that she had been lucky enough to know true love. She also knew that she had learned the meaning of freedom, liberty, and justice through the incredible young man she so adored. All these things had meant nothing to her before she had known Teg, and she knew that, even if she was never to see him again after his departure, she had much to be thankful for. So it was that she forced herself to smile and make what might be their last hours together as bright as she could. She tried to convey optimism. "When you've won, Teg, what will you do?"

"What do you mean?"

"Well, for a start, where will we live?"

"I really don't know. When I was first going to see the valley, with Mictor, I saw the most beautiful countryside imaginable. I imagined how wonderful it would be to live there as a free man. The valley itself, where The Forum is, is beautiful. There are superb houses there, you won't believe how luxurious they are. There are excellent crops and gardens, everything you could want. But somehow, I don't think I'd want to live there."

In his heart, Teg knew that he would love to live in the very place where they now sit. Still, he knew it would require many years of hard work and would be far removed from the comforts and luxuries available to them when they had achieved their aims. Ever since he had first seen this place, with its wild roses, lemon balm and apple mint, sloping grassy surrounds, and remnants of majestic rooms and passageways, he had loved it. He remembered how he first came to it with Zack, Daniel, and Jon to collect herbs and roots. Since then, he'd thought of this place and how it might be again, and it was here that he'd brought his new wife to languish in the gentle beauty of the ruins. He loved Elene too much to want to deny her any of the things her heart might desire, and so he ducked her question by asking her instead, "Where would you like to live?"

"Well, I haven't seen the places you've seen, although I know from the way you talk that they must be beautiful. I'd be intrigued to see the houses in the valley you tell me are so grand."

She paused and looked embarrassed and almost fearful before continuing, "I suppose you'll think I'm silly, Teg, but, to be absolutely honest, I'd give anything to live right here."

Happily, he kissed her, a warm kiss that became urgent. He led her back to where they had lain before. The bird had returned to the tree and resumed its musical salute to the day, but neither heard it.

Mictor looked as though he was about to cry. He faced Teg as they stood by the side of the vehicle. Jason was already inside, having said his farewell, with a tearful Margarita watching from the entrance to the hospital.

"Well, Teg, the moment has come," the old man said in a voice that trembled with emotion.

"I'm going to be fine, Mictor, don't worry."

"It's so hard to believe. I used to dream of a moment like this, but I never ever imagined I'd live to see it. Take care of yourself, my boy; I've grown very fond of you."

"And I of you, Mictor. I like to think of this day as the beginning of the end of something you started."

"I failed Teg, you won't fail."

"You didn't fail, Mictor, because you tried to do something. It has taken a long time for you to see it reach fruition, but remember, those men who are out there, those who leave with me today, and I; we are Mictorans!"

As they drove away, the hospital and the people there dwindling in the distance, Teg knew that his words had made the old man very happy. He felt a surge of affection for him that almost brought tears to his eyes, and then he turned to the front and set his mind on the coming adventure.

"I've been summoned to see the Second President this afternoon," said Antony.

He and James were in the courtyard that Teg and Valdor had crossed to gain access to The Forum. They knew that Tegs forces were mustering somewhere on the edges of the valley, and their tension had increased with each day as they feared that something would go wrong. The recent disappearance of two policemen, entirely without trace, had sent Aaron into a frenzy of anger, and he had become even more convinced that rebellion was in the air. His anger had been mainly directed at his Second President as he suspected that Delmo would be pretty happy to take over the mantle of President.

Antony and James had been expecting Delmo to increase his efforts to discredit David, and they guessed that that was the reason for the latest summons that Antony had received. Although worried by this latest development, James tried not to show it.

"Don't worry about it, my friend. Just a bit longer, and things will be resolved, one way or another. All you must do is stall Delmo for another hour or so.

"The trouble is I think he suspects that I am stalling, and I doubt that he'll be able to contain his anger if he thinks I'm stalling again."

They heard marching feet approaching from within The Forum.

"We better not be seen too much together", said James" That sounds like one of the patrols. They might think we're cooking up some kind of conspiracy if they see us talking together too much. I'll see you later."

As James headed for the door, Antony moved quickly to the side of the courtyard and sat on one of the benches provided there. He sat down and sprawled out, endeavouring to give the impression of someone who had been lazing there for some time. As James reached the door, it swung open, pulled by one of the police squads who had come marching down the corridor and halted at the door. Smiling, James stood back to let the squad pass through, but they remained where they were except for their leader. Antony tried to make himself as inconspicuous as possible as he heard the squad leader address James.

"Attendant James, we have been sent here by the President. You are under arrest!"

Teg was stunned. "Under arrest, when did this happen?"

Unfamiliar with the radio, he failed for a moment to release the transmit button and missed the first few words of Antony's reply. The missing words, however, did not detract from the message's content, and Teg's heart sank as he listened to the disembodied voice from within The Forum building.

"A smart policeman had an excellent memory. He just happened to have been on the previous inventory inspection. He noticed that an extraordinary number of weapons appeared to have been issued. We always knew it was a risk, but only if they could have waited another day."

"What's your position on this?"

"That's what's puzzling me at the moment. I've been expecting to be summoned to explain why the computer sheets show that the weapons in the supplies department are apparently correct when the police themselves say they have yet to receive the number that has gone. I was supposed to see the Second President this afternoon. Still, he's been in an emergency meeting of The Supreme Council since James was arrested. I've now got to see him a couple of hours from now."

"We weren't due to start our move until tomorrow; it looks now as though we're going to have to start earlier than that. We'll start work tonight; all is well, and we should be able to move in by first light in the morning. What about James, what's happening to him?"

There was a prolonged moment of silence. Teg was about to fiddle with the controls, thinking his radio had failed when Antony's voice was heard once again, filled with despair. "He's been handed over to the Interrogator."

This was the real thing, and the expressions on the men's faces reflected that. They had gone about their work with grim determination, and already, after just three hours, the results of their labours were evident. Teg was with the group at the top end of the valley, near the lake. He crouched now within a large clump of bushes and small trees and watched the men working in perfect harmony.

A large hole had been dug on the side of the small clearing within the course, nearest the fence about forty feet away. A trench was being dug from this hole, and it was already pushing between the bushes and would soon be in open ground. The large hole enabled a couple of men to retrieve the soil being passed back down the trench to pass it up to men on the top, who then distributed it under and around the trees and bushes on the other side of the clearing. Progress had been rapid at first but had slowed for the moment as the roots that intertwined below the surface had to be cut away.

The ground beyond the bushes sloped gently up to the fence. They had the advantage of the small rolling hills providing a natural valley to aim their trench, offering additional concealment. In one of the trees above them, a man was concealed. He would whistle gently at intervals to indicate that a patrol on the other side of the fence was at its nearest point to them. At such times, operations would cease for a few minutes and then start up again as quietly as possible until the patrol was a reasonable distance away. Brief radio messages from the other two sites told them that equally good progress was being made.

About half a mile back from where Teg crouched, a thick forest concealed his main force of a hundred men. They lay in disciplined quiet, concealed from all but the closest scrutiny. Their weapons, which ranged from a few sophisticated guns to the most primitive spears, ready at their sides.

Chapter 45

Every so often, they would look towards where they knew their squad leader was concealed, radio at his side, but they knew that barring emergencies, they would only be called to move just before dawn. It was a measure of their discipline that they were prepared to lie there for so long, quiet, and unmoving. Although the troops knew the chances of discovery were remote, they also knew that if they should be seen, the whole operation could be doomed, which they didn't even want to think about.

Antony sat across from the Second President as he had been ordered to do. He tried to appear relaxed, but his concern for James and his situation made it difficult. What was even more unnerving was that, for a couple of minutes, Delmo had said nothing, merely sitting there and staring at him intently. It had seemed like a couple of hours to Antony, and he was wondering whether he should make some attempt at conversation when Delmo startled him by suddenly rapping out a question, "What do you know about this business with this Attendant, James?"

"I'm not sure I understand the question, Second President."

"You know that he's been arrested?"

"Yes, sir."

"Do you know why he's been arrested?"

"No, I don't, Second President, I really haven't any idea?"

"He's been arrested because it appears that many weapons have been removed from the Supplies Department - the Department that he controls."

"That - that sounds serious, Second President."

"Sounds serious? It is serious, you fool! What I want to know is how the stock sheets provided from the central computer, which are your responsibility, show that the weapons that were in the Supplies Department were apparently correct."

An icy feeling had settled in Antony's stomach, and his legs felt as though they would fold under him if he tried to stand. He had known that a moment like this was always likely to come, and he had often wondered how he would face it. Now he knew. He had never imagined he could feel so frightened. He made a conscious effort to appear innocent and confused.

"That doesn't make sense, Second President, with all due respect, sir. I can only assume the computer has been tampered with."

Delmo looked hard at him. With an intense, calculating look, Antony was convinced that the Second President didn't believe him but wasn't prepared for his following words.

"Who do you think might have tampered with the computer?"

"I really don't know Second President; I wouldn't have any idea."

Delmo grinned an evil, satisfied grin. He looked pleased with himself as though finally he had found what he had been searching for a long time. He leaned forward. "Isn't it possible it could have been David?"

"David, sir?"

"The Third President, you idiot!"

"I don't think he knows anything about the computer, Second President."

"Perhaps he doesn't. Perhaps though, if you were to tell the President about how David had taken such a big interest in the computer in recent months, he'd likely believe you, don't you think?"

Antony stared with grudging admiration at Delmo. He had to admire how the Second President's scheming mind had latched onto the latest crisis in The Forum to rid himself of his rival. With the President's paranoid mind, he would only need to believe James if he testified that David had been learning about the computer. The President would feel his suspicions of a planned rebellion were justified and that David, as the ringleader, had manipulated the laptop to obtain arms for his planned insurrection. In theory, it distracts The Forum's attention. At the same time, the final preparations for Tegs attack were being made. The only problem was that Antony was fully aware that, in his present frame of mind, the President would no doubt suspect him of being part of the conspiracy, perhaps seeking to ingratiate himself with The Forum betraying his co-conspirator. The prospect of condemning David to the President by lying was not attractive.

"I don't believe you have much choice", Delmo almost sneered.

"I don't understand sir."

"If you can't persuade our dear President that David tampered with the computer, I shall have to tell him it was you. I leave it to your imagination as to what that might mean."

It didn't need much imagination, and Antony knew that his chances of stalling until the attack were slim. "If I do as you say, Second President, what's likely to happen to me?" he finally asked, hoping to find a way out of his dilemma.

"Then we would perhaps find some way of rewarding you."

Although his expression showed that he expected the scenario to follow the same lines as Antony had predicted, for a moment, Antony felt a stirring as he recalled the nature of the reward he was likely to receive and the fact that the means of that reward was the reason he had fallen into Delmo's clutches in the first place. He thought of Carla, and a faint hope stirred inside him. He risked it because he was on the brink of disaster anyway.

"Knowing that I might not emerge unscathed from my testimony to the President," he said carefully, "it might make it easier for me to make that testimony if I could enjoy my reward beforehand."

"You seem to forget, Antony, that if you don't give that testimony, then I will give a testimony of my own."

Antony knew that he was risking Delmo's wrath, but he knew it was his last chance, so as confidently as he could.

"With all due respect though, Second President, it is my testimony that will lead to the downfall of the Third President."

Antony felt the clutch of fear at his heart as Delmo's feature contorted with sudden rage, then almost as quickly, the rage was gone, replaced with a grudging smile.

"You have some nerve, Antony, you do indeed, but that's something I can admire. I can well understand your longing for the delectable

Carla, and, as it is very likely the last time you will enjoy her charms, I shall not deny you it." His face became hard again, his voice cold as he finished, "But remember, before the night has fallen, you must stand before the President and give your testimony."

It was becoming hard to see now, although there was still sufficient light to distinguish the dark gash of the trench cutting up the slope towards the fence. The front end of the trench was only about three feet from the wall and would need no more than an hour's work to reach it. The only concern was how deeply the wire mesh was embedded in the ground. Reports have been received from the other two teams that they were in similar situations. The primary group of men were concealed in the trees and bushes that ran parallel to the fence near the strip of grass that led along to the main gates. The trench was being cut behind a slight hump in the ground, which concealed it from the direction of the gatehouse but not from directly within the fence. They had gambled on the fact that only a little patrolling was done here to the main gates as the permanent contingent of guards was considered security enough for this area.

It had been agreed between Marcus and Teg that the major resistance would initially come from this end of the valley, and therefore, the main thrust of the attack would be here. Marcus himself was with this group, and, like Teg at the top of the valley, he was delighted and impressed with the discipline and efficiency of the men, both those who dug the trench and those who waited.

Marcus was aware of the risks they were taking as he looked along the line of the trench from where he crouched beside the bush. Although it was now quite dark, anyone who came close to the fence would easily see the trench. Although this hadn't happened so far, Marcus was only too aware of how disastrous it would be if the trench was discovered and felt like breaking through and launching his attack now. He knew, however, how important it was not to jeopardise the other groups by precipitate action, so he finally compromised. He called the leader of the digging squad and explained what he proposed.

"We'll carry on to the fence now and hopefully get through. We'll make the hole big enough for just one man at a time to get through; that way, we'll minimise the chances of it being seen. We'll send only half a dozen men in, and they'll be there mainly to guard against accidental discovery. However, a couple of them can make a start by looking for that alarm cable. We won't be able to send the rest of the men through yet because there'll be nowhere to conceal them; we want to wait to blow the whole thing. You get that trench under the fence; I'll organise my men."

He tried hard to think of how it might have been. He tried to think of what it would have been like to be free. He very nearly managed to capture the image of a mountain stream and grassy hills leading to beautiful vistas when the pain once more seared through his brain. His body arched against the restraints as he fought not to scream. A strangled panting escaped from his clenched teeth as his sweat-streaked head rolled from side to side. The pain faded, and as his body slumped back, he felt the nausea rise in him, the taste of bile in the back of his throat, and his stomach heaved up and down in violent spasms as he fought not to vomit. He felt warm breath on his face, then smelled the foul stale-wine odour of Garon's breath as he leaned over him. He opened his pain-dimmed eyes and looked with fear and loathing at the cruel face that sneered down at him.

On the screen of his mind, he suddenly saw a picture of policeman Tanner as he had first seen him, and he knew that this man had done that to him. His mind seemed to scream, "That's what he's doing to me!"

Most horrifying of all to him was the realisation that, despite the sickening, excruciating, dehumanising pain he had suffered, the torture had barely started. He prayed for instant death because he knew that what was to come would surely turn his mind. It was with almost detached awareness that he noted that Garon made no effort to question him, being content merely to inflict as much suffering as he could upon a being condemned the moment he had been given into his charge. The pain came again, sudden, shocking, and this time extracting a short, sharp scream from him. It had become a point of honour to him that he would not scream, and he clamped his teeth hard and fought not to fail again. His mind sought escape in thoughts of better things, and he prayed that the attack on the following day would succeed. Too late for him, admittedly, but he felt a comforting satisfaction in the thought that he had, in some small way, been a part of something good and noble before his destruction at the hands of this evil maniac. Once more, the pain receded, leaving him trembling and sick. He felt the perspiration running out of every part of him, and he was conscious of it pooling on his closed eyelids. When he opened his eyes, they blurred with perspiration as it spilled over onto his face. He heard a ringing in his ears, and the booming of his heart seemed like a drum inside his head. He listened to a discordant, harsh noise and momentarily didn't realise it was Garon's voice.

"You think you are courageous, don't you? Well, let me tell you, my friend, so far, you have suffered nothing. Do you think you can avoid screaming do you?"

He reached over, and then his hand came into view, holding an implement that James could not possibly have recognised but that he knew instinctively was evil. "This, my fine brave friend, will guarantee your screams. Don't worry that your screams will be unmanly because when I finish this, you won't be a man anymore anyway."

James clenched his teeth and squeezed his eyes shut as Garon laughed evilly and leaned over him. He felt his weight lurch across his body, the coldness of the metal against his thighs, and everything was still. All but a slow, very warm movement across his shoulder. Opening his eyes, James stared, fascinated at a bright red ribbon of blood that flowed across his upper body. He slowly traced its source back over the slumped body of Garon to the knife that protruded from between his shoulder blades. James raised his eyes and stared beyond Garon's body to where Valdor's white face stared back at him.

The policeman's boot was obviously well cared for, its polished surface catching and reflecting the light from the open doorway of the gatehouse. The wearer of the boot now stood, talking to a companion, about thirty feet from the gatehouse. They had met as one had been heading towards the small building, and the other had emerged from it, seeking fresh air. They stood on the edge of a group of small straggly shrubs that dotted the gently rolling slopes above the complex entrance. Although he didn't know it, the toe of the policeman's shiny boot rested on a triangle of cloth that protruded from under one of the bushes.

Had he noticed it and had cared to trace it to its source, he would no doubt have been astounded to discover that it was the cuff of the sleeve of the man who lay, hardly daring to breathe beneath the bush. The man knew that, somewhere behind him, another man lay similarly concealed, hardly daring to breathe. The night seemed so quiet during each pause in the conversation between the two policemen. The man under the bush was convinced that his heartbeats must be audible. The two men had crawled under the fence an hour before. There had been exultant grins among the men who clustered around Marcus as the patch of grass just inside the wall had slithered down into the trench. The dark patch of the hole showed clearly even in the pale light of a partial moon. They had waited a few minutes to ensure that no patrol was around, and then the six men selected by Marcus had run, crouched low, along the trench. The first two carried trenching tools, which they pushed under the fence ahead of them, and then the first one and another of the men were inside the wall. As their dark shapes moved swiftly across the grass inside, Marcus silently prayed that none of them would be discovered before the leading group of men began to go under the fence in about three hours. The latest messages from Teg and Peter at the other two locations had indicated that they would be ready to move at first light. As far as Marcus was concerned, the next three hours would be the longest he had ever known.

The policeman's boot moved away from the sleeve, and, very slowly, the arm was withdrawn under the bush. A few seconds later, the policeman glanced down, and all he saw were his shiny boots. And then the two policemen turned away and strolled towards the gatehouse. When they were sure the policemen were at a safe distance, the two hidden men let out long, pent-up breaths. They waited until the gatehouse door had shut behind the two policemen before they began to move. Crawling on all fours, using the overlying bushes as cover, they reached the top of the slope and then moved downwards.

When they were reasonably sure that they were below the crest of the hill, they rose to their feet, thankfully stretching their cramped limbs. Looking around carefully, they began to move towards the road to the barracks, which was concealed from them, some half a mile away, by the intervening trees and hills. Alert to the possibility of a vehicle suddenly appearing along the road, they ran stealthily parallel to the road until they saw a small stone building ahead.

The building had no windows, and its single door was on the opposite side of them, the word 'Store' stencilled upon it. The nature of the building was unimportant to them; what they were concerned with was, hopefully, somewhere among the ornamental shrubs that banked up against the end wall. When they were close to the building, they were dismayed to see how small the shrubs were; they would provide hardly any cover while they worked. One of the men crouched by the corner of the building, looking up and down the road, while the other crawled among the shrubs. There was relief and satisfaction as he found the small white peg pushed into the ground. Valdor had done his part. He freed the trenching tool strapped to his back and began scraping at the ground where the peg had been. Every little sound seemed magnified in the pre-dawn quiet, and his colleague glanced back anxiously as small stones in the ground clinked against the blade. They both felt incredibly exposed and knew that if a vehicle should come around the bend in the road, about two hundred feet away, at any speed, their chances of avoiding detection were remote. The man digging worked urgently, scraping at the ground like a dog burying a bone, and then, all at once, his trenching tool resisted his pull. He looked down and saw the cable stretched tightly across the blade that had slid underneath.

"Got it!' he whispered hoarsely and began scraping with his hands until he could get to the cable easily. Reaching into his pocket, he produced a small, very sharp knife. He began to carefully strip away the outer sheathing on the cable. Gradually he exposed the two different coloured inner sheaths and worked at the surrounding plastic until he had exposed a sufficient length for him to be able to slip the knife blade between the two wires. Turning the knife until the blade's sharp edge was against the wire, he licked his lips nervously and then jerked the knife upwards, severing the wire. He paused, holding his breath, expecting something dramatic to happen. Nothing did, and carefully, he cut the second wire. The alarm had been disabled.

"I'm sorry, Carla, this is most embarrassing; you'll have to give me a bit more time."

"Antony had never felt less like making love and, for the moment at least, was not displaying the ability to do so. Not that he wanted to.

His main object now was to stall for time. When Carla's skills had nearly succeeded in achieving their objective at one stage, he had successfully resisted by thinking of the fate that awaited him once he left this room. Carla grew angrier by the minute, whether through frustration at her lack of success or annoyance at the time she was wasting. He wasn't sure, he did his best to try and placate her.

"I suppose I got overexcited when I knew I was going to see you again, it made me too tense. It'll be alright soon, though, rest assured."

"I'll have to go soon, whether you're ready or not. I don't know what's wrong with you, but you're acting strangely. Have you been up to something?"

"Me? What could I have been up to?"

"I don't know, but anything's possible the way things are around here lately."

"Oh, come on, Carla! You know me,"

He froze as the beeping sound intruded. He cursed inwardly as Carla's eyes widened, and she jumped up from the bed. Moving swiftly to the table, she moved aside the pile of books from which the sound was coming and snatched up the police radio with a shout of triumph.

"So! You have been up to something."

"I don't know what you mean", he blustered, pretending astonishment at seeing the radio.

"I bet you don't" she sneered. "We'll soon see about that!"

So, saying she made for the door. Antony rose to follow her and immediately tripped on the trousers that hung around his ankles. Embarrassed and afraid, he quickly pulled his pants up and rushed for the door. As he pulled it open, he was confronted by an excited Carla who turned to the policeman she had fetched from down the corridor and said triumphantly,

"That's him, there he is, I want him arrested!"

The policeman pulled his gun and pointed it at Antony.

"I'll have to ask you to come with me, sir, you too, miss," he said, gesturing to Carla.

"With pleasure, I want to see what happens to this traitor."

They marched in silence along the corridor, around the corner, and along another corridor. Every so often, Carla glanced at Antony and sneered maliciously.

They stopped outside the door to Garon's chambers, and as the policeman pushed the door open, Carla turned to Antony and said, almost with glee, "Well, this is one place where you'll have no trouble responding, my friend, but I doubt you'll get the pleasure from Garon that you would have got from me."

They marched to the staircase and went down, past the torture chamber and on down to the cells. The policeman made Antony halt outside one of the cells and gestured for him to enter. As he opened the door and stepped inside, the grin was wiped from Carla's face as the policeman suddenly pushed her in the back, sending her staggering into the cell. Also entering the cell, the policeman closed the door behind him. Carla stared in astonishment as a half-naked man, smeared with blood, rose from the cell's simple bed and, smiling broadly, clasped Antony's hand.

"Antony, how good to see you; what on earth are you doing half-naked?"

"It's a long story, James. I know full well why you are half-naked; thank heavens you're okay."

"Well, from what I can see, we both owe our deliverance to our good friend Valdor here. You seem to be in the thick of things, my friend!"

Valdor grinned, holstering his gun as he pushed Carla to the bed and made her sit down. She stared at the three men in baffled anger and then exploded, "What the hell do you think you're playing at? You must be mad. Let me out of here."

She rose from the bed and started for the door, only to be shoved back roughly by Valdor.

"Sit down and shut up," he snarled, tension showing as the events of the past few hours began to unfold.

"When Garon finds you here, you'll be sorry,"

"That's a good point," Antony said. "What if he does come back?"

Almost casually, James bent down and lifted the edge of the cover hanging from the bed, gesturing underneath. Stooping, Antony stared at the stiffening body of Garon, his blood congealing in an untidy pool around his body. Unable to resist, Carla also bent and looked and then cowered back against the wall, her hand to her mouth, fear now very evident in her eyes.

"You're a cool one," Antony said admiringly to James, who had just as casually thrown the cover back into place. Although he spoke quietly, there was an unusual hardness to James' voice as he replied, "After what that bastard did to me and was going to do to me, I would gladly have stuck the knife in him myself."

"Oh, it wasn't you then who…."

He turned and looked at Valdor, who shrugged.

"I had no choice; I don't think James would argue with that. In any case, he's no loss to the world, that evil bastard."

Antony stared compassionately at the man who had undoubtedly saved James and, at the same time, had avenged himself for the obscenities inflicted on his friend.

"Please don't think I will criticise you, my friend. It seems we owe you more and more, James and I. I know Teg will be delighted to hear what you have done for us."

"Teg?"

They had almost forgotten Carla's presence until the name burst from her lips. They turned and stared at her as her eyes widened again in fear and consternation. "I've heard that name; Delmo's talk of him. He says he's a troublemaker, a traitor, and a rebel who ran away from the town. What's he got to do with all this? He's only a boy, isn't he?"

Without a word being exchanged, the three men realised that Carla now had to be silenced, at least until Teg's hoped-for attack had been completed. As if reading their minds, Carla began edging towards the door, only to be stopped as Valdor stepped smartly in front of her.

"We should kill her really," he said to the other two and looked back at her dispassionately as she gasped in horror.

"That really shouldn't be necessary," James said, reluctant to become an automatic killer, "we'll tie her up and gag her; it should only need to be for a few hours."

They tore one of the sheets into strips. They grappled with the violently protesting Carla until they had her subdued, her hands tied behind her back, her feet joined together, and her mouth closed tightly by a gag that still permitted her to breathe through her nose. Her eyes were wide with terrified pleading as they pushed her under the bed alongside Garon and dropped the cover back into place. The three men grinned nervously at each other, and Antony sat on the edge of the bed, surprised to suddenly find his legs trembling. He smiled at James, reassured that his friend was not severely hurt.

"What are you doing in the cell anyway?" he asked, curious now that he'd had time to consider the question "And how come you're covered in blood? I thought at first that you'd been badly hurt."

James related what had happened to him and told him about Valdors timely arrival. Realising the predicament they were now in, they had hit on the idea of hiding Garons body under the bed. James then lay on the bed, keeping Garons blood uncomfortably on his body. They reasoned that if anyone looked in the cell, all they would see would be the apparently badly hurt prisoner and wouldn't be too keen to hang around. That way, James was safely concealed until the right moment. They sat in the cell, discussing everything that had happened so far. Occasionally, Valdor would slip out of the cell to check that all was quiet above, and thus, they passed the time. A close companionship had sprung between the three men, and they spoke excitedly about what life might be like for them. It was Antony who voiced their doubts. "It all seems too incredible," he said, shaking his head. "I really find it all too hard to believe."

Valdor was about to comment when he jumped, startled, as the radio he had taken from Carla and which she had taken from Antony's room began to bleep stridently in the confines of the cell. Picking it up, Valdor pressed the receiver button. Into the cell, surprisingly clear, considering they were below ground, came a voice that had them standing, staring wide-eyed at each other.

"We're coming in!" said Teg.

It was eerie how quietly it was done. One by one, the men crawled under the fence and moved swiftly across the open ground to where the nearest trees and bushes provided cover.

They hoped to avoid any encounters until they'd get as many men inside the fence as possible. Teg had gone under the wall in the first few minutes and now lay under a bush on top of a slight rise in the ground. To his right, the lake's placid surface looked as though it was steaming as a thin sheath drifted over the water. On the edge of the lake, directly ahead and about two hundred yards from where Teg lay, was a thick stand of bushes, looking almost black in the dawn light. Within these bushes, Valdor had concealed some of the guns he had taken from the supplies department. Teg knew that they had to get to the guns as soon as possible but also knew that the chances of being seen, even this early in the day, were much greater once they began to cross the open ground. He looked back to where his men were still coming in under the fence; about half of them were through. Then, all heads turned faintly; from far down the valley, the crackle of gunfire could be heard.

"Well, it's started," Teg said, trying to sound matter-of-fact, but a tremor in his voice betrayed him. He was still finding it difficult to believe they had started their attack. He turned to the men nearest him and gestured towards the bushes at the lake's edge. "We'd better get moving; let's get those guns."

They were up and running immediately and Teg felt excitement as they sprinted for the lake. They were almost halfway to the bushes when the man just before Teg stumbled and fell forward. Thinking he had tripped, Teg started to grin as he dodged around him. Then, his grin faded as he saw the blood rapidly staining the man's tunic. Instinctively, Teg threw himself to the ground and, looking around, saw that the others had done the same. Then, the ground seemed to shudder as the men on either side of him opened fire. At first, Teg couldn't see what they were firing at, but movement caught his eye. He could clearly see one policeman behind a tree, his gun smoking as he poured a fusillade of bullets in their direction. Nothing had prepared Teg for the noise of the guns, and he realised with surprise that, for the moment at least, he was feeling no fear; he could see another policeman now, further to the right. He was lying on a hilltop, under a bush, and had stopped firing. Teg realised that the man was talking on a radio, and that could only mean that reinforcements would be here soon.

"We've got to get those guns" he shouted, then shook his head with frustration when he realised that no-one could hear him above the clamor of guns. He knew they would be sitting ducks when enough policemen moved along the ridges and surrounded them.

Ducks! The thought made him begin wriggling backwards. The vicious buzz of bullets flying over his head made him flinch. Still, as none came lower, he guessed that the firing men couldn't aim sufficiently low because of their position. He returned safely to the top of the slope where he'd waited earlier. Rolling down the hill until he judged he was safe, he got up, ran, and crouched back towards the fence. The last of the men were inside now and lying on the ground, obviously not knowing what was happening. As Teg came panting up to them, they clustered around him. He explained briefly what was happening, and then,

"I want some men who can swim."

Nearly all put their hands up. He made a brief chopping motion, dividing the men into two groups, the larger group on his right. He explained what he planned to do to the group on the left. "We must get to those guns before they get reinforcements out there. We can't reach them across open ground, so I intend to move inside the fence until we're level with the lake. The lake's shape at this end is such that if we enter it about a hundred yards from the end, we'll only have about a quarter of a mile to swim. We'll come up directly behind the bushes where the guns are. The same bushes will stop them from seeing us. Right, let's go. As they ran off, the gunfire to their left was muffled by the intervening trees, and Teg could clearly hear the faint but obviously intensive gunfire at the other end of the valley. It had nearly been a disastrous start for Marcus. Only a few of his men were inside the fence when a police vehicle came down the road towards the gatehouse.

Unfortunately, some of the men were crossing open ground at that moment, and from up on the hill, the policemen could clearly see them. They immediately accelerated and were soon screeching to a halt outside the gatehouse. The urgent sound of the vehicle attracted the attention of the men inside, who came pouring out when the two men from the car began shouting and pointing.

Marcus had already sent an urgent order back to the fence that no more men would come through now, and those inside had frantically sought cover. They were just in time before the policeman appeared, ranging along the top of a ridge, already firing aimless shots that passed harmlessly overhead. Once they had settled down, though, their shooting became more purposeful, and within a few seconds, one of Marcus' men had fallen back with a scream of agony as a bullet tore through his shoulder.

A cold rage filled Marcus, and without thinking, he jumped up, prepared to charge at the enemy single-handedly. One of his men grabbed at his leg and pulled him back down just as a hail of bullets whipped through the air where he had been standing. Realising how stupid he had been, he nodded at the man who had saved him and turned his attention back to the front. Then their luck began to change. Marcus stared in amazement as the police vehicle he had recently seen coming down the road suddenly came roaring along the top of the ridge on which the policemen lay. To his astonishment, the speeding vehicle was driven directly at the policemen lying on the hill, forcing them to dive frantically out of the way. Once past them, the vehicle was pulled around in a tight turn and roared back towards the startled men. One of them jumped up and began running for a small group of trees. Taking careful aim, Marcus fired and yelled with triumph as the man's arms went wide, and he was bowled over, landing in an ungainly position, his head half blown away. Seeing this, the other policemen also ran, but they ran in the direction of the gatehouse. The one bringing up the rear looked back over his shoulder, his eyes wide with fright as the roar of the vehicle neared him. Realising he couldn't outrun it, he turned, dropped to one knee, and sighed his gun at the car. Before he could fire and with appalling suddenness, the front of the vehicle had reached him. The watching men winced as his body was smashed through the air, a jumbled welter of flying arms and legs that crashed to the ground, an instantly still, bloodied heap. Marcus signalled the men at the fence to start coming through again as a group began converging on the gatehouse. The vehicle came slowly across the grass towards him, and he felt slightly sickened as he saw the crumpled front of the bloodied remnants that clung to the grill, mute testimony to what had happened. Marcus realised that he had forgotten about the two men who had gone in earlier to cut the alarm cable, and the thought made him feel guilty as they climbed, grinning out of the vehicle.

"Well done, great stuff", he enthused, patting them on their shoulders, "You came just in time."

"We saw the vehicle coming down and then heard the gunfire. We had no guns, so we used what we could find."

He looked back to the crumpled body of the man they had struck, and then suddenly, he shook his head and rushed for the cover of a bush where he could be heard being violently sick. By the time Marcus reached the top of the slope overlooking the gatehouse, the rest of the men who had run to it were pouring a hail of fire against it. One look was sufficient for Marcus to signal them to stop as their bullets rebounded harmlessly off the bulletproof windows; as the sound of the guns ceased, they could hear the crackle of gunfire from other parts of the valley. Ruefully, Marcus realised that cutting the alarm cable wasn't necessary, the barracks would have been well alerted by now by the sounds of fighting. Then he reflected that if the two men hadn't been where they were, they'd all be pinned down still, their campaign grinding to a halt before it got going properly. The rest of Marcus' group was streaming over the hills now, up to where they guessed the barracks would be a hive of frenzied activity. Instructing the small group of men around the gatehouse to keep the men inside pinned down, Marcus followed the other men as they raced towards the barracks. They paused at a group of trees level with the store where the cable had been cut and grinned triumphantly as plastic-wrapped guns and ammunition were recovered from under the bushes where Valdor had hidden them. The weapons having been distributed, they raced on, looking more than ever like a real army.

The water was icy cold and had taken Teg's breath away as he had lowered himself into it. He looked around at the other men as they began swimming. They had all stripped to their underpants, and three men had been left to bring their clothes around the lake when it was safe. None of the men relished spending the next few hours in cold, wet clothes.

Once he had started swimming, Teg found the water quite refreshing and enjoyed the swim until he remembered why he was there. He glanced at the bobbing heads around him, looking oddly black against the shimmering surface of the water, which was now catching the radiance of the rising sun.

The sound of gunfire from over the trees intensified suddenly. From how it was concentrated in one direction, Teg guessed that reinforcements had already started to arrive to face the small group of men he had left on the hill. He forced himself to swim faster and saw the other men doing the same. Then suddenly, the soft bottom of the lake was beneath his feet, and within seconds, he was stumbling out of the water. The air felt frigid on their bare skin, and the men quickly headed for the big clump of bushes now directly in front of them. The sound of the guns firing was deafening and covered any noise they might have made as they sought and found the packages of weapons. There was far more than Teg had anticipated, and he realised just how much of a risk James had taken, it wasn't surprising he had been found out. Having armed themselves, Teg and his men crawled through the bushes until they could see through them. There were four vehicles parked haphazardly down a road that Teg recalled led directly to The Forum building. Two men were standing by the cars, one of them talking into his radio. Perhaps twenty other policemen were spread out at various points, and they were sending a constant rain of fire to where Tegs men lay. From where he was, Teg could have shot six of the policemen quite easily, but looking at the vehicles, he gestured to the men with him.

"Three of you come with me. I want to try to capture those vehicles if I can. The rest of you wait until you see that we're behind the vehicles, and then you open fire on that lot out there. Good luck!"

With the three men, he ran back through the bushes to the lake and along the water's edge until they came to another clump of bushes. Using these as cover, they cut away from the lake so that they were near the road when they emerged from the trees. Ducking low, they ran beside the road until behind the vehicles. When he ran up to the nearest one, Teg heard gunfire shattering from the men in the bushes. The two men standing by the furthest vehicle spun towards the source of the gunfire, astonishment on their faces. As they turned, one of them, glimpsing movement, spun around and saw Teg. Dropping into a crouch, he reached for the gun that hung on his belt. Without stopping, Teg brought up his own gun and fired. The policeman flew backwards with the force of the blast. He cannoned into his colleague, who had been unaware of what was happening behind him. As he stared and nearly fell, Tegs bullets also found him, and he slithered to the ground, almost tiredly, his body falling across his colleagues' legs.

The concentrated gunfire from the bushes had surprised the policemen on the ridge, and they soon realised they were hopelessly exposed. Already, several of their number lay dead, and two others were so severely wounded they'd take no further part in the proceedings. The rout was completed when first one, then another and, finally, all the surviving policemen broke and fled straight towards the vehicles where Teg and the other three men crouched.

On Teg's instructions, they held their fire, thinking that the policemen would surrender. Then the running men saw the two officers lying on the ground, obviously dead, and then the four men crouched by the vehicles, they wavered, surprise and then fear on their faces, instead of surrendering though, they raised their guns and, still running, opened fire. One of the men alongside Teg fell back with a sharp cry of pain, the side of his leg seeming to explode in a red mist as a powerful bullet tore through it. The rest of the incoming fire was wild, inaccurate, and short-lived, as Teg and the remaining two men sprayed a deadly fire across the line of advancing policemen. The sudden silence was incredible as the last one fell, and they ceased firing. Teg shook his head to clear the ringing in his ears. As he rose to his feet and began to walk slowly and warily towards the fallen policemen, he could hear again from the other end of the valley the intense crackle of distant gunfire.

"Will you bloody well do what I tell you - put me down and get over there with the rest of them!"

Hal's anger was natural enough, although the pain was fighting for control of his mind. Also, there was fear.

They had felt exuberant when the last of his group had come under the fence to the south of the slave compound. It had all gone without a hitch, and they were half a mile into the valley, only a few yards from the cache of weapons that Valdor had left for them before they saw anyone. A police patrol of three men had come running along a road about a hundred yards ahead, heading towards the sound of gunfire that filled the air at the bottom of the valley. Knowing that the most important thing was to get the hidden guns, Hal turned and began to wave his men into hiding. One of his men, a young man no more than twenty, had not seen his signal and had run into the open. The running policeman had almost missed seeing him but one of them stumbled slightly, and as he staggered sideways, he saw the young man running towards him. Although the young man carried only a simple spear and a knife, the policeman hadn't hesitated. He had dropped to one knee and opened fire. The young man had thrown his arms wide and danced a grotesque dance as the bullets found him, kicking him first this way and then that. He hadn't died immediately but had lain screaming on the grass.

Hal had immediately known that the young man was doomed, but the screams had unnerved him, and without thinking, he had run to his aid. Hal had taken only a few paces when the whipping sound of high-velocity bullets cracked the air around his head, and then it was as though an enormous hammer had smashed into the top of his leg. There was no pain at first, and despite the blow, he couldn't understand why his leg would no longer support him. Hal realised he was lying down, his head reverberating with unheard noise. Gradually, his hearing began to return, and there was a buzzing. A humming, and then, almost as though his ears had suddenly been unblocked, the shocking sounds of battle were all around him. He could hear the shouts of his men, the occasional rattle of gunfire and the final despairing moans of the young man who lay a few feet from him who died in a vast pool of his own blood. Hal could hear Peter shouting,

"The guns, get the guns!" He could hear the flat crack of the occasional shot from the primitive guns that a few of his men carried. For some reason, he couldn't understand, Hal felt almost a sense of euphoria as he lay there in the middle of the battle, and he even felt relaxed enough to start drifting off into a peaceful, warm sleep. Suddenly, his body quivered, and he was startlingly awake as an incredible volley of gunfire opened very close to him. In a detached way, he realised that the gunfire was coming from his own men and felt vaguely pleased that they had found the hidden weapons. Satisfied that all was well, he decided to get another night's sleep. Someone was annoying him, shaking him, shouting at him. He opened his eyes and stared at the blurry image of Peter. Annoyed at being woken up, he was about to protest when he realised that the firing had stopped.

"Hal, how are you feeling?" Peter queried anxiously.

"Fine, just fine". He was curious about the reason for Peters question and was about to ask when it suddenly hit him. Somebody moved his leg, and what had been a numb, unassociated part of him was suddenly aflame with agony. Unbelievable pain flooded up through his body. He felt perspiration burst out of every pore, yet his face felt icy cold. He could feel the scream building low down inside him as he struggled to raise his head and look at where two men were binding his legs together. At least they were binding together one leg and the remains of what had been a leg. Then the scream came, startling them all. High-pitched and agonised, it soared, screeching into the air, and then choked off as he turned his head and was sick. Then came merciful oblivion. The next thing he was aware of was bumping and bouncing as he was carried over somebody's shoulder. His leg was hot with pain, but his mind was coping with it, shutting out as much of it as it could. The jolting of his body was making him nauseous. He called out to his bearer to stop and was relieved when he was laid gently on the cool grass. He looked up, surprised to see that the sun was now relatively high in the sky. The suns radiance was suddenly blotted out as Peters face appeared. He looked desperately anxious as he stared down at his colleague, and his voice was hesitant as he asked, "How are you doing, Hal?"

That was when Hal had told him to leave him, knowing that Peter should keep up with the other men directing the fighting. He smiled at the warmth in Peters voice when he replied, "There's nothing to worry about, Hal; they're behaving magnificently; they don't need me."

Hal smiled wanly up at his friend. He was aware now of just how weak he was and guessed he had lost a great deal of blood. Despite the sun, he felt cold and began to shiver, his teeth chattering.

"Hang on, friend", Peter said gently and stooped to lift him again.

Hal gritted his teeth, determined not to cry as the jolting began again. He closed his eyes when the uneven motion of the ground beneath him made him feel sick, but he opened them again when the noise beneath Peters feet changed. He just had time to register that they were crossing a road when, with a groan of despair, Peter stopped. Then Hal heard the decelerating whine of the police vehicle stopping beside them. He felt a surge of affectionate gratitude towards Peter for gently lowering him to the roadway despite the fear that must be assailing him as the vehicle doors opened. He heard the booted feet approaching and tightened his eyes shut, afraid of revealing his sickening terror to the enemy. It was like a dash of cold water in his face when Jason said, "They told me you needed my help, they were undoubtedly correct.

"Why don't we just keep them pinned down in there?" The question was directed at Marcus, who had returned to the hill overlooking the gatehouse after assessing the situation at the barracks. His men had met fierce resistance as they had moved across open ground about a mile from the barracks. Several had been killed, with few casualties on the enemy side. The situation had been desperate for a while, but to everyone's relief, reinforcements had arrived from Hal's men. They could distract the well-trenched police sufficiently for Marcus' men to pull back to safer positions, bringing their wounded with them. Aware of the threat to them from two directions, the police had made an orderly withdrawal and were now fighting a rearguard action at the barracks.

"We don't want any pockets of resistance remaining if we can help it." Marcus told his companion as he studied the gatehouse carefully. "We want complete control of this place, including the main entrance."

"Well, how we're going to get them out of there, I don't know" The gatehouse had bulletproof windows on all four sides. Beneath the windows were firing slots through which the muzzles of several guns protruded. No shots had been fired, and the stalemate looked like continuing. In the silence, Marcus crawled carefully forward until he reasoned he was within hailing distance of the men inside. They could see their shadowy forms behind the reflective glass and sensed that they turned to look in his direction as he shouted to them.

"We are taking control of this whole valley. You are defeated, and the days of The Forum are over. Come out without your guns, and you will be treated fairly. Come out now."

He ducked instinctively as the men inside responded by firing at him. The elevation was too much, and their bullets flew harmlessly overhead as he crawled back to his men.

"We've got to think of some way of getting them out of there", he murmured. "They've got radios in there, and as long as they can report that they're resisting, they'll encourage the others."

"I've got an idea, sir," one of the younger men called. Marcus smiled uncomfortably at the use of the title. It was not something he insisted on, but he had noticed that more and more of the men were using it.

He called the young man over.

"What's this bright idea of yours then, young Damien?"

Damien looked suddenly uncertain, as though what had seemed a brilliant idea a moment ago was now perhaps not so clever. His words came in a nervous rush.

"I thought, sir, that the police vehicle, it's got a chemically powered engine. If we could make it bulletproof somehow, at the back, that is, we could back it up to the gatehouse against one of those ventilation grills, and the chemical fumes from the exhaust might force them out."

Almost out of breath after his rapid discourse, Damien waited somewhat apprehensively for a response. Marcus, meanwhile, was studying the wall of the gatehouse. He hadn't noticed before that at a low level along the walls were a series of small, slotted grilles. He suddenly felt a surge of excitement and, turning, clapped Damien on the shoulder.

"Good man, we'll try it! He exclaimed.

"How are we going to make the back bulletproof, sir?"

"How about filling it with wood, sir?" one of the other men called out, and immediately, Marcus knew that was the answer; within minutes, the sound of snapping branches filled the air as half a dozen men moved among the bushes and trees. They packed the vehicle's back seat with green wood within a very short time. What had seemed a lot of material turned out to be less when it was piled onto the seat, and they had to make another two journeys before the back of the vehicle was complete. It was clear that whoever drove the car would be at grave risk should anything go wrong, and rather than delegate somebody, Marcus was about to climb into the driver's seat when Damien came forward.

"Sir, let me do it, please, it was my idea".

Marcus was about to refuse but saw the look in the young mans eyes and, with misgivings, relented.

They watched with bated breath as Damien swung the vehicle around in a big arc to approach the gatehouse at one corner across flat ground. He had driven to within twenty yards of the building. He was turning the vehicle to put its back towards it before the first bullets were aimed in his direction. He quickly reversed, using the wing mirror to guide him. Misjudging, he crashed backwards into the wall, and the watchers could see the stacked timber jolting forward, some of it piling onto his head. The engine was running quietly, the vehicle's tail against the wall. Two of the guns inside the gatehouse could be turned sufficiently to fire at the front portion of the car. Marcus became concerned as he saw holes in the driver's door and Damien didn't come out the passenger door as expected. Marcus had resigned himself to the young man's death or severe wounding when suddenly there was a roar from the engine of the vehicle. The roar was repeated and then became a steady rhythmic sound as Damien gunned the accelerator, revving the engine and increasing the flow of toxic gas into the vent at the base of the walls.

As the men watched and waited, they first knew of any success when clouding began to show at the tops of the windows. The men inside the gatehouse could be seen moving about, and then suddenly, the door opened, and they raced out, staggering slightly from the effect of the gas. They clearly had no intention of surrendering, their guns chattering even as they ran. After hesitating, the men on the hill began to mow them down. As the gunfire ceased, the continued rhythmic roar of the vehicle's engine seemed startlingly loud. Rushing over to the car, Marcus yanked open the driver's door. A pile of splintered branches fell at his feet as the roaring of the engine stopped. The front seat was a solid heap of timber. Still, as Marcus frantically pulled it out of the vehicle, Damiens's head suddenly pushed up through the pile.

"Did it work, sir?" he asked, grinning. Marcus was staring down at the bullet-riddled timber at his feet. He wondered what would have happened if Damien hadn't crashed the vehicle into the gatehouse.

"Yes, son," he said, shaking his head in wonder, "it worked."

The courtyard looked different in daylight. Teg found it hard to believe that so much had happened since he and Valdor had last walked across that stretch of ground between the tall cylindrical pillars. The major difference now was that hastily erected barricades had been put across the spaces between the pillars, and the weapons of defending policemen protruded from them.

Teg knew that the situation was the same at all the entrances to The Forum building. He had stationed a squad of men at each gate, and each squad leader had a radio. Teg was frustrated that they had been in position for three hours now. Still, apart from the occasional exchange of ineffective gunfire, the situation seemed stalemated. He was aware, from incoming radio reports, that a fierce battle was taking place at the barracks. Casualties were heavy on both sides, but Marcus, who had returned to the barracks after the capture of the gatehouse, felt confident that they were slowly gaining the upper hand.

Other minor fights took place at various points in the valley as scattered police patrols had amalgamated and set up defensive positions. Teg instinctively knew that The Forum building could be defended for days, and he was aware that reinforcements would be coming from the town.

Although his men were fighting superbly, Teg knew there were limits to their resources, and adding fresh, fully armed police to the enemy side could undo all that had been achieved. They had to take The Forum building. A head appeared briefly above the barricade across the open ground, and a couple of guns near Teg sent a brief but inaccurate burst of fire. As the deafening roar of the guns faded, Teg realised that his radio was beeping.

Putting it to his ear, expecting to hear the voice of Marcus or one of his squad leaders, he was surprised to listen to the well-remembered voice of Valdor. Teg could almost see him now walking along the front of the building on that tense, nerve-racking night, and he grinned as he listened to him. The grin morphed into a look of hope as Valdor asked. "Are you at the courtyard, Teg?"

"Yes."

"You must hold your fire; whatever happens, hold your fire, do you understand?"

"Understood."

Chapter 46

Teg quickly passed the message along to the men behind the trees grouped opposite the courtyard. Tensely, they waited. Time passed, and nothing happened. After a few minutes, Teg had assumed that something had gone wrong. Then he saw that the glass door at the far side of the courtyard was opening. From where he lay, he could only see the top few inches of the door, but the moment it had opened, there was an eruption of gunfire from within the courtyard. Instinctively, Teg and his men ducked, but they realised that the gunfire was being contained within the courtyard and watched in astonishment as the policemen behind the barricade began to jump up and turn so that their backs were towards the barricade. Almost immediately, they were staggering and slumping as bullets stitched patterns across their bodies. Abruptly, the firing stopped. The scene at the barricades was like a picture from hell, with broken, bleeding bodies draped in grotesque postures while a great cloud of gun smoke eddied into the courtyard. The sound of weapons being cocked sounded on either side of Teg as first one then a second man appeared through the smoke and stood at the barricade looking across to the trees.

"No!" shouted Teg as the guns were raised and ready again. Rising to his feet, he ran across the open ground as James and Antony began pulling the barricade apart. Teg felt like hugging the two men, and that is what he did as he reached them. They were both stunned by what they had done, and when Teg began enthusiastically thanking them, they gestured behind them.

"You can thank Valdor for that," James said, "In fact, you can thank Valdor for a lot of things."

Teg looked to where Valdor stood, propping the door to the building open, sensibly keeping watch on the internal corridors. Teg crossed the courtyard and faced Valdor while waving some of his men over. He felt a surge of emotion as he realised just how much the policeman had contributed to the campaign, and his voice was choked as he managed to say, "Thank you, Valdor, thank you."

"My pleasure, Teg," he said, grinning and then gestured down the corridor. "We'd better get moving. I saw one of them on the radio as we started shooting. He probably got off enough to alert them that something's wrong here."

"Right, "said Teg, gesturing to his men to join him. He directed them to portions of the dismantled barricade into the corridor and to set them up at the first intersection in either direction. Having instructed some men to man the makeshift barricades, he dispatched two groups in different directions to find their way to other entrances and, hopefully, repeat the successful maneuver that Valdor, James and Antony had just carried out. With about twenty men and the two Attendants accompanying him, Teg asked Valdor to take him to the President's quarters.

"They'll be in Supreme Council chambers Teg," he explained. "They went into emergency session when the first gunshots were reported. Whatever you do, be careful, they'll be well guarded."

The building was even bigger inside than it had appeared, and they followed seemingly endless corridors before emerging into a glassed-in walkway that ran around three sides of a substantial internal courtyard. gardens and fountains. At the far end, a broad flight of white steps led up to several what looked to be solid silver doors. As they paused at the intersection, there was a rattle of gunfire from across the courtyard. The glass immediately in front of them shattered into a million pieces, and two of Teg's men fell to the floor. Dropping to their knees, some of the men endeavoured to drag their wounded comrades back down the corridor, but as more bullets thudded around them and into the already wounded men, they had to retreat, angry and frustrated as they saw the bodies jump and twitch as more bullets ripped into them. Having regrouped out of the line of fire, they clustered around Teg, looking to him for guidance. Stunned by what had happened, he was slow to react momentarily. There was an awkward silence, and, feeling ashamed of himself, Teg forced himself to take command. "Did anyone see where the fire was coming from?" he asked.

"Behind the columns at each side of the steps," one of the men answered, "I think there's only one man at each position."

"Is there any other way of getting to the other side of those doors," Teg asked Valdor.

"There are other entrances, but they're all similar to this one; you'll have the same problems" Suddenly, Teg was inspired. "Can we get on top of these walkways without exposing ourselves to those guns?"

"The only way I can think of is to go back to the outside and come back over the roof."

"Right, you come with me, Valdor; the rest of you wait here. Be prepared to get around one of these corners if need be, we don't want to lose anymore of you."

They ran the whole way, skidding around the final corner only to see their own men raising their guns behind the barricades. "No, no, don't shoot!" yelled Teg and, without stopping, hurdled the barricade, Valdor following. At Teg's command, two strong-looking men stood close together against the building wall at the side of the courtyard. Another man was hoisted up to stand on their shoulders. This man was able to hold onto the guttering at the edge of the roof with one hand whilst cupping the other one down at his side so that Valdor could clamber up over the men, using the cupped hand as a foothold and hoist himself onto the roof. Lying flat on the roof, he reached down and assisted Teg in joining him. Their guns were then passed up to them, and they ran, crouched, across the roof.

The immensity of the building was even more noticeable up here, the grey roof stretching out enormous distances. Parapets and dips in the roof showed many internal courtyards, but there was no mistaking the one for which they were heading. The roof of The Supreme Council chambers was at least ten feet higher than the surrounding levels. Huge high-level windows were set into the raised walls. The large decorative chandeliers that decorated the main chamber could be seen hanging down through them. Fearful of being seen by the policemen in the courtyard, Teg and Valdor kept well away from the edge of the courtyard. Sending Valdor to the left, Teg headed right, and they ran around the courtyard, parallel but on opposite sides. Reaching the wall of The Supreme Council chamber, Teg closed in on the parapet of the courtyard; carefully looking over, he could see the roof of the walkway some six feet below him. Looking to see that Valdor was in position, he climbed onto the parapet and lowered himself to the roof. Keeping back against the wall, he knelt and crawled along the roof. On the other side of the courtyard, he could see Valdor doing the same, and he waited until he was in position before lying flat and inching forward until he could see over the edge.

The broad staircase was to his right, and he could clearly see the policeman lying flat behind the column at the far side, his gun poking through the stone balustrade. The man seemed totally unaware of Teg's presence until, just as he pushed the barrel of his rifle over the roof's edge, he looked up. His eyes widened as he saw Teg and then the gun, he panicked, trying to pull his own gun back to swing it around. In his panic he swung it around too soon and banged it against the balustrade. For a moment, Teg had been reluctant to open fire on such a sitting target. Still, as he saw the other man's frantic movements and heard the short, sharp stutter of Valdor's gun, he pulled the trigger. He watched as dispassionately as he could as the policeman's body slewed around sideways with the force of the bullets. Even as Teg pulled his gun back, he could see the bright pool of blood that flowed from under the body and poured over the white step. Shaking himself mentally, he turned and edged backwards over the roof and, holding his gun in one hand, lowered himself by the other and then dropped into the courtyard. He glanced to his left and saw a similar pool of blood flowing over the right-hand side of the steps and knew that Valdor's aim had been as deadly as his own. Hearing Valdor drop to the ground on the other side of the courtyard, he spun round just as James, Antony and his men poured through the space left by the shattered glass. Signalling them to spread out, Teg ran towards the silver doors. There were four sets of doors across the top of the broad staircase, and between each set was a silver column wide enough to conceal a man. Running up to the second set of doors from the right, Teg crouched there while Valdor ran up to the set of doors on the far left.

When they were both in position, they reached for the door handles. They turned them and pushed the doors. To their surprise, the doors were unlocked, and as they swung open, they jumped back behind the protection of the pillars. The rest of the men were crouched at the bottom of the stairway, and when Teg peered cautiously around the edge of the column and, seeing no sign of anyone inside, ran into the building, they raced up the steps after him. They were in a low-ceilinged lobby with more doors in front of them. Moving to the side walls, they cautiously edged forward. There were small windows set into the doors, and through these, they gazed in awe at the splendour of the chamber within. The room was vast, with elegant tapering columns in a circle at the centre holding a domed roof.

Around the chamber were sculptures of men who had once ruled The Forum, and the living man who now ruled it was visible at the far end of the chamber. Aaron, the President, sat in regal splendour on an oversized silver throne-like chair. Delmo and David, the Second and Third Presidents, sat on each side of him. Ranged behind them were eighteen Attendants, and standing at each side of the assembly were two guards in ceremonial uniforms, their guns held across their chests. There was no movement or talking among The Forum members, and Teg knew with a tingling certainty that they were waiting for him to walk through the door. Slowly, he pushed the door open and walked forward, sensing rather than seeing the rest of his group doing the same. He stepped forward slowly, his gun held ready. Glancing to each side, he saw his men spread across the chamber walking in line, staring in fascination at the long-hated and feared Supreme Council and other Members of The Forum.

Teg advanced through the circle of columns, glancing up briefly at the beautiful silvery-grey glass that topped the high dome. He stopped about twenty feet away from the big stage on which The Forum members were ranged, and without looking, he knew that his companions had also stopped. Teg was puzzled by the calm way The Forum waited. As he gazed at the surprisingly benign-looking features of the three silver-haired men, his mind went back to the beginning. He remembered how they had appeared on the view wall in Jason's house, how they had praised him and honoured him, and how they would have had him killed. Like a fast-running film, events of the past year flashed across Teg's mind. He saw his grandfather again standing at his window in abject misery because his grandson had dared to question The Way. He recalled their flight, their capture, and their unexpected release.

Teg thought warmly of Elene and of The Wastelands and the settlement. He recalled Mictor's kind face and Daniel's sneering one. He saw again the ravaged body of Tanner and the delicate child face of Melinda. He remembered staring in fascination at the agonised face of teacher Johansen. He thought of Valdor, James, Antony, and all the brave men who had fought today. He thought of those who had died or been hurt, he thought of those who would soon be free. And all because of that day when he had wondered why.

"So, you are Teg!"

It was a statement rather than a question. Although he hadn't heard the voice since the night in his grandfather's house, it was instantly recognisable, jerking Teg out of his reverie.

Teg stared up at Aaron and smiled slightly, his expression not betraying his heart pounding and his pulse racing. "Yes," he said solemnly, "I am Teg. The Forum is finished, and you will surrender yourselves".

The old man looked at him with a frankly admiring look, which became almost regretful as he said, "I think not, young man. I suggest that perhaps it would be better the other way around. You have been rather careless."

There was something in his voice as he made a simple nodding gesture that made Tegs blood run cold. Slowly, he turned and looked to where the old man had gestured. There were groans of dismay from Tegs men as they looked back towards the end of the chamber where they had entered. Now, they saw a balcony above the foyer they had come through with a staircase at each side. Policemen stood along the whole width of the balcony, everyone had a gun trained at Tegs party. One glance was sufficient for Teg to know that they would be annihilated before any of his groups could do anything. So, when Aaron crisply ordered them to lay down their weapons, he was the first to do so, hoping to avoid slaughter.

When he turned to face The Forum again, he saw with a shock that Aaron's face had undergone a transformation, and the benign look had been replaced by one of hateful evil. "So," he sneered, "the boy thought he was a man, did he? Did you really believe you could overthrow the might of The Forum?"

Teg was feverishly wondering whether his other squads had entered the building. Instinctively, he glanced over his shoulder, but all he saw was the line of policemen who had now come down off the balcony and were lined up behind him and his men. As if reading his mind, Aaron sneeringly advised him, "I shouldn't wait for any of your men to come to the rescue, my men can keep them outside. You only managed to gain entry because of these traitorous dogs here!" The President rose to his feet, his voice almost shrieking, as he pointed at Valdor, James and Antony.

Aaron walked to the front of the stage, his long white robe brushing the floor. He stared down first at Valdor, then at James, and finally at Antony. He seemed to lose control for a moment, snarling at them, "Traitors, traitors, filthy traitors!"

Teg admired the three men as they stared up with only contempt on their faces, although he imagined they must be feeling the same sick, despairing fear of failure. Suddenly, Aaron turned and with a mocking smile and almost imperceptible nod directed to one of his policeman. A single shot echoed through the chamber. Instantly Valdor collapsed to the floor like a rag doll and before Teg and his men had time to react Aarons voice rang out.

"No matter if you are traitors or rebels, whatever you may be, you are all worthless dogs. It is a well-known fact that removing a leader destroys the pectus of the followers. You will find young Teg, as I have just shown, that all you have done is ensure an early death for your followers. I wonder if they will think so highly of you then."

Teg felt his spirit crack and his legs became weak as he took in the sight of his friend Valdor crumpled on the floor. Teg moved over and knelt beside him and took his hand. Valdor looked up at Teg and between rasping breaths said, "You must finish this Teg. I'm sorry I can no longer fight beside you my friend, it has been an honour." His last tear rolled into his hair and his eyes closed. As Teg placed Valdors hand gently by his side he whispered, "I 'will' finish this Valdor I give you my word."

Standing he saw the look of devastation and fear on James and Anthony as they looked away in sadness and resignation.

Aaron was about to say something more when Teg stopped him by speaking out.

"You talk of traitors or rebels. You should talk of evil and corruption, for that is what you are. If not us that stop you, then one day someone else will because the human spirit must be free. The human spirit must know liberty and justice. Your evil, self-serving corruptness denies this basic truth, but one day right will triumph!"

Aaron's face had become mottled with anger as Teg spoke, and now, he angrily slashed his hand through the air and bellowed, "Enough, I'll hear no more of this traitorous nonsense. Take them, take them!"

Immediately, the policemen began herding Teg and his group to one side, forming them into a line. They began to prod towards a set of silver doors to the left of the podium. As they approached, two Attendants ran and opened the doors, and the prisoners were marched into yet another courtyard. Like the other one they had come through, it was beautifully laid out with fountains, flower beds, and shaded seats. The difference with this one was that it was surrounded by solid walls, the only break in them being the doors they had just walked through. Puzzled as to why they had been brought here, Teg turned and saw that The Forum, led by Aaron, had followed them into the courtyard and assembled in the centre. He was pushed suddenly and told roughly to move. He looked around and saw that his men were being ranged along the side wall of the courtyard, and the sickening feeling that rose inside him strengthened as the line of policemen moved away from them and knelt facing them, their guns at their shoulders.

Aaron stepped forward, walking between two kneeling policemen, and stood facing Teg. His voice sounded thin in the open air and echoed hollowly around the courtyard's walls.

"You look surprised, rebel. You undoubtedly did not think I would let you live? You have learned the lesson the hard way, but you have learned it nonetheless. Now, when those who dare to challenge us hear the just fate that has befallen you, they will understand the futility of resistance; the Way will always triumph."

There was silence for a moment as Aaron glowered triumphantly along the line of prisoners, reserving a particularly vicious look for James and Antony, who stood together and stared defiantly back at him.

Aaron was about to say something more when the pattering sound of approaching rain made him look into the sky. His expression was puzzled as he saw no sign of rain clouds. He shook his head and started to speak again, "Had we more time, I can assure you that your deaths would not have been so easy, I would..."

The pattering sound became almost thunderous and could now clearly be distinguished as coming from within The Forum building. All eyes turned towards the doors and Aaron stared open-mouthed as the doorway seemed to explode outwards in a mass of running, barefoot slaves.

The line of policemen jumped and frantically turned to face the wall of humanity that rushed at them. Some of them managed to loosen off a few shots that echoed thunderously around the courtyard and tore into the bodies of the leading slaves. Still, then, the sheer weight of numbers overwhelmed them. They went down under a punching, kicking mob. It was brutal, it was merciless. Years and generations of pent-up hate exploded as the slaves fell upon the policemen who were suddenly fighting for their lives. Pressed back against the wall, Teg and the other suddenly reprieved men watched in horrified fascination as the courtyard heaved and ran with the sights and sounds of vicious, hand-to-hand fighting. Their guns gone, knocked from their hands and irretrievable beneath the writhing, grunting, cursing welter of bodies, the policemen fought desperately with fists and boots. Their skills and their fitness were more significant. Still, the sheer fanaticism of the untutored slaves was overwhelming, and as fast as one fell, another would take his place. One by one, the policemen fell and remained still. Gradually, the frantic activity slackened off. The groans of the injured and dying became audible. Almost unbelieving, Teg stared around at the carnage.

In the far corner of the courtyard, surviving members of The Forum cowered, surrounded by a hostile but unmoving crowd of slaves. The principal fury had been reserved for the policemen. However, here and there, the body of a Forum member sprawled among the flower beds. Hardly recognisable was Delmo, his white robes contrasting vividly with the bright red stains of his blood. Teg saw David among those in the corner and was just seeking out Aaron when a movement on the ground and a howl of fury made him spin around. As though in slow motion, he saw the bloodied face of the President of The Forum as he arose from among a tangle of bodies. He was clearly very badly hurt, his face white where the blood hadn't smeared it. His lips were drawn back in a snarl, and the howl he made was almost inhuman as he faced Teg, a discarded gun in his hands. As if in a dream, Teg stepped forward, hands out before him as if hoping to ward off the bullets. As he moved, trancelike, his thoughts were all at once of Elene, and as he saw Aaron's finger tighten on the trigger, he closed his eyes and whispered her name.

There was a yell, a crushing blow to Tegs side. As he staggered sideways, eyes now open wide, he saw the old slave who had pushed him aside throw himself onto the barrel of the gun just as Aaron pulled the trigger. In a grotesque tangle of bloody arms and legs, the two men crashed to the ground. The gun fell silent as Aaron's head crashed upon a marble step, and his howling finally stopped - forever. As if waking from a dream, Teg darted forward and kneeling by the side of the two men, gently turned the slave over. At first, Teg thought the man was dead and knew in any case, as he looked at his dreadful injuries, that his death was not far off if he still lived. Teg reached out and took the old man's hand, and as he did, his eyes opened. He smiled weakly at Teg, then looked past him. Turning, Teg saw that Jon, the leader of the slaves, had come to kneel beside him. The old man didn't seem to be in pain, the massive shock to his body having dulled him. Tegs voice was choked with tears as he looked down again and said, "You saved my life, my friend, how can I ever thank you?"

The old man looked at Jon, then back to Teg. There was a strange, hopeful, almost pleading look in his eyes as he said weakly, "Perhaps, young Master, you could also name me."

The man's eyes were already clouding, and Teg knew he had only seconds to send the man to his rest with a dignity he had never known. He thought quickly and, leaning down, whispered through his tears,

"Your name shall be Jason, for you are a good man."

The old man smiled and tried out the name.

"Jason," then his eyes closed for the last time.

"He's gone," said Jon "he was a brave man."

"You were all brave, I'd resigned myself to failure, I'm afraid. How did you persuade the slaves to join you in the end"?

Jon smiled and looked down at the old man.

"I told them that they would all be given names if we won."

Roger, Jason, Antony and James were there. They sat at four separate desks spaced out across the grass that separated The Forum building from the trees where Teg had hidden with Valdor what seemed a lifetime ago. Teg sat at another table, some twenty feet behind the others.

Marcus sat on one side of him. They had been there for hours as four long columns of slaves had filed up to the desks to be given a piece of paper upon which had been written a name.

Each slave took a sheet of paper and lined up at Tegs table to present the slip to one of the two men. They, in turn, would solemnly shake the slave's hand and welcome him or her as a free person using their given name for the first time. It was a simple ceremony, but the delight on the part of the slaves at being given a name had invested it with an importance that outweighed its simplicity. Something was touching about how the slaves would walk away repeating their names to themselves whilst staring at the piece of paper, which, with a few exceptions, they could not read.

It had been four days since the decisive battle and a lot of hectic activity. Relays of vehicles had been travelling to and from the settlement, bringing first the relatives of the wounded men and others who wished to come to see the valley. Other vehicles had been dispatched to the town carrying squads of Marcus's men. Not knowing what the reaction of the people in the city would be to the fall of The Forum, Teg had deemed it wise to have armed men there before they found out. He smiled as he thought of how the final humiliation had been dealt with at The Forum and looked admiringly at Marcus, who had devised the plan.

When the police reinforcements from the town arrived, they met with a scene of normality. Armed policemen manned the gatehouse, and police vehicles were to be seen patrolling the roads. The surprised new arrivals were informed that the trouble had been short-lived and that they should proceed to the barracks to eat and rest before returning to the town. It was a calculated gamble on Marcus's part, allowing many vehicles full of armed policemen into the valley. Still, the deception had proceeded without a hitch. By erecting a barrier at the barracks entrance and ensuring every driver displayed his credentials, a security check that seemed ordinary, Marcus's men ensured a few minutes gap between each vehicle parking. As each crew member left their vehicle and was directed to the dining area, they were disarmed and imprisoned.

The last slaves passed through, they were no longer slaves and looked bewildered by the fact. It was a relief to stand at the tables after long hours, but the pleasure that the ceremony had given had made the whole thing worthwhile. As Teg and the others gathered, they knew that the real work was beginning. So much must be done to dismantle the last vestiges of The Way, to remove the lingering influence of The Forum. Tiredly, they began to walk towards the courtyard, which had become their usual entrance into The Forum building. As he entered the courtyard, Teg found it hard to believe that only a few days before, it had been a blood-soaked, body-strewn battlefield with many lives, including his friend Valdor, lost. More vehicles had been arriving alongside the building. Teg was almost at the corridor door when he heard the familiar voice. "Teg, Teg, wait for me."

Suddenly, it seemed a lifetime since he had seen her. She was even lovelier than he remembered, and he stood transfixed as she ran, seeming to float across the courtyard. As she drew near, she slowed and then stopped, bewildered by his lack of reaction and uncertain expression. Then he was moving, running to her, and the uncertainty, the doubts, the fears, and the past were swept away as their arms enveloped each other in a desperate embrace of reunion and love.

The party was in full swing, the crowded room reflecting the popularity of the man who circulated from guest to guest, accepting their good wishes and offering them his. His face did not betray the turmoil in his mind. As he had approached this day, in the last weeks of his sixty-fifth year, he had found to his surprise that the thought of his Dying Day, which previously had seemed so natural and perfectly acceptable, was now causing him disquiet.

He was aware that his doubts had taken root many weeks, months before, when the town had been scandalised by the defection of the physician Jason. He had been there on that fateful night and had shared the awe of the others when the great honour had been bestowed on Jason by tThe Supreme Council. He had also shared the shock the following day when his non-appearance at The Sanctum had become known. He had envied Jason the honour bestowed on him but, ironically, now that it was rumoured that he too might receive just such an honour, he realised that he envied Jason his life and freedom more. Concealing his thoughts, he moved among his guests and tried hard to show composure and pride when the view wall began to sparkle with static. The room became hushed, and all eyes turned towards him. His wife, hardly daring to believe her husband was to be honoured, gazed around at her friends and then at her husband, her pride and happiness making her radiant. The screen suddenly cleared, and there, as though it was an extension of their home, was The Supreme Council chamber. There were murmurs of surprise as the people in the room saw not The Supreme Council or members of The Forum but a group of ordinary people. There were gasps as faces were recognised. Murmurings arose as the watchers suspected that all was not as it should be.

"Surely that man there is Jason!"

"And isn't that the teacher: Johansen."

"Who are all those people - where is The Supreme Council?"

Then silence fell, as it fell in every home. In other houses, people grumbled, some good-naturedly, some not so, as whatever they watched on their view walls faded. Preparing themselves for some homily or other, or perhaps one of the more frequent exhortations from the President to be alert for so-called rebels, they too gazed in wonder at the unusual scene. They, too, fell silent as a tall, good-looking young man walked into view. The young man seemed vaguely familiar to some, particularly those at the party, who had been Jasons friend. They didn't associate this mature-looking young man with the boy who had fled with Jason, all they did know was that as he stood there, looking confidently at the camera, he looked very much as though that was where he belonged. They sensed it even more when he spoke with quiet but firm authority.

"My name is Teg."

ABOUT THE AUTHOR

John Houseman was one of 7 children, he grew up in the streets of London, England. It was here he met his wife. They married and had four children. In 1983 he and his family emigrated to Melbourne, Australia to begin a new life adventure. A family man and electrical engineer he was someone who always liked to challenge himself so in his spare time he enjoyed trying his hand at gardening, dressmaking and cooking. Being someone with a high IQ he loved solving crosswords and dabbling with writing. The completion of Teg was another accomplishment of a vision he had for himself to create and write a novel.

www.ingramcontent.com/pod-product-compliance
Lightning Source LLC
Chambersburg PA
CBHW031031030726
47497CB00004B/1094